MW00939618

Dear Kirk,

Pursuit

To my dear brother
in Christ & an
inspiration to me,
Hope you enjoy this!

John

J O H N   O W E N S

ISBN 978-1-0980-2593-9 (paperback)
ISBN 978-1-0980-2594-6 (digital)

Copyright © 2020 by John Owens

All rights reserved. No part of this publication may be reproduced, distributed, or transmitted in any form or by any means, including photocopying, recording, or other electronic or mechanical methods without the prior written permission of the publisher. For permission requests, solicit the publisher via the address below.

Christian Faith Publishing, Inc.
832 Park Avenue
Meadville, PA 16335
www.christianfaithpublishing.com

Printed in the United States of America

Chapter 1

Decker's Dream

In the dark, Detective Lou Decker crouched alongside an open door. He peered in. Ramon Garza stood there rocking and mumbling in a rapid, pressured Spanish to someone Decker could not see. "Six months chasing this madman, finally, here he is in front of me." *Garza laughed and began swaying maniacally while turning a machete in the fireplace blaze.*

Decker drew his Beretta. He brought it to bear on Garza. The detective did not hesitate. A floorboard creaked as he stepped through the door. The killer turned to see the detective enter the room. With a scream, Garza charged, swinging the wicked blade downward at Decker's head. Decker jumped to the side and the machete missed his head by inches. Garza gibbered as he stumbled and fell to one knee. Decker brought his gun down hard on Garza's skull, knocking him cold. He handcuffed Garza and turned him over. Decker then picked up the machete and tossed it toward the fireplace. The detective pulled a Kimber Lite from the back of his belt. Quickly, he stuffed it into Garza's sweaty right hand and blam! *He fired a round into the wall shattering a door jamb.* "Missed that baby, didn't ya? Thought you'd want it back."

The detective looked across the room. There was a child lying there, bound and hooded. He ran to the youngster, bent down and freed him. As Decker worked, the young boy looked up at him with terror in his eyes. A growling laugh came from behind. Lou turned to see the source of the boy's fear. Instead of Garza, a large reptilian form advanced toward

Decker. Wings flared and the monster's huge mouth gaped open. A roar blasted through the room knocking Decker down.

*****

Ring. Ring. The sudden noise caused Decker to shout "Hey. Hey!" He sat bolt upright in the lounge chair. He clawed toward consciousness, bolstered by the sensation of a growing puddle in his lap.

Ring. Ring. He reached for his cell phone. He had dumped a nearly full bottle of Budweiser onto his pants. Quickly setting the bottle upright, he now came fully awake. After the third ring Decker realized that it was his house phone that was ringing. Getting up from the lounger, he dumped his lap full of beer onto the floor. An expletive resounded through the room. *Another mess.* He walked to his desk and picked up the phone.

"Hello, Detective Decker?" came the voice on the line.

"Yes."

"This in Linda at central dispatch. I'm sorry to bother you at home but I've had several calls from a man who wants to get in touch with you. He gave his name as Herb Van Doss. He identified himself as your brother-in-law. I tried to take a message, but he says it is important. He says he needs to talk directly to you. He asked for your home phone number, but of course, I didn't give it to him. I figured that if he doesn't have it, that's a good reason for not giving it to him. He isn't buying the idea that you've been out sick for five days. He insists that we are not giving you his messages because you haven't called him back, which is true, but I thought I ought to let you know since he keeps calling. Is it okay that I called you?"

"Yeah, sure. Thank you."

"Detective, will you be back to work soon?"

"Don't know." Decker thought about his hearing that had been rescheduled for next week. It had now been rescheduled three times. Decker wondered himself if he would ever wear his badge again. "Hope so. Thanks, Linda."

Decker went to retrieve a rag to sop up the spill. *Herb…as if things weren't bad enough already.*

He looked at the clock. It was past four in the afternoon. He had been watching the Detroit Tigers lose another game, but he had dozed off. The game was over now. A TV psychologist was trying to keep a group of skinheads from coming to blows. *Just like work.* He laughed.

Decker picked up seven empty beer bottles. He carried them to the kitchen. He felt a wave of disgust with himself. He was never a daytime drinker. In fact, had rarely drank alcohol at all before his wife Maggie's death several years ago. *Falling asleep in midafternoon. When have I ever done that?*

Decker picked up his cell phone, masked his ID and dialed Herb's home. A part of him hoped Herb had called from work so he could just leave a message. No such luck.

"Hello."

"Herb? It's Lou."

"You are one tough guy to get a hold of. Your old home phone number was disconnected, so I called the station for your number. Geez, Lou, that gal was no help at all. She kept telling me that you were sick. Well, since you finally called me back, can I assume you're on the mend?"

Seeing no need to fill Herb in on his current situation, Lou lied. "Walking pneumonia, I'm taking a few days off." Giving an obligatory but rather lame cough. "Don't take it personal. The dispatcher was following procedure."

"Lou, this is important. Shelley's disappeared."

"She's gone? When?" Lou was more annoyed than concerned.

"Almost two weeks now."

"Did she go, like, on a vacation with girlfriends or something?"

"Of course not. I wouldn't bother you for that. What do you mean 'or something?'"

Lou did not take the bait, so he didn't respond. Decker realized that his suspicions must be obvious—even to a blockhead like Herb. Not for the first time did Lou hope that Shelley finally had enough of this jackass and left him. Herb and Shelley had always had what one might call a tumultuous relationship, punctuated by shouting matches and drama. There were many brief periods of separation.

Lou had always let his sister live her own life. She was an adult; if she wanted to live with someone who routinely screamed at her, well, that was her choice. However, last autumn, Lou had noted a sudden change in Shelley's general disposition. He also noticed what looked like bruises on her neck.

This enraged Decker so he spoke to a friend in the department about the situation. The friend agreed to pay Herb a visit. He posed as an old biker friend of Shelley's. He remarked to Herb that he had run into Shelley and noticed the bruising on her neck in conjunction with her general malaise. He then spelled out clearly just what things would befall Herb if the boys ever suspected that he laid a hand on Shelley. The officer reported back to Lou that Herb was the soul of indignation as he denied any issues at all with his marriage. Apparently, Herb took this admonition to heart as Shelley's demeanor normalized, and no further marks were observed.

During the family Christmas get-together, Herb mentioned that he had a disturbing conversation with one of Lou's lowlife criminal informants, judging by the man's accent and poor grammar. Lou feigned innocence, remarking, "I come in contact with hoods every day. That's part of my job." Actually, it wasn't, but Lou had plausible deniability. Herb's expression suggested that Herb had figured out Lou was behind this. Decker later advised, "You know, Herb, Shelley used to run with a rough crowd before she met you. I might take whatever the man said to heart." Herb went deathly pale at this warning. Lou wondered whether it was from fear or anger, but in any case, there was no further evidence of abuse.

Now Shelley was gone—again, but Lou's cop sense whispered that this time might be different. "Okay, tell me what you know."

"Not much. She just left."

"Herb, you called me, but if this is serious, and if Shelley turns up injured or worse, you *will* be suspect *numero uno*."

"C'mon, Lou, settle down. Can you come over so we can talk here, in private? I have some things to show you that might be—evidence. That is, if you are well enough to travel."

Evidence of what? Normally the thought of visiting Herb for any reason, other than to spend time with his sister, would have prompted an immediate refusal. But this call and Herb's concern were unusual, plus Lou's radar had been activated. Something might really be wrong. This development, however unpleasant, might provide a respite for his ongoing devolution from duty, routine, and responsibility.

"Guess so, but I can't get there until about seven thirty." Lou remembered that he should cough occasionally, so he gave a short one. "If you give me a line of BS or act evasive, I'm out of there."

"No, really, Lou, we need to talk." Herb coughed back, and he chuckled.

"Okay. Seven thirty. I'll stop for some burgers on the way. Do you want any?"

"Whatever you're having, as long as you are paying. Remember, I bought last time."

Decker almost said aloud the *last time*. He could not remember when Herb had ever picked up the tab for anything,

Herb continued, "Just kidding, Lou. Thanks. It'll be on me. That's the least I can do. See you later."

Decker wondered if he might be going a bit hard on his brother-in-law, but he was still irritated from his sudden arousal, and his sympathy quickly disappeared. Lou wanted to let the remains of his beer buzz dissipate, so he showered, drank three glasses of water, ate a raw egg, and sat down to pay some bills online.

Chapter 2

Reverend Willie's Dilemma

"Are you about ready, sugar?" a rich baritone called out from the front room.

"Give me five minutes, honey." Minnie Hammer struggled to pull the blue dress down over her head. The looseness of the fit confirmed that she had definitely lost weight since the cancer came back. Arthritis in her shoulders and hands made shimmying into dress-up clothes, however loose, a dicey job. Trying to peer out the neck of the dress, she stumbled to one side and caught herself on a chair.

Finally, the dress slid down into place.

Minnie considered herself in the mirror. Smoothing the loose folds of material over her stomach she giggled, "My, my girl. You certainly are a sight. Seventy-four years old and still a knockout."

Minnie was happy. Tonight, she and her beloved husband were headed to a prayer and healing service. Not that she expected any healing herself, but it felt good to get dressed up again. She couldn't wait to wrap her friend, Clarice, in a big hug. She wanted to chat with all of her old friends. She needed to smile, laugh, and talk about grandchildren—all those things she had missed so much. *This should make whatever comes later a lot easier to bear.* The isolation of the last months during her cancer treatment had taken a great toll on her.

At the age of seventeen, Minnie became Mrs. Willis Hammer. She followed him off to seminary school. Those were hard years as the Vietnam War had split the nation. Stability seemed years off, especially so for struggling young families. They persevered, and upon graduation, the Reverend Willis P. and Minnie Hammer headed north to the shores of Lake Michigan to take the position of junior pastor in a small Baptist church. Then Willis received his summons to military duty from Uncle Sam.

"Ready, dear." Minnie walked toward her husband, who held out her sweater.

"Better put this on, there's a chill in the air tonight." Concern creased his face.

Minnie knew that his anxiety wasn't solely for her. His health was not the issue. Willis P. Hammer had finally decided to step down as pastor, after over forty years of service. He was troubled. He sensed that it was time; however, "Reverend Willie" had been unable to find someone suitable to whom to turn the church over. Long ago, he and Minnie had hoped that their son Martin would follow in his father's footsteps, but that dream did not materialize. Martin had been a rebellious teenager. After some unspecified trouble in college where he was majoring in communications, he suddenly dropped out to join the Marines. Martin had seen action in the chaos of the Middle East and came home a changed man. His time there left him quiet and purpose-driven. Though he still declined the ministry, Martin finished his degree program in eighteen months. He took a job at a Grand Rapids radio station. At least WCRS was a Christian radio station, Martin's parents mused.

For Reverend Willie, finding a replacement was a difficult chore. He set a high standard for the church's next pastor. Over the first couple years of his search, he had no applicants at all, despite continual prayer and fasting. When a few prospects began to appear, they were either clearly unfit for a pastoral position or decided that small-town life was not for them, and they left on their own.

Tonight Rev. Willie was troubled because he had decided to inform his current junior pastor, Timothy Love, that he should look elsewhere for a permanent position. It was not that Rev. Love was inept or wanted to leave. More than once Love had stated that he knew he had been "sent" to this church for a purpose. He had a facile mind—quick to quote scripture or offer words of counsel. Yet there was something in the younger man that Rev. Willie could not trust.

He detected an underlying disinterest in the lives of people in the church. Love could not disguise this. After many prayerful nights, Willis understood that this one also would have to go.

"Honey, after the service, I'd like you to ride home with Clarice. I might be a little while. I need to have a talk with Tim Love."

"Okay." Minnie laced her hand with his and gave it a squeeze. She had hoped that this was finally the one, but at least the source of her husband's discomfiture had now been made clear.

Midweek services were held twice per month. Attendance fluctuated based on seasonal farm responsibilities, weather, and other personal factors, but the church was nearly full this evening. The mood of the congregation was upbeat. At the conclusion of the service, attendees milled around talking, laughing, and planning visits. Reverend Willie laid his hand on Tim Love's shoulder. "Tim, can we go to my office? We need to talk."

"Pastor, not here, please. You've been very kind to me in my time at Shoreline. I think I know what you want to talk about. But please not here. I have a restaurant picked out where I might repay your kindness in part, and we can talk in private. Besides, when do clergymen ever turn down a free meal?"

The old man had to chuckle. "Good point. Minnie fed me already, but I'm up for coffee and a slice of pie, or two."

"That sounds like a plan." Both laughed now.

As Rev. Love went to get his car, Pastor Hammer shuddered in the cool night air. *I certainly hope he doesn't think I'm going to turn the church over to him.*

The men found a booth in the corner of the nearly empty cafe. Each turned up his coffee cup. The waitress filled them and took their order.

Rev. Willie took a sip. He was about to speak when a plaintive voice cried out, "Padre! Sacred Elder, pleease help me, I neeed you." A phony pidgin Mexican accent distorted the words. Rev. Willie looked around the room. There was an elderly Hispanic man sitting at a nearby table with his leg in a cast.

"Please come here, most Reverend Willie. I neeed you." The elder clergyman was startled. He did not recognize the man. The pastor arched an eyebrow. He turned to his junior cleric, "Excuse me for a moment," and walked over to the man's table.

As the Reverend approached the old man, he realized on closer inspection that the leg was not in a cast. It was wrapped in many layers of newspaper held together by masking tape forming some sort of crude splint.

"Good evening. Do I know you?" Reverend Willie asked.

"Perhaps. I've been around for a long, long year," he responded in a singsong voice. "I know many of your parishioners very well. But then, maybe we met long ago, under different circumstances."

For a moment, the reverend was jolted back to an encounter during his hitch as an army chaplain in Vietnam. *No, that's not possible.* "Well, in any case, you seem to know me. How can I help you? What can I do for you?"

"I neeeed you to heal my broken leg, pleeease." A cross between a smile and a sneer twisted the old man's face.

"Broken leg? You have no crutches. Those are newspapers taped around your leg. This is no good. You need professional medical help for a broken leg."

"My, my, Padre, do I sense 'an underlying disinterest' in my life?" The words hit Reverend Willie like a slap. "Now don't get all het up, Padre, Reverend Love assures me those healing hands of yours can do the trick."

Reverend Willie looked over at Tim Love who held up his hands palms up, grinned, and then spun a finger around his temple. Shaken, Reverend Hammer turned back to the old man. The pastor was now totally discombobulated. He mumbled, "I will be glad to pray with you." He laid his hand on the old man's shoulder and prayed for healing. While Rev. Willie prayed, Timothy Love poured a vial of thick amber liquid into the senior pastor's coffee.

The old man mimicked, "A-a-a-a-amen-n-n-n. Thankee. Now go drink that coffee before it gets cold. Hey Padre, I'm better already!"

As he returned to his table, Rev. Willie heard the old Mexican mumble, "Hmmm, I think this prayer worked better than those for your wife." The reverend quickly spun around. The man's mouth was stuffed with a large dinner roll. He chewed with exaggerated jaw movements and rolled his eyes comically, as if from extreme pleasure.

"Do you know that man?" Rev. Willie dropped into his seat shaking his head.

"Not well, but yes, his name is Miguel. I hired him to do lawn work several times. He just kind of…appeared. He looked like a lost soul, so I put him to work. Why?"

"He says you told him I could heal his broken leg."

"Why would I tell him that? It doesn't look like he has a broken leg anyway. Look there he goes now."

Reverend Willie looked as Miguel shuffled toward the door, now minus the cast and in no apparent distress.

"Maybe he was just drunk." Love stared down at his coffee as he stirred in more sugar.

Reverend Willie had lost his appetite for pie, but he drank the coffee in several gulps. The men sat quietly for several minutes. "I wonder if this is one of those artisan coffees, it's a little too sweet for my tashte, but it's real shmooth. I like it!" His voice carried loudly throughout the room as he slammed his cup down on the table.

The Reverend Timothy Love, junior pastor of the Shoreline Baptist Church leaned across the table and fixed his erstwhile mentor with an icy gaze. "You wanted to talk. So let's talk."

Reverend Willie found himself feeling fogged in. He tried to utter a coherent response.

"Cat got your tongue, eh? Well, that's okay. I'll talk for both of us. You don't have to worry about firing me. Oh, I'm not leaving. I told you before that I came here on a mission. That is still true. Unfortunately, at least for you, you may have no role in this mission. Your refusal to move on voluntarily has, well…caused us to revise our plans. However, I'm going to take you to the 'top of the mountain,' so to speak, and make you an offer. If you accept, fine. If not, that's okay too. We have a consolation prize. Time to go."

Reverend Willie found himself unable to speak. His mind was jumbled, but he was aware of the young cleric coming around the table, taking him by the arm and lifting him roughly to his feet. He felt someone grasp his other arm. He saw the old Mexican grinning up at him. As they semi-carried him to the exit, Tim Love handed the waitress a fifty-dollar bill. "He's had a long day." Love made a tippling gesture. She snapped her gum and shrugged her shoulders as they stumbled out.

Love and Reverend Willie rode in the back seat while Miguel drove. "You see, Pastor, we have big plans for *our* little church. Your time is quickly nearing its end. The church of our fathers is becoming a thing of the past. People want relevance, not platitudes. They want to feel good about church. They want to socialize. They want that 'easy-believism.' Look at the successful TV ministries. Count the number of times that those preachers mention sin, hell, or even Jesus during their programs. Studies show that it's a total figure of 4.3 times per show. Just enough to qualify as 'Christian' programming, but not enough to stop the cash from flowing in. And that doesn't include their book, DVD and 'relic' sales."

They arrived at a point on a high bluff overlooking the big lake and pulled off the road. Miguel came around to help Love get Rev. Willie out of the car. They lifted Rev. Willie over the guardrail and stood at the edge. Holding the swaying old pastor upright, they surveyed the beautiful night sky.

Tim Love pointed to the north. "You can see our church there, right? This church that you toiled to help build for forty years. It's on life support. You know it. Attendance dwindles by the month. Your congregation is aging and dying off. Outreach programs consistently fail. Within two years, this church will go under." Love paused a minute, not really caring if Rev. Willie understood any of this, "but we have an answer to this dilemma. We are arranging to purchase that bit of shoreline property there behind where the church sits. We will build an amphitheater for this church's rebranding as the Congregation of Light. We will have healing, yes, actual healing services that will draw overflow crowds and build *our* kingdom. Money? No worries, I have backers with more than adequate resources. Well, enough jabber. It's decision time, Reverend? Are you ready to join the new church?"

The old man's fog was clearing. Though he still could not support his weight he looked straight into the eyes of Timothy Love. "No...never."

"Aw-w-w, wrong answer, Reverend. But you do get the consolation prize." The old man looked quizzically at Love. "Flying lessons." Love gave Reverend Willis P. Hammer a push. In the dark, they did not see the look of peace on his face as he plummeted to the rocks below.

Miguel looked over the edge. "Remember me now, Padre?"

Reverend Willie never felt a thing.

Chapter 3

Herb's Dilemma

For an "old guy," Lou was pretty computer savvy. His job partly had forced this on Lou, but he had always been an eager proponent of embracing new technologies, especially if they helped him put away bad guys.

His mind wandered. He considered his current predicament; his suspension due to "irregularities" in his arrest of the child-killer Garza. His thoughts were a jumble as he considered this but rushing over at Herb's house was out of the question. *Getting pulled over with beer on my breath would be the end of my career.*

After a while, Decker felt he was back in normal operating mode. He started to his desk intending to grab his badge and service pistol, but remembered he was not currently in possession of either. He went instead to his bedroom where he holstered his backup piece. He was still licensed to carry, just not as a police officer. Decker opened the door, turned off the lights, and stepped out. *Time to go see what this is all about—and grab a hamburger. Man, am I hungry!*

Grand Rapids traffic was usually light through the evening hours. Including the stop for a sack of White Castles, Decker arrived at his sister's home in Grandville a bit early. He looked at his dashboard clock noting the time. Lou considered sitting in his car for five or ten minutes to get a start on the sliders, but being a detective, he noted Herb standing in his open door and tapping his foot.

I guess eating alone is out of the question.

Herb scoped the bag in Decker's hand as Lou walked up. "I thought you were bringing hamburgers, not those—things."

Decker laughed. "Only the finest."

They both went into the den where they sat down. Lou asked, "Whatcha got to drink?"

"Bud or Coors?"

"Got any iced tea or soda?"

"Iced Tea? Soda? If not beer, I expected it would be bourbon for a famous, hard-boiled Grand Rapids dick." Herb was trying to be friendly, but his attempt at humor only irritated Decker, who recalled his own afternoon indiscretion.

"Ice water will be fine."

"I think Shelley has some of that Faygo Rock'N Rye. She drinks that stuff by the case."

"No. Thanks. Just ice water."

Herb returned with Decker's ice water. He plopped into a lazy-boy. Herb reached into the sack. He pulled out two double cheese-burgers and then launched into his story.

"Lou I think your sister got religion," Herb began.

"Unlikely." Lou knew that his sister had little use for organized religion. As children they had been forced to go to church at least twice a week, and though Shelley often claimed she was a spiritual person, Decker saw little evidence of it in her life. In this, Shelley was like him, but without the cynicism nurtured by his years of police work.

"No, I'm serious. She seems to have joined a cult."

Decker was growing impatient now. This was obviously a waste of his time; however, he decided to let Herb run with it for a while. Just long enough to finish his burgers and make sure his sister was not in any real danger. "Explain."

Stuffing a third burger into his mouth, Herb continued mashing his words. "Effy ha'c'mpl'in'd boot pak 'ain." He stopped, chewed some, swallowed and then started up again. "Shelley has had back trouble longer than I've known her. She told me years ago that she had fallen off a motorcycle as a teenager. Her back had never been right since. Until about two years ago the pain had only flared up occasionally, and never really put a crimp in her lifestyle." Herb stopped chewing and talking. He took a deep breath. "Then the back pain started worsening. It was hitting her on a regular basis. The pain would sometimes land her in bed for days at a time. Rest didn't help. She would never take anything stronger than Tylenol. We tried doctors, massage, chiropractors. Heck, we even tried some old Chinese guy who gave her a bag of stinky herbal medicine and stuck her all over with needles. That was the low point. His so-called 'ancient cures' really began to mess with Shelley's mind. You should remember that time period, it was about the time I got a sit-down with your goon. Yeah, I know you were behind it, but—"

"Why didn't she, or you, tell me that this was going on?"

"Because she said not to. She said our private life was nobody else's business. I think she didn't want to worry you of all people— just wait a minute, Lou. She said you knew about her old drug problem after the injury and did *not* want you to think she had relapsed, or maybe she really just didn't want you involved in this."

Decker nodded. He looked away at the wall. Lou was now unsure where this was headed or how joining a cult fit in, but so far, he didn't like it.

"Look, Lou, I'm not a complete idiot. I know you've never liked me, but I really didn't much care as long as my life with Shelley stayed our own. Besides, I don't think you actually like anyone anyway, so I never worried about it. Frankly, I never liked you much either. That's why I waited so long to call you." Herb was glaring at Decker.

"Why didn't you talk to the local police?"

"I did. At first, they said it was too soon to file a report, but I knew it wasn't too soon, so I pushed until they promised to look into it, but I haven't heard a word since. I couldn't decide whether the officer thought I was a psycho killer or just some poor schmuck whose wife left him."

"Did he say anything that made you think that?"

"Not really. Just his manner. He seemed totally unconcerned. He had this smirk. That's when I decided to call you."

"Go on."

"Shelley began going online. You know, looking at 'back pain' websites and going to chat rooms. About two months ago, she said she met a woman who had been living with chronic pain for years. The woman told Shelley that her pain had been 'taken away.' That's how she put it, 'taken away' by a healer. As they talked, Shelley realized that this healer was operating out of a church about twenty miles from here in a small town on Lake Michigan. The woman told Shelley that she had thought this was BS or a con until she saw him work with her own eyes. She told Shelley about a veteran from her hometown whom she knew was actually paralyzed get up and walk around without his wheelchair. The woman then went back to a healing service where she had her fibromyalgia 'cured.' She urged Shelley to go to a service because this church was "the real McCoy." But Shelley wasn't ready to bite. At first, Shelley resisted, but after a while, the pain wore her down to where she figured she had nothing to lose. So she went to a midweek healing service. I did not go with her figuring this was another waste of time, but when she came home, she was smiling and pain-free. She walked around the house bending and twisting, even jumping, to show off her lack of pain. I was surprised to say the least, but happy for her and presumed it was a temporary cure. I expected her to be hurting again by morning. I asked what the healer had done. She said all she can clearly remember was being jolted in the back repeatedly by one of the healer's assistants while the healer mumbled 'prayers' over her. She nearly blacked out, and she fell forward into a second assistant's arms. She remembered being stood up and the pain was entirely gone."

"And was she back to her usual painful state in the morning?"

"No. She wasn't. In fact, I watched her get more agile, even more youthful, right before my eyes for the next few days. It was weird."

"She attributed all this to that healing service? No drugs or spinal manipulation at all? Sounds like some kind of hypnosis to me."

"I thought so too, but yep, she bought into it totally. She began going to church there three times per week. Then she began to insist I come along—saying that my 'drinking problem' and 'anger issues' could be eliminated. Of course I got pissed off. All she wanted to talk about was how wonderful Brother Love—he is the pastor—is and what he could do to 'cure' me. Brother Love this and Brother Love that. I've seen his kind on TV, so I dug in my heels. I told her that I didn't intend to share my wife with some charlatan, church or no church, and she stormed out."

"You haven't seen her since?"

"No, she came back later that night. I was already in bed. She snuggled in next to me and said she didn't want to fight. I said okay. I didn't want to fight either, so I kissed her and snuggled back. In the morning she seemed preoccupied. I could see in her eyes that something was not quite right. She then told me that she had been selected to go on a weeklong retreat with the church to learn healing techniques. She half-heartedly asked if I wanted to go. She knew I couldn't. I had used all my vacation time taking her to the failed treatments. When I said 'no,' she seemed, well, relieved. She asked if I cared if she went. Watching her walk and function without pain for the first time in years, how could I refuse her? I asked who was going? She said several women from other congregations of the fellowship. Mrs. Hickey, the local congregation secretary, would do the driving. All in all it should be quite a learning experience. She was really excited. She left two days later."

"Okay, so you haven't heard from her nor seen her since she left for the retreat."

"Not exactly. Actually, she did call that evening to say she had arrived safely at the rally point. I asked where she was. She was not sure but thought she was in Ludington. She said no outside communications would be allowed during the sessions except in emergencies. Everyone in the group was required to give them their cell phones for the remainder of the trip. I thought this was a little strange, but I held my peace. She said if I had an emergency, I should call the Manistee Congregation of Light, which I presumed was a sister church, otherwise she'd be back in about a week."

"So did you call that church? When? What did they say?"

"Yeah. I called when I began to get worried—she didn't show up when she said she would be home. So I called."

"And?"

"I didn't have a number, so I went online. Couldn't find a thing. Then I called information and had the same result. No record of any Congregation of Light, in Manistee or elsewhere around here. By now, I was getting panicky and called the police department in Manistee. They weren't aware of any such church or group in the area. They suggested I check the area hospitals if I were worried about an accident. I did call the hospital later, but there were no accidents. It had been a quiet day in the ER."

"Did you call the local police department then?"

"Well, no. I went in. I explained the situation and that's when they told me it was too soon to file a report, and I should sleep on it. That there had probably been car trouble, or they were too tired to drive and would be home in the morning. They suggested I come in if she did not show up. I don't think they were taking me very seriously."

"Why did you think that?"

"I could hear sniggering in the background."

"Hmmm, not very professional. Did you try the local church—what was its name?"

"Lakeshore Congregation of Light. It used to be the Lakeshore Baptist Church, back when Willis Hammer was the pastor. You probably know about that fiasco from your job."

"Nope. I don't recall it."

"It was in the news for a while. Back then, even I thought it would have prompted a more vigorous investigation. The pastor had supposedly gotten drunk. Then he committed suicide by leaping off a bluff and landing on rocks at the lakeshore. When they looked into things, they found some church money missing. As I recall, it was about seventy-five dollars. To me, that seemed like a measly amount to drive a real embezzler to suicide. The kicker was no one else had ever seen him touch a drop of liquor. I knew his son from the military. He works at a radio station in Grand Rapids. Once I ran into him in town, and we had drinks. I asked about his dad. He said his father was neither a crook nor a drunk and loved his work with the church. He had also met Rev. Love, the replacement pastor who told Martin that his father had planned the renovation and expansion of the church you now can see along the shoreline. Martin laughed at this, citing the church's poor and elderly congregation. That didn't sound like an embezzler to me. Martin admitted that his father had briefly flirted with alcohol as a young man but after 'hearing the Lord's call' became a lifelong teetotaler. Martin claimed the investigation had been sloppy. He felt that as soon as his father's past alcohol issues and the missing cash came up, they just closed it down. He believed that this Brother Love, who had come there as a youth pastor, was involved. Love has been there as head pastor ever since. As soon as Love took Dad's pulpit, the whole direction of the church 'changed from Bible teaching to weird things,'" he said.

"Nice side story, but it doesn't mean much to me. I guess churches have to adapt to the times like any other business to stay relevant. What was this 'evidence' you mentioned, Herb?"

Herb left the room and came back with a brochure. Decker took it and looked it over. It described the Midwest chapter of the Congregations of Light's ongoing series of "healing skills" retreats in Northern Minnesota. Lou asked, "This isn't where she went, was it? We were talking about Michigan, not Minnesota and, besides, this conference brochure is from last summer."

"But this proves that they do hold retreats and conferences. You understand that, don't you? What if they took Shelley to Minnesota?"

"You haven't said anything to suggest that is the case, have you?"

"No, not really."

"Did you talk with Brother Love?"

"I tried, and that convinced me something is going on here."

"What do you mean?"

"I went to his office and his secretary told me that he is not currently taking appointments, but I could speak with him after Wednesday's service. Now what kind of pastor doesn't take appointments? I've never heard of anything like that. It's absurd. So I thought I should be cautious. I introduced myself to the secretary. I asked if my wife had registered us for the Minnesota Retreat. She replied that registration was not open yet. I asked if there was a mailing list and she looked at me oddly. She hesitated, then said yes and wrote 'Mailing List' at the top of a blank sheet of paper. She had me sign with my phone number and email. I did and handed it back to her. When she looked at it, I thought I saw a look of recognition pass over her face. Thinking I might catch her, I asked if last week's retreat had been a success. She gave me a hard look and answered that there had been no retreat last week. I was really getting steamed by her lies and said, 'I know there was. My wife was there! She went to your church's retreat, and I haven't seen her since! What's going on here?' She said she had no idea who my wife was, where she was, or what my problem was. Before I could say anything else, this hulking goon stepped into the room from a door behind her. He asked if there was a problem. I said no, but there soon would be if I didn't get to speak with Brother Love. I asked if that were him. He gave a low, growling chuckle and said, 'No, I think you should leave now.' The secretary added, 'I don't know what your problem is or what you think is going on here, but I'm going to call the police if you don't leave now.' The brute took a step toward me, and I thought it prudent to retreat."

"Have you gone to a service?"

"Not yet."

"I would suggest you stay away for the time being. I think it's time for me to speak with Brother Love up close and personal." Even as he said it, Decker remembered that at this time, he had no official standing, but there were ways around that. He asked Herb, "Anything else?"

"Yes, one more thing." Herb reached in his pocket and pulled out his mobile phone. He punched the screen and a screenshot of a map with a blue pin popped up. The pin was located offshore in Lake Michigan near Ludington. "I'm not sure if this means anything or not"

Seeing Herb's phone screen, Lou already understood what this might mean, he asked, "Is this a phone locator app?"

Herb nodded. "Shelley's phone"

"When was this screenshot taken?"

"The evening she called. But all this indicates is where the phone was last active."

"Have you tried locating her phone since?" Decker suspected what the answer would be.

"Several times. Now, I get no response. Blank. Nada."

"Herb, text that screenshot to me. Give me a day or two to see what I can come up with, and I'm sorry about this—everything." Decker folded the flyer and added, "I'd like to take this with me."

"Okay. Just find her."

Decker walked to his car. His distrust of Herb was fighting a losing battle to a creeping sense of unease—one helped along by his cop-sense, intuition, or whatever it should be called. The drive back home was quick with Decker replaying the conversation over in his head looking for inconsistencies and points of inquiry. As he pulled into his driveway, he decided to call this Brother Love in the morning and arrange to speak with him.

Decker ate a spartan breakfast of black coffee and yogurt as penance for the previous afternoon's indiscretion. This decision left him with a case of heartburn, and his mood was turning increasingly foul as the telephone rang.

"Decker." Came a statement, not a question. "McAvoy here."

"Morning, sir"

"I just wanted to bring you up-to-date on your situation, not because I miss your charm. You've always been a pain in my keister, Decker, but the brass has decided to put your case on the fast track for dismissal—over the objections of internal affairs, I might add. We are shorthanded here as usual, and we need everyone on deck. It didn't hurt that the perp copped a plea and dropped his complaint against you. You must have a guardian angel with awfully big wings, Decker. The skinny is that you should get your badge and gun back next week."

"That's good news, Captain."

"From my perspective, it's mixed at best. Hahaha. Good to have you back aboard, Lou. Just try to keep your ducks in a row. Stop in, and we'll get the paperwork going."

"Roger that, Cap, and thank you."

Decker felt like he had just won the lottery. Twenty-four hours ago, he would have thought it less than fifty-fifty that he would ever see his detective shield again. Now, out of nowhere! "I'm baaack!" he shouted. "*Or at least I should be soon*," he added quietly not wanting to jinx himself.

Decker picked up the phone. He punched in the number for the Congregation of Light Church.

"Good Morning, Lakeshore Congregation of Light. Sister Mary El speaking. How can I help you?"

"Good morning. My name is Lou Decker. Sister, is it? Are you a nun?"

"Goodness no. We use the terms brother and sister for all the followers of the light here."

"Oh. Mary El, is that for Mary Ellen."

"No, it's Mariel, but Brother Love has an odd sense of humor. He insists on calling me Sister Mary Elephant."

"Like the old Cheech and Chong bit. I get it, and I suppose the Brother Love name comes from Neil Diamond."

"I'm sorry. I don't know Mr. Diamond. He doesn't work here. I don't understand how his name might be connected to Brother Love. How can I help you, Mr. Decker?"

"I was wondering if I might set up a time to speak with Brother Love."

"Concerning?"

"It's a rather private matter I'm afraid."

"My, my, aren't we mysterious."

"Not really, it's just personal."

"His schedule is completely full until the middle of next week. So if—"

Decker interrupted. "I could just swing by later today. It will only take a few minutes."

"Definitely not. He's isn't in today. Wait a minute. I see there is one cancellation for tomorrow morning. Would you be able to meet him at Leon's, say ten thirty?"

"Sure. Pencil me in."

"Do you need directions?"

"No, I know the place. I'll even buy him breakfast. Thank you."

"I wouldn't be so quick to make promises, Mr. Decker." She chuckled.

Decker then called to set up a meeting with Herb's friend Martin Hammer. He left a message when there was no answer, and he went outside to cut the grass.

Chapter 4

Strange Fire

"You're listening to WGRC-FM, Grand Rapids Christian Talk Radio, and this is the Spirit Warrior Show with your host Martin Hammer. Next up on this hour's segment is Rock Rollins, winner of awards in numerous subgenres of contemporary Christian music over his long and prolific career. Rock's hits range from the Christian Folk classic, 'Hey, there's a Jonah on this Bus!' to his latest Christian urban rap offering, 'Who Dat 'Postle?'"

Martin: "Rock, it's great to have you here on the show today."

Rock: "Thanks, Mark."

"Uh, it's Martin. Rock, you have been called one of the fathers of the Christian music movement, yet you have had your share of both fans and detractors. How would you answer those critics who point to the repeated accusations of copyright laws infringement?"

"Accusations. No one has ever proven a thing in court."

"Sorry, *accusations*. However, your music has been called 'a rip-off of classic rock melody lines,' by music critics: one of whom pointed out that 'Creativity in so-called Christian music should be more than substituting spiritual buzzwords for the word "baby" in some old rock and roll tune.' How would you answer these attacks?"

"Attacks? Critics? Bull! Can I say that on this show? Hey, I don't worry about critics. What *critic* ever sold out the Iowa City Municipal Auditorium, or had ten or twenty kids pulling their hair and leaping about in a spiritual mosh pit, and screaming for more of my Christian jams? How 'bout that, Marvin?"

"It's Martin. I believe the criticism about the 'Christian mosh pit' came from your father—"

"The Book says, 'A prophet is always dishonored in his own house.'"

"Well, that's not exactly what the scripture says."

"And I've got one more word for the *old* man and his *old* world of hymns and *old* Christian music—relevance."

"Let's play part of the cut 'Christian Gangsters—Party in da Faddah's House (Higher Power Groove).' Then we'll have you comment on the meaning behind the song, okay?"

"Sure."

A monotone bass thumps for twenty seconds, *Thump. Thump. Thump. Thump.* then a semi-growling voice joins in, "Hey, unh, ugga-ugga-ugga, uhn, hey! *Par-Teee* [backgound falsetto kicks in]— in the Faddah's How-ooose! Hey-yo…ugga-ugga-ugga…higher POW-WUH…ugga, yo,yo,yo."

"Rock said it before, brother—relevance."

"Relevance? To what?"

Rock's lips had become a thin, taut line, and he glared at his host. Martin, sensing that this interview was quickly spinning out of control, felt a rush of panic. Martin had been under scrutiny from his bosses, since a memorandum came down from the advertising department. It was becoming increasingly difficult to sell ad space on programs with "poor demographics."

Martin changed the subject. "Well, Rock, your career certainly has demonstrated staying power."

"Certainly." Rock's face relaxed a bit as the interview appeared to shift toward the fluff he had expected.

"I remember the early days, Rock. I was a big fan from the beginning—back when your first album, 'Out of the Darkness' went platinum—and there were actually record albums back then. Suddenly, you were touring as a lead-in act for such great Christian favorites as The Publishers, The Hellfire Extinguishers, and Amanda Garnett. Can you tell us what really happened at the Ypsilanti concert that got you, er, dismissed from the Spiritual Extravaganza Tour, although I might add you were ultimately exonerated to your fans."

"Sure, Marty, it was like this. During my set, you might remember that some old dude rushed the stage shouting some Spanish blabber. I had no idea what he was saying, and security hauled him away before he could reach me. It was in the middle of my debut performance of 'Corizon del Hierro' which meant 'Heart of Iron' as I recall. I thought that was the end of it, but then he crashed my post-concert interview. He began raving again. He charged me, grabbing the mic. I asked my bass player, Segundo, what the man was so worked up about. Segundo told me that the man was calling me a lot of not-so-nice names. This loco man claimed I had stolen his song and changed a few lyrics. He was taken then, taken away again by security."

"As I remember, he was taken away in an ambulance after you broke his jaw—"

"Purely self-defense—"

"And knocked him out with the microphone."

"I said, self-defense, and as you said, I was *already* exonerated. Besides his jaw wasn't broken. He just had a hairline crack and who's to say that wasn't done when he was dragged offstage?"

Martin said, "Okay, moving on, from here, your career hit a temporary slump until your first comeback album, 'Back from the Darkness.' You scored bigtime with a revolutionary sampling technique on 'Honky-Tonk Women (go to Hell).' And the country-inspired, 'Mein Home, Ali Baba!' Fans embraced your music, and you were headed to the top once more—until the Little Rock concert. What was that *really* about, Rock?"

"After the show, I was still all keyed up, you know. I decided to take in a movie with a new acquaintance, to unwind."

"You know what scripture says though, Rock. Bad company corrupts good character."

"I'll say. This girl looked at least twenty. There was no way I could know she was thirteen years old and a preacher's daughter. We just went to the drive-in and watched, I think it was, 'The Shoes of the Fisherman.' Anthony Quinn gave a great performance as the pope or maybe he was the president. He personally prevented WWIII with his charisma. I guess I should have realized Rock was being set up when she didn't seem very interested in the historical truth of the movie. In any case—nothing happened."

Trying to muster sympathy for his guest, Marty opined, "Guess we've all been there, Rock. But on the bright side," Marty continued, "while you were in jail, you finally took time to pen your personal '*Mein Kampf*' where you detailed the tribulations and temptations of stardom—even in the world of Christian entertainment. I was a bit puzzled when you compared your incarceration to that of the Apostle Paul, but the governor of Arkansas read your book and was so moved that he issued you a full pardon, with the comment, 'I don't see that this boy has done anything that I wouldn't do. He surely deserves another chance.' He commuted your sentence and then you spent the next year in seclusion, Rock, or as you said, 'on a spiritual journey.' Where were you at this time?"

"I was holed up in a trailer outside of Barstow, California. It was my time to fast, introspect, and get the creative juices flowing again. The highlight of this experience occurred on returning from wandering in the Mojave for four days and writing what I think was my most meaningful piece up till then: *Purple Haze of Eternity*."

"Critics point out that that song appeared to describe the desert sequences from 'The Doors' movie, more than a spiritual journey. Another likened it to a description of a rather dull, bad acid trip."

"I would answer that all spiritual journeys share certain aspects."

"Of course, but not all include lizards and shamans. In fact, didn't you yourself compare your journey to that of 'my cousin, Jim Morrison.' Being a cousin of the Lizard King himself, perhaps you can enlighten us with some insights into his life which might suggest he was, in fact, a Christian."

"I *said* he was the cousin of a college fraternity brother."

Again, Rock's face was tightening up, but Marty pushed on. "Another song from the album, 'Gimme Kiva,' purported to be about 'the dark night of the soul' but seemed to reflect personal recollections of going through DT's or withdrawal. Personally, I had thought it was about a brand of coffee popular at the time—"

"I don't need this harassment, *or* this second-rate interview. We're done here." And with that, Rock Rollins walked out.

"We will take a commercial break now and be back with open lines. Unfortunately, it doesn't look like Rock Rollins will be taking questions with us, but you can catch him tomorrow night in Holland at the fairgrounds for night three of the 'Ottawa County Fair Concert Series.'"

Martin stood up, stretched, and removed his headphones. He called out, "Three minutes, Casey." And headed for the break room noting that Casey had already started the scheduled string of commercials. Martin got a glimpse of Rock Rollins standing in the lobby bent over the receptionist's desk. Rock was writing furiously. Rock then handed a paper to the receptionist and stormed out, pausing only to grab a handful of WGRC logo pens from the cup on the desk. Martin called out to Rollins, hoping to smooth things over a bit, but Rollins ignored him.

"Mr. Hammer," the receptionist chirped with the trace of a smile, "Rock Rollins left this for you." Martin walked to the desk and was handed a picture of Rock Rollins in concert. He wore a white hooded gown with what were supposed to be giant plastic wings attached to his back. He was bent over and apparently shouting into a handheld mic, but whether his posture was due to performance antics or the ungainly wings was unclear. Across the top of the photo was printed: "Rock Rollins Los Angeles, Wild Angels Tour—1997." Across the photo were the words "To all my Brothers, Sisters, and Fans. Keep shouting at the Evil—Love, Rock!" However, a line was drawn through these words and scrawled in pen below was: "To Mark Hammer, Kiss my—. *Sincerely*, Rock."

"I think this will look good on my wall." Martin observed. Rock Rollins looked more like a disheveled Klansman coming in for a hard landing than an angel. Martin's mobile phone beeped, and he saw he had missed a call. He listened to the message. It was from a Detective Lou Decker who asked to meet him when available for a drink. The detective said that he wanted to talk to Martin about the "Congregation of Light" church. Martin was somewhat intrigued and decided to call the detective back during his next break. Returning to his console, Martin caught the last of a commercial where his voice urged listeners to hurry over to Joyous Joe's Used Car Boutique and get to know "Guido—the caring Christian car salesman." Martin was routinely asked to do voice-overs for station commercials. As he listened to this particularly amateurish production, he tried to decide whether it was because of his rich, baritone voice or just the station's attempt to save money. In any case, the commercials generally sounded cheesy and the narrative forced. When he read the script, he wondered who, if anyone, vetted these businesses before "blessing" them on-air with the "Christian" label.

The bumper music faded out as Martin began, "In our next segment, we are honored to have as a guest, a local entrepreneur, Hector Wiley. Mr. Wiley is opening The Christian Juice Bar, a first for Grand Rapids that will feature local talent as dancers. He is calling out to young women between the ages of eighteen and twenty-five to audition for the ensemble and additionally, is looking for a man of dignity and presence, preferably about forty-five years old to portray the King David in'the planned evening pageant hours. Performers will receive a negotiated wage and tips. Mr. Wiley…"

Chapter 5

Breakfast Meeting

The next morning, Decker walked into Leon's House of Pancakes forty-five minutes early for his appointment with Brother Love. This was his customary professional habit, one he used to check out the meeting place. The breakfast crowd had cleared out by this time leaving plenty of open space for discussion without eavesdroppers and with good sight lines for Decker. In fact, there was only one other patron in the place. A middle-aged man sat at the counter pounding down coffee and chaining Marlboro's. At 10:15, Decker looked up from his third cup of coffee to find an elderly Hispanic man looming over his table—if looming is the proper way to describe a man who stood about five feet tall.

"Can I help you?" Decker asked.

"I don't know, senor. Are you Detective Decker?" The man spoke with a thick accent of a Mexican bit player in a B western.

"I am, but I don't know you, do I?"

"I no theenk so. May I seet down? I am only a tired old man, much too old to work the fields. That is work for the young men, don't you theenk?" Decker noted the old man was dressed in the manner of a field hand. He wore soiled white pants and shirt complete with a red neckerchief and beat up wide-brimmed white straw sun hat. For a moment an image of the Pampalona Bull Run flashed before Decker's eyes. The old man was sweating profusely as he took a seat across the table. The detective was immediately assailed by the reek of sweat and…tequila?

"But you did call and set up a meeting with me, didn't you?" The old man continued.

"I don't know if this is a mistake or a joke. I do have meeting, but with Brother Love."

The Hispanic man looked up from the table and transfixed Decker with his gaze. The whites of the man's eyes glowed with an eerie yellow energy. "Well, who do you theenk I am—his gardener? Perhaps you were expecting someone more like—him" The Hispanic man nodded toward the chain-smoker at the counter

"Hardly."

"No, not him. "He responded testily," Him."

Decker followed the old man's eyes again to the door this time. There was an elegantly dressed man standing just inside who looked to be surveying the room. As he looked toward this man, Decker suddenly felt dizzy and sick to his stomach. The air seemed to ripple in front of his eyes, and Decker could see that the distinguished gentleman was now looking directly at him. Decker looked back across the table to address the old farmhand but saw no one there. He looked around the room and the gentleman who had just entered was now seated opposite him.

"What—?"

"Oh, that's Miguel, my driver, and no, we don't have a burro tied up outside."

Looking up, Decker was flummoxed. There was the old man. He stood near the exit, hat in his hands, nodding and smiling broadly, exposing discolored and missing teeth. Vertigo slammed Decker again, and he struggled not to vomit.

He grabbed the edge of the table to steady himself and said, "I don't know what you're doing, but it isn't funny, and I don't appreciate it."

"Miguel might disagree. As you can see, he is quite the joker. But, hey, let's not dwell on that. You didn't ask for a meeting to sample Miguel's prowess as an amateur magician. Detective, may I call you that, you look a little green. Were the eggs a bit off?"

"No, I'm just having coffee. It was that switcheroo. I'm not sure what you did or how you did it, but I'm better now."

"Let me order you an omelet then—it's the least I can do if we've somehow affected your nutrition. You can't be expected to go around beating confessions out of suspects on an empty stomach."

"Now wait a min—"

"No! Please don't take offense. I fully support you. I understand that sometimes, uh—'initiative' is needed to get a job done. For example, putting Garza behind bars was a real coup. Somewhat costly for you, I think, but a coup, nonetheless."

"I really don't like the tone of this conversation."

"Detective Decker, relax. We're on the same team. You might not understand that now, but let me assure you, you will. And I can also assure you that you will be back on the job next week."

"Now you've lost me." Decker thought the man a bit theatrical, even for a preacher. This prediction about work struck him as odd given his conversation from earlier that morning.

As Decker was about to comment on this, Brother Love continued, "Don't trouble yourself. I have it on good authority from highly placed sources. After all, you're not the only one who does their homework, and in my line of work, it pays to have some powerful patrons."

Decker decided to let that hang for now. He was impatient to get to the topic which prompted this meeting in the first place. "That's kind of why I requested this meeting—to discuss just what is your 'line of work.'"

"Well then, I'm sure that you did your homework as well, detective, and you certainly know I am the worship leader and pastor at the Congregation of Light Church. Are you looking for a place of worship? Or might this be some kind of interrogation?"

"'No' to the first question and 'not yet' to the second. All I'm interested in is getting information on the location and condition of one of your followers."

"Oh, they don't follow me. They hear the call and turn to the light."

"Whatever. This probably could have been handled with a brief phone conversation yesterday when I called, but your secretary *suggested* that we speak face to face. She set up this meeting. So let's get down to it, Brother Love, can and will you give me information on the whereabouts of Shelley Van Doss?"

"I will say that you are not the first to ask me about Sister Shelley. Just what is your interest in her—she is a married woman you know."

"Of course, I know. Sister Shelley, as you call her, is my sister—by blood, not mumbo jumbo."

"In that case, I'll ask what is your official standing in making such an inquiry? You see, I don't think you have any."

Decker's agitation was apparent as he leaned in and said in a low voice, "If I find that anything has happened to her, you'll hope that when I find you, I have official standing."

"Settle down, please. You are making me nervous. And you certainly did not need to bring a handgun to this meeting." Love's face suddenly feigned terror. "Please don't shoot me."

"What handgun?"

"The unregistered one in your belt at the small of your back. Let me guess—Beretta 91A, 9mm. Serial number 87604. The one that was originally registered to Keno Gartinson of Ecorse, Michigan, but stolen from him in 2014. Picked up later that year by you at the scene of an arrest and used as a 'throwdown,' I mean backup piece ever since. There are currently four rounds in the magazine and a fifth chambered. Did you think you were David going after a modern-day Goliath and his four brothers?"

Decker was dumbfounded. *How anyone could have known this was—impossible.*

Love looked directly into Decker's eyes. "No, not impossible, detective, I told you I have powerful friends." Love rose from the table, turned away his penetrating gaze, and walked toward the door. "I hope to see you at Wednesday night's service. I'll have the acolytes rope off a prime seat just for you—and Herb, if he cares to join you. You might get your questions answered or at least, you might get some help before you develop a fatal booze habit."

Miguel bowed low, swinging his hat and looking at Decker with a grin and those crazed eyes before turning to follow Brother Love out the door.

Chapter 6

Love's Recruits

After the breakfast meeting, Brother Love drove directly back to his office. He walked through the reception area, instructed his secretary that he did not want to be disturbed for any reason during the next hour, entered the office and closed the door. In spite of his bravado this morning, the cleric was rattled. He walked over to his bookshelf and picked up a large volume. Opening the front cover of the false book he removed a hidden flask. Love stared at it for a long moment and then replaced it.

Replaying the meeting, *This one is no fool. He is not one of the Others. But he has a strong will and a sharp mind. He won't be turned or scared off easily. I think it would be wise to obtain some extra assistance.*

Brother Love dimmed the lights. He sat in the center of the red circled star woven into the center of his office rug. He crossed his legs and began a series of deep abdominal breaths to clear his mind. He began to meditate. After a short time began a soft chant, "Pingala…"

His entreaties for help were heard, and he got a clear mental message that his request would be granted, and he would shortly receive two helpers. He was then given the outline of the plan needed to get them.

*****

For Eddie Blake and his cousin Dickie Gant, life was, as Eddie's father summed up his own life, "just one damn thing after another."

Both boys were born into what might euphemistically be called working-class families. However, few adults in either family had held a job for more than a week in his or her lifetime. And the parents of these two were more interested in nursing a beer bottle than children. Neither boy would ever be called good-looking, nor was either gifted with any particular talent or high degree of native intelligence. As the years passed, Eddie grew thick and powerful while Dickie became a tall, sinewy scarecrow. But despite their dissimilar appearance, they were kindred spirits. Of the two, Eddie was the natural leader being almost a year older. He was stronger, with a more keenly developed cruel streak that fueled a precocious surliness.

By the time junior high rolled around, both boys were struggling to pass any of their classes, but in an era of dumbed down students and "no child left behind" education, ineptitude in scholastics was only a minor obstacle. When weighed against the option of keeping these obnoxious morons around for another term, what sane teacher wouldn't find enough academic achievement to pass them on. If only one could make a living playing violent video games or listening to hard-core heavy metal music, Eddie and Dickie would have been on the road to become millionaires. It was also during this time that their antisocial behavior spilled into their lives after school. Drug use began, and they turned to small-time drug dealing to fund this. Petty theft evolved into burglary. Fights on the playground became violent assaults. Both quit school in tenth grade, when Eddie figured out that "school is for suckers." Living in a small town just outside Grand Rapids, Michigan, the boys' escapades consistently gained the attention of the local police. Each developed an impressive juvenile rap sheet and spent some months in detention. At the age of twenty-one, Eddie was sent to Jackson Prison for grand theft auto and felonious assault on a seven-year hitch that turned into ten years due to continued behavioral issues while incarcerated. During this period, Dickie served seven years in two stretches for robberies (one time dropping his wallet at the crime scene), but mainly, he lived on the dole, shot pool, drank whatever alcoholic beverage was at hand and sired bastards.

Supposedly rehabilitated by the corrections system, Eddie was released from prison and took a job in a metal fabrication plant. He thought he might as well put his experience making license plates to use, but again was foiled. After nine days on the job, Eddie had a disagreement with a fellow employee over break times. In the subsequent scuffle, he landed a punch to his foreman's jaw that put Eddie back on the street. It was while awaiting his preliminary hearing that Eddie decided to go for the gold. He met Dickie at the Moosehead Bar, and over several beers he outlined for cousin Dickie his master plan to achieve financial independence for both.

"Every Thursday night, after Bingo at the VFW, two old guys load the take into canvas bags and head over to the night drop at the bank. An old guy back in the joint told me that sometimes there is over $30,000 in the bag on a good night."

"No way." Doubted Dickie.

"Not from the Bingo, bonehead. The game is just a front. My buddy said that unknown to the general public, this particular VFW post has particular members that have been heavy into the rackets for about fifteen years now. Numbers, babes—"

"The VFW? That's crazy! Those guys sponsor kid's baseball and—"

"Sure, they do. And where do you think they get that kind of moolah—dues? Think about it, what better group to muscle in on the mob's turf than a legion of army-trained killers?"

"Legion—like the American Legion too?"

"*No*, jackass, just this VFW. Are you in or not?"

"In what?"

"We hit these guys on the way to the bank, and we're set, man."

"Set? On thirty grand? I go through that in booze, dope, and cigarettes in a year."

Eddie was surprised by Dickie's resistance and backpedaled a bit. "I didn't really mean the word 'set' literally, like in 'set for life,' Dickie. It's just a figure of speech. With thirty Gs, we can blow this hick town and go out to LA and get a seat at the table. You know, get in on the real action, live in style—beautiful women, movie stars, primo weed and none of these freakin' Michigan winters."

"I don't know, Eddie. I've never shot anyone and—"

"Dickie, when did I say anything about shooting anyone? All we'll have to do is wave our pistols around and those old coots will piss their pants, drop the money bags, and head for the hills."

"But what if they don't?"

"Don't what? Piss their pants or head for the hills?"

"Don't drop the bags. Think about it, Eddie. What if they don't just give it up? These guys are veterans. What if one of them was with that guy in Vietnam—Crowley or what's his name. You remember he killed a whole town of them Viet Congs. Plus, I don't wanna have to shoot no war hero—or worse, he might shoot me."

"They will."

"Huh? They will what? Shoot me? I don't know, Eddie?"

"No, lunkhead, they'll drop the bags and run. I guarantee it, and what's to not know? Are you in or not, man?"

"I just don't know."

At this point, Eddie became aware of a man in a dark suit sitting a couple of tables away. This stranger stood out at the Moosehead not only because of the suit, but also due to his wearing wraparound sunglasses in the dimly lit bar. He sat with his head slightly cocked as if he were taking an interest in their conversation. Eddie was not fond of snoops and snitches in general, but here, as he and Dickie planned their caper, Eddie became enraged. He lurched from his seat and bolted over to the man's table to confront this interloper.

"Getting an earful, buddy?" Eddie demanded.

"Pardon me? What?" answered the stranger.

"What? What? What? Are you deaf—or just nosy?" Stormed Eddie. "My cousin and I aren't stupid. We see you sittin' here staring at us and taking it all in. What are you? Some kind of narc?"

"I'm sorry. I don't quite follow you. Can't you tell that I'm—"

But Eddie had no inclination to hear the man out. He was at the end of what little patience he had. First, Dickie, refusing to fall in line like he always did, asking a million stupid questions, and now this twerp was trying to make him. He lunged at the man, slapping his sunglasses from his face and sending them skittering across the floor, before the stranger had finished his sentence.

"Blind."

Eddie looked at the man and recoiled. The stranger's eyes were a chalky gray, and it became clear even to Eddie that the man was not staring at anybody—or anything. "Uh…sorry, Pops. Wrong guy," mumbled Eddie as he retrieved the stranger's shades and handed them back.

The stranger said nothing. Slowly he reached down, picked his cane from the floor and got up from the table. Everyone in the bar stared at Eddie as the blind man made his way out—tapping as he went.

"What are you lookin' at?" Eddie mumbled to no one in particular. He felt the burning flush in his face, not feeling embarrassment so much as agitation from the sudden exertion and subsequent surprise.

"Way to go, Eddie. I hope this isn't uh…what's the word, a foreomen, of how your big plan will work out," said a flustered Dickie. "Geez, Eddie, hitting a blind guy." In his mind Dickie continued, *that's gotta be a new low—even for you.*

The meeting ended on that sour and uncertain note. Dickie promised to think things over. But Eddie was not ready to cut bait. He figured Dickie would finally come around. So he started planning the particulars for their big score.

Three days later, Dickie, having run out of beer money, rang up Eddie and said simply, "I'm in."

"Good," said Eddie. "Here's how I figure it'll go down"

Dickie listened as Eddie rambled on, presenting a sketchy scenario devoid of any real planning other than provoking a confrontation, waving guns in the air and collecting the loot. He was stunned as Eddie then outlined a surprise element of the plan. "Tonight, we'll hit that 7-11 off the interstate in Whitehall for practice."

"Practice?" said Dickie. "How does taking down a convenience store give us practice for collaring two old bagmen?"

"It'll get us used to handling the guns when the pressure is on."

"What? Eddie, you said there wouldn't be any shooting."

"Listen, I know. There won't be, but as great as our plan is, we still need some kind of trial run, especially with the possibility, and

I mean just a possibility of using guns. I don't wanna go back to the joint because one of us panics." By this, he, of course, meant Dickie. Eddie then cut off any further discussion with the pronouncement that he would pick Dickie up at 11:30 p.m. and the admonition to "bring a mask."

At 12:15 a.m., Eddie arrived in his old Nissan to pick up his partner. Dickie came trotting out of his house laughing and wearing a red mask with yellow wings on the side. Eddie noted that his partner was just unsteady enough to raise a concern over how much bottled courage Dickie had imbibed.

"Call me the Flash," Dickie said as he clambered in, his breath reeking of whiskey.

Eddie told him to take off the mask as they drove away and asked, "How much have you had to drink?"

"Two shots—for luck, I say. Nothing more. I'm fine. Steady as a rock."

Eddie raised a skeptical eyebrow, but he planned to carry the ball anyway and, well—Dickie always could hold his liquor. He focused on the job at hand through the fifteen-minute ride to the specified 7-11 and decided that Dickie should just stand in the doorway as a lookout. They made one loop through the parking lot. There were no customers inside. Eddie turned off his lights and parked the car in the empty furniture store parking lot next door, "In case they got cameras," he said, oblivious to the fact that he had just driven right past any exterior cameras the convenience store might have.

Slipping on their masks, they exited the getaway car and jogged over to the 7-11. Throwing open the door, Eddie shouted to the startled clerk, "Nobody move. Hands up." Dickie moved just inside the door looking out for any would be late-night shoppers. The clerk, a young man who had been reading a paperback, was so startled that the book flew across the room as his hands shot up into the air. "Take it all," he pleaded, "don't shoot. I won't look at you."

"On the floor," Eddie shouted. He moved toward the counter. Then a click came from behind him down an aisle. He spun around and saw a man aiming a very large handgun at his face.

"Drop it," the man said. "I'm a police officer. I don't want to shoot you, but I will."

"What?" Dickie, confused, overheard. "Why you tellin' that kid you're a cop, Eddie?"

Dickie's voice caused the cop to glance in his direction and in that split-second Eddie made a decision. He swung to face the police officer and brought his gun up and *boom*. Eddie heard a loud report that seemed to fill the store. He felt something pound into his belly driving him backward against the potato chip rack. Before he could bring his gun up again, there was a second boom. And then a third and suddenly his arm went numb, and he dropped his gun. He felt his legs weakening and began to sag to the floor. "Dickie," he screamed. "Help me." As he turned, Dickie's back was framed in the doorway as the erstwhile Flash attempted to beat a quick retreat. Two more booms filled the store, and Dickie flew forward onto his face and lie still. Eddie looked up and noticed the lights seemed out of focus. A voice said, "Get up. You're all right. Call 911. I'm Officer Rod Evans. I'm an off-duty cop. Make the call, kid. Now! Oh yeah, tell 'em to send the meat wagon."

Eddie passed out. He drifted in and out, dreaming of sirens and aware of a terrible pain in his belly. He felt cold and didn't seem to be able to move. He dreamed that he was tied up.

He came to in a brightly lit room with a man in green scrubs standing over him. Eddie was unable to move and realized that he was too weak to talk and barely able to flutter his eyelids; however, he could clearly hear what the man was saying. "This one has bled out. I don't think there's anything we can do for him. We'll have to let him go and concentrate on saving the other one"

Let him go? Let who go? The doctor seemed to be talking to someone just out of Eddie's field of vision. Suddenly he realized the doctor was talking about him. As Eddie strained to turn his head and tell them not to give up, he began to panic. *No, I can't die*, he said in his mind. *Nooo*, he silently screamed. He became aware of another voice in the room—Dickie's voice. This voice was screaming in terror and pain. Dickie was wailing over and over again. "I can't move.

I can't feel my hands or feet. Somebody, anybody help me! Nooo. I don't wanna die. Help me! I can't move."

The man in green spoke again, "Oh, the other one, he'll probably live, but if he does, he'll be a quadriplegic. You can see on the X-ray where the bullet got his spinal cord." He was holding up something dark on the edge of Eddie's vision.

Again, Eddie strained to see who the man was talking to. As his panic reached a new level, a face came into view, hovering directly over his. All noise in the room seemed to cease. The man began to speak to Eddie. Suddenly, he was aware that he had seen that face before, and when the man spoke, he recognized the blind man from the bar. But this man had eyes. *How can this be? Am I seeing things?*

The man spoke clearly and distinctly. "Yes, it's me, my friend, and yes, you are dying. Listen very carefully since we don't have much time and you must make a very important decision. In about three minutes, which is the time you have left to live, a tanker truck will go out of control, leave the highway outside this small ER and crash into this building. It will explode and very likely incinerate everyone in this building—except me, of course. This then is your choice. You can either lie here on this cart, live the rest of your rather short time left on earth in agony, and then proceed into the afterlife directly to hell where you will continue in torment forever. Or you can leave your old life behind and come with me as my servant, live a long, prosperous life and spend eternity with me. Be assured this is no joke, and you are not hallucinating. You now have about two minutes left to decide—so choose quickly."

"What about Dickie?" Eddie tried to ask but didn't have the strength to move his lips.

"Dickie made his choice. He is walking out of here with me." The stranger answered Eddie's unspoken question.

"But I don't know you." Eddie whined

"Yes, you do. Thirty seconds now."

Suddenly the fear became overwhelming, and Eddie felt utterly lost. He seemed to stand on the edge of a precipice in an ice-cold gloom. Below he could hear screams of agony and insane cursing and moaning. Eddie *knew* that any moment now he was going over that edge into the abyss. In desperation, he thought, *I want to live. I'll take your deal.*

The stranger took Eddie's hand and pulled him effortlessly to his feet. Eddie's fear was gone in that instant. Suddenly, Eddie, Dickie, and the stranger were standing some distance away from the building. They watched as a tanker careened off the highway, slammed into the little hospital building and exploded violently. Dickie began to giggle. Screams came from the building as it was immediately and unnaturally engulfed in the inferno. Eddie later heard that several people, including two robbery suspects, were burned alive and beyond recognition, but that the off-duty policeman who made the collar survived with terrible injuries. In the distance Eddie detected sirens. The stranger said, "Come now." He turned around and walked toward a black late model Mercedes. As Eddie walked toward the car, he was overwhelmed. He still felt a slight ache in the gut but could find no wounds. As he checked himself, he noticed he was dressed in a nicely tailored suit. Eddie looked over to see Dickie coming along as well, dressed in similar clothing and walking with a herky-jerky motion, as if he were a marionette. *Well, that still beats being a quadriplegic*, Eddie thought. He also noticed that Dickie had somehow aged. He looked as if he were in his late fifties. As he bent to enter the car, he caught a glimpse of himself in the side view. Startled, he recognized the face of his old man.

Chapter 7

Decker and Hammer Meet

The day following his meeting with Brother Love, Lou Decker found himself back again at Leon's for his meeting with Martin Hammer. He decided on a different table. It was again mid-morning, and the eatery was nearly empty. The man who had been at the counter reading a newspaper on his last visit was this day sitting in a corner booth with his head buried in a tabloid. Decker could just make out this week's headline: How to Know If Your Significant Other Is a Reptilian.

Decker smiled to himself. The information in that article might have been useful back in college. Martin Hammer walked in at the scheduled time, directly over to Decker, and introduced himself. The men shook hands. "Detective Decker. I'm Martin Hammer." Decker smiled and nodded. "I spoke with your brother Herb, and he tried to get me up to speed on the investigation after you and I talked. How can I help?"

"Two things first. Herb is my brother-in-law, not my brother. Second, there is no investigation—at least not officially. I've agreed to make some inquiries into the alleged disappearance of my sister, who happens to be Herb's wife."

"I see. I'm sorry about your sister. Frankly, I was surprised to hear from Herb at all. I really didn't know him well in the Marine Corps, and before that, not at all. He kind of latched on to me in boot camp. I found Herb kind of annoying, but we were all homesick and needed each other to make it through. After basic training, our paths crossed a couple times before I was deployed. We ran into each other here in town a while back, but nothing since. Then I got this call from him."

"Herb tells me you have a rather successful radio program here in Grand Rapids. I'll admit I don't have much experience with 'Christian' radio. Are you a radio-evangelist? If that's even a job."

Martin laughed. "No, no. I host an interview and call-in show. We try to present issues of contemporary interest for discussion with a scriptural perspective. For my guests, I get all kinds. Interviewing 'Christian celebrities' isn't much different from interviewing TV reality show players. But I guess in your line of work you know that people are people. The show might be entertaining, but I'd be hard-pressed to call it 'successful.' How can I help you, Detective?"

"Call me Lou. Have you eaten? How 'bout some lunch?"

"Just a lemonade, I think. Call me Marty."

Decker raised his hand and the waitress came over and took their orders. When she walked off, Decker began. "I was told that your father was the pastor of Lakeshore Baptist Church. I was hoping you might fill me in on what happened, and how it became the Lakeshore Congregation of Light."

Martin looked down and took a swallow of water, it was apparent that it was a struggle for Marty to control his feelings.

"I don't see what my father's career as a pastor has to do with Herb's wife leaving him."

"Shelley."

"What?"

"Her name, my sister's name is Shelley. And if I thought that she had just run off we wouldn't be here. Honestly, I've wondered many times why she hasn't done that exact thing. But now I have some concerns about her safety. Especially after talking to this Brother Love character whom I understand took over the church after your father…died."

"Took over is right, but Dad didn't 'die.'"

"Excuse me? Do you mean he's alive?"

"No, no, Dad was murdered. He didn't 'die.'"

"Sorry, I was trying to be considerate. Didn't the medical examiner rule it a suicide?"

"Yes. Based on the findings of alcohol and drugs in Dad's system—and from testimony from Tim Love and that Mexican henchman of his."

"Miguel?"

"Miguel? Manuel? I don't remember his name. He seemed like he could speak about twenty words of English in this thick, phony sounding Mexican accent. Then, *presto*, the police show up to take his testimony, and he sounds like a combination of Henry Lee and Bill O'Reilly."

"What was their testimony?"

"That Dad was depressed over the slow demise of the church. That Dad had a plan to rejuvenate the church. Supposedly, they were going with a different worship format and starting a building program. However, I know for a fact that Dad had no such plan. He had been unable to find a young pastor to partner with and eventually succeed him. Plus there was not enough money for any 'building program.' The way Love phrased it suggested that there were irregularities in the bookkeeping, but that was never pursued as far as I knew. I guess Brother Love had done sufficient damage to Dad's reputation that everyone was eager to move on."

"Specifically, they said that Dad had become 'intoxicated' and insisted on driving up to the bluff and laying out his grand vision. Dad then supposedly expressed extreme remorse over his lack of success in raising funds. While there, Tim Love told Dad that he planned to move on, Dad then suddenly jumped off the bluff. They said they never saw it coming. Love said he had thought my dad's turn to alcohol was a reaction to my mother's recurrent cancer, that this and other stressors in Dad's life had led to drinking on the sneak. Something, of course, only Love and this Miguel had observed. And this Miguel, where in heck had he come from? They found several half-full bottles of cheap gin were stashed around Dad's study. No one had an explanation for the drug findings. But does it seem reasonable to you that a responsible seventy-year-old pastor would suddenly develop a taste for PCP when his wife was dying of cancer and had less than a year to live?"

"Hardly."

"There's something else. My mother had collapsed when she heard the news. Chemotherapy had weakened her heart, and she suffered a massive heart attack on the spot. She was in a coma for a week or so but woke up and was fully coherent for a few hours before passing on. During that time, she asked that I tell her the real story as I understood it. When I gave her the official version, she actually laughed. She said my father could never abide the taste of gin and sometimes even the smell would cause him to retch. Back as a younger man, after Vietnam, he had briefly developed a problem with alcohol, but he was a straight Bourbon man. After he received deliverance from that problem, he never had a drink for over forty years. Personally, I never knew him to touch a drop. Even the communion wine was grape juice at Lakeshore. When I told her about the PCP in Dad's system, she positively howled and said that any M.E. who bought that must have taken a snort himself. She died a few minutes after that. She had a peaceful smile and just fell asleep. Her last words were, 'I'm right over here, Willis.'"

"So you think the whole thing was planned out in advance and staged to cover up a murder?"

"Yes, I do"

"And the change in the church since?"

"Oh, I don't doubt that was planned too, but not by my dad. Love wanted control of the church to take it in this direction for his own reasons. Dad would never have stood for it."

"Even if the church were dying?"

"No, not even if the church were dying. Dad was a Bible preacher who taught from the Bible alone. He viewed his calling as preaching the gospel to the lost and helping the church family develop their relationship with Christ and each other."

"You're losing me here, Mr. Hammer. I understand the first part but aren't there many approaches—some new and novel—to fostering that development. TV preachers seem to always be hawking some new idea or book. Couldn't your father have made a decision to try some new methods?"

"Pardon me, but you didn't know my father, detective. He couldn't even stand contemporary Christian music being played during services, let alone allow people to howl like animals or hop around the sanctuary as if they were kangaroos. Not even if healings were seemingly produced. He had seen this before in other churches. He called this kind of thing 'strange fire' and would have nothing to do with it."

"What about this Brother Love?"

"I know he was on his way out. Mother said that the meeting on that night was initiated by Dad for the purpose of giving reverend, or 'Brother' Love as he calls himself now, his walking papers. In addition to potential character issues, Dad once remarked that there was something odd about Rev. Love's work record, but I can't recall if anything specific was ever mentioned."

"Do you remember where he was prior to coming to Lakeshore?"

"That I do. Bucyrus, Ohio."

"Is there something special or unusual about Bucyrus?"

"Only the name as far as I know. I remember that early in his time at Lakeshore, Love told me that he was from there. I mentioned that I had gone through the town a couple of times on my way to the Mid-Ohio racecourse, and Love's eyes lit up. Love and I had both gone to that track to watch races, separately of course. We talked about the cars and races we had seen, but all he wanted to talk about were the car crashes, especially ones involving fatalities and the great conflagrations that sometimes occurred. I thought it strange that he compared these events to old testament sacrifices to Baal."

"Who?"

"Baal was an old testament god of the Canaanites who demanded human sacrifice in the form of being burned alive."

"Not a cheery thought."

"Nope, Love was a creepy guy from the time I met him. I'm surprised my father didn't give him the boot a lot earlier, but maybe he had kept it under wraps around Dad."

Decker leaned back in his chair considering this. He then reached across the table to thank Martin Hammer for agreeing to this meeting and to shake his hand. "I've got a better idea now of where to look next. You've been very helpful."

As the men stood to leave, Martin said, "Let me know if I can help further."

Decker turned back to Martin after a few steps and said, "Martin, how would you feel about going with me to one of Brother Love's services? If nothing else, it might prove to be cheap entertainment."

*****

In his car, Decker called in to the bureau. Captain McAvoy came on the line. He told Decker that no further action on his reinstatement had occurred. Captain McAvoy then admonished Decker to keep his pants on.

"Captain. I'm not calling about that. I'm looking at a couple of locals who might be involved in a human trafficking operation. Can you reauthorize my computer access code so I can work remotely and not have to drive in, please?"

"Why haven't I heard about this before?"

"It's really preliminary and there's really nothing to tell yet."

"I'll give you seventy-two hours, Lou. Then I want a preliminary report on my desk. We can talk then about formalizing an investigation—if it's justified. Remember, you are still officially suspended and are not authorized to represent this department in any way."

"Yes, sir. I'm fully aware of that. Thanks, Cap."

"Okay, later. Gotta run. Some of us actually have jobs, Decker." The line went dead.

On arriving home, Decker fired up his computer. He tried some general searches. He queried Timothy Love, Rev. Timothy Love and Brother Love in the police and public records and came away with nothing. Not surprising. If Love were involved in the shady side of life, it wouldn't be unusual to keep a low profile or employ aliases. Next, he tried "Congregation of Light." Wikipedia alone came back with a brief description: "a nominal Christian sect first appearing in

Ohio and the American Midwest in the early 1990s…an emphasis on services involving extended periods of chanting, meditation and alleged manifestations of direct divine intervention…healings, many of significant documented injuries and illness, have been reported, though none have been substantiated."

Decker then checked a list of churches in Bucyrus and was surprised to note that there was no Baptist church listed. However, there was a Mid-Ohio Congregation of Light. Perhaps this was a nod to the old racecourse. He decided to call the PD in Bucyrus and try to reconcile this coincidence. He looked up the number online and punched it in on his mobile.

"Bucyrus Police, this is Officer Wyatt. How may I assist you?"

"Hello, officer, my name is Lou Decker, I'm a detective with Grand Rapids, Michigan PD, badge number 658. I was wondering if there was someone available who might be willing to give me a little background information on your city? Nothing sensitive. I'm just trying to cross some t's in a local investigation."

"Let me put you through to Sergeant Tedford. He's lived here all his life. I can see him at his desk, feet up, and drinking coffee. Just a minute."

"Thanks."

The call was transferred, and Sgt. Tedford picked up. "Larry Tedford here. What's your question, detective?"

"Thanks for taking my call, sergeant. I was wondering if there is a Baptist church in your town?"

"Wow! A religious detective? Why? Are you planning to move here?" He guffawed at his own joke, then added, "No, we had one until a while back. I think it is now run by that outfit called the Tabernacle of Light."

Lou ignored the jibe. "Congregation of Light?"

"Yeah, that's it. Funny thing as I recall. The pastor, who lived here for ages, was found dead one morning in his office. Heart Attack was the verdict."

"Was there any suspicion of foul play or poisoning."

"Well, it *was* odd. We had some questions at first, but—nope. He was sent down to Columbus for a forensic autopsy, and it showed a clean toxicology screen and a definite cardiac event. Apparently, the old pastor's ticker just timed out."

"Can you tell me why a forensic autopsy was done?"

"Well as I said, we had some questions and the church board had noted some irregularities in their church's finances and suspected the junior pastor of theft."

"What came of that?"

"Nothing. The money, all $273 was found a week later in a bank deposit bag that the old man must have dropped between his desk and the wall when he collapsed. Officer Jones got heck for missing that."

"Do you recall the name of the junior pastor?"

"No, he left town immediately in a huff, and the flock found itself without a shepherd and a big mortgage for a new building program to pay. To me, he sold out to that congregation group."

"One more quick question, then I'll let you get back to work. Does the name Timothy Love ring a bell?"

"Say, that was it. That's the name of the junior pastor. Funny that he couldn't turn his cheek when his church people questioned him. He turned out to be something of a local. Raised over in Mansfield."

"Anything turn up on him?"

"No, after about $273 worth of investigating on him, the only thing we could find was that he had a clean record. No tickets. Not even an overdue library fine. Nada. He didn't seem to have many friends which I thought was strange for a clergyman and his acquaintances considered him a bit odd—which doesn't."

"Did he have any ties to the group that took over."

"Dunno. He was out of here in a flash. As far as I know, he is still gone."

"Thanks, sergeant, you've been a real help and cleared up some of my concerns."

"Glad to help, detective. You know as I think back there was something else peculiar—the death scene."

"You mean you had other concerns? What were they?"

"There was a look of terror on the old pastor's face as if he had just seen Old Nick himself, and the place smelled like there had been a campfire burning in the office all night. Like a mix of wood, cooked meat, and sulfur. No burns on the body. No signs of fire, ashes, or smoke anywhere. No residue at all. Just that smell."

"Thanks again." Decker recalled Martin Hammer's remark about Love's enchantment with fire. Decker realized that maybe all his concerns had not been cleared up.

Chapter 8

Lou and Herb II

"Time to check in," Decker mumbled with a distinct lack of enthusiasm. He realized that there was no avoiding another conversation with Herb, who had called several times per day, presumably for updates.

Following his conversation with Sgt. Tedford and being stonewalled by the folks at the Congregation of Light, Decker realized that he lacked available sources for information about his sister's alleged disappearance. It might be a stretch, but he also recalled that Herb had mentioned a paralyzed veteran whose ability to walk had been restored through Brother Love's ministrations. Though Decker understood this was secondhand information, there was the possibility that Herb might know the person's name. If so, Decker could interview the gentleman directly. What struck Decker as incongruous was that everyone in Michigan, if not the USA, should know about this miraculous healing by now. He expected that such an event would make front page on the tabloids, and likely, the New York Times as well. Thus it would be visible at every grocery checkout lane in the country. There was also a chance that Martin Hammer would know the identity of this paralyzed vet who might have been an attendee at Hammer's old church. Finally, if that failed, he would try to tap official sources—once he was reinstated and if a real case developed. At this point, Decker was reluctant to give up what little momentum he had, so he decided to call Herb. Besides, he would update his brother-in-law, killing the proverbial two birds.

"Herb? Lou."

"I was just going to call you, Lou."

"Why? For an update? I told you I'd call when I had something to tell you. What's up?"

"Got a letter from Shelley today."

"Oh. So it's all settled? Where is she?"

"That's just it, Lou. Nothing's settled. I'm really scared after reading this. Can you come over to look at it?"

"Herb, just tell me, what does the letter say?"

"What if they are listening in?"

"Who?"

"The congregation"

"Herb, don't get carried away. The only people who might be listening are from the NSA. Unless you start throwing words like 'jihad' or 'bomb' around, they couldn't care less about this conversation."

"I guess you're right. It's just that if the congregation knows about this letter, then I think she is in real danger."

"Just read it, Herb."

"Okay:

'Herb, I am scared. They took our phones, jewelry, and purses when we got on a big boat right after I called you. They aren't letting us communicate with anyone outside this camp or compound or whatever it is. There is absolutely no religious instruction going on, just endless manual labor, weird talks at all hours and now, extended meditation sessions. We are fed just enough lousy food to keep us from starving, and I think our drinks are being drugged. Two days ago, one gal said she was leaving. They said "okay" and took her away in a van. They said no one else would be allowed to leave until our training course was completed. She showed back up yesterday stumbling, filthy, and half out of her mind with fear. The staff "welcomed" her back with a lot of attention. They cleaned her up, putting her back in her regular work group as if nothing at all had happened. All she does now is wander around mumbling. She refuses to talk to anyone. Whenever we ask the staff when our time here will end, we are told "soon, you are making excellent progress," but toward what?

Herb, try to find out where we are and come get me. You need to get Lou to help in case you need some "official muscle" I think we are in northern Minnesota or Wisconsin. We hiked about an hour as a "recreation period" to a mandatory half hour "swim" in a big icy cold lake—which I am assuming is Lake Superior because they would not tell us.

I have got to close now. A young man who delivers supplies to the compound and makes small repairs has promised to smuggle this letter out to mail it. He thinks it is going to my dad. He thinks I'm sweet on him. I haven't told him I'm married, but don't get angry, Herb, nothing has or will happen. Maybe, it was a good thing that they took my wedding ring. I'm scared… and my back is killing me again. Love, Shelley'"

"I'm assuming there was no return address. Was there a postmark on the letter, Herb? Did it look like the letter had been opened?"

"The letter was wrinkled and smudged. It looked like he carried it around in a toolbox for a while, but it doesn't look like it's been opened. I think I can make out 'Min or Man' on the postmark, but no date. What are we gonna do, Lou?"

"After we hang up, you are going back to the police. Tell them everything you just told me and show them the letter. I am going to the Congregation of Light healing service tonight. I'm going to try to get some answers. Herb, I'm worried too. We'll talk tomorrow after

I follow up a couple leads tonight. By any chance, do you know the name of the paralyzed vet you mentioned when we first talked?"

"No."

"Okay, I'll get back to you, Herb."

"Lou, I'm counting on you. I don't think the cops are going to help me. And Lou, thanks."

"We'll talk tomorrow."

Decker immediately rang up Martin Hammer at the studio. After waiting for a few minutes, Martin came on the line. "Martin Hammer here. I'm on the air so make it as brief as you can please."

"It's Lou Decker. Sorry to bother you at work. I'll be brief. Just wondered if you are up for a field trip?"

"What do you have in mind?"

"Tonight. Congregation of Light service, 8:00 p.m."

"Why not? My social calendar is open, and I could use some entertainment. You won't believe this, but Brother Love's secretary called today and asked if I would be interested in having him on as a guest. My first impulse was to shout, 'Hell no!' but I bit my tongue. You do that a lot doing a radio show like mine. Guess it won't hurt to size him up for an appearance either. I can leave the station about six."

"Great! I'll pick you up. We can stop for some dinner on the way. My treat."

"Sounds good, so long as it isn't Leon's again. I know the chef there."

"One last thing, Martin. Do you know of a local veteran who regained the use of his paralyzed legs after one of Love's show?"

"I recall a bit about that—no particulars other than he was injured in an IED explosion in Iraq. The story made the rounds at the station about a month ago, but I thought it was hogwash?"

"Was his name mentioned?"

"Maybe. Not that I can remember, but it may come to me later."

"See you at six."

"You are listening to the show, right?"

Decker pretended he did not hear the question. He hung up.

It was nearly 7:00 p.m. when Martin Hammer emerged from the studio building and got into Decker's car. "Sorry I'm late. I got a call from the program director as I went off the air. He wanted to discuss my 'lack of enthusiasm' for scheduling Brother Love as an on-air guest. Seems that his wife is a member of the Congregation of Light. She has convinced him that there are real miracles occurring at these services and that it would 'liven up the show' to feature such a prominent local personality. It's a puzzle to me how he knew about my lack of enthusiasm. However, when I explained tonight's errand, he seemed more than placated—enthusiastic, even."

"Sounds like this trip will serve you well. In any case, we better just stop and grab some burgers since we're running late."

"Fine with me."

Ten minutes later, as they pulled out of White Castle, each munching a double cheeseburger, Martin observed. "I had suspected that you are a man of rare discernment, and now, your taste in fine dining has now confirmed my opinion. I love these things."

They entered the amphitheater at the Congregation of Light and were met by a man with a big grin who shook Martin's hand a bit too long and vigorously. "I'm surprised to find *you* here, Martin. I just can't wait to see your reaction to the new direction here at 'Old Lakeshore.'"

"Nice to see you too, Neil. This is Lou Decker. He's the real reason I am here tonight."

"So you are the famous Detective Decker. You're not from the bunco squad are you?"

Neil guffawed at his own witticism.

"No, I'm not. Major crimes." The man looked away from Decker.

"Lou, this is Neil Hathaway. He was my dad's bookkeeper for years."

Hathaway interjected, looking at Decker. "Word came down to keep an eye out for you. Brother Love has had a special seat reserved— especially for you. And I guess you can squeeze Martin in."

With this, Hathaway led them to a side aisle and pointed to a small area in the middle of a pew three rows from the back. "Best seats in the house for our special guest."

Sitting here would put Decker and Hammer between two enormous couples, each of whom were arguing loudly and directly behind a tall man with the largest afro Decker had ever seen.

"Not funny, Neil, we can find some seats for ourselves."

"Wasn't meant to be *funny*, Martin. Fend for yourselves then." Hathaway took a few steps and looked back at Martin, "You always were a bit entitled, weren't you?" Neil turned and walked away.

"Nice fella." Lou observed.

"Well, we thought so until he got caught with his hand in the till. He should be grateful that Dad and the congregation never pressed charges."

Chapter 9

Clarice Bodkin's Miracle

Clarice Bodkin was looking for a miracle.

Seventy-three years old, widowed, with eyes dimmed by diabetes and her mobility slowly being drained by arthritis, Clarice had received a hammer blow at her last doctor visit. The doctor said that her kidneys were beginning to fail. What did that mean, she asked? At the mention of the word "dialysis," terror and apprehension surged. The last thing in the world she wanted was to spend her remaining days tethered to a machine. So Clarice Bodkin began to pray for a miracle.

A week later, that miracle glimmered on the horizon when Clarice got a phone call from her cousin, Agnes. Agnes lived "up north" in the fruit belt between Muskegon and Grand Rapids, where she now took care of her adult son, Raymond, who had become a paraplegic due to an accident while in the military. That is, she took care of him until a month ago when he suddenly regained the use of his legs at "of all things," a tent revival meeting. Agnes told Clarice that Raymond had not gone expecting anything at all, much less a miraculous healing. He only went to stop the continual nagging of a friend who had noticed a creeping gloom around her son. The friend believed a dose of spirituality might help Raymond. As she was totally unprepared for any episode of divine intervention in her life, Agnes had fainted on the spot when her son strode through the door that night. Tears of happiness rolled down his cheeks. After being revived, it took Agnes the better part of an hour to make sense of her son's narrative. Boiled down to essentials, Agnes learned that the "miracles" performed at the service ranged from the usual—"curing" headaches, asthma, back pain, etc. to the seemingly impossible in her son's case. While there was no actual restoration of missing body parts, the faithful were assured that "through the power of the Spirit" such phenomenon would manifest in good time. Furthermore, this "apostle of healing" was based right there at what had been Clarice's old home church—the Lakeshore Baptist Church now called the Lakeshore Congregation of Light. As Agnes saw things, fending off diabetes and kidney failure certainly wasn't in the same realm of difficulty as curing paralysis, or restoring an amputated leg, so Agnes suggested that maybe a good time for Clarice's own miracle would be during tonight's service, right there in her own backyard.

When Clarice questioned Raymond on the phone about the "healer," he spoke to her with a dull concreteness, "Why, God, of course."

She thought it a bit unusual that when she pressed the issue. "Of course, of course, but who was the human agent through which your healing occurred?"

Raymond replied, "I think he called himself Brother Love." Raymond spoke in an indifferent tone with a hint of annoyance. Clarice wondered that someone healed of paralysis would be a bit more eager to know who had helped him? She was considering pressing the issue further, but Raymond had already handed the phone back to his mother.

"I can't keep that boy down. Hey, don't look a miracle horse in the mouth." Agnes observed, torturing the old aphorism. "In any case if it's a real healing, it must be from God, right?"

"I guess…yes, you're right; no matter." Clarice decided. "As long as the Holy Spirit shows up tonight, and this Love fella is for real." She thought that the name sounded familiar. Clarice decided to call her oldest friend Minnie to ask if he was the new minister selected by the church board to succeed her husband in the pulpit, after Reverend Willie's unexpected death, but she remembered that Minnie has passed on as well.

"I sure miss Minnie."

*****

So there sat Clarice Bodkin, alone, hands folded in her lap in the fourth row, mumbling an old hymn along with all the others as an incongruously showbiz-type song leader opened the meeting. Many of the faithful visibly fidgeted in their seats, bored by the same old attempts to breathe some life into these eighteenth century compositions. They were already impatient for the real show, the thing they had come for, the healings. By the time a man that Clarice assumed was an associate pastor came out to introduce the healer, Clarice was having second thoughts about all this. The atmosphere was now more like the gym before a big basketball game than any church service she had ever attended.

"Brothers and sisters, seekers and skeptics, and y'all infirm in search of—restoration. In the name of *my* Lord, I greet you and present his anointed apostle of healing—Brother Love."

Thunderous applause erupted, mixed with shouts of "Glory," "Hallelujah," and "Bring it, Brother!" The lights then dimmed, and the emcee swung around, hand outstretched, in anticipation of Brother Love's entrance. After a time, the din lessened, but no one appeared. It was then that Clarice noticed the building of a low, barely audible murmuring. Like some kind of Gregorian Chant, she thought, but with soft musical accompaniment. The chant grew slowly in volume as people looked around for its source. Suddenly, a man was there, standing next to the young pastor who gave a startled jump as he recognized Brother Love.

As more applause and "hallelujahs!" erupted, two men strode out onto the stage, one extremely tall and thin, the other shorter and muscular. They flanked the healer, standing slightly to the rear, with faces obscured by shadow. As the emcee left the stage, Brother Love raised both hands to the people asking for quiet. The noise subsided. With only the continuing chant audible in the auditorium, the Healer began: "Good evening, everyone. My name is Brother Love. My birth name was Timothy Larkin, and I was blind from birth. For fifteen years, I was blind in body and spirit, but after my encounter with the power, I was no longer the same person. I gratefully received this new name—my true name—along with my sight."

"Although you may not realize it—many, if not most of you, are looking for this same healing touch. You may think you are looking for physical healing—to restore arthritic joints, to regain hearing, or sight, or be cured of some other sickness. You wonder where the vigor of youth—and maybe your hair—went."

A murmur of laughter went through the room.

"And you want it back. Don't you."

A few in the crowd muttered affirmation. Apparently, not enough for Brother Love as he balled his fists, thrust up his hands and shouted, "I asked you a question—*don't you*!" Clarice was stunned by this outburst, as he had looked directly at her. She sat staring as this time, many answered, shouting back in agreement.

Clarice stared up at the figure onstage. He was dressed in khaki trousers and a white shirt with sleeves rolled up to the elbows. He looked working class; *this is probably what the Lord would look like if he were on earth today.* Although she normally detested confrontational theatrics in church, she, nevertheless, found herself intrigued by this man. She sensed an unusual depth of sincerity in this man— whatever his beliefs.

Brother Love continued. "I know others of you are here because you think you can manipulate your God into making you rich, or powerful, or sexually attractive. No, that's not what you *call* it, but that's the reality isn't it. You've all heard some greasy-haired, silver tongued—or is it the other way around?"

There was laughter from the crowd. "Some… *Preachers* tell you that your God wants all his children rich in this life and all you need do to lay your hands on those riches is 'claim the promise!' Sure, we all have, but in truth, some of you don't really want God at all. What you really want is a genie that can make you rich. Who will take all your troubles away in this life and the hereafter. Maybe, just maybe you've even been told that if you aren't rich, the *real* reason is sin in your life."

"Now I challenge you to show me where it says this in scripture. Here's my Bible. I will give *one thousand dollars—cash*—to anyone who will come up here right now—and show me where you are promised a life of material wealth in this world." He stood slowly waving a thick black book over his head while the auditorium went dead silent

The healer slowly let his head drop, facing the floor. The background music began to rise in volume, as he shouted, looking out again to challenge the people. "You can't do it! There is no such promise in here." He wiped a bead of perspiration from his forehead with his Bible hand. He continued, "If you hold any of these attitudes, even though your attitude is wrongheaded and an abomination, I won't ask you to leave. You best reexamine yourself and get with another group of people here tonight, those who are seeking. Some seek the *real* God. Some seek his power in their lives. Some seek a blessing or a new path. These, my brothers and sisters, these are those who wait on this power in humility…and in faith.

Clarice felt moved by what she was hearing. It was as if he were speaking directly to her. But which group was she in? She certainly didn't expect to get rich here tonight. In fact, the thought of ever getting rich "off God" was disturbing. If she were honest, though, Clarice pegged herself as more in the first group than the third—with the desire for a cure, even if from a genie, paramount. Reflecting on this, Clarice felt a sudden profound sadness. The music had settled once again to the background, but it resonated within her and intensified her emotions.

Brother Love was again speaking when Clarice heard him call on those who wanted true blessing to empty their mind. "Contemplate the source of power in this world. Join in the holy chorus as that spirit moves you." The preacher declared, "It may take five minutes or five hours—or five days, but we will wait on that Spirit of power. When he comes, as surely he will, renewal, healing, and power will come as well. Is there anyone here that thinks waiting on the power for five days is too long—for a lifetime of re*wards*!" The preacher pronounced the last syllable [wahds], shouting like some backwoods country preacher. Clarice watched a number of people give a start at this outburst, but what Love did next was truly disturbing. Brother Love stood on one leg and slowly leaned over forward at the waist bending nearly to a right angle. His jaw thrust forward in a truculent, challenging manner, he squinted with one eye in an exaggerated manner, and suddenly with a laugh like Popeye, muttered, "Ack, ack, ack. I didn't think so." As he lurched upright again. The tension in the crowd released in laughing and clapping while the organist played a few runs on the keyboard. Clarice did not join in this laughter. She began to wonder if she should even be here.

However, Clarice decided to try to get into the flow. She closed her eyes and began to empty her mind, thinking only of Love's words and what her faith had meant all through her life. Yet the harder she tried to recall milestones in her spiritual life, the more her thoughts seemed to ramble disjointedly. After a time, she noticed that several of her near neighbors had joined in the chanting—softly at first but with increasing gusto. She resisted a strong impulse to join in. The words would not come into focus although she sensed familiarity. She tried again to focus on her faith, trying to not be distracted, but there were now little alarm bells tolling in her mind. She looked at her watch. Nearly an hour had passed! How had that happened? Had she fallen asleep? Her mind was a racing jumble, but her body felt warm and thick, as if half of her wanted to fall asleep. Clarice sensed that behind the sonorous chanting, which was now taking on an incoherent and increasingly dissonant tone, was a presence that was trying to intrude on her thoughts and mood in a persistent and definitely unpleasant manner.

Clarice became aware that her shoulders were trying to jerk up and down, but without a fluid rhythm—not quite in time with the chanting. As fear began to flood Clarice, she looked from side to side. She was surrounded by people who appeared to be jerking up and down, some leaving the floor to a height of two or three feet, as if they were marionettes being pulled suddenly upward and then slowly lowered to the ground. Furthermore, many of these same people were violently rubbing and scratching at the sides of their head and ears as if tortured by a terrible itch. She opened her mouth to scream but the sound she made was drowned out by an increasing cacophony of what had begun as a worshipful chant, but had now degenerated into shrill cries, moans, and guttural animal noises. Looking up, she saw that Brother Love drifted through the air toward her. He floated slowly, legs frozen in a sitting position, feet several feet above the heads of the worshippers, his arms and hands outstretched as if playing ragtime on an unseen piano. He traveled along with his head back, and his mouth wide open. All at once his head snapped forward, his eyes popped wide open, and his mouth formed a wide circle. Then from his mouth came the sound of electric thunder.

The lights went out for Clarice Bodkin.

She lay on her back now onstage. She had no memory of going up there. She looked up at an oddly smiling face surrounded by other faces—some smiling—no, grinning, others reflecting amusement. The room was dead quiet. No music, no chanting, no barnyard noises. All was normal with no hint of the insanity she had just witnessed. Had it been a dream or hallucination, she wondered?

The tall man she had seen earlier, barefoot and wearing what appeared to be a plain suit of black pajamas reached down and touched her forehead as Clarice attempted to sit up. "Rest a minute, dear. You had a seizure, but you should be fine now. Brother Love spoke the word of power and you were healed."

"But I don't have seizures—"

"That is right! Not no more, you don't have seizures!" the man bellowed to the crowd, who responded with raucous cheers and applause. "You are cured!"

Clarisse braced herself to stand, but the gaunt man again reached down and this time with one hand took her elbow. She felt her body become momentarily rigid at his touch, as Love's assistant effortlessly lifted her to a standing position. She was hit with a sense of nausea as she stood, feeling as if she might fall again.

"No ya don't." The man chuckled, snapping his fingers up at her face. "There. That should do it."

She saw Brother Love standing offstage with his back turned, wiping his forehead with a handkerchief. A muscular man, dressed like the tall, skinny one, helped Clarisse into a wheelchair and began to wheel her offstage. As she passed Brother Love, he gestured for his assistant to stop. Brother Love leaned over Clarice and said, "You *know* you don't belong here. Don't come back or you might wind up with something worse than a bad pair of kidneys. Your kind is not welcome here!"

As the man pushed the wheelchair toward a side door, Clarisse again swooned. She woke up sitting alone in the parking lot next to her car. Tears were rolling down her cheeks, and she could hear a rumbling murmur from the direction of the building, but it also came from inside her head. In the distance, people ran in and out of the sanctuary, some of whom threw themselves on the lawn and appeared to be eating the grass. She lurched to her feet and fumbling with the door and noticed that it was ajar with the keys in the ignition and the engine running. Climbing in she grasped the steering wheel. She saw a very large, bushy-haired man in her rearview mirror drooling and stumble-running directly toward her car from the amphitheater. "That's enough for one night." Clarisse put into drive, punched the accelerator spraying nearby cars with gravel as she exited the lot.

Chapter 10

Lou and Martin's Take

Decker and Hammer sat waiting for the big show to begin. Martin looked over at Decker and remarked, "I saw a lady who was a friend of my mom's seated up toward the front. Boy, I'm really surprised to see her here in this crowd."

"Why?"

"Well, she was what you'd call 'old school.' That type just wasn't the kind of Christian you would expect to have anything to do with this circus."

"Sounds a bit judgmental, Martin."

"Nope, not meant to be, I'm just surprised. That's all." At that moment the lights began to dim, a man walked out onstage, and the crowd began to settle.

"Well, we'll see…here we go."

Martin had anticipated the bizarre spectacle with amusement, but as the service proceeded, he rapidly became bored by the theatrics. Then the crowd began to wail. Many rose to "dance" with spastic, herky-jerky gesticulations and his mood changed to apprehension. He began to notice a sour metallic taste in his mouth. Looking over at Decker, Martin could see that Decker remained seated but was bent forward from the waist at an impossible angle and was snoring loudly.

Martin could now feel himself becoming drowsy and momentarily closed his eyes. Suddenly, he came fully awake to a warning voice from somewhere within. As a roar from the crowd died away, Brother Love encouraged the faithful to proceed outside for a moment to fellowship and to take nourishment from his words and the lawn. He also thought he recognized his elderly lady friend being pushed offstage in a wheelchair.

Hammer made a snap decision that it was time to go. He did not know what all this going on was, but he knew this wasn't like any Christian service he had ever attended or heard described. He looked over at Decker, who had begun duck-walking back and forth, up and down the now nearly empty pew and hopping from seat to seat. Decker was still snoring loudly. Martin tried to grab Decker by the arm but missed. A second attempt was successful, but Decker flapped his arms wildly as if trying to take flight and Martin found he could not awaken Decker. Martin pulled him up and half-pushed and half-carried him from the arena. "Detective, wake up!" Hammer yelled in Lou's ear. "Decker! Decker, wake up!" As they exited, Decker began to show signs of coming around, but when the command to come back in and "see what the Spirit can dooo" blared over outdoor loudspeakers, Decker began a stumbling return to the tent. Martin grabbed him face on and shook him roughly until Lou Decker suddenly came fully awake.

"Watch it. What the—" Decker blurted as he nearly tripped over a woman on her knees who appeared to be eating grass directly from the lawn. Nearby, a gaunt elderly man was tussling with an extremely fat woman over a tuft of sod that both apparently felt would prove a very tasty morsel. Then she landed a roundhouse that sent the old man stumbling backward into Hammer.

"Time to go."

Decker turned back in time to watch the two stage assistants through the open doorway. They carried an elderly man up onto the stage and laid him out flat on his back. Decker tried to get a better look at the heavier of the two men, thinking that there was something about him that looked familiar.

Reaching their car, Decker said aloud, "Man my back is sore. Did you punch me?"

Hammer looked at him and smiled. "No, it's all on you. Actually, I hadn't pictured you as that limber, buddy."

"What do you mean?" It was apparent to Hammer that Decker did not remember his contortions. "And why are we leaving now? We came to get a handle on this crew and here, things have just begun, and you're dragging me out."

It was obvious that Decker did not remember *anything* that had gone on. "Lou, we were there for over an hour."

Decker took that in with a skeptical grin. "Bull." But after checking his watch, his face clouded up. "What happened in there?"

Hammer shrugged. He decided to spare Decker the details of his behavior. "You seemed to take a nap for a while, and when Brother Love sent the crowd outside to, uh, graze, I thought it was a good time to leave."

"Don't give me that. I was not asleep, I was…meditating." Decker's brow furrowed. "But I was…dreaming. A really strange dream." Lost in thought, Decker sat there for several minutes staring out the windshield.

"Do you want me to drive?" Martin asked.

"No, I just was trying to recall the dream. It's pretty much gone now, but I recall it as…well, I'm not going to bore you making you listen to my dream."

"Not a problem, Lou, if it would help you recall it, fire away."

"No, like I said, it's pretty much gone now. I just remember feeling—menaced." Lou punched the ignition button and began to pull out of his parking place.

"Like a duck in the sights of a hunter?"

"What? No."

Hammer chuckled. "Just reminded me of something. Maybe, I'll tell you the story someday."

Lou didn't hear Hammer's comment since he had already returned to his unsettled thoughts. He recalled that Herb was somehow involved in this dream, but he could not remember anything more. In his rearview mirror, Lou got a glance at two men pushing an elderly lady to her car in a wheelchair and thought, *It looks like we're not the only ones leaving the party early tonight.*

Chapter 11

Herb's Adventure

Herb Van Doss was not a patient man. Although normally phleg-matic, Herb could summon a surprising level of energy when aroused, and nothing aroused Herb like someone taking his property. While Shelley was not his property, the prospect of losing her was having a profound impact. The thought of being alone and not having her to bring him a beer when he summoned her, or to listen to him gripe about those "stinking Detroit Lions" was clearly not acceptable. He had already forgotten that Lou had asked him to go back to the police department. He had also forgotten that Lou promised to call him in the morning with an update after tonight's visit to the con-gregation service. Herb sat down in his rocking lounger and began to stew. After his fifth beer, he suddenly remembered the brochure he had palmed during his visit to Brother Love's office. He got up, rushed to his desk and grabbed the pile of papers there, which he had taken to calling his "case files." Riffling through them, he found the brochure. It featured an aerial view of an idyllic looking campground near the shore of a large body of water. In the picture were cabins, and a swimming pond showing youthful, happy campers jumping in off of a diving board. There was a large log hall and a garden plot. The phrase "nestled in the Minnesota Northwoods along the pictur-esque Lake Superior shoreline" jumped out at him. He knew at once what he had to do.

He went to his bedroom. Tossing things out of the floor of his closet, Herb found his old duffel bag from his service days. Throwing it onto the bed, Herb began to stuff it with things he might need for this trip. Never much of a traveler, he packed one pair of underwear, three pants, socks, and several old golf shirts. Realizing he might need a coat, he searched out his old Marine field jacket. *This should show them not to mess with me,* he thought. Trying it on, he felt that either the jacket had shrunk, or he was considerably bigger than he used to be. He could not even get the zipper together. "Probably too hot anyway," he mused tossing it back into the closet. He settled on the only other jacket he could find. It was a pink, black, and day-glow green nylon windbreaker with "Ye Olde Village Pump" emblazoned across the back. This was a souvenir from his honeymoon in Florida and seeing it made him miss Shelley even more.

I need a weapon. Owning no gun, he walked to the kitchen where he hefted Shelley's nine-inch chef's knife waving it back and forth like a pudgy D'Artagnon. *No, this won't do. They would probably take it away and use it on me.* He placed it back in the knife block. Then he remembered the revolver-shaped lighter he had been given as a gag gift during his cigar-smoking phase. He trotted downstairs and there it was, sitting on an old, broken TV. *Yes, this baby might just come in handy if I need to scare some of those Bible thumpers.* He pulled the trigger and a six-inch blue flame shot from the barrel. *Whoa, this will light up those congregationers. Heck, they'll probably think it's some kind of ray gun.* He went back and tossed the "gun" into his bag.

Herb then walked out, looked at his car and, surprisingly, made a logical decision. Driving this unreliable car would take too long, plus the possibility of it breaking down was very real. He went back into the house and pulled out an old Yellow Pages. There were several small airlines that flew out of the Gerald Ford Airport. One might have a flight to Duluth or at least a connection through Minneapolis tonight. Herb was lucky. Superior Air had a flight to Duluth that evening at six. He gave the clerk a credit card number to hold his ticket and then started to dial Lou. Then he stopped. *Why should I call Lou? Lou had never called him with any progress report. I have to practically beg for any help at all.* He decided to just leave a note at the house which Lou could find. That is, if he cared enough to even stop by. *I should have gone into police work,* Herb thought, scrawling,

"Gone to get Shelley. Flying to Duluth. Don't bother coming. We'll be back in two to three days" on notepaper and taped it to the front screen door.

Herb's lucky streak continued as he arrived in Duluth about eight o'clock and rented a vehicle. The SUV was bigger and pricier than Herb would have preferred, but, heck, this monster was intimidating, and he was on a mission. Herb set out on Highway 61 along Lake Superior. He stopped at a "Mom and Pop" cabins motel in a lakeside town named Castle Danger and mused on the potential irony in this name. He turned in about midnight and set the alarm for 6:00 a.m. Herb slept fitfully. He awoke feeling drained and half-rested. Herb decided to roll over and sleep for another hour. *Gotta be sharp for this job. Wouldn't do to be half asleep if things get touchy.* He rolled out of bed at 9:30 and ambled across the street. There he fortified himself for today's mission with a half-dozen doughnuts and an XXL coffee—black.

Herb asked the doughnut clerk if she had ever heard of the Congregation of Light campground, and the young goth girl replied that she had not. After further discussion, she told him there was an old "church camp" of some type about twenty miles up the coast off to the waterside. She was unsure if that was what he was after as no one had used the place for several summers as far as she knew. He thanked her and left, now with the conviction that he was approaching the end of his journey.

The sun was brilliant, reflecting off Lake Superior as he passed breaks in the trees. The forest grew thicker and wilder by the mile. A short time later, a weatherworn sign for Camp Wendigo appeared on the right. It stood next to an overgrown turnoff heading toward Lake Superior. Turning east, he was now driving with the sun shining directly in his eyes through the windshield, and he barely missed a deer standing in the middle of the path. After about half a mile, he entered what had once been a clear-cut area with some residual gravel and log bumpers which indicated it had once served as a parking lot.

Herb stepped out of the truck cab. He realized that the camp layout and buildings did not match the brochure, and he quickly decided he must be in the wrong place. *Gee, I hope that wasn't a stock photo in the brochure or this may prove a wild-goose chase*—He got back in his vehicle, put it in reverse and began to back out without looking. There was a loud *thump*. Someone yelled, "Hey, watch where you're going, dummy!"

Herb threw the SUV into park and jumped out. Puzzled, he could see no one. Looking around he saw a large heavyset man dressed in what looked like a lumberjack costume stumble out of one of the old log buildings. The man slammed the door shut behind him. He trotted to where Herb stood.

Herb said, "Sorry, I didn't see anything. Everyone all right?"

The lumberjack looked at Herb. "What are you talking about? I'm fine!"

"I heard a noise and a yell. I thought I'd hit someone."

"No, not me."

Herb looked around again. He saw no one else. Herb decided that he must have hit some small animal. He was opening his mouth to voice this to the stranger, when the logger pointed down under the truck. "Must've been him."

A very tall, thin man had wriggled out from under the driver's side of the car. He was dressed entirely in black with a fly fisherman's hat, that he took off to brush away the copious dust which coated him from head to toe. He jumped to his feet spryly and looked at Herb. "Are you Art Fleming?" The man reached out to shake Herb's hand.

"No, I'm Herb. Herb Van Doss. Geez…are you all right? I never saw you."

"Of course. Better than all right! It's a beautiful morning, isn't it? Are you with Mr. Fleming's party?"

"No, I'm afraid I don't know Mr. Fleming. Sorry."

"Sorry that it's a beautiful morning or sorry that you are not Art Fleming? Well, that makes us even, haw-haw-haw. Mr. Fleming scheduled a fishing trip with us on the lake today—but he was supposed to be here between 6:30 and 7:00."

Herb looked closely at the tall man thinking the man looked familiar. "Do I know you from somewhere?"

"Doubtful. But somewhere is a pretty big place. It was probably my brother there. People are always confusing us."

"No. I remember you from back in Brother Love's office."

The lumberjack chimed in, "My brother said you don't know him, so I'd leave it alone." Turning to the tall man. "Don't you remember that Art baby was supposed to bring his boat?"

"Oh yeah, the thirty-footer with three 350 horsepower outboards. A real beauty. Just the thing for our little lake." And the tall man turned and gestured to the water.

Herb burst out laughing at this. "You mean that—pond? I thought you meant the *big* lake. You know, Lake Superior."

"Nope," replied the tall man keeping a straight face. Then the two began to laugh uproariously. "Lake Superior."

"Tell you what, my fine Mr. Herb. Since Mr. Fleming appears to be a no-show, Eddie here and I will take you out on the best durn fishing trip of your life—and at half price."

"Sorry, gentlemen, I didn't come here to fish. I've got to be running along."

"How about for quarter price?"

"No, thanks, I've really gotta go."

"Wait, wait, wait—fifteen dollars—all day. We furnish the gear, beer, and snacks."

Herb turned to get into his SUV. He found that Eddie the lumberjack had stepped between him and the door. "Excuse me," said Eddie. "Hold on now, pardner. My brother has made you one heckuva offer. What do you have to do that's so important you can't kill some fish with us? If he has no customers, how is he going to pay for that box of dynamite? That stuff isn't cheap, you know."

"Dynamite?" Herb looked around, wondering uneasily who these lunatics were.

"Yup. Beats poles, nets, and all that messy crap any day. Guaranteed catch." Put in the tall man.

"I don't think that's even legal," offered Herb.

"We here at Bang-Up Fishing Trips Incorporated are duly authorized by the state of Minn-e-*soh*-ta to sell annual and daily fishing licenses!"

Herb was losing his patience now and attempted to step around Eddie when the lumberjack reached out and grabbed his shoulder.

With uncanny ease, Eddie spun Herb around and bent him backward over the hood of the SUV. "Okay. Forget the fishing. Are you going to answer my question?"

"I-I-I did."

"Did not."

The tall man, Dickie, answered, "Eddie, he did!"

Eddie replied, "Did not. What was his answer, then, Dickie?"

The tall man theatrically removed his hat and screwed up his face as if considering a profound mystery. Scratching his head, he mumbled, "Hmmm…" then blurted, "'I-I-I did!'"

Dickie then also moved in on Herb. "Then why did you come?"

Herb was annoyed by the intrusiveness of this inquiry. "I don't see that this is any of your business."

Dickie suddenly looked as if he would burst into tears any moment and Eddie turned away and slumped his shoulders. "Any of our business? You come tearing down the path onto our property, get out to look at our lake, then jump back into that—that monster truck. You even run me over. Then you refuse my generous offer and call us criminals. Is this how you treat your friends?"

"No, I'm sorry. I don't mean to be rude, but my wife is missing, and I'm looking for her. She was being held prisoner at a church camp somewhere along the lake."

"Wow, that doesn't sound like any church I'd want to attend," said Eddie

"Is there a ransom? Did she stiff them at the offering?" chimed in Dickie.

"Did she refuse to pass out door-to-door literature for them?"

"How about the airport? Did she mess up the chants at the airport?"

Herb cut in. "Stop already. This is serious. I'm looking for a group called the Congregation of Light. Now if you can help me, fine. If not, I'm leaving."

"Well, why didn't you say so in the first place," exclaimed Eddie. "Come on into the cabin, and we'll draw you a map of where their detention facility, haw-haw-haw—just kidding— where their camp is."

Gripping Herb's shoulder tightly, Eddie steered him toward the log cabin. Herb groaned as he realized that he forgot to put his "revolver" in his pocket this morning.

Chapter 12

A Morning Chat

Arriving home, Decker decided that he could wait to call Herb until the next morning. Lou was a bit queasy, and he felt a nagging unease over the events of the evening. Lou realized that he had learned nothing useful and could actually recall very little of the evening's events. Hammer had brushed off his request to fill in the gaps in his memory, responding that it was a supremely boring evening with typical church music and a boring "pep talk" from a flaming egotist intent on spouting his own ideas instead of the gospel. Not one person was healed, nor in Hammer's opinion was anyone even helped. Hammer admitted that he must have nodded off himself and awoke just before they left. Before parting, they agreed to meet in the morning. They planned to take a run out to Martin's friend, Mrs. Bodkin's home for a chat. While Decker suspected this would prove a waste of time, he decided to go along as Martin was adamant that the old lady would be able to offer useful comments as an actual participant in the service. Martin said that Clarice had once been sharp enough to qualify for a spot on the TV show "Jeopardy," but could not go to L.A. due to lack of funds. Decker wondered if she still would even be functional, if not "sharp." In his view, her attendance at the previous night's service did not speak to a highly developed intellect. But then, of course, he chuckled as he had also been in the crowd. In the end, Decker had agreed to a breakfast date and to an hour or two indulging Martin Hammer, who had been kind enough to accompany him.

Decker set the alarm for 6:30 and went to sleep.

He slept soundly, but not restfully, having spent what seemed like hours in dreams of running. First, he was running to Herb's house for some unknown purpose. For some reason, as he neared his destination, Lou lost his way and began to jog aimlessly. He then found himself sitting alone in a duck blind, quacking and working his arms like a duck in flight, as if these silly actions would bring in his quarry, but to his surprise, it worked. A large duck flew into range right in front of him and hovered right there. Decker reached for his shotgun, but instead he found his service handgun sitting on the bench next to him. He picked up the pistol and noticed that the "duck" had now grown to an extraordinary size and was coming directly at him. He also noticed that the duck's face resembled that of a grinning Ramon Garza—or did it belong to Miguel, Brother Love's henchman? As the beast neared, Decker raised his weapon and fired. Click. He realized then that there was no magazine in the gun. The giant duck was now so close he could feel the air from the beating of its huge wings. Seized with terror, Decker turned and burst through the back wall of the blind. He was again running up Herb's street toward Herb's house. Decker looked back and was startled to find the duck still pursuing him. Finally, he reached Herb's house, bounded up the steps, and raced across the porch. He was knocked off his feet by a peck to his back from the duck. Lou turned and threw his weapon at the monster and managed to crawl into the house and slam the door. He did not think to call out to Herb, but the house phone immediately rang, and Lou picked it up nearly shouting, "Hello, hello."

Herb's voice came through in a dull flat tone. "Lou, I need you now. Why aren't you here helping me. They are going to hurt me, Lou. Lou." The line went dead. Decker was suddenly aware that his alarm was ringing. This was not like his usual wake up routine, as he felt as if he were "coming back" from another place. There was something in his mouth. He wiped away a pillow feather. Lou was confused as he had always bought foam pillows. Decker laughed at this and put the silly dream aside. "Afraid of an old Latino duck," he muttered

Decker was ravenous. At breakfast, he ordered "Leon's Famous Farmer's Feast" consisting of four eggs, bacon, ham, sausage, three large buttermilk pancakes, hash browns, a jumbo biscuit, and as much coffee as he could choke down. Throughout the meal Decker and Hammer chatted about their impressions of last night's service. There was nothing new. This consisted merely of reviewing their previous conversation until Lou remarked that his back and legs were quite sore. This caused Hammer to splutter a bit of coffee out and give Decker an odd look. Hammer was glad that he held his tongue as Decker related enough bits of his "waking dream" to justify the soreness. Again, Martin decided to wait to tell Decker about his bizarre behavior the previous night.

With breakfast finished, they rode out to Mrs. Bodkin's trailer home. Hammer had volunteered to drive, as he knew the route, so they left Lou's car at Leon's near the back of the lot. The ride out went quickly and there was little conversation, except that Hammer found himself whistling one of the discordant hymns from last night and Decker asked the name of the tune saying it sounded vaguely familiar. Hammer became aware of what he was whistling and answered that he did not know.

Decker said, "Hmmm, I don't remember that one either, but the tone is pretty strange for church music. Sounds more like something off of a Hitchcock soundtrack than a hymn."

When they arrived at Clarice Bodkin's door, Martin knocked on the screen door. He called out, "Mrs. Bodkin?" Martin stepped back off the metal steps to the ground.

A few seconds later, an elderly lady looked out at the two men. Her face broke into a wide smile. "Why Martin, Martin Hammer. You are a sight for these old eyes. I don't recollect seeing you since your graduation party, but I'd know you anywhere. My, you are the spitting image of your daddy, God rest his soul. Come in, come in, and who is your young friend?"

This comment brought an amused snort from Decker who was now totally convinced that this old lady was either batty or going blind. He wondered whether Mrs. Bodkin was picturing a Willis Hammer of forty years ago, or if she thought Martin had aged considerably. They stepped into the clean and surprisingly airy trailer which was furnished with old but serviceable furniture.

"This is Mr. Lou Decker, ma'am."

"Sit down. It isn't often I have gentlemen callers these days—and two at once." She chuckled. "Would either of you like a cup of coffee or tea?"

Martin said, "Coffee would be nice. Black is fine. Thank you."

"None for me, ma'am," Decker answered. "Thanks."

"How 'bout a glass of ice water, Sergeant Decker?" Mrs. Bodkin persisted.

Decker and Hammer exchanged a glance. Neither one had indicated that Decker had any rank or job in any organization.

"Ha. I may be old and live alone," Clarice said as she brought Hammer his cup and sat down, "but that doesn't mean I'm slow on the draw. I don't know if you are a sergeant or not, but one, you carry yourself like a person of authority. Two, I'm not so dumb as to think that *two* adult men are going to drop by to chitchat. Three, you look very familiar. I think you are that policeman I've seen either in the newspaper or on TV."

Decker reddened slightly for some reason he didn't quite understand. It isn't that they were going to try to pull a fast one on this pleasant old lady. He remembered the publicity he'd received for the Garza collar. "It's detective, ma'am. Decker."

"Ahh, I know. Just an old woman having a bit of fun. When you get to be as old as me, fun becomes a precious commodity."

Decker found himself warming to this lady. He understood a bit why Hammer had thought her observations about both the service and on the miraculous healing might yield a nugget or two.

"Well, Mrs. Bodkin, the detective and I do have a couple of issues that you might help us with."

"Since I haven't gotten a ticket in twenty-three years nor have I shot anybody in the last few weeks, I'm at a loss as to what I might know that could help you."

As agreed in their drive out. Martin would ask the questions. "First, we saw you at the service at the 'old' church last night. We wondered if you know of any 'miraculous' healings that have occurred there. Second, would you know of a young ex-serviceman who regained the use of his legs after being paralyzed. We also would like your impression of the preacher, Brother Love."

"Please don't call that place a church. Your father would be rolling over in the grave. A gate to hell is what it is. He's no fraud, Martin, you're looking at this wrong. He's pitching for the other team. First, I don't know what you think about your father's death, but you know your dad and my Louie were best friends for years and this—preacher—was on his way out the night your father died. Louie knew this for a fact. Everything about Rev. Willie's death bothered him. He was convinced that Brother Love was somehow responsible. However, Love had an alibi. Two men on the deacon board vouched that they were with him on the bluff. Both gave sworn statements, oddly, both disappeared shortly afterward."

"What about Neil Hathaway?"

"Come to think about it, Louie thought he was involved, but I can't remember how."

"Please go on, Mrs. Bodkin," piped in Decker.

"Well, this Rev. Love might be many things, but he is *not* a fake. He taps into a power. I don't *know* where it's from or how he does it, but I have my suspicions, and it is real, make no mistake."

"What makes you say that, Mrs. Bodkin?"

"Because I was there last night. I saw it with my own eyes, and I experienced it firsthand."

"As we said, we were there, Mrs. Bodkin, and Martin recognized you. That's why we came to you today," Decker put in. "But we didn't see any demonstration of any kind of power, all we did was apparently sleep through a boring church service."

"Well, that's not quite true, Lou."

"What do you mean, Martin?"

"Just please tell us what you experienced, Mrs. Bodkin." Martin quickly changed the subject.

"Okay. First off, the music was not like anything I ever experienced in a church."

"Roger that." Martin seconded.

"It had a dissonant, ominous quality which I now believe was to lull us into a trance state of some kind. I guessed that he would make a pitch for money or cure some planted patients of their asthma or some such, but that didn't happen. Instead the darndest thing did happen. I saw it with my own eyes, and I know it was real. People started doing this bizarre spastic dance, being jerked around like puppets. Up and down, up and down. This went on for a bit. Then people started bending and straightening up over and over and over like those Jews praying at the Wailing Wall, but as if they were on speed. The pastor then told everyone to go outside and eat something or other, I think it was the lawn, but this was after he came for me."

"What do you mean 'he came for you.'"

"He kind of floated toward me. He looked like an insane bar-room piano player and shouted something at me. I passed out. Next thing I knew, I was on stage. The crowd was applauding and then I was wheeled out to my car. The last part is kind of hazy, but there was definitely some kind of power working there. I know it, Martin. I know how this sounds. He said, I don't, no, 'my kind' did not belong here. What did he mean by that?"

"Not sure, but I think it was an unintentional compliment, Mrs. Bodkin."

Lou was quickly becoming lost here. It was as if Clarice and Martin were speaking in a foreign language.

Suddenly, Hammer turned to Decker. "Look, I know that if I had told you what was really going on last night you would have thought I was either kidding you or crazy. But you, Lou, were one of the dancers."

The hair on Lou's neck began to rise in spite of his forced grin. "C'mon, you called her last night and set me up—"

"No, Lou, it's true. You were 'dancing' exactly as Mrs. Bodkin described. Then you were duck-walking along our row of seats, quacking. You were in some sort of trance."

"But you told me you had fallen asleep as well."

"I know I did, Lou. Do you remember awakening?"

"Vaguely. Yes, just outside the amphitheater."

"I practically had to drag you out. I think you would have begun chowing down on the grass if I hadn't persisted in focusing your attention on me. Do you remember trying to return to the show."

"No, not really."

"Lou, I'm sorry. I'm really sorry for holding back. I know you think this is all a load of crap, but it is real as anything in your life. If you are pissed at me, I get it. Sorry. I just did what I thought best."

"Martin, I'm not mad at you. This isn't my first encounter with Brother Love. I know he can make it *seem* that he has some kind of power, but—"

"Think, Lou, your sore legs and back. Do you really think you got that from a dream? And the duck, can you see a connection?"

Decker was deep in thought as he considered whether there actually might be something behind all this mumbo jumbo.

Mrs. Bodkin said, "You were there then, Martin. You know that I'm not making this up."

"Yes, Mrs. Bodkin."

"What about your friend? Why doesn't he remember anything?"

"I think that you and I were protected by our faith in Christ. I'm not sure why he was susceptible."

Lou suddenly stood up. "Thank you for your help, Mrs. Bodkin. Oh, we just wanted to ask one more thing, do you know of a young paralyzed vet who regained the use of his legs after ministrations by Brother Love?"

"Yes, detective, I do know him, but not from the church. His mother is my cousin, Agnes Pibble. His name is Raymond Pibble, and, detective, it's no rumor or tall tale. I've seen him walking myself. They live near Lake Michigan, but I don't think he'll be much help with whatever it is you are looking into. If you wait a minute, I'll write out Agnes's phone number. She can put you in touch with Raymond."

"Thank you."

The ride back to town was quiet as Decker tried to process everything he had just been told. Martin made a few attempts at starting a conversation, but he was met only with desultory replies or nods, so he left Decker to himself.

Chapter 13

On the Road

After picking up his car at Leon's, Decker headed to Herb's house. Lou's mind was replaying Ms. Bodkin's narrative. He was also trying to make sense out of his strange actions last night. He realized that he had experienced the metallic taste once before. It was at Leon's during his meeting with Brother Love when the Reverend and Miguel were playing switcheroo. "Odd." He chuckled. "And I thought it was just Leon's cooking." He tried to let it go, but his confusion increased when he considered that he was mentally stronger than most of the people whom he met on a day to day basis. Yet here were two civilians, and one a little old lady at that, who were able to resist Brother Love, while Decker failed—twice. Martin Hammer had hinted that Lou was not protected by a spiritual faith that apparently, Martin and Mrs. Bodkin shared. *Yeah, right, substituting one form of superstition for another. Not much of a plan.*

He called his office to check in and was going to leave a message for the captain, but what should he say? "Hey, Cap, I spent last evening quacking and duck-walking through the pews at the church of insanity?" He hung up before the call was answered.

As he drove up Herb's driveway, Lou noticed that Herb's car was not there. He was about to drive home when he noticed a small piece of paper taped to the front screen door. He parked and got out. He walked onto the porch and as soon as he read the note, he regretted not calling Herb last evening.

"Gone to get Shelley. Flying to Duluth. Don't bother coming. We'll be back in two to three days."

Lou pulled out his mobile phone and dialed Herb. No answer after five rings, so he hung up. A moment later, he tried again. This time seven rings then a voice, "Hello, Herb Van Doss here. Who is this?" Lou began to answer but was interrupted by the sound of Herb laughing. "Gotcha! Leave a message, and I'll get back." Lou left a request for Herb to call him ASAP.

Lou entered the house using the key that he knew his sister kept under the mat. He looked about for a clue as to whether Herb had left last night or was leaving today. There were dishes stacked in the sink as usual, so that told him nothing. He went back to the porch and emptied mail from the box. Circulars only. No help there. Going back inside, he found a pencil and paper pad on the table. Looking closer, he could identify indentations, but they could not be deciphered. He shaded the paper with the side of the pencil and read, "Superior Air to Duluth 6:00 p.m." Okay, Lou had a starting point now. He pulled out his cell and dialed Superior Airlines at Grand Rapids Ford Airport.

"Good Afternoon, Superior Airlines. How may I help you?"

"Hello, this is Detective Lou Decker with the Grand Rapids Police Department. I need to know if Mr. Herb Van Doss has booked a flight to Duluth."

"I'm sorry, but we can't give out that information over the phone."

Decker had expected this response, and he made a snap decision. "Okay, I'd like to book a seat to Duluth for tonight's 6:00 p.m. flight." Looking at his cell, he noted that he'd have ample time to run by the house and pack.

"Uh, we don't have a Duluth flight tonight."

"Did you have a six o'clock flight yesterday?"

"Yes, we did."

Well, that answered the question of when Herb had left. "When is your next flight please?"

"We have a flight tomorrow morning at 8:15. I see there are a lot of open seats. Would you like me to book you on that flight?"

"Yes, ma'am." Lou gave his credit card number and TSA travel information. He was now headed to Duluth and from there—where? *Good grief, now I've got two people to track down.*

Decker closed up Herb's house and headed directly home. He finished packing in about half an hour then realized he still had time to contact Raymond Pibble today. He'd like to get that out of the way before he left in the morning for Minnesota, so he called the number given him by Mrs. Bodkin.

"Hello, Mrs. Pibble?" Lou asked.

"Yes, who is this?" came a female voice.

"My name is Lou Decker, ma'am. I'm a detective with the Grand Rapids PD, and I'm looking into the activities of a church group in the area. Mrs. Bodkin said your son has had some experience with the Congregation of Light. Do you think I might speak to him please?"

"Oh, Clarice said you would be calling. You can certainly talk to him, but you'll have to call the Cushion and Cue. If he's awake, he's there, not here—except to borrow money which he either drinks up or loses shooting pool. I don't think he's a very good player."

Not being much interested in Raymond's gaming skills, Lou thanked Mrs. Pibble and hung up after she assured the detective that Raymond had indeed regained the use of his legs after visiting "that church."

As he considered this, Lou decided that he wanted to put eyes on the miracle man, so he looked up the entry and found the address of the Cushion and Cue Family Fun Center. It took about twenty five minutes to reach the place, and from the outside, he was astonished that it might actually live up to the "family" tag in the name, but when he swung open the door, it looked to Decker like any other pool dive in the country. Dim lights, a dark wood bar, several dining tables, six pool tables, and a jukebox. There were swinging saloon doors at a hallway entrance leading to rest rooms. A pay phone was visible on the wall.

There was an elderly man sitting at the bar nursing a drink. He held his head down mumbling to himself. The bartender took a swipe at the bar with his towel and looked up at Decker as Lou approached the bar. "What'll it be, Mac?"

Lou pulled out his wallet and showed his police ID to the bartender. "I'm not here to hassle you or your customers. I just need a few words with Ray Pibble. Is he here?"

The bartender was inclined to try to make a quick buck. "What's in it for me?"

"Well, you'll be able to take pride in assisting in a police investigation, and there's the other option."

"What's that?"

Decker bluffed. "I can arrest you for hindering my police investigation, and I will have some colleagues from the health department down here in about twenty minutes to shut you down for a week or two."

"I like plan A better."

"Good. Can't say that I'm surprised, I've always been impressed with the analytical skills of our city's bartenders. Where is he?"

The barkeep indicated across the room with his chin.

There was only one table in play at the moment with a rough looking biker type playing a hipster. The biker type did not look happy as the hipster was making shot after shot.

"Which one?"

"Not those guys. Slow Raymond is leaning against the jukebox. Over there."

Decker noted that the bartender's use of the word "leaning" was apt. Raymond appeared draped over the top of the old Wurlitzer and was attempting to bob up and down to the beat of Grand Funk Railroad's "We're an American Band." Lou walked over to him.

He called to Raymond three times in an increasingly loud voice. The third time he yelled in the dancing man's ear. Yet Raymond, in his own world, did not even acknowledge Decker. "All them Chacquitas in Omaha…" the song blared. Decker took Raymond by the shoulder, spun him and forced him down into a chair. He reached behind the jukebox and pulled the plug.

"Hey!" came simultaneous shouts from Raymond, the old barfly and the biker. The biker took a step toward Decker. "I like that song!" Decker pulled his sport coat back just far enough to show his 9 mm. as he pulled out his wallet and flashed his ID to everyone. The barfly turned back to his drink and the biker gave Decker what was supposed to be an intimidating glare as he resumed his game.

"For the record, I like Grand Funk Railroad too. It's a shame, I know, but I need a bit of quiet to finish my business here, then I'll plug the jukebox back in and leave. Thank you for your cooperation."

He pulled a second chair around and sat straddling it facing Raymond. "Mr. Pibble?" Raymond nodded, clearly intoxicated. "Do you know who I am?"

"No, should I? I can see you're a cop. I ain't done nothin' wrong."

"No, you shouldn't, and I'm not here to arrest you though I imagine it wouldn't be difficult to find a reason if I took a close look at your—activities."

"What do you want. I'm just a disabb…disavul…crippled vet. I served my country, and I don't deserve to be hassled." Raymond was clearly having trouble speaking. Lou was wondering if this would turn into a fool's errand.

"Mr. Pibble, all I need is a bit of information. Then you can go back to your dancing. I understand you were injured in the service."

"Injured? I lost the use of my legs in that damn army." Tears formed in the corners of Raymond's eyes and Decker began to feel pity for this young man. "I was on my way back to base camp from another useless roust when an IED went off. I woke up six days later in Germany unable to walk."

"I was also told that you regained the use of your legs after seeing a faith healer named Brother Love."

"Yeah, I thought so too." He gave a bitter laugh. "But his cure sure isn't lasting. My legs have started to get weaker every day now and some mornings I can barely get out of bed. At this rate I'll be back in my chair in two weeks."

"When did they start going—bad again?"

"Right after his two 'men in black' came over. A couple weeks ago."

"Did they do something to you?"

"No, they wanted me to become some kind of poster boy for Brother Love, you know, going to all those church services with all that weird shouting, and I said 'No' I wasn't interested."

"Did they threaten you in any way?"

"No, they just told me they would check back in a while to see if my mind had changed. They were very sure of themselves, but I'll tell you I'd rather be back in the chair than deal with those creeps."

"Okay. Thanks for your help, Mr. Pibble. Have you considered going to the VA?"

"The VA Spa? Hell, those clowns will give me an appointment for next February and when I show up, I'll see some foreign quack who won't give me anything, or they'll just lose my paperwork again. No thanks."

Lou got up to leave. He shook Mr. Pibble's hand and reached into his wallet. He pulled out his business card and a couple twenty-dollar bills and handed them to the young man. "Thank you and good luck"

Raymond looked at the money and asked, "What's this for? I don't need no handouts."

"Get some pool lessons. A friend says you need them. And the card, if those two men come back, call me—while they are with you if possible, okay?"

"Sure thing. For another forty dollars I'll facetime you."

As Decker walked to the door, he saw a small smile creeping up Raymond's face. His eyes followed as the young man lurched back toward the jukebox on unsteady legs. *That's not the alcohol,* Decker thought.

Chapter 14

To the Shores of Gitchee Gumee

Decker turned in early that evening. He woke up just before his alarm went off at 5:00 a.m. Having packed the previous evening, he had plenty of time to have a cup of coffee and a roll before heading to the airport. Prior to heading out, he dialed the police station and asked the desk sergeant to leave a note for the captain that a personal emergency had come up. Lou had to go out of town for a week or so. Lou would call the captain with details when things became clear. He then asked if the desk sergeant might ask Lou's departmental secretary to run a credit card search on Herb Van Doss for activity for the last two to three days in Minnesota and to call him immediately if anything popped. The sergeant, who was one of Lou's friends, agreed, and they rang off.

On the way to the airport, Lou did something he had never done before. He tuned his radio to WCRS. Knowing that it would be hours until Martin Hammer's program, he was surprised to hear an advertising spot with Hammer's voice. He announced that today's guest on the Spirit Warrior Program would be none other than Brother Love. This surprised Lou a bit as he was acutely aware of Hammer's negative take on the preacher. Then he recalled Martin's reason for being late to leave work yesterday.

Guess the boss's wife got her way.

All went well checking in to his flight. He flashed his Police ID to the ticket agent and asked if Herb Van Doss had booked a two-way ticket, and if so, had he had booked two seats for the return flight. The agent surprised Lou by tapping a few keys informing him without hesitation that Mr. Van Doss had only booked one ticket, one way to Duluth. As Decker feared, this suggested that Herb was on a hunting trip. Decker had been holding out hope that Shelley had somehow escaped or gotten word to Herb where he might come get her. But such wasn't the case.

Lou was pleasantly surprised when he saw the aircraft that would make the fifty-seven-minute hop to Duluth through the jet-way widow. It was a two engine, modern business class jet, smaller than a 727, but infinitely better than the '60s vintage prop-driven cattle car that he had imagined. As Lou boarded, he chuckled at Superior Air's garish color scheme of sky blue and crimson with a large, angry-looking beaver glaring out from the plane's tail. Entering the plane, Decker noted there were only about a dozen passengers and took his seat in 8b. As expected with this half-full flight, 8a was empty. Right before the attendant closed the door, a gargantuan man came hustling in, red-faced and huffing. "Thanks for waiting," he said to the attendant, who smiled back at him. Decker had a sinking feeling when the man stopped beside him and looked over at the empty window seat next to him. The man made a sour face, rechecked his boarding pass, shook his head and turned and plopped down in the empty 8c, across the aisle. Decker let out an audible sigh, and both men looked at each other and laughed.

"The term Airline service is becoming an oxymoron," the man said.

"I really don't fly enough to know," Lou responded.

The man stood to put a briefcase and trench coat in the overhead bin and plopped back down nearly overflowing the seat. Lou sat staring ahead, eyes half closed as he listened to the usual preflight safety lecture. He had not brought a book to read as the flight was a short one and he thought he might try to doze. His cell phone chimed. A message was coming through, "Call station." Lou tried to dial, but the flight attendant admonished him, "Please turn you phone off or to airplane mode, sir. There would normally be internet available, but this plane is in the process of being upgraded, so we are out of luck. Sorry."

Lou returned his phone to his pocket and said to himself, *The text did not specify an emergency, so I guess it can wait an hour.* His giant row mate leaned across the aisle and said, "Bad timing. Hope it wasn't too important."

"Nope. Routine business I imagine."

"Well, thankfully this is a short flight. We may hit some rough weather though. The Weather News Channel said a big storm was moving toward us from Canada this morning. They even named it 'Elmo' as I recall."

Decker laughed. "Elmo? Like the muppet? Doesn't sound like much of a threat."

The stranger joined in the laughter. "It's kind of goofy to be naming rainstorms anyway. I have a friend who calls these people the 'weather terrorists' and that sure seems the case here. My name is Scott Nash." Mr. Nash reached a beefy paw out to shake Decker's hand.

"Lou Decker."

"And what prompts you to fly to Duluth, Mr. Decker. Business? Or pleasure?"

"Kind of both actually. I'm going to hunt down a relative, and I'm involved in an investigation. I'm a police officer in Grand Rapids. A detective actually."

"I trust the relative is not your quarry."

"No, nothing like that, ha-ha, though sometimes I would like to shoot him. And you, Mr. Nash, what do you do?"

"I'm an investigator and writer for America's Fortean Life magazine. I trust you've never heard of this publication?" Decker shook his head and Nash continued, "I was trained in comparative theology, but I decided to spread my wings a bit. I've always loved writing and, actually, I didn't know what my magazine was about, when I took the position."

Decker eyed this man and decided he looked more like a WWE wrestler than either a theologian or writer. "No, sorry. Fortean?"

"As in Charles Forte. He was sort of the 'father' of paranormal studies. Like a real-life Fox Mulder in his day. We serve a limited clientele, so I'm not surprised you don't know of our 'very important' work." He chuckled.

"Oh."

"I'm headed up to Lake Superior to investigate sightings of a sea serpent the locals call, 'Soupy.'"

"Oh."

"Even if it's a hoax or just a dead end, my boss thinks we can at least get a feature story out of it. Funny, we ran a story last summer on a creature in Lake Michigan called Mitch. We did one the previous year on a monster living in Lake Erie called Earl. As you might guess, both managed to elude me, but hey, as I said, we have a *very* hard-core demographic who loves Loch Ness Monster-type stories."

Lou had been only half-listening to this as he formulated the question he wanted to ask. "Mr. Nash, have you ever investigated any religious cults who practice faith healing?"

"Not per se, but I have looked into shamans and alleged miracle cures done in the name of God."

"And what was your conclusion?"

"Conclusion? I suppose it's still an open question, but so far, I've mostly found fakes, and quick-buck artists. You know the kind who evoke a sense of guilt or expectation in their audience and then sell them the promise of a miracle—a magical swatch from the genuine Shroud of Turin for $9.95 plus shipping and handling—which normally doubles their take. I guess it's pretty harmless to the pocketbooks of the gullible, but it's tremendously profitable in the aggregate to the salesmen. The real tragedy is that the harm which the inevitable disappointment will do to a soul can be devastating."

"You said 'mostly.' Are you saying that there are genuine healers from God?"

"Well, I've experienced some pretty strange things. And maybe, I should say that people I trust have seen some dramatic cures, although the medical community dismisses them all as phony, psychosomatic or the patient's own mind doing the healing. There are cases though, that I honestly just don't know—and there are cases where darker forces appear to be in play."

"Do you attribute any of these to a divine power?"

"Hard to say. People do crazy things in the name of religion and then use the persona they have cultivated to invoke God as justification. Does that mean they are all fake? No, it doesn't, but scripture is clear that you will know people by their fruits. Most of those whom I know seem to have an angle. Mr. Decker, just because I write for a rag that caters to the weird curiosities of our readers does not mean that I think we either understand everything or that we even have the capacity to understand. I'm sure that you've experienced things that you cannot explain in your line of work."

"Touché. I'm currently working a case with a 'Fortean' kind of angle. Thank you, you've been very helpful to me."

"Well. Then perhaps this has been a divine appointment of sorts. All I'd say is to keep an open mind, Mr. Decker, and remember, with God, all things are possible."

The sun continued to shine as Decker exited the plane and bid goodbye to Mr. Nash. However, as he looked off to the northwest, he could see a darkening horizon. On his way to the rental car desk, Decker pulled out his cell phone and dialed his departmental secretary.

"Grand Rapids Detective Bureau, LaShiqua speaking, how may I help you."

"Hi, it's Decker. You called."

"Oh, hi, Detective. I got some hits on the Van Doss card in Minnesota. Just three, but I thought they might help. The first was from two nights ago. A room rental at Harry's Tourist Cabins in Danger Castle—$29.67."

"Just the places, please. I don't need to know the amounts." Decker decided that Harry's was probably not a five-star accommodation.

"Okay. He spent a few bucks the next morning at Castle Doughnuts the next morning. But I think you might want to know more about the next charge."

"Lay it on me."

"Menard's Garden Center, yesterday in the afternoon for $3,951.66."

"Geez. Can you pull up that bill detail?"

"Sure, just a moment. It lists a chain saw, two pairs of work gloves, a bundle of workshop rags, and a small off-road four-wheeler."

"Thanks, Herb didn't mention that he was opening a tree trimming business." Hearing no response, Decker continued. "That's a joke, LaShiqua. I'd say that purchase waves a big red flag."

"Oh, wait. Another charge just popped up. Two pies and two cokes from 3-Pie Betsy's in Harbor, Minnesota. Same town as Menard's."

"Sounds like Herb worked up an appetite. Thanks, LaShiqua, and please text if any more charges come through."

"Will do, Detective, and welcome back."

"Bye now." Decker had yet another mystery now. Why in blazes would Herb buy such items? He could think of several reasons, and a chain saw? He did not like what that might suggest.

At the rental counter, he decided on an SUV. If he needed to follow a trail into the woodlands, a sedan might prove useless. He hopped in and headed north along the lake. First stop, Harry's Cabins.

*****

Martin Hammer leaned back in his studio chair and sighed. Now, in addition to the hassles of the last-minute scheduling change, his engineer had just suddenly gone home sick, so Martin now had to run the control panel as well. It was nearly one o'clock and his guest was nowhere in sight. Martin was queueing up his show's theme music, an instrumental cover of The Doors's "Waiting for the Sun (Son)," and rehearsing today's introduction when Brother Love strode into the studio. Martin waved him to the opposite chair in the broadcast booth. The guest mumbled, "Sorry I'm late," as he took the chair.

From the corner of his eye, Hammer saw his boss enter the control room with a Hispanic man dressed in an expensive suit. Hammer did not recognize this man. The boss leaned over the console, pushed a button and said to Martin, "I'll handle this end, Marty." He began to roll the intro.

Love noted Hammer look quizzically at the Mexican and Love said, "That's my attorney, Miguel Lopez de Atocha Gonzales y Ramirez. I did not realize that he was friends with your boss. He insisted on coming along to ensure I don't make any verbal missteps. Heh, heh." Hammer failed to appreciate any humor here, but he smiled, nonetheless. His boss pointed his forefinger at Martin, indicating the intro was ending and Martin hit the switch on his microphone and went live.

"Good afternoon, brothers and sisters. Welcome to today's Spirit Warrior Program. Thanks for tuning in. I think we're all in for a real treat today. We have a surprise guest in the studio. He's something of a local celebrity and the visionary behind this area's fastest growing church movement, Brother Timothy Love. The good brother heads the Congregation of Light for those of you who might not know." He looked across the desk to Brother Love who surprisingly had taken out a pack of cigarettes. He was removing one when Martin shook his head vigorously. Love looked surprised, and he fumbled the cigarette. But then he replaced the cigarette in the pack which he wadded up and stuffed back into his shirt pocket while pantomiming a look of mock horror.

"We apologize to those of you who tuned in today expecting to hear from Terry 'Bugs' Bonham whom you might remember from the original CSI credits as the insect wrangler for the show's star Gil Grissom. Rest easy, we have already taken steps to reschedule that 'Bugger.'" Brother Love and Miguel laughed uproariously at this slightly off-color attempt at humor. They chortled so loudly that Hammer had to hit the mute button. There was apparent dead air for fifteen seconds until Brother Love and Miguel could control themselves. Martin then continued. "In our second hour, we will take calls for Brother Love, and in our final segment, we will have Grand Haven's own Biggie Dark, star of the touring production of 'Milhous, Our Quaker President,' the charisma-award winning musical. He's promised to give us a live rendition his solo, 'NWO—A World of Sin.' Now a word from our sponsor, Dr. Hans Weinberg, our caring Christian Podiatrist who will walk that extra mile in your shoes with you." *Who writes this copy?* Martin wondered.

The bumper music came up, in this case a rumbling Nixonian baritone singing the signature tune from "Milhous."

"It's Sodom and Gomorrah they be bringin' on in.

Turning our Nation to the land of sin.

But we are the Watchmen on the Walls.

We've got the gumption and we got the…"

And faded away.

Martin Hammer had decided to play it cool with Brother Love, and the first hour went off without a hitch. Hammer was polite, if reserved. He tossed a series of softball questions at the preacher who was allowed to spout self-serving babble without challenge. Near the end of the hour, Love made the announcement that the church's "Lakeshore Sanctuary Amphitheater" would be opening within the month and encouraged his radio audience to watch for the date. At this point Martin asked whether there would be a large grassy area surrounding the venue as the flock would no doubt appreciate a snack bar. Brother Love's cheeks began to redden, and Martin tried to put him at ease by commenting "Just a little joke between friends." This placated the preacher, but Martin could see Senor What's-His-Name glaring from the other room.

When the show resumed, Martin announced that they would now be taking calls. Oddly, the calls came in one at a time and for about thirty-five minutes there was a steady stream of complimentary, fluff calls praising Brother Love's compassion, his vision and healing skills. This was clearly not Hammer's usual audience. Hammer had the impression that Love's "attorney" was screening the calls. The man whispered into the boss's ear to make sure only shills got through. As this travesty proceeded, the calls became more and more outlandish with one caller claiming that he won a half million dollars in the state lottery after attending a prayer service, and he was giving this as a "reverse tithe" to the Congregation of Light. Another claimed that Brother Love actually raised her husband from the dead, after the man had collapsed during an extended song session.

Then everything suddenly went south.

Martin thought the voice of the next caller sounded familiar.

"Hello, Martin and Mr. Love. Preacher, I was at your service the other evening, do you remember me?"

"Well, not precisely, ma'am. There were a lot of people there—"

"That's odd. I wasn't just a face in the crowd. I wasn't hypnotized by your music. I wasn't jumping around like an idiotic puppet or eating grass outside. But you singled me out for special attention. I was the lady from the fourth row that you took up onstage before showing me the door. You didn't cure my dandruff or gingivitis, but you did cure my seizures—which, frankly, I never had. Do you remember me now, Mr.—?"

Miguel was yelling at Hammer's boss, telling him to shut this down, now Martin could hear him through the sound-dampening glass. Brother Love momentarily stared like a deer in the headlights, then a look of malice came over his face which scared even Hammer. He mouthed something to Miguel. Miguel nodded and the lights in the studio went black and all the equipment shut off. A few seconds later, the dim emergency lighting kicked in, and Hammer caught sight of his guests walking out of the studio.

Hammer muttered, "Mrs. Bodkin, thank God." And started to laugh.

His boss stuck his head in and asked, "What's so funny, Hammer? This is a disaster."

Hammer nodded his head and thought, *I hope so.*

Thus, ended the day's programming at WCRS.

Chapter 15

Castle Dangerous

The run up to Castle Danger went quickly. Decker was a bit surprised that northern Minnesota reminded him so much of Michigan's upper peninsula. Giant pines, impressively large granite rocks and sandy soil, with glimpses of big Lake Superior waves crashing against the shore. All in all, the area was very pretty. A storm was now quickly moving in from the northwest as the sky darkened rapidly. During his ride, Decker decided that his first priority would have to be finding Herb. Then together, they would work on getting Shelley back. As he pulled into the check-in parking spot at Harry's Tourist Cabins, the first big raindrops hit the pavement and thunder rumbled.

Inside, Decker was greeted by an older, balding man with wire-rimmed glasses. The man was sitting on a stool behind the desk reading an old Louis Lamour western novel. "Can I help you?"

"Hello, my name is Lou Decker. I'm a detective with the Grand Rapids Police Department, and I'd like to ask a couple questions if you have a moment?" He fished out his ID and showed it to the clerk.

The clerk put his paperback down, glanced at the card, and raised his eyebrows. "Go right ahead, lawman. I'll do my best to shoot straight as long as the answers don't violate the Hosteler-Guest Privacy Laws?"

Decker was about on the verge of either laughing or asking if Minnesota had a statute to that effect. "I can get a warrant if—"

The old clerk broke out in laughter. "Hold your horses, young man, just having some fun. Ask away."

"Were you working the desk two evenings ago?"

The clerk assured Lou that he was working; in fact, he said that since his wife went into the "home," all he pretty much did was work when he wasn't with her. He looked at his guest register and confirmed that Herb had checked in late two nights ago. The man remembered that Herb departed early the next morning, leaving the key in the room. The clerk was clearly much more observant than he appeared. He gave a detailed description of Herb down to the ratty Converse All-Stars that Herb always wore and an accurate portrayal of Herb's sometimes irritating vocal mannerisms.

Decker thanked the man and turned to leave. As the clerk picked up his book again, he peered over the top, and called out "Sheriff, do you want me to rustle up a posse? The boys and I could corral that rascal pronto. We could string him up right across there on the doughnut shop marquee."

"No, he's my brother-in-law, and I doubt if he's a person of interest to anyone else. Under the circumstances, a lynch mob might be a bit extreme. But if he does show his face around here again, I would appreciate a call, pahd-ner." Lou placed a business card on the desk and walked out.

The storm was building to full fury as Lou hopped in his rental and dashed across the street to the doughnut shop. The Goth girl was again behind the counter and after official introductions, Decker asked the girl if Herb had come in on her shift. She said that he had been there and recited his order from memory, concluding with "No Tip." Decker asked if he had indicated to her where he might be headed, as he was a stranger to the area. She remembered that he had been asking about the location of an old church camp.

"Congregation of Light?"

"That's it. I don't think I've ever heard of that church before—it must be really old. Ten or fifteen years at least."

Decker let that pass.

"I did tell him about an old, abandoned camp. My girlfriend once told me it was called Camp 'Wings to Go.' It's on the lakeside, up the road about twenty miles. I told him no one had used it for years. He thanked me and left. Is he a criminal or something?"

"No, just my brother-in-law." There was the hint of disappointment on her face.

Decker bought a cup of coffee and tipped her a five for the information. By now the storm had unleashed its full wrath and the rain was coming down so hard that Decker could barely see his SUV in the lot. Decker was soaked by the time he piled in and decided that he was not going to be able to do any useful investigating until the storm blew past, so he headed back across the street.

"Good to see you back, lawman. More questions?"

"Nope, I'd like a room."

The clerk eyed Decker suspiciously. "Oh, you met Misty across the street. We don't rent rooms by the hour."

Decker looked at the clerk incredulously and burst out laughing. "No. no. You think—it's for me, just me, for tonight."

"In that case take your pick of rooms. You can tell people are not beating down my doors."

The clerk handed Lou the key to unit number three. Decker had recently watched the movie "Psycho" and decided to skip the cabin next to the office. As he turned to leave, he asked, "Do you have internet?"

"Of course, what do you think we are, hicks? We even have a *local* dial-up number."

"Dial-up? You mean with a telephone modem?"

"Yep. The best available. If you know the right people and have the bucks, you can still get whatever you want in America."

Decker shook his head. He could not tell if the old guy was joking or serious.

Opening his door, he ascertained that the clerk was not kidding about the internet service. There it was, a dial-up modem sitting on the desk next to the twenty-one-inch black-and-white "portable" TV. Decker had not seen nor used a dial-up modem for nearly twenty years and decided that he would do better to just use his 4G cell carrier. Otherwise, looking around the room, everything appeared neat and very clean, if a little dated. There was an air-conditioning unit in the window which might be useful in drowning out traffic noise even if it were not needed in this storm. The bed was a queen with a firm mattress and two "my pillows." He plopped down and opened his browser. His connection was a bit slow but serviceable. The rain pounded on the roof. Decker's eyes grew heavy as he laughingly looked for "Camp Wings-to-Go" on his browser.

Decker woke up at 4:45 p.m. The storm had blown out, and it was quiet now except for traffic noise. Lou turned on the TV. He went all around the dial and could only get three stations clearly, one of which was Canadian rip-off of Sesame Street featuring a singing blue Muppet-type moose, a lisping walrus, and "Big Pelican." He dialed back to option one, a local station in Duluth. The news was coming on. As he lay there, he became alert when the news anchor said, "In our top story, the Minnesota State Police are attempting to discover the identity of a man found wrapped in fishing line, who apparently drowned today in a pond at an abandoned campsite off of highway 61 just south of Harbors." The TV showed a tarped figure being loaded into an ambulance and then shifted to a hefty man dressed in waders and speaking to a TV reporter. "Yah, da man, he must have been one inept fisher, to, ya know, get all tangled up in his line like dat and fall in and drowned." Lou's neck hair stood on end as he thought he recognized the man. Was he from the Congregation of Light service? The anchor came back on and said that the witness had stumbled on the body as he and a friend were setting out their gear to fish for crappie. It was not only a mystery who the deceased was, but how he got to the location as no vehicle has yet been recovered. "In other news…"

Decker dialed the front desk and asked for the phone number of the MSP. He dialed the number, Minnesota State Police Harbors branch. "Minnesota State Police. This is officer Haukom."

Lou introduced himself, and he asked if the "fisherman's body" was at that facility. When informed that it was, Lou told the officer that he might be able to identify the body and said he'd be there shortly. Decker bolted from his room and hopped into the SUV. He gunned it onto the road adding yet another rubber patch to the lot as he departed.

The Harbors branch of the MSP was housed in a log cabin type building. It was on the southern outskirts of town and backed up to the forest. At the rear of the building was a windowless extension. Upon entering, Decker saw that the station had a front desk, an office area and two holding cells. Decker showed his ID to Lieutenant Haukom and was taken through to the morgue area in back. When the tarp was pulled back, there was Herb, lying there, no longer wrapped in fishing line, but with numerous thin, linear marks along his face, neck, and hands.

Lou identified the body and, as he explained his errand to the extent of coming after Herb, he noticed a look in the MSP officer's eyes that showed he might have some questions about Decker's role in this death. Decker then produced his boarding pass from this morning's flight, and the officer relaxed. Looking at Herb on the table, Decker felt sadness and growing worry about his sister.

"What do we know?" asked Decker.

"Well, he was supposedly found by the man who called it in this morning. He and his buddy discovered Mr. Van Doss as they were arriving to fish."

"Do you believe him?"

"We don't have any specific reason to disbelieve him. But several things don't quite fit. Our homicide unit is looking at the case."

"What things?"

"Well, for one thing, we don't have a lot of major crimes here—just occasional cabin break-ins, meth cooking, bar fights and such. We haven't had a murder in these parts since 1957. Then there was the motive. At this point we are going with a robbery or drug deal that went bad. We found no wallet, phone or ID on the body. Then, why was he fishing in this stinky pond on private property when there are 10,000 lakes in the state—or so our state motto says? How did he get here? Where is his vehicle? Why was he fishing with an antique rod and reel with no bait found anywhere? Why was he wearing a fly-fisherman's hat, that was so large that it came down over his ears. Finally, why wear an oversized red-and-black checkered coat that looked like something out of the costume department from a lumberjack movie?"

"What about the fellows who found Herb? One was being interviewed on TV. I think you'll find that they do not check out."

"We wondered about them too, but they had a solid alibi for last night and this morning. We estimate the time of death to be either of those times. Cause of death, possible asphyxiation by drowning, but he did have a laceration and swelling to the back of his head which appear antemortem. He was said to be found face down, so we don't think the injury was from a trip and fall. The body will be shipped down to Minneapolis for a forensic autopsy, so we expect to know more after the ME has a look. But back to the two men. They aren't locals but their ID's looked good, and they weren't in our system. They gave their names as Jud Heathcote and Jon E. Orr, according to the paperwork. In fact, they even had current fishing licenses. Just one thing bothers me, detective. Why were all three men fishing in this particular pond? It's all a little too neat. I told them to stick around for a day or two, and they gave me the name of a local place, Charlie's Tourist Cabins, where they are supposedly staying. It's about fifteen miles down the road."

"I know the place." Lou's cop sense told him that Herb was murdered and to him, these two guys were likely to be the killers. He decided to hold his tongue and let the MSP do their job without muddying the water.

"Would it be okay if I take a look at the scene?"

"I think the crime techs, such as they are, are finished, so I don't see any reason why not. It is private land, but as I recall, it's owned by an out-of-state trust, so I don't expect anybody to hassle you. If they do, just flash your ID or badge. You can tell them you were sent there by Lieutenant Haukom, MSP and give them my number." He handed Decker a card. "And thanks for your help, detective. You'll find the place a few miles north, before you get to Harbors. There is a broken, nearly unreadable old wooden sign reading 'Camp Wendigo' at the entrance road. The whole area is pretty overgrown."

Lou thanked Lieutenant Haukom and filled out some forms. As Decker walked toward the door to leave, the MSP officer asked, "Why was Mr. Van Doss really here, detective?"

Decker decided to level with his law enforcement colleague. "My sister is, was, his wife, and she recently became mixed up with an off-kilter church bunch. She supposedly came here to a retreat in Minnesota. Herb read me a letter that indicated she was being held against her will. While I was occupied doing some background work on the church, he decided to take matters into his own hands and flew over here to find her. How he wound up at that old camp, I haven't a clue. But I know fishing had nothing to do with it."

"Had he gone to the police with this?"

"Yes, he had, but with no proof, they didn't listen the first time. I had instructed him to take the letter and go back to the station, but apparently he jumped the gun and decided to go off himself."

"I'll get this into our network right away, detective. I guess I don't need to tell you that if you think of anything else that might help. Please call."

They exchanged thanks again and Decker left the station.

*****

Decker decided to run into Harbors. The storm appeared to be reforming, and with that promising an early dusk, he decided to check out Herb's Menard's purchases and maybe visit to the pie shop this evening. Arriving at the Menard store, Decker went directly to the customer service desk where he showed his credentials to a young woman with a name tag reading Ruby, Asst. Manager, and asked who might have sold the equipment purchased with Herb's card. "You're in luck. Calvin made the sale, and he's still around in the back. He's getting ready to go home." She picked up a handset and asked Calvin to come out to the service desk. A moment later a bushy haired young man appeared around the corner and asked somewhat peevishly, "What is it Ruby? You know I'm two hours over already, and I have to get back here at 5:30 to open up."

"Detective Decker, this is Calvin Wood." Turning to Calvin she said, "Calvin, Detective Decker. He has some questions for you!" she said accusingly. Turning back to Decker, "Would you like to use my office. It's a little more private if you need to turn the screws on this rascal."

Decker couldn't help grinning and the assistant manager burst out in a laugh. "I don't think it'll come to that, ma'am. Just a couple questions about a purchase."

"Which one was that?" Calvin asked.

"This morning a man purchased a four-wheeler chain saw and some smaller items. Could you describe him?"

"It wasn't a him. There were two men. Kind of an odd pair, but their card went through, so no big deal to me."

"What did they look like?"

"One was tall and wiry, the other was shorter and heavy, but not fat, muscular, like a body builder or laborer. The tall one did the talking. It was strange but the other guy hung back and seemed to be picking up everything he looked at and holding it for a time like he was planning to either buy it or pocket it."

"Did they take the big items with them, or are they going to be delivered."

"Oh, yeah. They took it all. I ran the hi-lo and carried the four-wheeler to their truck. It was the biggest pickup I've ever seen and brand-new. Jet black. A really cool ride for these two dips."

"Okay. Thanks for your help."

Calvin added one more comment. "I asked them how they were going to get the four-wheeler out. It's really heavy. The big one said they had a hi-lo at their lake home and then laughed at me. I thought they were pretty strange."

"See, that wasn't so bad. Meet you at home in an hour, honey," Ruby called out to Calvin.

"Okay. Careful. I'll get dinner going."

"My husband," she said to Decker.

At the sound of the word "dinner," Decker realized that he was ravenous. He decided to do double duty at the pie restaurant. He drove up the road another half-mile and saw another of the ubiquitous log cabin motif buildings in the area. He entered and found a booth. A waitress came over almost immediately and said, "Hi, I'm Mollie. I'll be taking care of you. Can I get you something to drink?"

"Coffee, black."

Decker looked over the menu and decided on "Chicken in a Basket." This proved a good choice as the dinner was delicious. Finishing his second cup of coffee, he ordered a piece of peach pie for dessert. He was brought a very large piece of the best peach pie he had eaten in years. Decker thought that he should call his secretary LaShiqua and tell her about this stupendous pie and coffee but realized she was too young to have watched "Twin Peaks." When Mollie brought the bill, Decker asked casually, "Have you been working all day, Mollie?"

"Yes, and my feet are killing me."

"Do you remember a customer buying two pies earlier today?"

"No, but Cody was manning the counter for an hour or so at lunchtime. We were swamped."

Mollie called to the back and a very pale white-haired gentleman who looked more like a Hans than a Cody poked his head through pass the window.

"What?"

"This gentleman has a question for you."

"What?"

"Did you sell two pies to a customer around lunchtime today?"

"Yes."

"Can you be a bit more informative? It would be helpful."

"Oh, in that case I sold them to a really fat guy who looked like he was going to eat them right here in front of me. Besides we mostly sell pie by the slice."

"Was he alone?" Decker asked.

"Yes, or at least I didn't see anyone with him"

"Did you notice what his vehicle looked like?"

"Nope. I was pretty busy. What's with all these questions, what are you—a cop?"

"Just looking for someone," Decker answered. "Thank you, both." He paid his bill and headed back to Charlie's. About halfway back, he pulled out his phone thinking to call Lieutenant Haukom, but he decided to wait till the next day after he looked at the scene. Then the sky opened up in a downpour.

Chapter 16

Camp Wendigo

The next morning was sunny with a clear deep-blue sky. It was a perfect day in the north country with no sign of the storms from yesterday. As Decker checked out, the clerk asked if he had ever been "to the Judy Garland Museum there in Grand Rapids." Lou replied, "I'm from Grand Rapids, Michigan, not Grand Rapids, Minnesota." And the men each had a good laugh. Decker stopped in at Castle Doughnuts to grab a couple of doughnuts and a coffee before heading to the camp.

On the way out of town, he passed the local library and decided to stop. It was small but had an extensive archive of the local newspapers in their various incarnations for about ninety years back. It also had high-speed internet. He signed into a computer and looked up the word "Wendigo." This was the name for a mythical beast from American Indian lore that was both a shape-shifter and a cannibal. Decker thought that this was a strange name for a church camp. There was not much else on the topic except the plot synopsis of a campy horror movie from the early 2000s, so Decker went to the newspaper section of the library and did a topical search for "Camp Wendigo" in the master index. He was rewarded with a list of articles listed as being stored on film.

These articles were dated from 1949 until 2003. He gathered the filmstrips and went to a viewer. He spent the next two hours learning about the camp's checkered past. Originally named Camp St. Paul, when it opened in 1948, it was the first nondenominational Christian youth camp in Minnesota and its facilities and programs were considered groundbreaking. In the early 1970s, Camp St. Paul suffered a steep decline in attendance, first due to the changing ideas of morality in the sixties. Then came the economic recession of the early '70s and its impact on America's middle class. In 1976, the camp was sold to a religious organization from Ohio called the "Lighthouse" and renamed Camp Wendigo. This group continued to operate the camp under the form of a trust, and Decker wondered if the Lighthouse might still be the owners of the property. Shortly after the new owners took charge, a string of mishaps occurred which eventually led to the camp's closure. Most serious among these were two children who went missing from the camp over a three-year period. Both were from out of state, as were most campers those days as saturation news coverage surrounding these disappearances had turned most local Minnesotans sour on the camp.

Decker learned that the camp closed for good in 1983 after a major fire burned a large portion of the camp to the ground, killing three campers and a counselor. The fire was determined to be accidental by investigators; however, several lawsuits were initiated by the families of the deceased. One was settled, and the rest were still in litigation when that article was penned. Decker learned from a subsequent news story that both of the remaining suits were suddenly dropped after one plaintiff died of drowning in a bizarre accident. He was reportedly visiting the camp and investigating on his own. Years later, in 1995, a newsman took up this story and after visiting several of the campers, now adults, he had discovered that all of them now recalled events surrounding the original fire as being part of some type of occult ceremony that might have gotten out of hand. This 30-year-old journalist passed away of a massive heart attack one day after publishing the article which exposed this part of the story. Again, local officials refused to investigate, this time maintaining that the journalist's death was ruled "natural," although unfortunate. Lou thought it odd that the story mentioned that none of his notes were ever found. At this point, Lou decided he needed to take a deeper look at the absentee owners of Camp Wendigo, but he could find nothing useful here.

Having finished at the library, Decker walked down the block looking for a place to eat prior to going out to Camp Wendigo. He stopped in front of a building with a faux limestone façade shaped like the Roman Coliseum and a red-and-green neon marquee flashing "Alto's Pizzeria—Best in Town." He decided that some pizza would hit the spot and entered. Inside, the movie "Gladiator" was playing on all eight large screen TVs with the roars of a tiger and the plebeian crowd competing with a Dean Martin soundtrack. There was an athletic-looking man throwing pizzas next to the oven. He smiled at Decker and waved in greeting. Decker was shown to a seat near a wall covered with a well-done mural portraying the Vatican. On the wall opposite were heroic renderings of a man, presumably a much younger version of the pizza-tosser striding down a football field cum colosseum holding a ball in one hand and fending off a midget clad in a puce jersey emblazoned with "PM" and stepping on a second. Lou ate slowly, thoroughly enjoying this Roman delight.

Decker then headed out to see Camp Wendigo for himself. As he rode, the sun was bright, his belly full, and he became a bit drowsy. There were no other cars on the road, and he turned on the radio. The strains of Procol Harum's "Conquistador" filled the car. A large, dark shadow intermittently covered the car as he drove and seemed to move along with him. He looked up to check it out. Above was what he assumed to be an extremely large buzzard flying along at such an angle that it blocked the sun. It appeared to look down at him and then resumed its flight. The radio blared "And though you came with gun held high, you did not conquer, only die." The shadow had moved ahead and veered off to the right toward the lake. Decker realized that these were not the lyrics he remembered. Gun? The lyric as he knew it was "sword." He felt a wave of nausea and came suddenly alert as the decrepit Camp Wendigo sign that he had missed on yesterday's trip came into view. The song ended with the final plaintive wail "I see no maze to unwind." And he shut off the radio.

He turned off the main road onto what would have been a barely discernible two-track a few days ago but was now clearly visible due to recent traffic. After about one-half mile, he came into a clearing with a pond as described by the police. He parked and got out. Across the pond, he could see a man looking at him. The man took off a large Stetson hat and waved it at Decker. He gestured toward a large log building about thirty yards from Decker, as if directing Decker to go there.

Decker decided to ignore the man. He walked to the edge of the pond. Many of the reeds and weeds at the waters' edge had obviously been crushed down recently, but to what end was not discernible. He bent over and looked closely at the ground. Scanning the area, he found a large brass button, but it looked old and was unfamiliar. Rubbing off some of the grime, he saw the face of Bozo the clown and determined that the button must be at least fifty years old. After about ten minutes of fruitless searching, from the corner of his eye he noticed what looked like a disruption in the tall grass off to his right—away from the pond. He looked directly in that direction and lost sight of it. Tilting his head, he scanned and brought it back into focus. He noted the direction and crabbed over toward it. When he got there, he could see that the weeds had definitely been pushed down and out of the way. *Something big moved through here.* He now saw an obscured path heading off toward a denser patch of vegetation on a hill about 200 yards away. He followed the trail and as he approached the hill, there was a tree line that marked the beginnings of the woods, just beyond the hill. A small section of trees appeared to be missing. At the tree line, most of the trees had trunks three to four inches in diameter and that the gap contained stumps which stood a few inches off the ground. They were cleanly cut off. He also noticed sawdust scattered about the opening. *These have been cut recently. Hmmm, chain saw?*

Decker continued about a hundred yards into the forest. Now the path was easy to follow as it was marked by the cut trees. About fifty feet ahead the path appeared to end abruptly, but as he neared this point, Decker could see that it actually made a sharp angle turn to the left. There he found a very large pile of all the branches and tree trunks cut to make the path. He walked up to the pile and pulled away several branches and caught a glint of chrome underneath. He spent the next twenty minutes pulling off the foliage. There stood what was presumably Herb's rented SUV. He looked inside. There was a bag from the donut shop wadded up on the floor and a large cardboard coffee cup in the holder. No sign of pie cartons. There was a rag on the driver's seat. Decker thought it was probably used to wipe down the car; he figured that if these killers were careful enough to dispose of their trash, no fingerprints would be found. Lou looked for a key, but he did not see one. He took out his mobile phone and took pictures of the vehicle inside and out. He then opened the map function and dropped a pin. He decided that it was time to give the MSP what he had discovered, but he was getting no coverage bars here. Decker shook his head and headed back to the clearing in the camp where he had parked his vehicle and dropped several pins along the way.

When he reached the clearing, two men exited the log building. One of them called to him, "Detective Decker."

He knew immediately that these were the same two men from the TV interview. They appeared as described by the witnesses at Menard's and the restaurant. Decker replied, "I'm afraid I'm at a disadvantage, gentlemen, as I don't think we've had the pleasure of introductions." The longer he looked at them the more convinced he became that they had been the men at Brother Love's side during the Congregation of Light service. He added, "I do have to hand it to your travel agent, though. I saw you two at the service Wednesday evening, and getting you here in time to murder my brother-in-law, Herb, yesterday is impressive"

The fat one was doing all the talking. He had a smirk on his face that Decker found as obnoxious as his attitude. "I don't know *what you* saw, but we did enjoy rousting Mrs. Clarice and would have gotten to you shortly, if you hadn't 'ducked' out and ran away. And while we're on the subject of travel, it doesn't look like you'll be doing any soon." He gestured toward where Decker had parked his rental. Decker turned. His vehicle was now gone.

"You are just so predictable, detective." He began to laugh at Decker's confusion as he looked all around for the SUV.

"Where is it?" Decker took out his phone with his left hand, and he drew his weapon with his right.

"Your friend borrowed it."

"My friend? What friend? I don't have any friends here."

"Well, we know that you've met Miguel. Don't you like him? He might not be so happy to hear that." The fat man called loudly across the lake, "Amigo, your friend the detective here, he says he doesn't like you."

At this point Lou looked across the lake. The man was comically holding his big hat up to his ear like a hearing horn. Looking at the man, Decker noticed his SUV which looked to be about waist-high there next to the man. Decker still could not see the man's face clearly, but he was becoming nauseous. His anxiety level rapidly increased. Decker leveled the pistol at the fat man and his phone suddenly rang. He answered. His ear was attacked by a bunch of Spanish sounding gibberish. The fat man translated, "He says the preparations are now complete and it's time for you to see Lake Superior from the air. I guess you get one last trip after all, Mr. Detective man."

Decker tried to hold his gun steady on the fat man, but Lou was suddenly extremely nauseous and dizzy. As Lou's gun began to wobble, the fat man began to hop from side to side with surprising speed and agility. "Careful with that gun, you might shoot someone," the man taunted. The tall man who had taken "cover," comically standing behind a sapling, spoke for the first time, "Though I personally would love to, *we* aren't going to hurt you. But if I were you, I'd be paying attention to him. I think you have insulted Miguel." He pointed across the lake.

Decker was now dealing with a severe case of disorientation and felt as if he would vomit at any second. His gun hand wavered, and he had dropped his phone, but he looked where the skinny man had indicated. Here came the man who had been waving at Decker. Incredibly, he appeared to be skating across surface of the open water with incongruously long strides. As the man reached the shore, Decker identified the face of Miguel, Brother Love's henchman except this Miguel looked about twelve feet tall and was heavily muscled. He bowed theatrically low with his hat in hand to Decker. His eyes radiated an eerie yellow energy and his face was locked in a smile.

"Bonus Deegas, mi…what is the word for a person who you thought was your friend but says he is not? Sorry, my Spanish is a bit rusty." The words came directly into Decker's mind as he realized that Miguel had not moved his lips. He was hit with a pressure in his ears and another surge of nausea. He was having difficulty concentrating.

"Now we can't have any of that," Miguel continued, this time verbally, and Decker felt his mind suddenly clear and nausea subside. "I don't want to be accused of tampering."

Miguel now looked into Decker's eyes and his face became serious. "Senor Detective Decker, Brother Love has already warned you off. You were clearly told not to get involved. In fact, he was offering you a place on the team, remember, back at Leon's? But you continue in your stubbornness and stupidity. We know that you do not believe in God. We know that you are a thoroughly materialistic man—what one might call a practical 21st century American man. A man stuck firmly in the here and now. Don't get me wrong, I get that. What has God ever done to show you that he really exists? But we, on the other hand, have shown you our power over and over, but you persist in explaining it away as ooga-booga or humbuggery. In the end, you'll wind up in our dugout, even if you don't want to play for any team but your own. But even we run out of patience, and frankly, you are becoming a nuisance, so since you insist on being so thick, let me show you something that might get through to even a dullard like you. Would you like to go for a little flight?"

Decker was convinced that he had lost his mind with what happened next.

Miguel began to float up into the air and at the same time lose his human form. His shape became at first hazy and then began to coalesce into a huge reptilian shape with huge wings that stretched out from his sides. He had an unearthly reddish green hue. The dragon threw back its head and roared with the sound of a hundred thunders. It craned its neck and inhaled with a great rush of air. Smoke began to issue from his nostrils. Decker emptied his magazine into the chest of the great beast. His salvo had no effect on the monster, and Decker threw his gun at the monster. He had the certainty that he would be incinerated in the next few seconds on the shore of this stinky fishing pond. But Miguel had other plans, he rose into the air and with several beats of his great wings traversed the lake. The dragon incinerated the SUV with one blast.

The two henchmen began to cheer and jump around as if they had just won the lottery.

The creature wheeled and then headed back toward Decker. He stopped in the air hovering on slowly beating wings and looked down at Decker, extending a giant claw toward him.

"Jesus," Decker said quietly. It was not spoken as an oath, rather Decker had now seen the impossible and was at the end of his rope.

The celebration suddenly stopped as the tall one cried out, "*The Word*," as if suddenly in pain. In his mind Decker thought a voice said, "No further."

Decker looked up. The dragon recoiled and withdrew his claw. "You know the rules. He belongs to us." He appeared to be addressing a bright light immediately between Decker and the beast.

Decker again was aware of a second voice, "As you do. You know that he is not yours until the moment of his death. You also know that he has neither committed to your side nor has he tried to end his own life."

The dragon roared again and began to beat his wings furiously. Decker turned to see the two killers running toward the log building, and he decided to make his break. He didn't know who, or what it was that stood between the beast and him, but he'd let them argue till next week if they wanted. He took off running full tilt toward Herb's SUV. As he ran, he realized that even if he got to the SUV, he had not seen any keys and would be cornered there. Understanding what one blast from the dragon had done to his vehicle, he didn't relish the idea of getting fried in a tin can. He ran past and continued his headlong dash for what felt like hours. The roar echoed once again. This time it was louder and came from up in the air. He knew that the coast was ahead. If he could reach it, he might climb down and hide in a cave or among the rocks. This was a thin hope, but it kept Decker going. He was totally spent when he stumbled onto the shoulder of an old road which ran along the coast. Another loud roar came, much, much closer now. He thought his lungs would

PURSUIT

burst and he wobbled on rubber legs across the broken pavement. He looked down and despaired. Here was a sheer cliff dropping straight down over 100 feet onto giant rocks scattered below and swirling water. Then he felt the roar as much as he heard it and the giant beast landed on the opposite side of the road. Decker reached into his pocket for his phone, then remembered he had dropped it. He pulled out only his wallet.

"No one to save you now, boy." The monster drew in a deep breath.

As the dragon inhaled, Decker turned, took two running steps and leaped out into the air over the cliff edge, dropping his wallet as he fell.

Chapter 17

The Fishermen

That morning out on Lake Superior just offshore was a fishing boat with two occupants. In the bow was a young woman holding a fishing pole as the boat tooled slowly through the light chop. In the back was an elderly man minding a pair of outriggers and steering the boat. It had been a slow day having hooked only one large salmon on an outrigger about 11:00 a.m. and nothing before or since. The woman called to the back, "Uncle, are you ready to head in? Looks like the fish are sleeping today, and I've been hearing thunder for the last fifteen minutes."

"Unnhh," said the old man who looked up at the bluebird sky quizzically. He too, had heard the noise, but it had not sounded like thunder to him; however, he agreed that they had spent enough time trying to coax the fish to bite. He began to haul in his lines while letting the boat engine slow to an idle. In his long life he had been through many storms. He had even been told of men being roasted by fire from the heavens on cloudless, sunny days, but this "thunder" was different. It sounded somehow…*alive.*

"Look there, Uncle!" The old man looked up quickly to where the woman was pointing, just in time to see a large object plunge into the lake. "Let's go! Quick now, Uncle. That was a man!"

The old man wondered where the man, if man it was, had come from. He had seen no plane. No parachute. No nothing. Surely, he must have fallen from the cliff high above. He jazzed the engine and their boat leapt forward toward the impact site. As they raced to the spot where the falling man had hit the water, the old man noted that the shore was rocky here. He marveled at the magnificent high bluffs, that could more correctly be called cliffs lining the edge of the lake. As he looked upward, there it was, a dot in the sky moving slowly away inland, but he assumed that he was just watching a large bird, or a visual floater and said nothing. As they neared the point of impact, he could see that there was indeed a man floating on his back in the water. There was blood streaming out from around the man's face. He decided that the man was probably dead. If the impact on the water didn't kill him, it was doubtful that he has missed the submerged rocks.

The woman reached out and snagged the man's head with her pole net. She gently held the man's head out of the water while the old man guided the boat alongside. Together they hoisted the man from the water and laid him. on the foredeck of the boat. The old man returned to the stern. He gunned the motor and they made a beeline for Harbors. She checked for a pulse on the man's neck. "He's alive, Uncle."

In the sky above, an iridescent green creature wheeled back from the cliff's edge. It looked over at the bright entity that flew unseen, to others in the sky alongside him, and said, "There you are, bright slave. Satisfied? I did not lay a talon on him. He jumped of his own accord. He's ours now."

"Perhaps," responded the other, right before disappearing in a flash of light.

The woman called ahead to have an ambulance waiting at the Harbors' dock, On the run back to shore the man remained unconscious. She noted that his breathing was regular and his heartbeat strong, but he was bleeding from his mouth and had bitten his tongue. She also determined that he had bled through his shirt from a laceration and the shape of his shoulder did not look right. She gingerly removed his jacket. There was an empty holster under the injured area. She took a fishing knife and cut away his shirt material from near the wound. Then she cut away the holster straps letting the rig fall away to the deck.

The old man called from the back, "Keep his neck straight, Lenore. Here, use this alongside his head." He tossed his floatation seat cushion over the windshield to her. "There's tape in the first aid box below." She decided that she did not want to leave the man and kneeled at the top of his head holding it. She put the cushion to one side of his head and neck to help stabilize him. She decided to keep her vest on as Uncle was driving the boat very fast. She looked into the live well and briefly considered using the Salmon to stabilize the other side of his neck.

The man's breathing continued deep and even, but he remained unconscious. She looked at his left pant leg which had ridden up over something. Concerned that it might be a broken bone, she pulled the material up. A small empty holster was strapped on his ankle. *Who is this guy?*. It *was* kind of a "James Bond" leap he had made.

The ambulance attendants met the boat at the marina. They thanked Lenore for the care she had provided. A policeman from Harbors asked Lenore if she knew who the victim was. She said that she didn't. While relating the story, an MSP cruiser pulled up and an officer got out. He walked over to the ambulance and looked in the back as the EMTs were getting ready to close the doors. All Lenore could catch was the EMTs response that "it's too early to tell." The state trooper then had a brief conversation with the local police-man who then smiled, nodded toward Lenore, and shook the troop-er's hand. The patrolman got in his car and left. The state trooper walked over to Lenore. He introduced himself. "Hello, Ms. Cloud? I'm Lieutenant Haukom, Minnesota State Police. Do you mind if I asked you what your involvement is in this?"

"Hello, Lieutenant. I'm Lenore Cloud, but I'm not sure what you are asking."

They went back and forth a bit before Lenore understood that he was asking for her version of what had happened to the man who was just taken away in an ambulance. She stated that she had seen the man falling from the corner of her eye, called out to her uncle who was driving the boat and they sped to where he came down in the water. She related the rest of the trip to Harbors a her observations of his injuries and the fact that he was unconscious the whole time.

"Frankly, I'm surprised he's alive, Ms. Cloud. Did you happen to see anyone else?"

"Falling?"

"No, at the top of the bluff. Someone who might have been with him?"

"No." She looked to her uncle who had come up from the boat carrying the holster and jacket. "Do you think he was pushed?"

"I wouldn't know one way or the other, ma'am." Haukom rubbed his forehead.

Uncle decided that he had seen an eagle or maybe nothing at all. He shook his head no when the lieutenant looked at him.

"Just a few more questions to you both if I may. Does the name 'Herb Van Doss' mean anything to you?"

Lenore answered "No." And her uncle again shook his head.

"How about 'Lou Decker'?"

Again, they both indicated no. Lenore said to the trooper, "Can I ask a couple questions?"

"Go ahead." As he took the holster and jacket from the old man.

"Who is he? Is he a criminal or something? And how did you hear about this? This doesn't seem like a state police type issue."

"No, he's not a criminal. He is a police officer, a detective in fact. He's here on a—vacation. His name is Lou Decker, and I met him when he stopped by our office in Harbors yesterday as a courtesy. He had indicated that he was trying to find a relative who decided to take a fishing trip rather precipitously. Decker said he might check out a lake in the area today. We monitor 911 calls and I drove here to check things out. I don't expect this was his plan."

Lenore sensed that there was much more to this than the state trooper was saying, but she smiled and held her piece. The trooper looked the holster over, "Nice rig. Custom. Was there a gun as well?"

"No," said Lenore. Uncle shook his head while looking at his niece.

"Well, thanks again. He could use a prayer or two if you are the praying kind."

Lenore nodded and Uncle harrumphed as the officer left. Her curiosity was now piqued. Lenore decided that she might just swing by the hospital to check on Detective Decker after they got home and cooked up that salmon.

Chapter 18

The Invalid

In fact, Lenore did not get to the hospital that evening. After helping Uncle clean and prepare the salmon for baking, she sat down and began to reread today's newspaper while he went about fixing the rest of dinner. She picked up the front page and quickly found the story she was looking for. There it was above the fold: *Unidentified Fishman Found in Local Pond. MSP Fears Murder.* She laughed aloud again at the headline, shaking her head she thought, *No wonder newspapers are doing poorly. If they can't proofread their own headlines, why should readers trust their content?* Moving on, she skimmed to the part which had drawn her attention after the events of the day.

"MSP spokesman Lt. C Haukom stated that the deceased was unidentified at this time and asked that any members of the republic who might have information bearing on the case to please come forward. He added that the MSP was not ruling out foul play and that the incident was under investigation."

Lenore sighed. *"Republic? Really?"* She then went back to the beginning of the story to refamiliarize herself with the particulars of the death.

"The MSP stated that they had received information concerning a man found in the shallows of the large pond at the old Camp Wendigo site, adding yet another chapter to the camp's grisly past."

She looked up and said to herself, "Sounds like maybe they have since identified the man as Herb Van Dyke, or whatever that name was. How is a detective from out of town involved in this?"

Lenore called her cousin Anna Tall Deer who worked evenings as a nurses' aide at the hospital.

"Anna can you tell me how Detective Decker is doing?"

"Let me check with his nurse and I'll call you back, okay?"

As she hung up, Lenore's cousin, Hank stuck his head into the room. "Dinner's ready." As they went to the table Hank commented, "Dad says the fish just weren't biting today. He thinks the man who fell from the sky scared them all off."

Lenore laughed and commented, "Maybe so, but that doesn't explain the rest of the day."

Uncle, who heard the last part of the exchange commented, "The fish in that sea are all connected. Just because one of their brothers took pity and gave himself for our hunger doesn't mean they did not know he was coming."

Lenny just smiled. Her uncle was a man who spiritualized everything. Lenore just could not think that way. She had followed the Jesus road since she was a child attending Enemy Swim church with her parents. She loved and admired her uncle. He was a truly good man who exhibited the essence of the Christian faith. She realized that no two souls experience God in exactly the same way, so she chose not to dwell on the strangeness of some of his ideas. Uncle had shown her only kindness since the day her parents were killed in a car crash near Waubay, South Dakota. She had heard it said that if there were only two cars on the reservation going anywhere, they would find a way to crash into each other. In this case, it was only too true. Her uncle Floyd and his bride Aunt Jessie White Sky took her in as their own daughter and raised her alongside their son Hank.

Dinner was fabulous. Fresh salmon cooked to perfection by a master game chef, and fresh greens and boiled red skin potatoes from their garden. Lenore was full, and after cleanup, she walked into the living room, where Uncle was watching a sitcom about a fictitious family in current day America. The cast of characters had been chosen from every fringe group in the country. The men were all slovenly idiots, incapable of even finding the front door without constant hectoring from the beautiful, accomplished women in the show. Any children who might appear in the scene would yell at and talk down to any adult they encountered. Hank followed Lenny into the room. Noting his father's sour expression, he voiced Lenny's thoughts, "Why do you watch this crap."

"Because 'Keeping Up with the Kardashians' is not on yet." His eyes twinkled.

That brought a smile to both Hank's and Lenore's faces. He went on, "I am simply witnessing the deterioration of the American male from those brave souls who tamed this continent, much to the distress of *our* ancestors. And, I might add, who defeated the Nazis into these squirrels. Why do those making programming decisions in this great country hold up these numbskulls to our children as ideals?"

"Wow. That's pretty rough. And I thought it was a sitcom. Are you convinced this is deliberate?"

"Maybe it is. Maybe it isn't."

The room fell silent. Lenore was startled by the sudden ring of her mobile phone. She listened as Anna related such information about the injured detective as she was able to finagle from the nursing staff. Lenore thanked Anna, asked her to keep her updated if anything significant occurred, and disconnected.

Uncle looked up at Lenore from his chair. He asked, "Well, how is the man who fell from the sky?" Hank looked on curiously.

"Uncle, there is a law called HIPPA which limits the amount of information available to outsiders, but Anna learned quite a bit. He got out of surgery about an hour ago. They had to put a pin in his shoulder. The cut there was pretty deep. He may have damaged the tendons or ligaments. Anna was not sure which. He has not awakened yet. They CAT scanned him all over and it looks like there is some swelling with a build up of fluid around his brain. They expect that to resolve without surgery, but until he wakes up, they won't know the extent of any injury. The good news is that there was no neck or spine injury and his chest and abdomen were normal on the scans. Anna says he will be in intensive care unit until he stabilizes. Even when he wakes up, they will keep him in the hospital for a time for IV antibiotics and observation. According to the nurses, the trauma docs were saying he was twice lucky. It is unusual for someone to fall from that height and survive, let alone to escape with the few injuries he has."

"And what is the second bit of luck?"

"That Uncle and I were there."

The old man looked away. "Hmmph...luck."

"Anna says no one has called about him yet, and his only visitor so far was an MSP lieutenant. Probably the man we met at the dock. But the detective is in ICU, so he cannot have visitors anyway."

After a few minutes Lenny said, "I'm pooped, I think I'll turn in."

"There is one thing I'm puzzled about, sis."

"What's that."

"If he fell into the water, wouldn't that soften the impact."

Uncle opened his eyes and responded for his niece. "You've done plenty of belly flops, son, think about how they felt from five feet."

"I see what you mean. Good night."

Chapter 19

Soul Searching

Lenore climbed into bed. She decided to read a bit before trying to sleep. She was about halfway through Frank Peretti's novel *The Oath*, but it was difficult to concentrate on the story as her mind was repeatedly drawn back to the events of the day. After several starts and stops, she put the book down and laid her head on the pillow. She realized that she was experiencing the adrenaline letdown which comes after a stressful event. She recalled Lou Decker floating face-up, staring at nothing. She kept flashing back to images of the man lying on her deck. Her hands were bloody, and she tried to hold his head and neck steady. She remembered the dead weight of his limp body being hoisted onto the stretcher and loaded into the ambulance. This was her first meeting with the ugly chaos that surrounds violent death since her discharge from the Air Force. Her mind wandered back through years to her training. Repeated drills and lectures. Endless hours of practice cutting open the metal hulls of mock-ups. Stumbling into training fuselages black with smoke, hauling dummies to safety in hopes of doing the right thing automatically when the time came. Finally, there was the horror and the sickening sadness of actual crashes. No one ever survived the heaps of burning metal and flesh that merged into a gruesome sacrifice to evil. She considered that war was always dressed up in patriotic imagery as it was projected into America's living rooms; always separated by miles from the awful actuality of this, this waste of the greatest of God's gifts—life. Few would ever understand the sensory reality of war's violence. Lenore had looked death in the face before. She had felt its cold claw reaching out. Today was more of the same—trying to save life, but understanding that her efforts, their efforts, might be in vain. Yet this time it was different. She prayed for quiet and peace. Eventually her mind settled, the nerves calmed, and she drifted off. No dreams. Just a moment of blackness interrupted by Hank's voice.

"Anna's on the phone. Do you want her to call back?"

"No, I'll take it. Thanks, Hank." She picked up her bedside house phone. "Hello?"

Anna told her that the "flying man" as he was being called around the hospital, was still unconscious, but his vital signs remained stable and there was no fever. The surgeons had decided that he would be moved to the step-down unit this morning because a car accident brought in two victims to the ICU during the night. There was an MSP lieutenant there again at the desk a few minutes ago. It was the same officer who had been there the previous evening. Anna had gotten close enough while pretending to stock carts to overhear him talking on the phone to the detective's boss. It sounded like Flying Man's department didn't know he was here nor that he had been injured. No one else had called or stopped in to see him. Anna promised to keep her updated and hung up.

It was Lenore's morning to run the front desk at Ohiyesa Lodge where she lived. The family owned and operated this resort on the grounds of their family property. It proved a busy morning with three families booking weeklong stays with guided fishing trips. There were numerous other calls and inquiries. She spent the time she was not on the phone, putting the finishing touches on her revision of the lodge's antiquated brochure. The parked cars in the old picture were 1960s era Fords and Chevy's with enormous fins and lots of chrome. The patrons appeared to be answering a casting call for a documentary on the hippie era. She had answered his question about the need for the expense of revising "a good thing." "Yes, I think it's time, Uncle." She was free in the afternoon and decided to stop by the hospital after her daily run. The hospital was only two blocks off her route and less than a mile from the lodge. As she ended the cool down phase of her run, she walked right up to the hospital lobby desk.

A neighbor, Shirley Sweet Grass worked the desk. She greeted Lenore with a smile. "Hello, Lenore. You must realize that you and Uncle have become celebrities. Your exploits in saving Flying Man are being put into verse by Elijah Black Horse. He promises to have your song ready to perform at next week's pow-wow."

"I can hardly wait. I remember his 'Song of the Peacekeeper' celebrating the drunken driver who crashed into the escape car of those boys who had robbed the party store."

They both laughed. "Anything new on the detective?"

"No, he is still unconscious, but the nurses say he's stable. The doctors are upbeat."

"Can I see him?"

"If you peek in Room 3, B Hall, I don't think it'll hurt anything. Just mind the nurses, but I guess I don't need to tell you that."

"Thanks, Shirley. I'm just gonna look in, then I'll be on my way."

Shirley turned her attention to an elderly lady in a wheelchair who had come up behind Lenore. Lenore moved off toward the step-down unit. She opened the swinging double doors and walked into the unit unmolested. There were only four rooms in this area. Two on each side of the nurses' station. No one was in view. She heard a moaning from room 2 as she passed by, but she resisted the urge to look in. As she approached room 3, a young nurse came out. Lenore recognized her as the younger sister of an old schoolmate but could not recall her name. Lenore looked in to see Decker, who lie on his back with his head slightly elevated and his shoulder bandaged heavily. He had a tube in his nose, and he was hooked up to a heart monitor which displayed a tracing and a plethora of numbers. She could see that the tracing pattern looked regular, which she knew was a good thing, but could tell nothing more from the information displayed. An IV bag dripped fluid and antibiotics into a blood vessel in his arm. The bed made occasional groaning noises as a pneumatic device shifted Decker's position periodically. The nurse looked at Lenore and smiled. "Hi, Lenore, good job with Detective Decker there."

"Thanks. How is he doing?"

"For all intents and purposes, he is either the luckiest man in Minnesota or someone upstairs seriously wants him to keep living. I've fished that area along the shore where you pulled him out and how he managed to avoid the rocks is a miracle in itself. Then to have someone in the area at that precise time—well, if I were him, I think I'd buy a lottery ticket as soon as I woke up."

"They *do* think he will wake up?"

"Yes, his coma was medically enhanced because his brain appeared slightly swollen on the initial CT. But a second, better CT Scan today showed that it is now normal sized. So he just got his last dose of sedative and barring unforeseen issues, neuro expects him to wake up in twelve to twenty-four hours. At least that's their expectation."

"How's his shoulder?"

"He had a hairline fracture and a deep laceration. Ortho washed out the wound and pinned the bone in place. He's bandaged, on painkillers, and IV antibiotics. Nothing that should cause permanent problems, but Dr. Niemi says he'll probably lose ten mph off his fastball." She laughed.

"Best case scenario, how long will he be in?"

"Best case scenario, five to seven days. But these things can be unpredictable. There was a lot of violence in his fall. From the height he fell, they estimate he was traveling maybe fifty or sixty mph when he hit the water. His shoulder probably hit a submerged rock, but maybe not."

"Anyone else stop in to visit him?"

"No one—at least not socially. The MSP was here. I heard them speaking with his boss. Apparently, there is no family 'available,' whatever that means. When he leaves, we don't know where he's going. I know Anna has been keeping you updated with what we can tell you under the HIPPA regulations, so we'll try to keep you in the loop through her, okay?"

"Thanks. Sounds great."

This last got Lenore thinking as well. He had no wallet. Was it left in a vehicle somewhere? Was he staying somewhere locally? How will he get money? Lots of questions. Lenore walked home. As she walked she looked up at light coming through the tall trees and thanked God that she and Uncle had been there.

The next twenty-four hours went by without change. Anna's reports were brief because there was not much to tell. There was no discernible change in Decker's condition for the better or the worse. At 10:00 p.m. the third night, Lenore received a call on her cell. It was the charge nurse from the step-down unit.

"He woke up."

"That's great—isn't it?"

"Well, he started to come around about an hour ago. His nurse heard him making a gagging noise, and she went in the room to check. He had his hand on the NG tube and was starting to pull. She grabbed his hand and called for help. A resident came to remove the tube right away."

"How was—how is he?"

"At first, he was groggy and really confused but his mind has been clearing as well as can be expected. He's on painkillers, so it was difficult to understand him, especially with the cut on his tongue. He kept asking where Herb and Shelley were, but no one here knows who or what he was talking about. As he has come around, his nurse has spent the better part of the last hour explaining to him what happened."

"How much does he understand?"

"Hard to say. At first, he kept repeating himself, asking where Herb and Shelley were. Carrie, his nurse, told him that only Lieutenant Haukom had been in to see him—and you. He repeated the name Haukom and asked if he were a state trooper. She told Mr. Decker that yes, he was, and an odd, sad look came over his face. He did not ask about this Herb again, but he attempted to clarify if anyone knew where Shelley was? We asked who she was, thinking she might be his wife or an ex because he wears no ring, but he just shook his head and said 'thithter.' He then asked several questions about you—like who you are and what was your part in this. He did not remember anything when we told him the story. He seemed to think that he should know you—you've never met online, have you?" she said with a laugh. "We asked 'what was the last thing' he remembered and he answered, 'I jumped.' He went silent then. About twenty minutes ago, he said he would like some pain medicine since his shoulder was killing him. He got a shot and he's sleeping now. You might want to come by in the morning if you're free."

"I'm working in the morning, but I'll come by in the early afternoon if that's okay."

"Sure, he'll probably be in a regular room by then, so stop by the front desk and check."

"Thanks for the call." Lenore was inexplicably happy and relieved at the same time. She said a prayer of thanks and called out to Hank as she felt the need to share this update.

Chapter 20

Camp Ohiyesa

Lenore spent the next morning working the desk again; however, business was slow and as she ruminated, her enthusiasm to actually meet Detective Decker began to fade. By the time she had eaten lunch, she was having second thoughts about even going to the hospital. After all, Lenore had merely done what anybody would have done in a similar situation. Did this give her the right to intrude on his private life? Definitely not. About 2:00 p.m., still torn between curiosity and propriety, she called over to the hospital. When the nurse told her that Detective Decker had just dozed off, she felt a sense of relief. Lenore said that she'd call back later. In this case, later became after dinner and when the phone rang it was Decker's nurse.

"Lenore, Mr. Decker had been asking after you all day, wondering when he might be able to thank you in person. He's now expressing doubt that this mysterious Lenore is ever going to put in an appearance—or maybe, that she is not even a real person."

Lenore laughed. She surrendered to her curiosity. "I'll be there in about a half hour."

It was a pleasant evening so after she helped Hank with the dinner clean up, she cleaned herself up and walked on over to the hospital. She stopped at the desk for a visitor's name tag and walked down the inpatient corridor to his room. The door was part way open as was usual with hospital rooms, and she knocked quietly.

"Come in."

There was surprise in Decker's eyes when he looked at Lenore. The surprise was so evident that it made Lenore start to blush.

"You must be the mysterious Lenore? Thank you. I don't know how I can ever repay your kindness."

"Ah shucks, sir." She looked down and scuffed her shoe. "'Tweren't nuthin.'"

The both burst out laughing at Lenore's clumsy attempt at humor.

"Well, now that we've got that out of the way." More laughter. "I'm Lou Decker, but you probably know me by my other name, Flying Man."

"My uncle calls you the Man Who Fell from the Sky. I think that might be more apt. As a flying man, uh, don't take this wrong, but not so great." Lenore wagged her hand.

Lou laughed again and had a smile from ear to ear. "This laughing is making my tongue hurt. In any case, thank you."

"You are certainly welcome."

"Please sit down. You must be a lot stronger than you look." Decker realized that he might have misspoken as she sat.

"I am. I wondered why you looked at me so odd when I came in."

She laughed at his discomfiture, and they both relaxed a bit.

"Sorry, I don't know what I was expecting, but from the nurses' descriptions of your prodigious feat of strength, I think it was Olga the Norse Opera Valkyrie."

"No, I'm not Scandinavian as you can clearly see. But I can make a hot dish as well as any other Minnesotan."

This puzzled Decker, who had never come across the term "hot dish" before.

"And I prefer raw bison liver to lutefisk." Lenore looked so serious that Decker was at a loss for words. Then they both burst out laughing.

"What in the world is a loot-a-fish?"

Decker was incredulous that anyone would voluntarily put lye-soaked rotting fish in their mouth. They sat there for an hour and a half, exchanging small talk until the nurse came in with Decker's nighttime meds. Decker declined the sleeping pill, but took the pain shot to go with his IV antibiotics. Shortly afterwards, he began to yawn, so Lenore said goodnight and left after agreeing with Decker's request that she return tomorrow. The closest they had come to discussing what had happened to Decker was when he asked her to relate the events of his rescue. As he listened, his eyes grew distant. She realized that something unsaid was troubling him, but she did not push. For his part, Decker was captivated by this lovely young woman who had truly performed a miracle in saving him.

Lenore went back the next evening. She brought Decker a book of crossword puzzles. It was one which she had purchased for Uncle and had sat in his book pile for months. "How's the shoulder?"

"Well, I've been told my chances of making it to the Big Leagues are over, but ice and ibuprofen are keeping the pain down. It's my mouth that is really sore. The nurse, Carrie, told me you bit my tongue while you were giving me CPR."

Lenore laughed. "Nope. Your breath smelled like a dead salmon. If I had to give you CPR, you wouldn't be here today." They both laughed.

"Well, I've now tasted every flavor of Jell-O possible and some I think the nursing staff invented just to punish me. I've also eaten so much oatmeal and soft-boiled eggs that you'd think I was teething. Don't people in Minnesota eat *any* solid food?"

"Well, now that you are speaking an intelligible form of English, you might ask someone to check that tongue wound and advance your diet."

Decker smiled and held up the book. "Thanks for this. Volume twelve number seven, eh? How did you know that I just finished Number eleven. If I wasn't carrying it when I fell, I must have left it in the rental." As he realized what he had said, Decker's face briefly darkened.

"I gave you credit for being more than a word-search type. I'd guess sudoku isn't your thing, either. So crosswords it is—are? My uncle says it keeps 'Old-Timer's' Syndrome at bay."

"Judging by you he must be what forty-five to fifty? Does dementia hit early in your family?"

"I certainly hope not. Anyway, Uncle is full of medical theories—most are unsound according to Western medicine."

"Really? I thought the crossword thing *is* Western medicine."

Lenore shrugged and smiled. "You mentioned your rental. Is that something the hospital or police are handling for you? You won't be cleared to drive for a bit and there's no sense in running up a bill. Where is it anyway?"

"Not sure…" Decker flashed back to the impression of seeing the SUV destroyed and burning on the opposite side of the pond. He decided to keep that to himself.

"Hmmm. Maybe these crossword puzzles are just the right thing then. I can send Hank along the coast road to see if you left it there if you want."

"Who is Hank?"

"He's my adoptive brother, a cousin by blood. He lives with his dad, my uncle, and me at Ohiyesa Lodge. It's our family-owned hunting-and-fishing retreat here on Lake Superior. Uncle owns it, but Hank and I pretty much run it."

"Oh. That sounds like—fun."

"It can be. But for the most part it's hard work. We cater to church groups and families, which increases our workload, but footloose adult males, firearms, and booze pose a risk that we won't accept. We have a children's program which has been pretty popular. In the summer, we hire college kids to act as instructors in archery, riflery, fishing, and woodcraft. After all, with a traditional Indian name, our lodge has a certain image to keep up."

"Ohiyesa is not your uncle's last name then?"

"Hardly." Lenore laughed heartily and went on to explain. "Ohiyesa, the name given to a mixed-blood Eastern Sioux, a Dakota, who was a Boston-trained physician by trade, and became an advocate for and a benefactor to the American Indian peoples among the general population, that is, in White American culture. He is a hero to Uncle and a blood relative to my mother. Whew! Enough history or I'll need a CT. What about your car?"

Decker shrugged. "I can hardly ask your brother to chase down my lost rental."

"Not an issue. He's always looking for a reason to get away from work. You do know that it is a tradition among Native peoples that saving someone's life gives you a lifelong obligation to help them, right?"

"No, I don't know that. Sounds like you've maybe got it backward to me." Lou chuckled. "What I know is that is a Chinese or Arabic or some kind of Asian adage, anyway."

Lenore laughed. "See, your memory *is* better than you thought. The crosswords are helping already."

At this point a large man in a long white lab coat came in with two younger men wearing similar but shorter coats.

"Hello, Dr. Niemi."

Dr. Niemi nodded to Decker. He removed the bandage from Decker's shoulder while addressing his residents. He put the shoulder through a range of motion exercise and inspected the wound closely while repeating the stale joke about Decker's thwarted baseball career yet again.

"Any pain, Mr. Decker?"

Decker was incredulous that a man who had just nearly bent his arm back ninety degrees could ask such a question. "No, I don't think it hurt you at all."

Lenore burst out laughing and both residents snickered while Dr. Niemi joined in. He roared. "Haw, haw, haw. Here is Dave Chappell in person." Then the entourage walked out.

"Looks like they may be releasing you soon. In fact, if you keep upstaging our docs, they may turn you out in the middle of the night. Where do you plan to go when you get out?"

Decker shrugged. "Not sure. I have some business to finish up here—then home, I guess."

"Uncle, Hank, and I have talked it over." Lenore lied. "And you are welcome to come and stay at the lodge until you are ready to travel." In fact, this idea had just come to her, but she was sure she could easily convince them. "We have plenty of open cabins for the next two to three weeks and there is very little hubbub to disturb your recuperation. Plus, you would be right here by the hospital to come in for rechecks—or whatever." She did not know where this last had come from.

"I'll think about it. You've already done much more than I could ever repay."

Lenore said good night and left with the sinking feeling that she had overplayed her hand. She genuinely liked this interesting and mysterious man and did not wish him to go. However, she was unaware that the attraction was mutual, and Decker had already made his decision—he could certainly find a much less pleasant companion and place to recuperate while he was getting his life back in order.

Chapter 21

R and R

The next three days were the longest of Decker's adult life. Lying in bed, he willed himself to heal, but his mind kept returning to the fact that his sister was still out there, somewhere, at the mercy of who knows what. Rest did not come easy. Lieutenant Haukom sent a trooper to get more information about Shelley, and the facts as known about her disappearance from Decker. This would facilitate making a formal report with national human trafficking authorities and the police departments who made use of their data sites. Decker had been out of bed for lengthening periods over the last three days. He sat much of the day in a chair at bedside making those phone calls necessary to replace his documents and credit cards.

Decker then called his boss. Lou was pleasantly surprised to note McAvoy's congenial tone. "It's good to hear your voice, Decker. As you might imagine, the call from the Minnesota State Police came out of nowhere, and it was quite a shock. You could have brought me into your confidence regarding the nature of your trip. I only learned of your sister's disappearance from a flag that the MSP put on their missing person report for your sister. It also named you and our department. That came as a real surprise."

"You're a busy man, Captain, I didn't want to bother you with what I was led to believe would be a quick trip over here to collect my sister and brother-in-law. When I left Grand Rapids, I understood that Herb, her husband, had found her, and I was coming to accompany them home."

"This Lieutenant Haukom from the MSP told me that your brother-in-law's death was likely a homicide. However, at this time, they have no solid leads. Knowing you, Lou, I suspect that you might have some ideas." A silence hung on the phone line.

"I've got a couple longshots, Cap. I am almost certain that the Congregation of Light outfit is involved in both Herb's death and Shelley's disappearance." *These are the type of "longshots" that make millionaires out of bettors,* Decker mused.

"Do you want me to send a couple men out there and see if we can shake something loose?"

"No, sir, in fact, I believe that they consider me out of the picture entirely, most likely dead. I don't have any reason to make them think otherwise. I should be back in a week or two. I'll fill you in if anything new develops on this end. In all honesty, all I have are suspicions at this point and my injury was purely an accident." He added under his breath *I should be dead.*

"Okay, then. Well, you understand that I don't want to hear that you've been hassling those Congregation of Light loonies. We don't need any bad publicity, especially where you're involved. And, if anything develops here involving them, we won't be waiting for your return to send in people. Is that understood?"

"I read you loud and clear, sir." Lou gritted his teeth at the subtle reprimand.

"Outstanding. Heal up and get back here ASAP. You already know we're shorthanded. I've filled out the paperwork for your reinstatement, so when you get home in it'll be right back to business as usual…and Decker I'll schedule you some extra range time so you can learn to shoot left-handed. Haha." Decker was about to respond that he was ambidextrous, but the phone clicked, and the connection went dead.

*****

Lenore got a call from the nursing staff at 4:00 p.m. "Mr. Decker has been discharged. He is ready to leave whenever you get here to pick him up." There was a touch of amusement in her voice as she

139

relayed this. Since Decker had informed Lenore that morning that he would accept the offer to recuperate at the lodge, she and Hank had been busy readying a cabin for the recovering detective. "Looks like he'll have to live with a few cobwebs, Hank."

When she pulled up in the lodge Humvee, there was Detective Decker sitting in a wheelchair under the entrance canopy.

"Wow, you don't waste much time getting out of here, do you?"

"Time is fleeting." He deadpanned.

Lenore couldn't help but notice three young nurses standing in the doorway waving and calling their goodbyes to the detective. "Your fan club is going to miss you."

"They'll learn to live with disappointment."

The ride back was brief. It was a pleasant late summer afternoon. Decker was a bit apprehensive as to whether he had overstepped in accepting this invitation, but when he saw two men, Uncle and Hank, waiting and smiling with a luggage cart at the ready, he laughed. Uncle helped Decker from the vehicle while Hank went to the back with the cart. He opened the lift gate and stared in. Hank looked at Uncle, who shrugged his shoulders. "Hmmm, a little light on the luggage. Guess you won't need the cart, Hank. Come to think of it, Flying Man, I don't recall that you had checked any baggage for your flight."

Decker laughed and exited the vehicle with a white plastic hospital bag and the book of crosswords in his hand. Uncle eyed the book suspiciously and glanced at Lenore. She was suppressing a grin. Lenore walked Decker to his cabin. He stopped on the porch and looked out at the panorama of Lake Superior. "Wow. With this view, I may extend my stay."

Lenore smiled and opened her mouth to reply, but instead she turned red with embarrassment as she could think of no response. "We are having you eat with us. Dinner in an hour or so. We figured to spare you the trauma of eating in the chow hall with the families' screaming kids. Hank cooked tonight, so I won't vouch for the meal, but we're having elk and wild mushrooms."

"Sounds good. I'll unpack and rest for a bit. That ride over was nerve-racking and exhausting. Elk? Really?"

"Nope, sorry, just kidding. Sloppy Joes, fries and salad—for real. But it is pretty good. We don't drink alcohol. Just so you know."

"No problem. I'm not a teetotaler, but I'm not a souse either. I'll have a beer once a month, mainly, to be social." *At least that's what I used to do.*

"Great, see you in a bit."

Lenore walked back up to the lodge house to set up for dinner. On the way, muted, happy chaos spilled from the dining hall. Dinner had concluded and the counselors were leading the kids in a variety of games designed to tire them out.

"Daughter." Uncle only called her this when he had something important to say to her. "I see you are…smitten with this man. You are a grown woman and able to choose your own path in these matters, but I would caution you. There is a darkness about this detective, and I detect a cold presence as well. It is not *connected* to him—but I warn you nonetheless."

"Thank you. I don't know how you know these things, Uncle, but I have seen glimpses of the same myself. I will be careful. Have you been hand trembling again?"

"No."

"Did you smoke him?"

"No. I did not attempt to read him in any way. These are only impressions. Just use that pretty head, daughter."

Hank came in. "Five to ten minutes."

Lenore finished setting the table and Uncle set out drinks for everyone. Fifteen minutes passed and no Decker. Hank volunteered to go to the cabin and get him. Hank knocked on the door and got no answer. He opened it. Decker lay face down across the bed. Momentarily alarmed, he rushed into the room. He shook Decker. "Detective! Mr. Decker!" Decker rolled over groggily and opened his eyes. It was clear to Hank that Decker did not at first recognize him and he backed off as Decker reached out toward his throat with his good hand. Hank easily blocked the move. "Mr. Decker, it's Hank."

"Sorry. I must have dozed off." Decker felt sheepish. "Is it time for dinner?"

"Un-huh, I was sent to get you."

They made it to the house without further misadventure and Lou was grateful that Hank had the grace not to mention the incident.

"Great dinner, thank you all. This spread sure beats hospital food. Jell-O for dessert?"

Uncle laughed. "You set the bar pretty low, Flying Man."

Decker tried to help carry the dishes to the kitchen but was refused in his efforts to assist in cleanup further. "Don't worry. Your time will come." Hank took the dishes from Lou's unsteady hands.

"Besides you looked pretty shaky carrying in the plates, and replacing the dinnerware is not in this month's budget…" Uncle shot a meaningful look at Lenore and asked cheerfully, "Are the new brochures done, Lenny?"

"Yes, I sent them off to the printer yesterday. I told him to do an initial printing run of 20,000."

"Twenty thousand?" Uncle looked alarmed until he noticed that Lenore was grinning.

She laughed and said, "Two thousand. Sorry, I mistakenly added a zero."

"I'm glad I left it in your capable hands, I think."

Decker and Lenore walked back to Decker's cabin. They sat on a glider out front. The night was pleasantly cool and clear. "These wonderful nights are pretty rare." Lenore looked out across the lake at the star-filled sky. "Perfect temperature, gentle breeze, good meal, clear skies and…"

Decker wondered at this comment. *Am I included in the wonderful part?* He noted again her lustrous black hair and beautiful profile. They sat for some minutes with neither speaking. Decker excused himself and went inside. He brought back a blanket for each.

"No, thanks. I've gotta head back. Morning comes quickly and I have horse duty in the morning 'cause our regular girl is sick. Breakfast is at 7:30. There is an alarm clock next to your rack. If you wake up hungry, I'll, er, we'll see you then. If not, you can wander over to the chow hall anytime. And there are always rolls and coffee out."

"Lenore—"

"Lenny. Uncle calls me Lenore when he is all serious. Please call me Lenny, and I'll call you Lou, okay? No more phony formality." They both laughed.

"Sounds good and I guess this way you'll know if I get serious with you, eh? Good night. And thanks again—for everything, Lenny." Lou raked his hand back through his hair and watched her walk away down the starlit path. He was somewhat surprised that after his long years on the force, he could still find beauty in the world.

Lou sat back down alone on the swinging chair and wrapped up in the blanket, he was also wrapped in his thoughts. He owed these people a lot, more than he could ever repay. He also considered that he might owe them the truth about why he was in this predicament.

*****

Decker slept in the next morning and wandered over for coffee after he showered. The water was tepid and reminded him of his Navy shipboard showers from his younger days. On the way back to his cabin, he noticed Hank sitting cross-legged near the bluff cliff. He began to detour over toward him, but as Decker approached, he saw that Hank was reading from a Bible. Lou decided not to disturb him. He headed back to his cabin and called the hospital to check if any of his replacement credit cards had arrived yet.

"Oh, Mr. Decker. Good morning. Yes, there are two business envelopes here for you. Let me suggest that you file a temporary change of address form with the post office, if you want to expedite receipt of your mail."

"That sounds like a good idea." *At least in theory.* He determined to either catch the letter carrier that day or borrow the lodge's internet terminal and make the change online. In the meantime, as Decker had nothing to do, he decided to walk over to the hospital. He had a general idea how to get there, but he stopped at the front desk to double-check with Lenore. To his surprise there was a young lady there whom Decker did not know. What Decker had understood to be a mom-and-pop operation was actually considerably bigger than Lenore had described. Chow hall? Horses? He had seen several large outbuildings and resolved to find out what mysteries they hid. The desk girl confirmed Decker's memory that he would need to go north on the road about a mile and take a right. The hospital was there sitting back from the bluff.

Hank came in and overheard this last part. "I'm going there to the pharmacy to get some medicine for Uncle. I'll give you a lift."

"Great, when are you going?"

"Now, if you're ready." Hank shrugged and pushed the heavy wood door open, holding it for Lou to follow him.

Hank went around to get the Humvee and picked up Decker at the front door. "I saw you walking by a while ago. You know, you could have come on over."

"It looked like you were into some serious reading and I didn't want to disturb you." Decker deliberately omitted mention of the book he was reading.

"No bother. I was just reading my Bible. There is a passage that I'm not understanding or that I'm afraid I'm not getting it right. It's called the Olivet Discourse. Ever heard of it?"

"Nope. My knowledge of the Bible is pretty limited. John 3:16 is about the only verse I can recall from memory."

Well, that's a good start. In fact, that verse sums up the whole shebang."

"Shebang?" *What an odd term to refer to the Bible.*

"We can talk about my confusion later, *if* you are interested."

From the corner of his eye, Hank saw Decker shrug.

They arrived then at the hospital. "Be back in about fifteen minutes, detective, meet you here." Hank headed to a small building across the lot.

Decker went to the front desk and collected his mail. He also collected two nurses who had seen him and stopped to ask how he was doing.

Arriving back at the car, Hank remarked, "You certainly have a following here, detective, just like Lenny said. Your notoriety is something novel to the locals. Haw-haw." Hank's laugh was deep and friendly, without a trace of sarcasm or envy. "Lenore told me that no one has picked up your vehicle yet. The old camp is only a couple miles down the road. Do you want to take a run by and see what's up?"

Decker was doubtful that such a trip would yield anything useful, but he had nothing but free time, so he agreed. At this point Decker was not comfortable sharing that he had watched the truck blasted to oblivion by a dragon, so he nodded his approval. They took the short jog out to the main road and headed south. Decker almost missed the sign for the old camp approaching it from the north. It was a lot closer to the camp and hospital than he had imagined. Hank turned off onto the two-track entry trail. He continued to the clearing and looked questioningly over at Hank.

"Across the pond." Decker directed and Hank nodded his head. Assuming they would walk from here, Decker was reaching for the door handle when Hank turned the wheel to the right and gunned the engine. His Humvee plowed right through the underbrush and reeds. Decker had not considered that the vehicle's high clearance allowed passage over rocks and debris, making it ideal for off-road use. In a couple minutes they were on the other side of the pond. In the middle of the small clearing where Miguel had stood was a large burned area with a jumbled pile of slag and metal scraps. Both men exited the vehicle and looked at the mess. Hank said nothing, but he flashed back to his time in Iraq where he had seen vehicles destroyed by RPGs and IEDs. This looked nothing like any of those. It made him think of God's fire blasting down from the sky to consume Elijah's sacrifice. "Hmmm. I can't identify any of those scraps as a car for sure, but that *might* be part of an engine block." He pointed to a lump of steel.

"It was an SUV…"

"Not anymore. I guess I'd just file an insurance claim as a missing vehicle and let them wrangle it out with the rental company."

"Sounds like a plan." Decker agreed. "You have some pretty rough vandals around here, I guess." He noted the look of incredulity in Hank's eyes. "While we're here. Would you mind taking a ride out to the back forty." Lou hoped that Hank had not caught the shiver that ran through him as he recalled the events of that day.

"No problem."

Lou directed Hank back to the clearing and over the ridge to where he had found Herb's vehicle. Hank realized that they were following a clear-cut path and gunned the engine over the crest and into the woods. He stopped at the turn. Lou got out and Hank followed over to a pile of cut trees, saplings, and pine branches. Hank could tell from Decker's expression that Lou was disappointed at not finding something he hoped for, as he moved the pile of branches. His vehicle? Hank caught the glint of chrome as Decker picked up a small object and put it in his pocket.

"Did you find what you were looking for?"

"No, but I guess I didn't really expect to."

They headed back to the lodge, each lost in his thoughts. Glancing at his passenger who sat staring out the window. Hank sensed Decker's unease. "You know, Lenny is a pretty good listener and she knows an awful lot about what goes on around here, and what she doesn't know, Dad probably does."

Decker nodded.

Chapter 22

Conversations

Friday, Decker returned to the hospital for a wound recheck of his shoulder laceration. He saw the chief resident rather than Dr. Niemi, who was in surgery fixing the pelvis of a car accident victim.

"Hey, doc, how does it look?"

"You are healing well. The wound shows no sign of infection. I'm going to take the staples out, then I'll tape it. You should still take it easy, except for rehab, don't lift over ten pounds until released to do so, keep the wound clean and dry, apply the antibacterial ointment in the morning and before bed for the next three days."

"Can I bathe?"

"Please do. Just don't lie in a tub or submerge the shoulder for five to seven days yet. No lake swimming for the rest of the summer."

"Don't worry I've had my share of Lake Superior for a lifetime."

"I really meant inland lakes. You look like a guy who goes for the gusto."

Decker then realized that the physician did not know how he was injured. "Yes, I am. Speaking of that, when can I resume throwing a baseball?"

"Puh-leeze. That joke is older than Doctor Niemi. You know, corny jokes and all, he's the best trauma orthopedist in this part of the country?"

"No, I didn't."

"He trained at the Mayo Clinic. Then went to the Twin Cities where he opened a practice. Yeah, he was a doc for the Twins and

Vikings. Then one day he quit, sold his practice, and came out here to the boondocks. You wouldn't know it, but residents are standing in line to train under him—even out here."

"Guess I was lucky he was on call when I came in."

"Yes, no doubt about it."

The doctor placed a small dressing on the wound, then told Decker he would get a prescription for physical therapy and a pain-killer—Decker declined the drugs. He wished Decker well and vanished through the door. Decker flexed his shoulder. It still hurt when he moved it, but not nearly as much as earlier in the week. Decker's range of motion was improving daily due to his adhering to his rehab schedule. Lou stood and pantomimed a quick draw. He lost his balance, nearly stumbling against the wall.

That evening Decker sat on the porch with Hank. It was the first time they had been alone since the trip to Camp Wendigo, and they began reminiscing about their pasts. Decker told Hank about his time in the Navy. He characterized his military experience as "brief and undistinguished" ending prematurely with a medical discharge after he had injured his knee. Lou had torn a ligament representing his ship in a football team against an army squad. He asked Hank if he had served in the military, sensing that he had.

"Six years in the Corps. Force Recon. Second Gulf War, Iraq 2004–5. I wound up in a mixed unit with army special ops guys in Tikrit. The Iraqis were beaten, so our mission had shifted to 'liberating' art objects and finding antiquities that Saddam had reportedly stolen from his people for personal enjoyment in his many palaces. It's funny, but when you think of Saddam Hussein, art connoisseur does not immediately come to mind. In any case, our convoy of five Hummers and two stake trucks had just cleaned out a residence and we were heading back to base. Our group leader had designated my vehicle to run point. About halfway home we dodged around a burning truck that was not in the road on our way in. The last thing I remember from that trip is a deafening roar, a blast of heat and the sensation of being jerked into the air. I woke up in Germany about three days later, so I know what that's like—to lose time, eh?"

"Geez, I guess you do."

"I had a concussion, needed some skin grafts for burns on my back and my right kidney was bruised. My eyebrows were singed off and my scalp had some bald spots, but it could have been a lot worse. I was told that we hit a mine with the left front wheel. The driver and gunner never had a chance." Hank looked at his shoes and continued. "I came back with some PTSD but here I am running a dude ranch with my dad and sister, er, cousin. This was the best thing that could have happened. Tell me, Lou, do you remember anything from when you were out?"

"No, not really… I think I may have heard voices."

"Do you recall what they were saying?"

"Not really, but I have the impression that they were arguing over something or someone."

"My memories are much clearer, detective. I remember being dead."

"I thought you said you were 'out'. It was probably just a dream, right?"

"No, I was dead."

Lou Decker stared at the younger man and could see an Indian warrior. Hank did not strike him as a liar or someone who would even consider drawing attention to himself with outlandish tales. Decker began to sweat. He recalled clearly the events in the bluff and the conversation he had overheard up there. He remembered Miguel and Brother Love's antics at the restaurant. There was just too much of this…this…whatever it was in his life lately. Decker was wandering through new territory without a map or guide. This made him very uncomfortable.

Hank continued. "I remember a moment of sadness that I was leaving my family and this beautiful world that the Creator has given us, but I was ready to go and already looking ahead. Then I was told that it was not my time and I was sent back to 'finish my task.' in this life."

"What task is that?"

Hank laughed. "I'm still trying to figure that out. In any case the next thing I remember was being back in my body with a bunch of medical people in scrubs standing over me and smiling. I was in quite a bit of pain from the burns and my chest and ribs were really sore. But the thing I recall most clearly is being so profoundly sad that I had to leave the beauty of where I had been and return here."

Lenore had walked up with a tray of iced teas, sat on an open chair and joined the conversation. "Then the knucklehead did not take the discharge he was offered. At least he was done with combat duty. They sent him back to the states and assigned him to a secret project."

"Secret project?"

"Yes, but not immediately. I came back to be trained as a gunnery instructor. During that period, I became aware that the concussion had changed me. I found that I could do mathematical computations at a, well, very fast rate."

"He has beaten computers—"

"Lenny, don't exaggerate. I began to use my new talent to win bets at the NCO club on base. One night there was an officer who sat there all night just watching me in do my thing, winning drinks for my buddies. As I was leaving, he approached me and asked if I could perform this 'trick' on command. I told him to try me. He laid out a complicated calculation that I did instantly. I didn't realize it at that time, but he was not interested in the speed or accuracy with which I could perform the operations, but rather, he had noticed that I was consistently giving my answer before people had finished giving me the parameters of the problem. The next morning my CO summoned me to headquarters and told me to report to Fort Meade forthwith. He handed me a flight voucher and said my orders would be awaiting me there. When I arrived at Meade, I was driven to a run-down Quonset hut. I was stunned. There was that same captain sitting at a desk—he had been waiting for me. He explained that he was going to give me a series of tests over the next several days. I was never told the purpose of what I was doing or whether I was performing well or poorly. But apparently, I passed, because after four days of guessing card suits, colors, and numbers and describing my surroundings during guided imagery sessions, I was welcomed into a special unit. We were designated as military 'remote viewers,' and for the last twenty-one months of my hitch, I served with that outfit. It was very strange for a marine like me to be tasked to do this seemingly hocus-pocus stuff, but we were getting results. I had been a guns and bullets guy, and suddenly I am in the 'Timothy Leary' brigade, without the drugs. I can't talk about many of the specifics because most of the targets we viewed were classified, but it was wild to say the least."

"What is 'remote viewing,' Hank?

"It's a way to acquire information about places, people or things. It is not magic or ESP, it is an acquired skill—a technique that an operator learns, in order to retrieve the desired or targeted 'information' from the collective unconscious. Remote Viewing, or RV, further postulates that basically all information is retrievable if a set of rigid protocols are observed. In a sense it is like the 'Matrix' of movie fame."

Hank noticed that Decker looked amused and doubtful. "I get that reaction a lot. But, Lou, let me assure you that this is as 'real' as that chair you are sitting on. Initially I was totally skeptical, but bear with me—after all, you asked." Hank laughed.

"Sorry. Please go on."

"I won't bore you with details of the procedures, but sometimes the task is performed alone and sometimes with a monitor. You are basically assigned a very specific target, generally unknown to you, with the intent of acquiring desired information on that target. We never considered the process as psychic or 'soul travel.' In fact, the procedure might resemble 'automatic writing' to an observer. However, in my experience, the best of our group did have something 'extra.' After a lot of practice, at times it was as if you were physically there looking on your target directly."

"You make it sound like a pretty good gig for a soldier. Did something happen?"

"What I can tell you is limited, but one day I was tasked with viewing a facility in South America for a three-letter agency. I was told that it housed a drug production facility, but our intelligence reports suggested that something more was going on there. I was tasked to do reconnaissance on the location. I located the target easily and had established a link, when I encountered something I had never seen before. There were two remote viewers from hostile nations present and they were 'looking' directly at me. I 'relocated' my attention within the facility in order to lose them, but they followed. My monitor suggested that I move to other levels in the building if they existed and just grab a quick look before leaving—which I tried to do. In the last room I entered was a Hispanic man standing before a group seated around a table. The men were from obviously diverse ethnic origins, but the speaker was addressing them, I don't know if this is exactly right, but 'psychically.' I could hear in my mind what he was communicating, but he was not speaking or moving his lips. He became aware of my intrusion immediately when I entered the room and he glared at me. The two psychic guards followed me in and flanked me. They tried to bind me, but I had the sense that they weren't very skilled at what they were supposed to be doing, and I easily moved away from them. However, I found myself unable to leave the room. The Hispanic man then raged at me and began to transform in shape. By this time, I was in a near panic, but training kicked in and I 'summoned' a side arm from the holster of one of the two guards to my hand. The handgun was heavy and looked somehow 'foreign,' but it had a trigger and that was all I cared about at the time. The shape of the leader was coalescing into a reptilian form and he was inhaling with great vigor. As I fired at the shape, he exhaled a flame which incinerated the guards beside me, but I detected a glistening light, in human form, in front of me blocking the fire. I stumbled backward and dropped the gun, but I had hit the entity and he howled in pain. I took this opportunity to again try to leave and was back in the control room in this real world immediately. I was lying against the wall and my shirt was singed, but I was unharmed. I smelled of smoke for two days after that, no matter how many showers I took. When I had arrived back at the base, I felt something beneath me and found the gun had somehow also 'come through' and was under me as I lie there. Not thinking, I pocketed it."

"Quite a story. Do you still have the gun?"

"I do. I'll show it to you sometime if you wish."

Decker knew now for sure that Hank was on to him.

Hank got up and stretched. "Think I'll turn in. I'll leave you two kids to put away the chairs and blankets. Remember Uncle is watching."

Both laughed. "Good night."

Hank took about five steps and turned around. He had a very serious and disturbed look. "There is something I need to ask, Lou. The damaged car. I've seen all kinds of destruction caused by bombs, RPGs and ordinance and I've never seen anything like that site by the lake. What happened to that car was not…natural, was it?"

"No, it wasn't."

Hank left and Lenny turned to Lou. "Hank is telling the truth. He is concerned about you."

"Yes. It seems to be a common trait in the people I'm meeting nowadays."

Lenore looked away at the moon which was just shy of full. "You sound as if that's a bad thing."

"No, that's not what I meant, Lenny. I've just lived my whole life in a different—world. What is tangible *is* what is real. All the rest is—was fraud, or BS. Now I've had to question all of that. It's just a shock."

"You can talk to me."

"I know." Lou reached over and squeezed Lenore's hand and she squeezed his back. "I was here looking for my sister and brother-in-law. She had joined what her husband thought was a harmless cult, but she got in too deep. She went off with them to what turned out to be a secluded camp—maybe Camp Wendigo, but I doubt it—and she was being held incommunicado. Herb found this out and, well, I think he has always wanted to prove himself. So he came over to retrieve his wife alone. He bit off more than he could chew and now he's dead."

"You probably don't know this, but Camp Wendigo has a pretty salacious history. When I was a kid, no one would even go on the grounds because they were all afraid of the 'evil spirits' there. I know they had many missing campers and pretty weird deaths."

"I do know. I read through forty years of articles at the library in Castle Danger. It appears to me that a cult was at work even then.

What I need to do is find the connection to the Congregation of Light that Shelley got messed up with."

Is Shelley your sister?"

"Yes."

"So do you know where she is now?"

"No."

"And she doesn't know that her husband is dead?"

"No. Or I should say not unless the Congregation of Light told her."

"Well, I've never heard of the Congregation of Light, but I do know some of those cults can play pretty rough. You're a detective, so I don't think you need my advice on finding your sister. But you can count on my help."

"Thank you."

"We've got a big day ahead of us tomorrow. We won't get to the powwow until around lunchtime, so I think we'll miss the giveaway. But we should hear some of the Drum Circle competition and catch the dancing."

"Dancing, like the Jerk or the Boogaloo?'" Decker smiled.

"Maybe. You'll see tomorrow."

Chapter 23

Powwow

Decker was up early the next morning, which was sunny and warm, promising good weather for the powwow. On the porch table outside his room he found a note and a small package. On the paper was written "For Lou Decker" with an arrow pointing to the package. He opened it up and inside was a new iPhone in a beautifully tooled leather case. On the back:

Flying Man
Ohiyesa Lodge

was rendered in neat beadwork. He marveled at the generosity of these folks as he admired the beauty of this gift. He went up to the office looking for Lenore, to thank her but found that she had gone into Harbors for the morning on errands.

Shortly before noon, the Humvee drove up and Lenore got out. He walked over toward her. "Good morning. Thank you for the phone and case. It is beautiful work. You didn't need to do that."

"No problem. Just be careful of the case, it doesn't offer much protection."

"Do you mean for the phone or me?"

"Either or."

Decker held it up and examined the case appreciatively. "If I decide to go flying again?"

They both laughed. "Kinda like that, yeah."

"Have you eaten lunch yet, Lenny?"

"No, but I'll grab something at the Powwow. What about you?"

"Nope."

"Great. You can try some 'muskrat on a stick' and fry bread."

Decker caught her smile and knew she was kidding him—at least about the muskrat. "Yum. Four drumsticks, I can't wait."

Decker carried Lenny's two shopping bags from the car into the office. Lenore reached into one bag and pulled out a large crimson pullover shirt and handed it to Decker. It had various colored ribbons hanging down from the yoke, both front and back. "We don't want the locals to think you are a 'wasicu' now do we?"

"A what?"

"A white person. At least that's what TV says." She grinned mischievously at him and nodded approvingly as he tried it on over his T-shirt.

"Certainly not. Behold, I'll fit right in now."

"Give me fifteen minutes and we can go. Hank is drumming at one o'clock, and Uncle has been there since last night. They had a sweat session and Uncle never misses those."

Decker went back to his cabin. He changed into the ribbon shirt. Lou looked over at the remains of his holster rig, sliced and lying on the desk. He strapped on his ankle holster out of habit and took it back off when he realized he had no firearm. *Man, I'm getting paranoid,* he mused, a bit embarrassed that the thought had even occurred to him given his situation. Lou walked back to the office. He waited about five minutes and Lenore appeared. She carried three small pouches with a fourth hanging from her hand on a leather thong. Lenore handed him the small pouches. "Here, put these in your pocket." She reached out and hung the fourth pouch over his neck. "This is from Uncle and me. We thought it might come in handy, eh?" She draped the thong over his head around his neck. She pulled out the front of his shirt and let the fourth item—a medicine bag—fall, concealing it from view.

"What are these? And what are they for?" Decker indicated the small bags. He was already vaguely familiar with the concept of medicine bundles, though he had never thought to need one himself.

"Those are gifts. If you speak with one of the elders it is polite to offer them a gift. Tobacco is good for all occasions. I think they will find these satisfactory."

"Who am I going to talk to?"

"Who knows? Forewarned is forearmed I always say."

It took about twenty minutes to reach the county fairgrounds which was the site of the powwow. Exiting the Humvee, Decker heard a happy cacophony of laughter, drumming, and singing. There were many young men and women in traditional native attire. He smelled horses and fried food. For the first time, Decker noticed that Lenore had slipped a shawl over her shoulders, and was sky blue with fringe and beading. It was decorated with bright images. One he recognized was the thunderbird. Others looked like lightning, the sun, and the moon. In the center of her back was a large USAF patch noting her service to the nation. "Nice shawl, did you make it?"

"Blanket."

"What?"

"Blanket, not shawl—and no, it was a gift on my return from the Air Force."

"Ugh."

"Wander around. You may recognize some of the nurses from the hospital. I'm sure they would love to chat with you." Lenore smiled. "I need to talk to my aunt and some friends for a bit. I'll meet you by the fry bread stand in, say, a half an hour."

"Yes, ma'am." Decker threw her a salute. He wandered over toward the drummers. Hank sat with four other men—two young and two older. Three wore old military shirts, now decorated colorfully. The fourth wore a ribbon shirt, not unlike Decker's. This man also wore a black beret festooned with military pins. The other three had Black Stetsons identical in cut with bands of silver conchos. Looking at the military designations, Decker realized that all of these men were serious players with special ops emblems on display. *I'll bet those boys could clean out any bar around here.* After about twenty minutes of wandering, Lenore came up beside Decker and took his arm. "I'm starving. Let's get a burger, sit down, and watch the drumming competition."

Decker, who just that morning had received his bankcard and withdrawn money at the office ATM, bought them each a bison burger, piece of salmon, fry bread, and lemonade. They wandered over to a shady area under a large oak and sat. The drum circles now began to form up out in the center clearing.

The shade was pleasant and the food tasty. Decker and Lenore fell into easy conversation. Decker nodded at Uncle who was up on the judges stand. "What's the story with your uncle?"

"He's a judge."

"But Hank is competing."

"It would be a big shame to Uncle if he even appeared to be favoring anyone. Last year, Hank's group came in fifth, ha-ha, after they had just won two other competitions."

"Oh. I imagine last year is not a subject I should bring up then?"

"Uh, no. I wouldn't think so."

They stood as one of the elders invoked a blessing on the proceedings. As they sat back down, Lenore identified him as another uncle from her mother's side. "Uncle Floyd, you did know his name didn't you, is my mother's brother [in law], as you would say."

Decker shook his head and Lenore laughed. She then began to tell a tale to Decker:

"Uncle Floyd does not have one drop of Native American blood."

Decker was stunned at this revelation. He opened his mouth and no words came out.

"But in his soul and life he is the epitome of the traditional Indian male elder. He had been trained as a welder and was working on a pipeline when he met and married my aunt Jessie White Sky. Shortly after taking me in he was laid off. The family packed up and we moved to Los Angeles, where he hoped to get a job in the L.A. construction boom. As chance would have it, Uncle Floyd Roselli, bronzed by working in the summer sun and having stereotypical native facial features, became a full-blooded Indian one day as he and Aunt Jessie were walking into Jerry's Deli for lunch. They were stopped by an elderly white stranger. This gentleman believed he had stumbled on 'the perfect American Indian couple.' He was a movie producer who had been unable to find an appropriate 'Indian' actor for a nonspeaking part in his big budget film. After listening to his plight, Floyd began to laugh, but Aunt Jessie was on the ball. She responded that they were Jessica and 'Sunka Gnaskinyan' or 'Wild Boar' Cloud. She told the producer that they were out in LA from South Dakota on a vision quest and felt mysteriously moved to come to this place. Floyd looked at his bride incredulously, never knowing her to lie about anything, but he wisely kept silent and he realized that the producer was eating every drop. She explained to the man that her husband spoke little English. To Wild Boar, the man's English words sounded like he was telling Wild Boar that the food here 'smelled like rotten fish.' The man apologized as Aunt Jessie spoke a few words in Dakota to Floyd—who had no idea what she was saying. However, when she nudged him and frowned, he put on a look of concern. The producer asked if 'Wild Boar' would be willing to stop by the studio in the morning to determine how he looked to the camera. Jessie muttered another few phrases and Floyd shook his head down once and said 'Ugh.' Jessie told the man they would be at the studio tomorrow and got the directions."

"What happened next?"

"Well, Uncle and Aunt Jessie showed up at the studio, Jessie all the while pretending to translate for 'Wild Boar.' This was the beginning of Uncle's career as a Hollywood actor. He got the first of many parts—all nonspeaking of course—in major motion pictures. Mr. MC Kupperman, the producer, went to his grave thinking my uncle Floyd was the ultimate Dakota warrior and constantly bragging on Uncle's native cunning in seeming to understand stage directions intuitively."

"How did you all wind up here?"

"Aunt Jessie hated the Hollywood lifestyle. Uncle knew that staying in the big city was killing her, so after big check from his role in 'Walking with Bears,' his only speaking role and last *real* acting job, they used the proceeds to buy the lodge and moved back here. Occasional roles still were offered to him, all nonspeaking. It seems the Hollywood bigwigs didn't want their 'Indian' sounding more like a mafia don than Sitting Bull. Ha-ha."

"That's a pretty good story. I think I recall him from that movie. I really enjoyed it. Was he the hopped-up warrior who attempted to kill the marauding grizzly with a knife and got mauled?"

"Yeah, but his life's story turned bittersweet then. Aunt Jessie died of cancer three years after we moved back. Hank and I went into the service and the lodge started to go to seed. When we returned, we decided to give him a year or two to get the place back running right, but we've been here since. Uncle, meanwhile, had turned his life around. He went native. He swore off alcohol and used his money as a generous benefactor to the tribe—especially at the giveaways. He is renowned for his generosity; by the way, that's where your phone came from. He has established medical clinics and programs for unwed mothers on the rez. The tribal elders took notice and ultimately adopted him into the tribe. I think that was the proudest moment of his life. He has studied Native culture since, become fluent in Dakota, and even taken courses in Christian theology on the internet. He is determined to hold and participate in a Sun Dance next summer, but at his age and in his condition, I'm not so sure."

A small boy approached Decker at this point and handed him a package about the size of a shoebox. Lou thanked the boy, who smiled and held his hand out. Decker reached in his pocket and pulled out one of the pouches.

"No." Lenore laughed as she grabbed his arm. "Just give him a dollar. He's a delivery boy. Besides, I think you are going to need those pouches." Decker paid the boy and he scampered away. Decker looked from the package to Lenore, who nodded that he should open it. He unwrapped the present and it was indeed a shoebox. He hefted it and looked to Lenny. "Cement shoes?"

"Just open it."

Inside the box was a handgun in an elaborately decorated leather shoulder holster modeled after his destroyed rig. He removed the handgun and inspected it closely. It looked similar to his old 9 mm Beretta, but the markings were unfamiliar. He removed the magazine and was surprised to see that it held what appeared to be gold tipped rounds. He replaced the weapon in its holster and closed the box. "Wow."

He realized at this point that this was the handgun which Hank had carried back. "Lenore, you know I cannot accept this."

"If you even try to return it, it will be a deadly insult. Besides, Hank has the best gun collection in the county. Clearly, he wanted you to have it—and knowing Hank, there is a reason behind it."

Just then the drumming started in earnest, soon the singers joined in from each team. This went on for about forty-five minutes while Decker was lost in his thoughts and heard little. Suddenly, the music stopped, and the judges awarded prizes. Various feathers and what looked like trinkets were given out along with more tangible awards like packaged beef loins and large salmon from the lake. These latter were then given by the winners to families having need of them. Hank's band came in second. Each member received an eagle feather and a very large fish that Lou assumed was a salmon. The audience hooted and hollered for the drummers and horns blared from the parking lot. Gradually, the crowd settled down and Uncle stood up and began to speak. Decker watched as the crowd went silent in respect and listened. Uncle was speaking in Dakota so Decker could not understand him. Uncle nodded several times in his direction while speaking. Finally, Lou distinctly heard his name.

"Stand up, Lou. Don't be rude. He's calling you up there." Lenore chuckled. "Now is where I think you'll need the pouches." Decker stumbled to his feet. He could feel his face reddening as everyone looked at him.

"Leave the gun here. You won't need it." Lenore chided.

Decker walked up to the front where Hank stood.

"Face the crowd, Lou."

Decker turned around as instructed. He could hear Uncle speaking over him out to the crowd.

He went on in Dakota for a couple minutes then asked Lou in English to face him. Lou turned again. Uncle put his right hand on Decker's shoulder and said loudly in Dakota, "Wicasa towanjiato wokonze unkawa wo!" The crowd began to yelp, howl, and many danced about making flapping motions with their arms. Uncle smiled at Decker warmly.

Hank said, "He has given you a tribal name very roughly translated: Man who fell from the sky for a purpose. Oh, by the way, he declared to the people that he has adopted you into the family. Now nod and give Dad and those two old guys flanking him the pouches of tobacco that Lenore gave you."

Decker did so and was immediately surrounded by men slapping him on the back and shouting their congratulations. Meanwhile the bedlam in the central clearing began to build as the professional drummers began and those present dressed as animals, or in other costumes began to dance in a large circle. Over a PA system came the call "Let's start things out with the teenage fancy dance." Lenore had moved up again besides Decker and held his arm. She steered him back to the shade. Decker asked, "Do I call him Uncle or Dad, now?"

"Dad, Uncle, Floyd, whatever you wish." She laughed.

Chapter 24

Change in Plans

As the dancers twirled and whirled, Decker enjoyed watching each become a wolf, a crane or whatever their "spirit animal" was. After a few rounds of fancy dancing, the caller bawled out "social dance" over the PA. The music started and Lenny tried to get Decker to go out into the circle with her, but he steadfastly refused. After a few urgings, she gave it up and joined a group of women in the circle. He couldn't take his eyes off Lenore as she gracefully bobbed, twirled, and danced around the circle. Hank came over and stood next to Decker. "Quite a sight."

"Yes, she is."

"I meant all the dancers."

"Oh." Decker reddened.

"Gotcha!"

Decker quickly changed the subject. "Thank you for the pistol and holster rig. I've never seen a weapon exactly like it. It is the one from your—trip, correct?"

"Correct."

"All I have left to give you is this." Decker reached in his shirt to pull out the medicine bag, but Hank grabbed his arm.

"No need. Everything's cool. That bag is something special that is just for you alone. Besides, that is from Dad and Lenny."

"Thank you, Hank. The pistol looks like its chambered for 9 mm rounds. I'll keep that magazine handy."

Just then the PA announced "Honor's Dance, Flying Man." And the gathering began to yip and hoot and stomp. Everyone looked at Decker. Hank grabbed one elbow and Lenore had the other. "Don't worry, just follow me." Hank shoved a gourd rattle into Decker's hand and pulled him into a lead position in the circle. "Do what I do."

The music began and Decker moved with the beat in a shuffling double step. He bobbed his head forward and back as Hank did and worked the gourd in time to the beat as he trudged around and around. He was joined by virtually everyone in attendance including an elderly man being pushed in his wheelchair by the young boy who had brought Lou his present. As he plodded along, round and round, Decker began to feel a lightening of his step and to experience a sense of kinship. Decker realized that he had missed this connectedness in the years since his promotion to detective. After a half dozen circuits, the PA blared "Veterans" and most of the women and all the children headed for the sidelines. Decker was suddenly flanked by people of all ages, including the man in the wheelchair, all interlocking arms and proceeding in a prowling, high step, stalking dance, bent over at the waist with heads searching first right, then left, then right again. Decker began to sync with the rhythm and lose himself when an MSP cruiser pulled up with lights flashing and stopped in the lot. Lieutenant Haukom got out and when he saw Decker, he raised his hand in salute, indicating with a wave that Decker finish out the dance. Another two circuits, then the PA announced women's choice. Decker thought there was a look of disappointment in Lenore's eyes as he walked over to the lieutenant.

"Fitting right in, I see."

"Yes. Going native, I guess. I'd better not stay too long. I'm starting to feel like I'm home."

"Well, as much as I find your 'dancing' entertaining, I'm here for another reason. I've brought some good news. Your sister was picked up in Las Vegas last evening. The report said that she wandered out to the strip in the company of a homeless woman who brought your sister to a LVMPD squad car that was stopped at a light near the Bellagio. The patrolmen noticed blood on her scalp, put her in their squad car and drove her to the hospital. When they tried to talk to her all she would say is 'Sister Shelley.' According to the officers she was in a daze. She is being held in the hospital for observation. But a social worker was able to break through and get her name. An officer checked wants and warrants, and *bingo*! She popped up on the missing persons database. The officers filed a report with their sergeant who called me about thirty minutes ago. She appears to be all in one piece and although she is saying very little, she seems to understand everything. Las Vegas is not sure if she should be traveling alone, so they are sending a jail matron with her on a flight tomorrow to Minneapolis. Do you have access to your cell phone?"

"No, I lost it in the accident, but I got a new one this morning. I can set it up as soon as I get back to the lodge."

Haukom laughed. "So this has turned into a vacation for you after all."

"I wish."

"Well, I'll text the arrival details and contact info to you as soon as it's finalized and sent to me. I assume you'll be using the same cell number you wrote on the forms the other day."

"Roger that, Lieutenant, and thank you. For everything."

"Great to meet you, detective. Let me know if any of this brouhaha leads back to my county here, and I'll keep you posted on our investigation." With that said, Haukom turned, hopped into his cruiser, and drove away.

"What's up, Lou?"

"They've found my sister, Lenore."

"Is she okay?"

"Don't know yet, she has a cut on her head, but otherwise she looks to be in one piece physically. Lenny, do you think you or Hank could drive me into Harbors so I can rent a car. I've got to pick her up in Minneapolis tomorrow." Lou's expression was turning sour as he realized that he would soon be leaving this place—and Lenny.

Lenny looked into Decker's eyes. "Are you nuts? You are in no shape to drive around the block, let alone make a four-hour drive down two-lane country roads that you don't even know. Hank and I will drive you. No, don't open your mouth. We wouldn't even think of letting you go alone. Besides where do you think you are New York City? There isn't a car rental place for fifty miles."

"What about Duluth?"

"Shut it, Detective. It's all settled. Hank and I will drive you."

"What ab—"

"Decker." Her face hardening.

The PA announcer told the people that today's main attraction, Elijah Black Horse would be playing in the pavilion in fifteen minutes. There was general whooping and waving of hats and arms, followed by more laughing and chaos. "Never heard of him," Decker said.

"Most of that cheer was ironic. He is a local self-styled troubadour," said Lenny.

"He likes to call himself the 'Red Bob Dylan.' I think you might find him—entertaining." Hank added. "Let's show our new brother some real Indian talent." Grinning at Lenore. They steered Lou by the arms to the pavilion.

Entering the viewing area, Lou was surprised to see so many people packed in. The only seating was a ring of benches around the outside "For the elderly and infirm," Hank remarked. The three took a place standing near the front, close to center stage. There were two people onstage. One was a very dark-skinned Indian man with a painted and feathered Stratocaster guitar. The other was an elderly woman in full tribal dress sitting toward the back behind a large drum. Flanking the two were the four biggest speakers Lou had seen since attending a "Rush" concert in the '80s. The speakers had all been painted white and decorated with horses and native designs in bright colors. Lou was about to say something when Lenny leaned over. "Don't be alarmed, Lou. The two big ones were blown by the band 'Rush,' a while back in a Twin Cities concert and the others don't work very well. Elijah bought them all for $200 from their road manager. It's all for the spectacle."

Lenny was right. Elijah started to play, and the crowd went silent in order to hear the music and song. He croaked out some remarks in Dakota. Lou picked up the word "wicasa" and all eyes look at him. Lenny and Hank were laughing, and the crowd began to whoop. Elijah launched into his song.

"He was as strong as a mule and wise as an owl.
he made the women swoon and his enemies
howl."

Lou overheard Lenore asking Hank, "Didn't he use that line in his last epic?"

"The women always swoon, Lenny."

Lenore laughed.

"He was a lawman of renown from east of the
sea.
Living in a pinewood and stone teepee.
With his pure black pony resting in back,
A hopped-up two-tone Cadillac."

The crowd roared so loudly most of the next verse was drowned out for Lou.

"His grandfather took the demon Custer's scalp."
More cheers and roars.
"The Mexican took his sister's magic herbs.
He vowed to his sis to get them back.
To the shores of Gitchee Gumee he took his
attack."

Elijah Black Horse spent the next fifteen minutes of this yarn, detailing an imaginary trip by Decker around the shores of Lake Michigan and up across Wisconsin. The fantastic tale included stops for help and guidance in numerous villages while running off various enemies of the locals. The song climaxed with a deadly battle on a bluff high above Lake Superior where he shot the Giant Mexican, who incidentally had defeated Muhammed Ali earlier in the tale, dead and recovered his sister's magic herbs. The hero then stood on the bluff, bellowed out his war cry and dove into the lake, intending to swim home. At this, the crowd roared out the war cry and several strong young men clapped Decker by the arms and feet and lifted him high above their heads.

"Careful of his shoulder," yelled Lenore.

Unheeding, the men ran in a large circle around the area carrying Decker who lie on his back, helpless. Returning to the spot where Lenore, Hank, and now Uncle stood, Lou was lowered carefully to the ground. Bewildered at this display, Lou began to laugh. Uncle and Hank helped him up. Elijah ended his song with a final stanza of the heroic efforts of Uncle and Lenore in fishing out the "Flying Hero," who was somehow now also dead, holding him up to Wakan Tanka and asking the Great Father to restore his life.

Everyone looked at Uncle and Lenny and waved and whooped. Uncle waved expansively and bowed. Lenny merely turned red.

"We can leave now," said Lenny.

Uncle observed to Lou. "It is important for a people to have laughter and heroes." As they headed home. Lou was wondering at Elijah's strange insights and his interworking of essential truths into this lurid and hilariously fantastic saga.

"He did keep the body count down this time." Hank laughed at his observation.

*****

The rest of the day was spent getting Decker ready for the trip. Activating his phone took ten minutes and he was greeted with thirteen "recent" phone calls, only two of which were of interest. The first was from Martin Hammer who gave a brief but humorous description of his aborted interview with Brother Love and concluded with a request that Decker call him as soon as he was able. He had now been here for weeks since he suffered his accident. He resolved to call Martin in the morning on the way to the airport. The second call was disturbing. It was Miguel's voice. "Detective Decker, I am disappointed that I haven't seen you since your rather dramatic departure from our meeting on the bluff. So I guess that means you are still among the living. Since I am sure we *will* meet again, I would only offer this advice. Stay out of our way, be careful of the friends you keep—and button your coat when you go out—it's getting chilly this time of year." This last was punctuated by a guttural laugh. "Adios, for now, amigo."

Decker decided to play this recording for Hank and get his take on the warnings.

Lieutenant Haukom was as good as his word texting the flight number and arrival time to Decker along with Shelley's traveling companion's phone number.

"Hank, give a listen to this if you have a minute. Is this the… creature from your trip?"

"Not sure. Could be. I was too busy trying to get out of there alive. I really don't know. Why are you asking?"

"This is whom—or what—I was engaged with in the clearing and on the bluff." Decker went on to detail his encounter with Miguel and the basics of this whole misadventure from the beginning. Hank's expression never changed. Decker realized that this might be one of a handful of people in Minnesota who might hear this story and accept every word as true.

"How much of this does Lenny know?"

"I told her the general story, but none of the facts surrounding my 'experiences.'"

"Lou, she's a big girl and she has seen more carnage than either you or me. My advice is to level with her. She can handle it. She has good judgement, she's discrete and might even offer some good advice. Also keep that special magazine handy."

"Will do."

"I've got a lot of 9mm rounds. Let's go out to our back range and you can get used to your new weapon."

They took turns firing the handgun. Decker liked its feel and balance and the lack of kick considering the heavy loads they were shooting. He determined that it shot true out to about one hundred fifty yards which he figured was about ten times as far as any target he would engage. Afterwards he broke the weapon down and cleaned it using some of Hank's gear. He then packed it away in a small suitcase he had purchased that afternoon along with two sets of clothes.

After dinner, there was a reception for the newest member of the family at the lodge. Many relatives and friends stopped in to visit and congratulate Lou and Uncle. About halfway through the evening Decker and Lenore took a walk out along the bluff rim. "Watch your step, Flying Man," called an elderly woman visitor, prompting raucous laughter from the visitors.

"Lenore, I appreciate all you have done for me and the friendship your family has extended to me. But I need to level with you."

Lenore stiffened up awaiting some devastating revelation, but Decker merely recounted the whole story as he had told it to Hank. "Geez, I thought you were going to tell me you were married, or a drug addict, or only pretending to be a detective."

Decker looked perplexed. "Naw, nothing *that* dramatic, although my history as a detective has been a bit iffy at times." He then related the story of the gun throwdown incident with Garza as the event leading to his suspension.

"But you were innocent, right?"

"No, I did what the perp said I did. You are now the only person on earth who knows that. You can destroy my career now." Decker had a strange, sad look. "But I've got to say that I would do it again. It was the quickest, surest way to take this crazy serial killer off the streets for a long time, if not forever. I'm not proud, but I'm not sorry either. I'm only telling you this because of the admiration that I have for your—moral code. And the affection I have for your family and…you. For whatever reason, I'm being forced to look at life a different way now. If all these people were brought into my life a month ago, I wouldn't have given them or their ideas the time of day. It's like maybe someone bigger, stronger, and smarter than me is trying to tell me something."

Lenore looked down at her feet, then into Decker's eyes. "Lou, we all, or most of us anyway, try to do the best we can in life. I know you have a lot of good in you, but good or bad, that's not the issue. I don't judge you. You are doing that yourself. It's God, Lou, he is trying to get through to you."

"I wish it was that simple, Lenny. I've seen nothing but hypocrites and con men using religion since I was a kid to manipulate people, get money, and advance themselves."

"Lou, I'm not talking about religion. We are on the same page there. This is basic to who you are. God is reaching out to you. Hank, Uncle, and I have been praying for you. I want you to know that."

He looked in her eyes and said, "Thank you."

Lou bent down and kissed Lenore. She kissed him back.

Chapter 25

MSP

Decker had agreed to meet Lenny and Hank outside the chow hall at 6:30 the next morning. The sun was up, but daylight filtering low through the pines reminded Lou that the days were already becoming shorter. He was sadly aware that soon he would need to go home.

"It's funny, but breathing this clean air makes me realize that I've never paid any attention the air quality around me."

Neither Lenore nor Hank responded, but Hank did a deep knee bend with an exaggerated deep inhalation through his nose. He gave out an exaggerated "Ah-h-h-h" as he exhaled. Everyone laughed. "Sis, do you remember what God told Abraham after he and Lot chose their areas to live?"

"Didn't He say that Abraham made the better choice."

"Yes, ma'am, He most certainly did."

"But was that because it was better to live in the country than the city? Or was it because Lot chose to live in Sodom?" Decker put in, surprising the others.

"Six of one, half dozen."

"There are multiple advantages to living away from big cities. Yes, I know there are also disadvantages. Harder to get to Walmart. Have to travel farther to museums to see weird sculptures. Less likely to meet friendly neighborhood carjackers. Ha-ha. I guess it's obvious where Lenny and I come down on this one."

"I wonder what Sarah thought of Abraham's choice?"

This question drew no response as the Humvee pulled away from the lodge. The silence was brief, however. It was broken by Hank. "I did something last night I haven't done in years."

"I saw you taking blank sheets of paper and pens into the back room," Lenore stated.

"Yes, I ran an RV session on your Mexican friend, Lou."

"Hank, do you think you should be messing around with—"

"Probably not. What I brought away was disturbing." Hank briefly related to Lenore the gist of Decker's phone message from the other day.

"And you just couldn't wait to find out, could you, Hank." She put in.

"What happened?" Lou was still unsure if this remote viewing was even real, but he figured if the military spent money and time on it, well, he may as well hear Hank out.

"I made contact with the target after a few minutes. I tried to get prayed up first."

"What were you praying for, Hank? That you could mess around with these powers with impunity?"

"No, it's not like that, sis. Of course, I prayed for protection and direction. Look, I was willing to let the Lord stop me if it was wrong. In any case, I don't want to argue with you. I've already been through this with Uncle."

"Did he know?"

"He came in during my session. One thing at a time."

"When I made contact with your entity, Lou, it was from a perspective that was kind of behind him. He was engaged in a shouting match with a man in khakis and a white shirt who stood near an intricate glowing diagram on the floor of what seemed to be a library. There were two other men in the room with the human. They were both prostrate on the floor and I could see the taller of the two shaking. It was clear that they were terrified, but of whom—the man or "Miguel"—I couldn't tell. I attempted to listen in to the argument, but at that moment, Miguel must have sensed my presence as he spun around and growled. He could not focus his gaze on me, but I heard him scream with rage in my mind, 'I know you! Get out of here or else.' The other man looked directly at me and said something. At this point, Miguel moved toward me, and I became very apprehensive."

"What happened then?"

"I left. Dad had come into the room and was shaking me by the shoulder. He asked if I was all right. I tried to play it cool and said 'Of course.' He said that I certainly didn't look 'all right,' that I was sweating and white as a Swede. I told him what had occurred."

"How did he react?" Lenore asked.

"Better than you. He said he had sensed in his spirit that I was in grave danger. Dad was looking all over the place for me. I told him what I had seen. He said to me 'There is a very dangerous darkness here, are you sure you want to get involved.' I said I was already involved. That I had been involved since I was in the Corps. 'Very well. You are a warrior, my son. The Great Mystery has your path already determined. I will pray for you.' He then told me that he believes the detective is also entwined in this, but without smoking him, his knowledge about particulars was scant."

"You know, detective, that my father is very fond of you. His giving you a name is a great honor. He has known from the beginning that you carry the promise of profound change for our family. It will either be great sorrow or great joy, but whichever is to be is between the Great One and you."

Decker could see tears in the corner of Lenny's eyes. "Well, let's hope I make the right choices." As he wiped the tears away.

Decker sought to lighten the mood by calling Martin Hammer. But before this, Decker briefly ran over the role of Hammer thus far in this. Lou described Martin's program as a Christian interview-call in show. Lenore then suggested that they call the station as crank callers for a laugh, but Decker told her that would have to wait till the afternoon. He dialed Hammer's cell number. "Hello, Martin?"

"Hi, Lou. You are one hard man to get ahold of."

"Sorry, I had to go out of town in a hurry."

"Oh, are you back now?"

"Nope, not for a bit yet. Your interview with Brother Love must have been a doozie."

"Yeah, you could call it that. Lou, I think I met the Miguel you had mentioned. He was pretending to be Love's attorney. But after Clarice called in and bearded the good brother, Miguel went into action and I think he took out the electrical service to the building. My boss tried to say that was a coincidence—right before he suspended me—but I don't think so. I do have some intel on their plans. Do you remember construction equipment back toward the lake the night we went to the service?"

"No. I must have been occupied duck-walking." Lou chuckled. Lenore and Hank shot questioning looks at Decker. Hammer laughed.

"It was in the area just northwest of the tent amphitheater. Love said on my show that in about a week from now the permanent lakeside facility, which is what I gather they were building, will open for business. The group has some special doings planned to 'dedicate' the facility."

"Martin, I have reason to believe that these people are not the fakirs and con men I've figured them for. Their goals may be much deeper, more sinister, and I think they killed Herb."

"You mean your brother-in-law is dead? I'm sorry. Is Shelley okay?"

"We're on our way to pick her up right now. I hope so, but I can't rightly say. Martin, I'll give you the full story when I get back. Right now, you best lie low and go to the police if the Congregation makes any move in your direction. My captain is somewhat in the loop now, at least as far as the mundane issues go."

"Okay, Lou. Again, I'm sorry about the death. See you when you get back."

As they neared the Minneapolis/St. Paul airport, Lou's cell phone rang. It was Lieutenant Haukom. "Detective? Haukom here. I just got a call from the Minneapolis police department. Seems they've found an SUV rented by Mr. Van Doss—or at least what's left of it. They were running a sting on chop shops in the Twin Cities and a vehicle matched the color, style, and VIN number. There's nothing for you to do about this, but I thought you might want to know. Was

Mr. Van Doss well-to-do? I'm told this vehicle rents with a pretty hefty price tag."

"No, he wasn't." Lou puzzled over this. "Thanks, Lieutenant. We are just pulling into the Twin Cities right now. I think we are about ten minutes from the airport."

Lenore nodded her head in agreement.

Decker opened his phone app and dialed the number for the matron who was accompanying Shelley. "Sounds like they're not here yet. No answer from Shelley's travel companion. MSP found Herb's car."

"Where was it?"

"Being parted out by a chop shop here in town. Apparently, the Congregation has embarked on a new fund-raising program.

"See, Lou, it pays to live a country lifestyle."

They entered the short-term parking lot and found a spot quickly. As they walked to the baggage area to meet Shelley, Lou noticed two men standing near the bottom of the incoming passenger escalator. One wore a police officers' uniform and the other a trench coat and fedora. They had not noticed Decker when he walked ahead of his companions and approached from the rear, calling out "Officer." After recognition dawned on him, the tall policeman spun to face Lou, and Decker instantly recognized him as the skinny man from Camp Wendigo. The heavier one was slower to turn, but Decker had already made the pair. "Officer, detective, are you meeting someone?" Decker reached up into his windbreaker and realized he was not armed. The heavy man said, "If you want you and dat skanky sister of yours to live, you'll back off." He drew on Decker.

Hank and Lenny had stopped about fifteen feet away. Lou threw his hands up. "You make a worse detective than you do a lumberjack." Lou shouted, "Police!" The people around noticed the gun in the heavy man's hand and start running in all directions, women screaming. In the distance, two real policemen were now running toward the confusion. Dickie looked and saw them approaching quickly and said to his companion, "We gotta go now! Come on, Eddie." They then ran across the walkway into an open elevator.

Lenny came over. "Obviously, they weren't policemen. How did you know them?"

"Nope. They are goons from the Congregation of Light. I met them at Camp Wendigo, the ones I think killed Herb. They like to play dress up. Fortunately, they aren't very good at it."

Decker noticed Hank eyeing the elevator lights. "Do you want to tell the cops, here are two coming right now," Hank asked.

"No. Waste of time. Other people can do that. We came to get Shelley. Let's stick to the mission."

Chapter 26

The Package

Decker locked eyes with his sister as she stepped onto the top stair of the escalator. He smiled, but she dropped her eyes. Shelley kept them averted until she reached the bottom.

"Hi, Lou. Where's Herb? They said family would meet me here. I assumed it would be Herb." She looked up at Lou with a sad, slightly confused look.

"Hi, Shelley." She hugged Lou tightly.

"Where is Herb, Lou?"

Decker took her by the hand. He walked her over to a row of seats near the wall away from the crowd. Lou held Shelley's hand as he knelt down in front of her.

"Herb is dead, Shelley." She looked incredulous and then slowly began to cry. Passersby must have thought they were witnessing the world's saddest wedding proposal.

"How? When?"

"After he got your letter, he took off without telling me. He wanted to bring you home safely, but by himself. He was 'found' dead by two men from the Congregation of Light posing as fishermen."

"He got my letter? Then it's my fault." Her sobbing made her following words unintelligible.

"No. It's not your fault. No, don't ever think that. Herb loved you, Shelley, and he did what any good, loving husband would do if they knew their wife was in danger. He wanted to rescue you, Shelley. I would have done the same thing myself."

She leaned onto Lou's shoulder. Lou just held her there and let her cry.

At the foot of the escalator, Lenore and Hank introduced themselves to the Las Vegas police matron and thanked her for her help. She acknowledged this with the comment, "No problem. I need to get away from Sin City every so often—even if it's only for a few hours." She then said that she only had twenty-five minutes till her return flight boarded and observed, "It doesn't look like I can add anything to this reunion, so I'll get going. Tell Detective Decker that she never said a word to me about what happened, but he has my number and is free to call if he wishes. Good luck with this. Sorry about how things worked out."

Lenore and Hank thanked her once again as she turned to take the escalator up to her gate. They watched her step off at the top and break into a run. "Big Airport." Hank observed.

"She must *really* miss Las Vegas," Lenny countered.

Decker looked over momentarily and started to stand up to leave, but Lenore signaled him to just hold Shelley as everything was under control. Decker looked around to make sure the two henchmen were not lurking about. *Why would they come here anyway? Tying up loose ends?* Decker did not like where that thought took him.

After a few minutes, Shelley's crying subsided and she looked at Lou as she held his hands. "It *is* my fault, Lou. I should have known that big dummy would try something harebrained. I was scared, Lou, I didn't mean to set him off."

"You didn't 'set him off.' He made a choice and ran into some very bad people. No one could have foreseen that."

Lenore and Hank had sidled over to be near Lou and Shelley as Shelley's crying had diminished.

"Shelley, these are two people I'd like you to meet. In the past several weeks, these people have saved my life and proven to be true friends."

At the phrase "saved my life," Shelley's eyes opened wide and she backed out of Lou's embrace. "What do you mean?"

Lou gave her an abbreviated version of Lenore's heroism in saving him from drowning when he "slipped" off a bank along the shoreline of Lake Superior, and Hank's help in his recovery these past weeks. For the first time, Shelley was aware of the padding on Lou's bandaged shoulder and his grimace when she hugged him tightly. "Lou, I know you. You came to help Herb, didn't you?"

"Yes, I did, but I was too late." Lou's face was drawn into a tight grimace as he struggled not to give in to tears.

"I also know that no one gets hurt the way you described—'slipping into Lake Superior,' and I've seen enough of that shoreline to know that there are big rocks and high cliffs everywhere. Not places to randomly take a stroll along the beach at water's edge."

"Well, I gave you the brief version, Shelley. These people from the Congregation of Light are dangerous. Dangerous in an insane, crazy way."

"How did Herb die, Lou?"

"At first the police announced that it was an accidental drowning. Herb had gotten tangled up in his fishing line and fallen into the shallow end of the lake and drowned."

"Lou, you know Herb hated fish, fishing, hunting and any of those things. His idea of an outdoor sport was to sit in the stands at a football game drinking beer—and even Herb wasn't clumsy enough to get tangled in a fishing line to the point he couldn't stand up."

This was the first time that Lenore and Hank had heard these details of the story. They looked at each other and Hank bit his tongue to keep from giggling. Lenore gave him a stern look.

"I know. I know. That was for public consumption when he was a John Doe. His autopsy showed that he died of blunt force trauma to the head. The manner of death at this point is undetermined. They are leaning toward homicide, but so far it looks like the killers have covered their tracks very well. In any case, things are still under investigation."

"But you know who it was that killed him, don't you, Lou?"

"I think I do. I've got a pretty good idea who was involved, but who the triggerman—or in this case, the rock man—was, I'm still working on that." All four moved off toward the parking lot. Lenore gave Lou the message from the matron and Lou thanked her.

As they reached their floor of the parking garage, Hank bolted away through the door in the direction of where they had parked. Hank was chasing the tall, skinny "policeman" who was running to a dark sedan, waiting with the door open a short distance down the row. Lenny had seen this just before Lou and called out, "Hey, you there! Stop!"

The interior of a nearby SUV was aflame. The tall man jumped into the getaway car and it sped away with a loud squeal of tires. The burning vehicle had been thoroughly vandalized with slashed tires, deep scratches, and spray-painted windows. There was a crude trident sprayed on the hood.

"That's not our car, is it?" asked a confused Shelley.

"No, but it is a dead ringer for the SUV I rented when I got first got here."

"Where is that car now?"

"Long story. Tell you on the ride back."

"Back to where? Are we headed to Grand Rapids?"

"No, no. We are going to my friends' camp. There are some things I need to do before I go home."

Shelley just shook her head, muttering, "Camp?"

Hank had returned. He was breathing heavily. "It was the same two guys. Sorry I couldn't get him." He bent down and looked closely at the symbol. "Hey, there is some writing here."

"You can't outrun a car, Hank," Lenore said. "What does it say?"

"Looks like it says, 'This your last warming Dick!'"

"Warming?" asked Shelley. "And they sure don't like Dick— whoever he is."

"They must have seen us coming and hurried to finish the message."

"He probably misspelled 'warning.' These two aren't Mensa candidates."

"I think he was referencing 'Dick' not as a name but as in 'Detective.'"

"They probably assumed that you, Decker, are a creature of habit and always drive the same vehicle."

"Let's hope we can whip up a few other surprises for them."

By now the flames were dying out as the oxygen supply in the closed SUV had been exhausted. "Like I said, these guys aren't geniuses."

"But they are dangerous. Let's not forget that."

A small crowd including airport security had surrounded the vehicle. Lou pointed at their Humvee across the aisle and a couple spaces farther on. "Nothing to see here. Move along."

Chapter 27

Summer's End

As the Humvee exited the airport, Hank turned on the radio. "How 'bout some tunes? We need to lighten up a bit. Mission accomplished. Shelley is with us and safe and we're headed back to base camp. No hostiles in sight." The voice of Don Henley filled the vehicle…

> *"A voice inside my head said*
> *Don't look back. You can never look back.*
> *I thought I knew what love was*
> *What did I know?*
> *Those days are gone forever."*

Shelley turned to the window. Her shoulders shaking as she wept silently.

"Maybe a different station, Hank." Lenny in the back seat with Shelley reached out and pulled her close. "It's okay, Shelley, it's okay."

"Sorry." Hank punched a button

> *"Please allow me to introduce myself*
> *I'm a man of wealth and taste."*

Hank switched the radio off. "Why don't we just talk for a while."

"Good plan."

They stayed silent for the next half hour until Decker broke the silence. Shelley had drifted off and slept soundly in Lenny's arms. "Hank, I've got to get a better idea of what I'm going up against."

"Agreed. Sound recon is the basis of any successful op. But we're going to have to mark out our objectives first."

"Our?"

"In for a penny, in for a pound."

Decker turned to the window. He didn't want Hank to see him choke up. He took out his mobile and dialed Lieutenant Haukom. "Hey, Lieutenant, it's Decker. The fishermen are still in Minnesota."

"You saw them?"

"Yes, they were waiting for Shelley at the airport, one dressed as a police officer and the other as a TV detective, but I don't think the LVMPD matron would have bought it. They looked more like a funeral director and an overweight flasher than real officers."

"A flasher?"

Hank laughed and looked at Decker. Lenny punched Lou from the back seat.

Lou continued. "Ow, sorry, a bad joke, Lieutenant. Just trying to lighten our mood here. Our driver has proven to be an incompetent DJ on this trip. Are you aware that there was a fire in airport's short-term parking garage?"

"No, but I'll check into it."

"It was them. They thought they were burning our vehicle, but they couldn't even get that right. You might pass on their description to the appropriate people, but my guess is that they are long gone."

"Will do. I don't think they would stay dressed up in those getups, but I'm glad to hear we got your sister back. Have a safe trip. Check back with me later if you would."

"Roger that."

"Ten-four," said Hank.

From the back came, "Over and out."

"What? Is there no privacy anymore?"

Shelley continued to sleep and the rest of the 175-mile journey went by quickly with Lenny, Hank, and Lou making small talk and discussing unusual cases that Lou had worked as a detective. "Seems like my workload in Grand Rapids is always going up, but the criminals show less and less imagination. Which, I guess, is good in a way. In general, now, I'm investigating theft, or robberies with the occasional home invasion. The trend I really fear is the overall increase in violence—random crimes against unknown persons, family holiday arguments that result in a beating or killing and the like." Decker gave a mirthless laugh. "That probably explains a lot about the way I am."

"Lou, you know our world is changing—and not for the better. So many drugs available, one-parent families, people out of work, kids being programmed in school rather than learning how to educate themselves."

"Sure, I see that change every day. Heck, when I first moved to Grand Rapids as a kid, the big TV news story of the day might be a community rummage sale or someone finding their lost dog. Now it's like any other big city—constant, unending violence. Something in American society is broken."

"Amen to that, brother," Hank opined.

They were about twenty miles outside Duluth when Shelley gave a cry and woke with a start. She looked at Lenny and pulled back violently, not recognizing her. "Shhh, it's okay, Shelley." Lenny kept her distance.

Lou turned back, "You're all right, Shelley. You're with us now. You were just dreaming."

Shelley nodded her head gently and wiped a wet spot from her cheek. Shelley noted a large wet spot on Lenore's T-Shirt. It appeared to dot the *E* in "Camp Ohiyesa." "Sorry about that."

Shelley pointed to the drool mark and Lenny laughed. "No big deal. I have about seven T-Shirts just like this one."

Hank chimed in, "She's a regular Charlene Brown."

Everyone chuckled except Shelley. "Must be a Minnesota in-joke." After a while Shelley offered, "I had a strange dream."

The others remained silent.

"I was back at the Church camp. I was hoeing in a big garden plot, but all that I could see growing were weeds. We were supposed to be digging out the flowers and crop plants, I think. I was having trouble because the ground was rocky and hard. Then a big Mexican-looking man dressed up like a gardener was standing in front of me. He had a really strange and—ugly grin on his face. He called me 'viuda.' I have no idea what that means. But he said, 'Viuda, you are doing a good job. Now you must bring that one to me.' He pointed to a plant that had your face, Lou. And he began to laugh. I looked back at him and there was a miniature Herb standing behind him looking confused and moving his mouth as if calling out to someone. I yelled to Herb, but he didn't hear me, Lou. I couldn't get to him." Shelley looked distressed and Lou responded softly.

"You know it's just a dream, Shelley. You've been through a lot and I don't even know the half of it. Nothing to worry about." Shelley sank back in her seat and closed her eyes.

"Viuda," Hank mouthed to his sister, who exchanged looks with him.

A short time later, they were turning into the tree-lined drive at Camp Ohiyesa. The camp was overrun by children this week as several churches from the Twin Cities had rented it for their annual retreats. Two seven-year-old boys ran alongside the Humvee waving in at the passengers and making monkey faces. The vehicle stopped under the canopy in front of the porch and Lenore jumped out. Immediately the two kids were wrapped in her arms as she bent down to them, all hugging tightly. "Luis, Farley. You two get better looking each year." They made the monkey faces again and laughed. "Ms. Lenore has some things she needs to do, now. I'll see you both at chapel. I'll have a special reward for you two 'watchmen' then." The young boys then extricated themselves from Lenore and ran happily away. This was a side of the young woman which Decker had not yet seen. It made him very happy.

Uncle came out and walked directly to Shelley. He surprised her by sweeping her up in a big bear hug that lifted her from the ground. "My daughter, you have had great trouble and sadness, but Camp Ohiyesa is not the place for any of that. You are welcome here. Let the spirit of our people and family comfort your spirit. Come in. Come in." He put her down. Shelley who was astonished to be engulfed by this giant Indian's arms had struggled at first, but when she saw the gentle light in his eyes, she relaxed and even gave him a tentative hug back. She smiled and said, "Thank you."

Lou thought it peculiar that Uncle had omitted God from his greeting but decided that he was merely demonstrating sensitivity to what Shelley had just been through. Uncle led everyone directly to the dinner table. Shelley sat next to Lou as an extra chair was now in place. Uncle said, "First the good news. Fresh dilled salmon for dinner. Now the bad news. I cooked dinner. Agnes Two Kettles had a stroke last night and may not make it. Her condition is listed as grave."

Agnes Two Kettles had been their cook since the day the Clouds had opened Ohiyesa.

Uncle bowed his head. Lou looked at Shelley who had bowed her head but kept her eyes open.

"Great Father. We ask that you touch the lives of the Two Kettle family. Please strengthen and comfort them. And let your powerful hand rest on Agnes. Thank you for the beauty of life and this dinner we share. We ask your direction and protection in the days ahead. Amen."

Dinner conversation was centered on informing Lenore and Hank about the developments at the Camp today. As there were no empty cabins or rooms this week, it was immediately decided that Shelley would bunk with Lenore.

After dinner, Shelley walked with Lou to his cabin. His shoulder ached and he wanted to take some ibuprofen. She sat on the porch swing, while he went inside. She heard her brother make a call. "Hi, Lieutenant." Pause. "That's good news." Pause. "Thanks, bye." Lou returned to the porch. "That was the MSP lieutenant. He says that video surveillance in the parking garage got a good picture of the tall, skinny guy while he was trashing that SUV. He agrees that it was indeed one of the alleged fishermen from the other day. They also got a plate number on the 'getaway' car. The local police found their car was abandoned on the top story of the parking garage. Airport video then showed the men boarding a plane to Detroit. The investigation is underway, and they have already contacted Detroit area police and transportation authorities who are checking security tapes there at the Detroit airport."

Much of this went over Shelley's head, but she asked, "What about the other guy?"

"He was smart enough to wear a hat and keep his face down."

Changing subjects, Shelley asked, "What did Uncle…mean when he prayed for direction and protection for 'us'? Protection from whom? And who is the 'us'?"

"Dunno."

"You know 'Uncle,' as everyone calls him, looks very familiar to me. He looks like that old Indian in the commercials for trash collection or littering, whatever, from TV a while back."

"Hmmm. Uncle Floyd was in the movies and did some TV as I understand it. Don't know about that commercial though."

"Floyd? That doesn't sound much like an Indian Name."

"Floyd Roselli."

"Sounds more Italian than Indian."

"No, he's Indian through and through. His Indian name is 'Wild Boar.'"

"Is this a joke?" Shelley looked hard at Lou.

"Well-l-l—kind of. He is the owner of the lodge and has been a beloved benefactor to his people here. It's a story that I can't do justice—ask Lenore."

Shelley said good night to her brother. She was really tired and after thanking him for coming to get her, she walked back to the main house intending to go to bed. As she walked through the residence to her bedroom, Uncle looked up from reading today's "Wall Street Journal." He smiled and said, "Good night. Sleep Well."

He is Indian, she decided to herself, staring at him. *Lou is teasing like he did when we were kids.*

In the bedroom, she found a toothbrush, hairbrush, washcloth and nightgown laid out for her on the bed. She took these to the adjacent bathroom and readied herself for bed. She noticed a book on the dresser opposite her bed and walked over to look at it. It had a leather cover with the words "Praise Ye the Lord, Hallelujah!" beaded into the cover. She picked up the book and opened it. It was a very old Bible in a language that she assumed must be an Indian dialect. On the presentation page was the name, "Ellie White Sky." Shelley wondered who this was as she dropped into a sound sleep.

Chapter 28

Meanwhile Back at the Ranch

Martin Hammer looked at the pile of mail that he had let accumulate over the past week, walked into the kitchen and retrieved the garbage can. He picked out all the circulars. He tossed them into the trash. He then picked up the letters one-by-one. Bills were placed in one pile, adverts thrown out, solicitations likewise and the rare item of personal correspondence opened right then. Three items caught his eye.

The first was a small note from Clarice Bodkin who apologized for the trouble she had caused Martin with her call. *Bless her heart.* The second was a brightly colored postcard from the Congregation of Light inviting "Occupant" to the official opening of their newly constructed Skyview Sanctuary on September 15. The form promised two tickets if sent back "immediately." This promised to be a gala affair with Rock Rollins leading the musical devotions. Rollins' new band the Capernian Skeptics would also debut songs from their new album entitled "Herod versus Pilate." Hammer chuckled and asked himself, "What in the world is that?" Hammer filled in the ticket request card and put it aside to mail later in the day.

The final piece of mail that caught his attention was a thick envelope with "Camp Ohiyesa" stamped as the return address. He almost chucked it in the trash thinking it was a solicitation, but something in his spirit compelled him to open the letter. It contained four typed pages. He skipped to the back which had Lou Decker's signature, then went back and read from the beginning. The letter detailed Lou's sudden disappearance: his chasing Herb, Herb's death, his encounter with the Congregation of Light "hit squad," his rescue and recovery and all the other developments. The final page contained a warning to Martin to stay away from the Congregation until he arrived in back in Grand Rapids. "They are hooked into a powerful something, that I don't quite understand yet." He asked that Martin go to his house and look for his father's old army logbook from Vietnam and send it to him. Martin should be able to find it in Lou's old sea chest in the basement. Lou closed with a request for Martin to check the health status of Raymond Pibble, the erstwhile paralyzed veteran. He was particularly interested in whether Pibble's ability to walk continued to deteriorate. Lou then wished Martin good fortune and signed off telling him that he was once again in possession of a cell phone. After paying his bills, Martin called Mrs. Bodkin, who was surprised to hear from him. "Martin, I didn't want to bother you, but I needed to apologize for you losing your job over my call."

"I'm only suspended, Mrs. Bodkin."

"Well, I guess that's better than it could be. There was a different show in your time slot now, and well…that's why I assumed you were out. The show is not very good. There is some man with a New York accent lambasting everything in modern life and every two minutes there is an ad from these local Christian lawyers…but I'm sorry anyway."

"Mrs. Bodkin, it's really no problem. I don't think I'm going back. Events have been going on here at the station that make me uncomfortable in that job and those things have challenged me to look at my life's path again."

"I knew it. They *made* you put that son of the devil on, didn't they?"

"Yes and no. I have to accept some of the blame. They were determined that he be given airtime. But I didn't have to go along and be the one to bring him on."

"Well, God bless you, Martin. You know your father would be thrilled to have you in the ministry."

"Whoa, Mrs. Bodkin. I'm not saying that."

"Pray, and think about it."

"I will. I just wanted to set your heart at ease. Your call was the best thing that happened to WCRS in a long time. Before I go, I wondered if you have heard from your cousin about how her son is doing these days."

"You mean Raymond. Agnes called the other day and said he's back to drinking heavily again—I doubt that boy ever stopped—and his legs are getting weaker. He wakes up in the night yelling, 'No, no, get away from me,' and screaming. She asks if he is having dreams about the war, and he just yells at her and tells her to get out and leave him alone. She's nearing her wits' end with Raymond."

"That's not exactly encouraging."

"No, it isn't."

"Well, thank you for that, Mrs. Bodkin. I'll let you go now."

"Martin?"

"Yes?"

"Some of the girls from church and I have started a prayer group to pray about that Congregation. I want you to know that we are praying for you too. Not sure why we were led to, but is there anything you would like us to pray for?"

"Thank you. Uh, please pray for Detective Decker if you would. He is in a serious situation."

"We will."

Martin then drove over to the address Decker had furnished. The house was a neat craftsman style in a residential neighborhood. Oddly, it had a very large cell tower just behind the lot. *Didn't Lou's wife die of cancer?* He found the key right where Lou had described and let himself in. The stairs were off the kitchen and he went down. Turning on a light, he moved a row of small boxes from the top of Lou's old sea chest. He rummaged through the chest and found the book. He sat down and wondering why Lou would attach any importance to this book. Martin opened it and glanced through it. When he saw a sketch on page 87, he read the commentary and understood why.

He took the book and drove to the nearest office supply store. There he had the clerk scan a copy of the relevant portions of the memoir for him. He then looked up the address to Camp Ohiyesa and sent it off next-day delivery. On his way home, he called Lou, who answered on the second ring.

"Decker here."

"Hi, Lou. Martin. Hey, I found your book and just sent it off next-day delivery. Let me know when it gets there."

"Great. Thanks. That was fast. Anything else?"

Yes. I spoke with Clarice Bodkin and she says Raymond Pibble is decompensating. His legs are going weak again. She also mentioned that he is drinking heavily and having severe nightmares. She chalked that up to his wartime trauma."

"Maybe. Hey, thanks for calling and sending that book off. I'll call when it gets here. Adios."

"Later."

*****

Brother Love sat fuming in his office. In front of him were Dickie and Eddie. The two henchmen hung their heads and absorbed the angry, epithet filled dressing down with apprehension. "You two incredible boobs. First, you kill the brother-in-law of a detective and go on TV to talk about it. Then you bungle your attempts to cover it up in every way possible. Finally, you burn some poor shmuck's SUV in the parking garage who has nothing to do with anything, and you, Dickie, your picture is on every police website in America and on all the Midwest TV news programs. What do you expect me to do? I can't protect you if the cops come calling. And if you screw up again like this, I'll—I'll feed you to Miguel." Love let that threat sink in. Both understood the import of that statement as they had seen Miguel in action.

"Get out!"

Both men hustled from the office with the door staying slightly open behind Dickie. Love got up and slammed the door loudly. "These idiots can't even close a door."

He went back to his desk and unrolled the plans for the new facility. He took a deep breath and let it out slowly, trying to relax.

He pulled out a preprinted checklist and noted there were only two unchecked tasks. They were the painting and finishing the electrical work. Love decided that he needed something to get him in a better mood and picked up his car keys to go out himself and check the project. He turned back around and in the chair opposite his desk sat Miguel. "Lighten up. You know, I don't appreciate you using me to threaten your help. Those nitwits are going to give me indigestion soon enough. There are a couple people you need to meet."

Miguel nodded to the side of the room and two apparitions appeared. "How can we be of help?" The older, a male, asked. The younger, a fit-looking, heavily tattooed female was clearly anxious as she shuffled her feet and looked around.

"I need you two to perform a task for me. There is a man named Lou Decker who was injured and taken to the hospital in Harbors a couple weeks ago. He was discharged and I believe he is staying somewhere in that area. Go to the hospital and find out where he is and get back to me. He might be hanging out with some locals. If you can, find out their names as well. I have something special planned for them."

The girl began to ask why he couldn't do this himself, but the man elbowed her. "Of course, always glad to help."

Miguel continued in a calm, measured tone. "I do not want to be 'known' in that area. The opposition is paying close attention to me at this time and I wouldn't want to tip my hand. I'll expect your report." He made a hand gesture and the apparitions vanished.

"Who were they?" Love got up to go and noted that Miguel was already gone.

The two from Duluth drove up to Harbors and went to the hospital that afternoon. They walked up to the desk. The woman identified herself as Decker's sister. Shirley the secretary told them that her access to hospital records is limited by law, and that she does not know who Decker left with. She reminded the woman that as his sister, "You should just call his cell phone. I'm sure he'll be thrilled to hear from you."

The man then suddenly leaned in and said loudly, "Why aren't you being more helpful. We are family and you aren't helping at all."

"I've already explained the situation to you. I can get my supervisor if you are unhappy with what I told you."

"Is she going to give us the information."

"Probably not, unless she wants to lose her job and face a possible federal lawsuit over violating privacy laws."

The man turned and muttering a curse, he left, with the woman still standing there. She then turned and walked after her companion. As she did, Shirley noticed a row of skulls and pitchfork tattoos on her lower leg. "Yeah, she's Flying Man's sister, and I'm his mother."

Shirley picked up the phone and called the camp and related the strange encounter to Lenore.

Chapter 29

A Widow's Tale

It was mid-morning when Decker had finished his stretching exercises, an adapted version of Tai Chi that his department called "Guy Chi." With his deconditioned body, even a brief workout brought out a sweat. *At least I'm eating right.* He showered and headed to the camp office expecting to find Lenny at the desk, instead he found yet another young Indian girl, this time sorting through the mail. She smiled at Decker "Good afternoon, detective, and all that."

"Don't start that good afternoon stuff with me, young lady. You know perfectly well that it's only 11:15. Where can I find Miss Lenny?" Decker smiled.

"She's at the dining hall. She's been pressed into KP since Auntie Agnes got sick."

"Thanks, and do something. At least try to look like you are working."

She giggled and Lou headed off to the mess hall. He went through the dining area where Hank sat holding an iced tea in one hand and reading "Rodeo Times" magazine.

"Never thought about you being a bull-rider, Hank,"

"Oh, I'm not. Just getting ideas for this weekend's activity."

"Isn't that a little dangerous for these city-folk?"

Hank looked at Decker with an expression of disbelief. "Well, detective, we don't have any bucking bronco's or calves to rope, so we have the kids ride sheep. They rope and 'rassle' the farm dog. They love it. Not the dog, particularly, but he is so laid-back he just enjoys that the kids are playing with him."

"Sheep riding?"

"Yup, the Camp Ohiyesa version of the Calgary Stampede. Maybe you ought to give it a try? When I was about five, Dad took me to a rodeo, and I rode the sheep. Stayed on three seconds before I fell off. I cried all the way home, but I got a Turkey feather for my efforts. My first and last attempt at rodeo."

"Quite a career. Where's your sister?"

"She's in the kitchen prepping lunch with Shelley."

"Shelley?"

"Yup. Shelley whipped up some great omelets for breakfast and did most of the cleanup herself."

Decker walked through the swinging doors into the kitchen. Lenny and Shelley laughing and standing on each side of a large steel prep table washing a great mound of torn lettuce in a steel colander for a large salad.

"Good morning, sleepyhead," Lenny called. "Can you bring those three lettuce heads over. Are you going to eat lunch with the *hoi polloi*?"

Decker brought over the lettuce. He washed his hands and began shredding it.

"No, Lenny, he's going back to take a nap."

"Yes, I just may, I always hated KP."

"Well, your sister is turning Camp Ohiyesa into a gourmet dining experience. If word gets around, we'll be forced to add 'foodie's week' to the schedule."

"Lou knows I can cook. Look how I fattened up Herb." A sad look came into her eyes as she said it.

"Even Uncle is eating lunch here and I don't think he's set foot in this building since 1990."

They finished preparing lunch and people began to wander in. Hank joined the line near the front and Uncle was not too far behind. Decker shrugged his shoulders and joined them. The salad was fresh and excellent as were the herb seasoned tomato soup and grilled cheese based 'Dagwood' sandwiches.

"Not a fancy lunch, but very good. I wonder if the prior quality of meals has had any impact on our camp attendance." Uncle looked thoughtful as they finished up and bussed their dishes.

"Good chance." Seconded Hank. He turned to Decker. "Lenny has always been a good cook, but, Lou, your sister is spectacular."

"What about Agnes Two-Kettles? Are you going to throw your old cook away with the slop?"

Uncle thought a moment and responded, "A good woman, but rather pedestrian in her culinary pursuits. In any case, I spoke with the doctors, and they don't think she can come back to work after this illness. I've already put ads in the papers from here to the Twin Cities. It's a shame in a way that we are now experiencing the 'revolution of rising expectations' regarding our cook staff." Uncle looked sideways at Decker.

The three men headed to the big veranda on the office building and settled down in the shade, each with a lemonade. They were watching a gaggle of campers wandering over to the archery range, dragging, swinging and a few carrying their bows and quivers normally, when the girls walked up and sat down in wooden rockers.

"Fifteen minutes. Finished already?" Hank asked. "A new record!"

"Finished till four o'clock. The dinner meat has already been marinating and the lunch cleanup is *fini*," said Lenny.

Uncle observed. "Agnes and her two nieces would be in there till 3:30 most days. Were we paying them by the hour, Hank?" He laughed.

There was a cool breeze taking the edge off the heat of the sun. In the shade on the veranda, Decker leaned back and relaxed. He was just dozing off when Shelley appeared and said, "Lenny thinks I need to tell you about *my* 'camping experience.' Or at least what I can recall."

She told the story up to the point of writing the letter to Herb, and then said, "Lou, I think this is where you lost track of me. We stayed at the camp, and I still don't know where it was, but it seemed like we drove quite a bit farther north than Duluth. And I don't remember ever hearing the word 'Wendigo' or seeing any signs indicating a name even though we walked out to a main road several times during our extended 'hikes.' As I said before, we worked every day to the point of exhaustion. We performed nonstop manual labor, much of the time on 'make-work' projects. At irregular times during the workday and sometimes even in the middle of the night, we were taken to a big building that looked like it was an old sawmill. It had a stairway leading to a basement room, referred to as the lecture hall for talks or what they called 'sessions.' God and Christ were never mentioned, which I thought odd for a church, and ethical issues were either blurred or ignored in these talks. I was having difficulty understanding the reason for this gobbledygook. Then the lecture was followed by an extended period of guided meditation and relaxation exercises. At first, the meditation eased the misgivings I was having about coming here and helped my body recuperate, but after a week or so, I began having terrifying dreams every time I would go to sleep—and this was true of everyone I talked to."

Lou asked, "Did the staff abuse you?"

"Did they hit us or assault us? Not me and not that I saw. Although the program was certainly not what I envisioned. Looking back now, I realize an inertia and increasing disinterest in even leaving the place and returning home had developed. About a week into our program, one of the ladies, Sally, began complaining loudly and stated she was leaving. I remember being surprised at the time that none of the workers tried to stop her. She walked out of camp down the road with her duffel bag over her shoulder. Three days later, they brought Sally back in the van. She was dirty, her clothes were torn, and she looked like she had been frightened nearly to death. After that she wandered through the camp mumbling to herself and avoiding eye contact and conversation with everyone. A few days after they brought Sister Sally back, our 'counselor' came into the bunkroom at 4:00 a.m., threw on the light, and said, 'Congratulations, you've finished your training here. Pack up and be ready to roll out in thirty minutes.' I remember assuming that we were headed home. As I entered the bus, I asked if I might call my husband. The counselor asked why. I said to tell him to expect me home later today. He laughed. 'Who said anything about home, you finished the first part of your training is all and we are moving on to phase two.' I told him I was finished with this crap and I wanted off the bus. He moved aside. As I stepped down to leave the bus, he put a hand on my shoulder and said, 'Remember Sally? She left.' This was the woman who left and then returned. I said 'Yes' and looked over. She stared vacantly at the window. He went on, 'You might wish to consider that you are nearly 100 miles from the nearest town, and you don't know where it is. You are also thirty miles from the nearest 'friendly' habitation. These woods are filled with bear, wolves, and two-legged predators. Heck, I don't know. We might not even be in the United States anymore. I guess I could call Herb for you and tell him that "you were unhappy at camp and snuck off on your own. Sadly Herb, we don't know where she went. Yes, we have the police and staff all out looking for her, but…"' Shelley, we managed to buy Sally back from some men for three bottles of gin. But sadly, no one will be here till next spring to do that for you. It could make for a long winter.' I took his hand from my shoulder and turned to walk to the back of the bus. 'You've got spirit, just like Brother Love predicted. That's a valuable commodity.' I sank into my seat and began to cry. I had not even considered that we might be in Canada and as I recalled Sally's expression when she returned to camp, I was terrified. I then remembered that Herb would be looking for me in Minnesota and I felt gloomier yet."

"So were you *in* Canada?" asked Hank.

"I don't know. We were taken to the camp in vans that drove for hours. Oh, and the windows were so dark that you couldn't see out clearly. Just like in the bus. And the drivers of both turned off the headlights several times during the trips and put on a helmet-type thing."

"Night vision. Sounds like a pretty sophisticated operation. Mental programming, high-tech gear."

"Well the bus was silent for a long time and then someone asked when we were going to stop—she was thirsty and hungry. The driver yelled back over his shoulder 'We're almost there. No stops till then. We're on a schedule and there's no time to lose. You can get drinks and sandwiches out of the boxes in back. And you women already know where the toilet is.' The woman kept up asking to stop and the counselor came back and sat down next to her. He opened what looked like a pocket flask and passed it to her. A short time later she had fallen asleep. Meanwhile, we passed out the sandwiches—chicken salad and PBJ—to the women on the bus. There were about twenty-five of us. There was also a case of water which we shared. Shortly after eating, I began to feel groggy and when I awoke it was nighttime, judging by the pitch-black. I had a headache and felt like a fool for not realizing that the food or water might be drugged. The box of sandwiches had been replenished and the water restocked. The woman who had been complaining was not on the bus anymore. So I assumed we had stopped. I then noticed that there were several new women on the bus as well as a few teenage girls. When I saw these young teens on the bus, I was really getting scared. As our original group began to wake up, one began to speak with one of the new women. The counselor was up in a flash 'No talking.' 'Why not?' the woman persisted. The counselor walked back to her and bent down to look her in the eye 'Because I said so' and he put his hand on a small club on his belt."

"How long had you been driving at this point? Did you make any more stops? Could you see anything outside?" Hank was fidgeting and clearly upset by the story.

"No, the windows were too dark. Yes, we made a couple stops for driver changes. I think, at that point we were about twenty-four hours into our trip. We finally stopped about eight or nine hours later, and the driver shut down the bus. We were herded out and across a dry, sandy parking lot into a warehouse-type building. As we walked, we were repeatedly told to keep our eyes to the front. Inside, was one very large rectangular room, like a school gym, with tables and chairs at one end and bunk beds at the other. In the mid-area was a living area with couches chairs and a TV. Restrooms were along one of the longer walls. There appeared to be one main door at the end opposite the bunks. Big men with guns stood by it, continually. There were two doors along the longer wall opposite the restrooms. When we entered, there were about fifteen women already there, but no children or teens. The counselor yelled 'Grab a bed and make yourselves at home.' On the way in, I had glanced toward the sunset out of the corner of my eye. I recognized a tower that looked like the top of the Stratosphere Casino up over a hill in the distance. Off to the south, as I reckoned from the sunset, there were many large electrical towers crossing toward the casino, so I guessed we were somewhere east or southeast of Las Vegas. The next two days dragged by and I spent my time trying to rest and plan for an escape if the opportunity arose. I have you to thank for that, Lou, it's what kept me sane. I'm sure our food was drugged because many of the women spent all day sleeping or just walking around like zombies. Some of them cried persistently and when two got into a fight over a magazine, they were dragged out through the side door and weren't seen again—at least by me. I quit eating during this time and drank only water from the sinks in the bathroom. There were new arrivals every day. Each evening, a group of women would be taken, usually five to six, into one of the side rooms and come out wearing expensive-looking, if somewhat slutty clothes and all made up. They would then be taken out the other side door. Usually only one or two would return. Some nights, women would be roused from their bunks and just taken out the main entry door. These never came back. During the fourth evening I positioned myself so I could see out the side door when the women were taken. I was pretending to be looking down at a magazine, so I wouldn't attract attention. I watched them being loaded into a small van like the ones that took us up to the camp. There was writing on the side, but I couldn't read it. I moved slightly sideways to change my perspective and saw a separate wing of the building. The inside lights were off but there was a blue glow and I could make out part of a world map on the wall. Beyond that wing were some towers. I remember a lighted sign out front that said 'Saturn Communications.'"

"Could you see what kind of towers they were?" Lou asked.

"Is that important?"

"Maybe." Hank already had his mobile device out and was punching Saturn Communications into the browser. "Got it."

"They looked like three or four of those big cell towers that are everywhere with a lot of metal gizmos and dishes attached. As I recall now there were also two of those really big satellite dishes near the towers. You know, like you see at cable TV places."

"'Saturn Communications is a cell phone provider serving those having discerning tastes. It is based in Las Vegas with branches in…' Go on with your story, Shelley, Lou and I can look at this later."

"The night after that, I was taken into the side room and cleaned up. My hair was washed and combed out and makeup applied by some hard-looking women. We were forced to take a pill of some kind. I managed to keep it under my tongue and spit it out later, but I still started to feel funny. I was then put in a tiny red dress and taken with the rest of the women out the side door to the van. I spit out the rest of the pill as I walked. By this point, I *knew* that we were headed to Vegas and my intuition told me there would not be a good outcome if I couldn't get away. I was really scared, Lou, and I began to pray. I'm sure I made all kinds of promises to God as to what I would do if He got me out of this. We pulled into a dark access road near the entry to a casino parking garage between giant buildings. When I got out of the van there was a limo waiting with the door open. I was terrified as I saw a large man standing next to it. He looked like a bodyguard. I said, 'Jesus, please…' and began to cry. The man with me turned and said, 'Hey, get out of here,' to someone nearby, who obviously was not supposed to be there. I looked to see who he was talking to and a homeless woman was stumbling toward us with one hand out. But she also looked strange, like she was glowing with this bright light. She held out one hand to my guard and he stumbled backward against the van. Her other hand was held out palm facing the 'limo thug' who now was oblivious to our presence. The woman took me by the arm and whispered, 'Run that way—*now!*' as she pushed me forward. I went stumbling up the road and found myself on the strip. The limo guy never even looked at me as I went past him. I was really dizzy by now, from the drug or what had just happened, I don't know. I was standing next to two Las Vegas cops and a different woman was holding me up by the arm telling them something and gesturing. I noted the same blue-white glow about this woman. Next thing, I'm in the back of a squad car and then at a hospital. As I sat there on the stretcher, my mind began to clear.

All I could think was, 'Thank God I'm free!' The doctors and nurses treated me very well, but I wasn't saying too much. They stitched up this cut on my scalp." Shelley pointed to the side of her head. "I still don't know how I got it. Later, I spoke to a mental health worker. I did not give her much information, and I think you know the rest." Shelley stopped talking and her head dropped. She was crying softly. Lenore leaned over and held her in a hug.

Uncle moved over and took both the girls in his massive arms and just held them. Lou noticed his lips moving but could not make out the words after "Wakan Tanka."

Hank nodded to Lou and stood up. Lou followed. They went to a log bench under some cottonwoods and sat. "Some story," Hank said.

"Sure is. More of the woo-woo I've been experiencing recently. All in all, she's a lucky girl."

"Lou, it's not woo-woo…or luck." Hank hesitated, choosing his next words carefully, but Lou interrupted.

"What do you have on Saturn Communications?"

Hank sat back and sighed. "Saturn has a pretty strange profile for a consumer cellular service." Hank chuckled. "Listen to what they offer customers from their website: three-year contracts, you must use their equipment—which, by the way—looks like an old flip phone from the picture on its site and costs $1000, no rollover of minutes, and $300 per month. And get this, they have over a hundred 5-star ratings."

"Doesn't sound like a very popular plan to me—unless you cater to a select, 'discerning' clientele. It's pretty obvious they are a front."

"Sounds that way to me. Prostitution, human trafficking. I bet if we looked deeper into this, they would hit the trifecta with drug distribution."

"It's sounding like the Congregation is a much bigger operation than a small-town bunco scam. I'm going to call Lieutenant Haukom and pass enough of this story on that maybe he can sell an investigation to the Feds."

At that point, the girl from the front desk walked up. "Mr. Decker, a courier just dropped this off for you and since it is marked urgent, I thought you might want it. Sorry to interrupt."

"Thanks, uh, I don't know your name."

"Laurie."

"Thanks, Laurie."

Decker tore the envelope open and beheld his father's old "army book" and exclaimed, "Yes!"

Hank recognized Decker's excitement but couldn't understand why an old army field manual would excite him. "Lou, can we talk a bit about what is going on here, I mean, behind the scenes."

"Sure, but let's do it later. I need to make a couple of calls and then I have some reading to do, okay?"

"Okay." Hanks face dropped as he thought of the story of the Apostle Paul, Felix, and the more convenient time. Decker got up, pulled out his phone and walked briskly toward his cabin.

Chapter 30

Apocalypse When?

Decker sat on the edge of his bed holding his father's army log. He rolled the book through his hands. He flipped through the pages. *If it's in here.*

Martin was years younger than Decker, but since their first meeting, Decker had been nagged by a recurrent feeling, *Have I met him, or seen him before?* He had called Martin Hammer to tell him the book had arrived and to thank him again. Decker left a brief message when Hammer did not answer. Decker put the feeling aside. He called Lieutenant Haukom. Lou explained his concerns about Saturn Communication being a front for human trafficking. Decker had been circumspect when relaying parts of Shelley's story, but together with Hank's characterization of Saturn's internet programs, he built a damning company profile.

"Lou, I'll run this by a friend at the Minneapolis FBI office. If he thinks anything is going on, you realize they will want to speak with your sister. Has she gone back to Grand Rapids or is she there with you?"

"She's here with me. We called yesterday and made arrangements to have Herb's body sent back for storage at a funeral home in Grand Rapids when the ME has finished with it."

"He's been done for a week, so I guess your brother-in-law is on his way home already."

"Guess so. Okay, I'll call you if anything else turns up, Lieutenant."

"Thanks, Lou. You might want to prep Shelley for a visit from the Feds. I don't think they can ignore this. I'm looking at the Saturn website right now. This is not what I'd call a customer-friendly business model, but now, at least I don't feel so bad about my cell plan." He laughed and hung up.

Lou lay back on the bed. He opened his father's manual and started reading. The first sections were basic information on various aspects of military life. Each topic was typically covered in lectures during basic training. After each section, were one or two blank pages for notes. After the final text section, came a lot of extra blank pages, which Lou's father had used for journaling. The first part of this briefly described his father's experiences at jump and ranger schools. It was obvious that his dad had been either too busy or too tired to spend much time writing other than noting some of his more interesting experiences. After this was a section on his time in Vietnam. Lou closed the book. He got up walked out to the bench under the cottonwood tree. *Nothing so far of much interest.* He sat on the bench seat and resumed reading. "I'm sure it has to be in here. It was the only thing he ever told me about his tour, and, of course, now I wish I had paid better attention."

"Paid attention to what, detective?" Uncle had come up behind him and came around to where Decker was sitting. "Do you mind if an old man sits for while?"

"Nope. Nice to have company." Decker did not realize that he had spoken aloud. He enjoyed being with the old man. "I have a half-formed memory that my father had tried to pass on something important to me, but I was too busy being a kid to listen."

"Many of us never take the time to listen, son. You shouldn't be too hard on yourself. I'll let you read in peace and just sit here if that's okay."

"Sure, I'd enjoy the company." Decker went back to the memoir. On page 87, he began to read carefully.

17 June 1968. Base camp-3 klicks west of Da Nang.
A week ago, Murphy, Crosby, and I were sent by chopper to a location near the Vietnam-Laos border. We were ordered to check on the

207

status of a detachment sent to deliver weapons and ammo to friendlies in that region. A Laotian warlord had been making incursions in-country and wreaking havoc on ARVN patrols. When radio contact was lost with our people, headquarters sent us to check things out. The flight over was uneventful, but by our flying time I reckoned that we were actually inside of Laos. In any case, lines on a map never meant much to either us or the brass, so we just dropped in and went to work. We figured that we could make it back to base in a couple days. After about an hour of recon, we located the spot of the last transmission and noted ARVN bodies strewn about, many having evidence of being badly burned. Murphy noted that we had never run into flamethrowers before and cautioned us to keep eyes open. We continued on a westerly path through the jungle thinking that our boys had been ambushed. We figured that if any were alive, they might be taken back to Laos, so we pushed on. About an hour later, we heard small arms fire. We immediately identified it as AK chatter and now moved up cautiously toward the engagement. About a half a klick onward we saw a clearing. On one side were a ragtag militia with several bound ARVN soldiers and a couple American "advisors" in tow. Across the field, were twenty to twenty-five pajama-clad slopes. They appeared to be picking off the Laotians, if Laotians they were, at a brisk clip. Suddenly, something came in from behind the Cong over the trees and the attackers began screaming and burning. At first, I could not see it plainly, and assumed it was some sort of helicopter set up with a flamethrower. As it got nearer, I could make out that it was some sort of flying creature. We immediately ran toward the remaining Laotians and Murph and Cros finished them off. The beast continued circling the Congs' position and then flew off toward the northeast, belching fire at Cong who had escaped his initial blasts. While Murphy and Crosby were doing their job, I ran to the group of Americans and uniformed ARVNs. They were all dead except one American. I cut him loose and saw that he was a chaplain. His uniform was filthy with several cuts. His nametag read *Hammer*. He pulled me down as the winged monster came cruising in with a roar and I looked up in time to see my comrades engulfed in flame. Hammer grabbed me and pulled me down as I attempted to raise my M-16 and take aim. "That won't help," he said. "Get behind me, now." He grabbed me pulling me forcefully behind him.

The creature circled around us and Hammer kept between the monster and me. He called out to it. "Your work is done here. I charge you by the name of God and his son, Jesus Christ to depart."

The dragon replied in a low growl, "I claim him. He bears no mark of protection."

Hammer yelled back, "He is under my protection. You know the law, you must withdraw. Or should I ask—"

The dragon roared and wheeled back a short distance clearly enraged. On both sides of us, I now saw bright, white luminous orbs taking up a position between us and the monster. They began a slow advance toward the monster, glowing, whirling and—singing in a language I did not understand. The music was magical and mesmerizing in its beauty. The creature screamed in pain and wheeled about, flying away roaring.

"We're safe for now, but we better get moving," Hammer said. "There are plenty of other dangerous things out there."

I was in shock and nodded, but just stood there. Hammer took my face in both his hands and looked into my eyes. "Focus, soldier." He read my name tag. "Decker, we need to get going, *Now!*" He walked over and bent down over the cinder piles remains of Murphy and Crosby. He grabbed their dog tags and said to me, "Your friends are gone. There's nothing left. You don't need to go over there, there's nothing you can do for them." He took my hand, pointed in the direction we had come and asked, "East?"

I nodded, and we moved out. I came back to myself rapidly as we walked. After half an hour, I was leading us back. When I turned around, I was surprised that only this strange chaplain was following me—not Murph or Cros.

It took us almost four days to get back to base camp. Along the way we spoke little, but as we made camp the first night, I asked him to tell me what had really happened. He recited the facts, exactly as I had experienced them, but from his point of view. When he was finished, he added "Yes, this was real. And if you don't want a section 8, I'd keep it to myself. You aren't in Kansas anymore, Sergeant Decker."

"Michigan." I corrected him, not recognizing the movie quotation and thinking he thought I was from Kansas.

"Whereabouts?"

"Grand Rapids."

"I'm from near Grand Haven. I'm gonna look you up after we get back. You can buy me and my Minnie a nice steak dinner."

"Got just the place."

He talked about God, his faith, and those things that chaplains talk about then, but it was strange because he was the first and only person whom I've ever met who didn't seem to have an angle. And after what we had gone through, I couldn't deny the power he called on. We parted back at base, and these events have always stayed fresh in my mind, haunting me for months in dreams and occasionally since. Sadly, my impression of him has faded, but I took his advice and I've never mentioned this episode to anyone since that time. I am not sure why I am documenting it here, but I feel compelled to do so. Martin Decker, USA."

There was one brief final entry written in blue ink on the following page.

17 June 1978.

Got a call from a Rev. Willis Hammer the other day. He called to say he was going to be in town today, ten years after our "adventure" and laughingly wondered if our families might go out for that steak dinner that I promised him. He showed up in the afternoon with his wife, Minnie, and their baby son, Martin. So we all went out, had a nice dinner and caught up on our lives. Talking to the Hammers was easy and I sensed the same faith and power in this man who had saved my life. He was the minister of a congregation at Lakeshore Baptist Church on Lake Michigan and invited us out to the services. Of course, I said we would come, but I'm not so sure I want to relive that day and so—we'll see.

My son Lou asked who these people were and what they were to us. I told him that Rev. Hammer had saved my life in Vietnam. Lou looked confused and disinterested, but my wife, Judy, said, "I didn't know that." I had never told her the story."

Lou put the book down and stared out at the lake.

Uncle saw that Lou had finished reading the manual and said quietly, "Is your father speaking to you, son?"

"Yes."

Chapter 31

Rodeo Clowns

Knock, knock, knock.

Lou opened his eyes. He stretched and moved stiffly to the door. He cracked the door open. The sky showed it was just past dawn. Lenore's face looked up at him.

"Lou. Good morning."

"Good morning, Lenny. I hope you didn't wake me up just to tell me that." Lou chuckled. "Not that I don't appreciate seeing you."

"No, Lou, the good morning was just a bonus. I came to ask a favor. Our rodeo clown, Buster Eagle, is in the hospital, so we are without a clown for the rodeo today."

Uh-oh. Lou started to close the door on Lenny, but she put a boot between the door and jamb. "Lou, you know I wouldn't ask if it weren't important. After all, what is a rodeo without a clown?"

"Lenny, dear, first of all I've never been to a rodeo, so I can't answer your question. Second, I've never, deliberately at least, been a clown. Third, you do know that I have a broken shoulder, right? I'm just not the rodeo clown type."

"Sure, you are. Besides, your shoulder seems healed enough for all your other activities and no one here knows who you are, so it really isn't important whether you're funny or not. This isn't stand-up comedy on a stage anyway. Your dignity will survive. Please, Lou. Shelley says you would be perfect. Puh-leeze."

Shelley? "How did she get involved in this?"

"She volunteered to be Chuck Wagon Cora!"

"What is this, a cast of thousands? Uncle has experience in the movies. Did he come up with this rodeo?"

"Well, mostly yes, originally, but it's sort of grown like 'Topsy' through the years. The little campers look at it as the highlight of the week. You don't want to let them down do you?"

"Me? I'm not letting them down. And what happened to this Eagle clown anyway?"

"Unfortunately, Buster has a fondness for the firewater. He spent last evening at the American Legion post quenching his thirst. He got into an argument with a short-tempered young man who objected to being referred to repeatedly as 'jarhead.' After what I understand was a further brief exchange of insults the stranger landed a solid right cross that busted Buster's jaw. Hence, Buster lies, jaw wired, in a hospital bed unable to either sing 'Rawhide' or do rope tricks for his fans." Lenny was biting her lip to keep from laughing.

"Ha-ha-ha. He could still do the rope tricks"

"Have you ever tried jumping around with a hangover?"

"Nope. I still don't see how this is my problem."

"Lou, if you don't do this. Uncle will have to do this, and he is…definitely not clown material. Can you picture the disappointed look on the kids' faces with this old guy hobbling around, telling 1950s era jokes with a philosophical twist, unable to even properly throw a lasso or even make a balloon animal?"

"I can't throw a lasso or make balloon animals."

"That's not the point, detective, and you know it!"

Decker realized that Lenny was losing steam and he decided to not let things go too far. "Okay. Okay. I'll do it. For you. But only because you said 'please'. I'll have to talk to Uncle and learn a few jokes."

"No, please don't. I'll send over a book of trail songs, campfire stories, and jokes. You should be able to glean a few nuggets from that. One more thing, can you play a guitar?"

"Guitar? Who am I supposed to be now, Gene Autry?"

"Never mind. I'll send over the book." Lenny turned and hurried off before Decker could change his mind. "Thanks, Lou!" she said over her shoulder.

Decker called out as Lenny left, "Send the book with Shelley. I wanna talk to her."

In spite of himself, Lou was a big hit with the campers. Dressed in greasepaint and wearing an orange fright wig under a beat-up giant sombrero and rhinestone encrusted chaps, Lou resembled a clown from the world of "It." However, the kids thought it was hilarious when he repeatedly stepped in animal manure. Lou was run down by "stampeding" sheep to the cheers of the onlookers. When he demonstrated the quick draw, his prop gun flew from his hand and hit Hank on the head—the kids thought that was part of the act. Finally, he was coerced into singing "Rawhide" with Lenny accompanying him on the guitar. He fumbled the words and his singing was so bad that the kids were howling with laughter.

"Perhaps I misnamed you, detective. Perhaps 'Heyoka' instead of 'Wicasa' would have been more apt. You are a natural," Uncle told him, a big grin on his face.

After the rodeo, everyone gathered in the mess hall for awards and the farewell chapel session. Decker came in, dressed in street clothes hoping no one would recognize him. A wild cheer erupted from the campers when Shelley yelled out, "Hey, everyone, here's our clown!"

Decker was called to the front by Hank to assist in passing out trophies, feathers and other trinkets. Hank pointedly rubbed his head and smiled. When the awards ceremony concluded, Uncle walked to the front and gave a brief invocation in both Dakota and English. He then turned the program over to Hank. It was a tradition at the Camp that the last devotional service be led by Uncle, but this year Uncle turned this responsibility over to Hank.

Hank cleared his throat. He began, "I consider it an honor that Uncle has turned the reins over to me for this final session. I have been a part of it for many years, but I've never had to come up with a message. As I thought about this, it dawned on me how important this task is. For some of you here, it might be your last chance to hear the Gospel. With this in mind I thought and thought about what to say today, but I could not come up with anything. Then today it hit me. As I watched our clown out there performing, I realized that this was a fine allegory for the Gospel. First of all, I want you to know that this year's rodeo clown has never done this kind of thing before. I know that it's hard for anyone to believe, but, yes, he is a rookie clown. In real life, he is a police detective from Grand Rapids, Michigan, who is also a first-time staff member here at Camp Ohiyesa."

Decker smiled to himself. *Now I'm a staff member.* Heads turned and looked at Decker, who was standing in the back between Shelley and Lenore. A voice called out, "He doesn't look like a detective! He looks like a clown!" One of the young boys yelled and drew a raucous round of laughter.

"Nonetheless, he is a detective. This is a position of sacred trust in Indian society. As a policeman, he is charged with the responsibility to keep us safe and enforce our code of justice—sometimes at great peril to himself. I know this man. He takes his responsibility seriously. Today when the man whom we hired to be our clown—"

From the crowd, "You mean that lame old drunk?" Again, a round of laughter. This time even Hank joined in.

"As I was saying, when our usual clown could not perform, this policeman agreed to sacrifice his dignity and position to make our rodeo complete by performing a task, for *you*, that he was neither trained for nor paid to do. In a way, this is a picture of the Gospel— that sacrifice of Jesus who was not obligated to leave his position nor give his life for us, yet willingly did this so we might be reconciled to God and have eternal life." Hank went on for a bit and as he ended, Uncle returned to the front, gave Hank a hug, delivered a brief benediction and dismissed the campers with the admonition. "Live your faith, trust the great Spirit and we'll see you all next year!" The campers filed out past Hank and the girls. Several shook hands with him and one even asked for Lou's autograph. Lou looked at Shelley and Lenore and smiled. "Maybe I made the wrong career choice."

Dinner was eaten late that evening. Under a darkening sky they enjoyed the last of Chuck Wagon Cora's bison meat sloppy joes. Off to the north, out over the lake, they observed lightning flashes silhouetting the thunderheads.

"No rain for us," Uncle stated.

"Nope." Lenore seconded. "But Ontario is gonna get a soaked pretty good."

As the storm moved off to the east, Decker observed the frontal boundary crossing the sky from west to east just offshore. He remembered the old adage from his navy days, "If you can hear it, fear it" referencing the ability of lightning to strike a substantial distance from an active, visible thunderstorm.

"Tell me, Detective Lou Decker, do you believe that thunder can be your friend?" asked Uncle.

"I'm not sure what you mean."

"Lenore here thinks that it was thunder that saved your life."

"How so?" Decker pivoted to look at Lenore.

"I wouldn't put it like that, Uncle. He means that it was the sound of thunder that alerted me to look up and I saw you falling."

"No, Uncle, you and Lenore saved my life, not thunder. Besides I don't remember any storm or thunder on that day. The sky was clear."

"Quite so." Uncle looked intently at Decker. "What we heard was not thunder, was it, detective?"

"No, but I don't recall ever saying that it was."

"Do you know what it was?"

Decker remained silent. He was deep in thought. *If I tell them the truth, they'll think I'm crazy.*

Shelley leaned over and nudged Lou. "C'mon Lou. You're holding back. What was it—a helicopter?"

Hank spoke for the first time "What Uncle is trying to draw out, I think, is are you going to continue to live your life as if it's a random series of unrelated events, but that everything is rational. Do you not understand the problems with that view?"

"That's a rather prosaic way of putting it, son. But yet, that is exactly my point. I think there was something in the air over the cliff that you find terrifying to admit may be real. Is this not so?"

Lou felt anxiety rising and his palms were sweaty. "I was being hunted by a...dragon." Lou looked up expecting everyone to be laughing or challenging him. Instead they all wore somber expressions. "He had me cornered on top of the cliff and I decided it would

be better to take my chance jumping rather than being burned alive."
He then looked solemnly at Hank and continued. "Hank, that is
what happened to my rental SUV. The dragon picked it up and
dropped it there and then incinerated it. You saw with your own eyes
what happened to it."

Hank said, "That explains the remains of the SUV better than
anything I was able to come up with."

"A dragon is a formidable foe," said Uncle. "By the way, this
confirms that I am not going blind or crazy. Mr. Decker, you are a
detective and a detective must be a hunter-warrior. You must go to
war prepared or you will fail—and in this case, you will probably die.
You must be protected. You must seek that protection from Wakan
Tanka."

"I don't have a clue what you are talking about."

Lenore looked over at Lou. "Wakan Tanka is a Dakota phrase
for God. It is usually translated as Great Spirit or Great Mystery."

"How can this Wakan Tanka protect me if I am not sure He
even exists?" Lou got up and walked away.

Chapter 32

Guns and Butter

Decker slept fitfully that night. At 4:30, after awakening for the third time, he decided to give up trying to sleep. He showered, shaved, and picked up the handgun that Hank had given him, took the cleaning kit and went outside to watch the sun come up. He decided to perform a repetitive task that he often used to clear his mind.

A light in the dining hall came on, and curious, Lou walked over. He peeped in one of the side transom kitchen windows. Uncle was moving about, gathering filter paper, coffee and filling the big urn with water. Decker turned away leaving the old man to his brewing. *Two cups of Uncle's coffee and I won't sleep tonight either.*

He sat down at a picnic table under a light outside of the dining hall and began to disassemble the gun. He wiped down each part and carefully oiled them. He then placed the parts on the table and looked at his watch. He noted the time, closed his eyes and began to reassemble the weapon. He worked quickly but could not find the magazine anywhere on the table. He opened his eyes. Uncle was standing there holding two cups of steaming black coffee and his magazine. "Don't do it, detective."

Decker laughed and accepted the coffee from Uncle, who had moved to the other side of the table. "I saw you when I was in the kitchen. Do you want to be alone?"

"No, not really. I always enjoy your company. You do know I wasn't going to shoot myself, don't you?"

The old Indian looked serious. "You seemed a bit upset last night." Decker was opening his mouth to object, but Uncle held up a hand. "White men do crazy things when they are upset."

The comment hung in the air for ten seconds. Then Uncle burst out in a great laugh. "Look at me, I'm a white man who became an Indian and bought a run-down camp." He swung his arm in a wide arc. "I go fishing with my daughter and what do we catch?" He eyed Decker and squinted.

"I wasn't upset. Uncle, I just have a lot on my mind, and I don't know what to do."

"You will probably do what you always do. Strategize. Gather your resources. Attack the problem. This has always worked for you in the past, so that is what you will do."

"You make it sound foolish."

"Not foolish, my son. But this time it is not enough. You and I know, and for that matter, Hank knows that this adversary is very dangerous. He is also very different than anything you have ever encountered. Yes, I do know Hank's story—how he was trained to see beyond these things." Uncle swept his arm out to indicate all their surroundings. "If you believe he is being truthful, you must acknowledge that he is on to something. He is concerned for you. Lenny is also concerned for you—and she knows her brother well and senses the worry which is not evident to others."

"What is it that you think I should do?"

"I only know what I would do."

"What is that?"

"Pray." The old man got up, reached for Lou's empty cup and said as he walked toward the building. "Lenny and Shelley will be along soon to prepare breakfast. I would suggest that you eat hardy today. You will need to fast tomorrow if you are going to participate in the sweat."

"Sweat?"

"Did I forget to tell you? There is a sweat in your honor tomorrow night. Be there or be square."

"A sweat." Decker repeated, watching the sun rise over the lake.

Decker took his handgun and headed back to his cabin. After putting the weapon away, he kicked off his shoes. He laid down on the bed. He was jolted awake at 8:30 by his alarm. He got up for the second time that morning, brushed his teeth, and rinsed his face. He headed to the dining hall, wondering what was on the menu for breakfast. Seeing Hank ahead he called out, "Hank, wait up."

Hank slowed and turned "Mornin'. Uncle says he told you about the sweat tomorrow night and you acted surprised."

"I don't remember hearing about a sweat before."

Hank laughed. "This is Dad at his best. He probably just came up with this. He told you it was in your honor too, didn't he?"

"Yes, he did. Makes it kind of hard to decline an invitation."

"Lou, sweat ceremonies aren't held in anyone's honor. He knew you wouldn't know that—at least until it was too late. Hank chuckled. They are important though, we use them as a time of purification, preparation, and focus. Christians express our feelings of gratitude to the Creator and ask for guidance and strength."

"I thought I made it clear last night that I don't believe in religion."

"It's not religion, Lou."

They sat at a long table in the hall heaped with pancakes, eggs, bacon, ham, juice, and dry toast. "Where's the butter, sis? And where is Dad?"

"We're out of butter and I don't know where he is."

Shelley was already sitting there digging in. "These pancakes are wonderful, Lenny, what are these berries?"

"Chokecherries. Hank, when you go out later, will you pick up twenty pounds of butter?"

"Okay. Lou, do you want to come with me to run some errands after we eat?"

"Sure, where are we going?"

"We'll run into town for the butter, then I need to find some saplings for the lodge."

Lou had no idea what "saplings for the lodge meant." "Oh, okay."

Shelley looked at Lou and said with a grin, "Better eat well, Lou. You're fasting tomorrow you know."

Lou screwed up his face at Shelley. "Ugh."

As Decker and Hank were getting in the Hummer, Laurie opened the front door. "Detective Heyoka! Shirley called from the hospital and said some mail came in for you and she'd have it there at the front desk for you when you can come by."

"Thanks, Laurie."

Hank laughed. "Man of many names, we can run by there when we go to the store, they're only a couple blocks apart."

"Sounds good."

*****

Aren't those the rude man and woman from yesterday? Shirley put down the mail she was sorting. "Excuse me, can I help you?"

The man turned around in a circle slowly. He looked around the room. No one was there. "As a matter of fact, you can." The woman sat down in a chair and reached down and clutched her ankle. "My wife here needs an ice pack. She slipped on your wet floor over there."

Shirley looked where the man was pointing. There was no water spill or difference in the floor from anywhere else. She decided not to argue with these two as she figured it would only cause a problem. She picked up an ice pack from the pile on her desk and walked over. "Let me get a wheelchair for her and I'll—" She never finished the sentence as when she bent down to apply the pack, the man thumped her on the head and the lights went out.

*****

As Hank pulled into the lot, a dusty brown sedan was exiting. "Funny but that looked like Shirley."

"Driving?"

"No, in the passenger seat with her head leaning against the window."

"Hmmm. I wouldn't know. You have a lot of unusual characters here, Hank."

Hank waited in the car at the entrance while Decker went in. Lou walked up to the desk. No one was there, but as he looked, he saw his letters, picked them up and turned to go. He noticed a candy striper walk into the waiting area and look about as if searching for something or someone.

Lou turned to her. "Are you looking for someone?"

The girl was startled by the question. "Uh. no."

"Isn't Shirley working today? Where is she?"

"In—the back." Not knowing Decker, she lied. It was the first thing she could think of, having been warned extensively to never give medical information to unknown people.

Decker relaxed. He waved the letter. "Tell her thanks."

"Yes, I will."

Decker briefly described the exchange to Hank, who nodded and put the Hummer in gear to drive away. "Hmmm. Must've been someone else." They drove down the coast to the old Camp Wendigo sign and Hank turned in.

"Why are we here?"

"I've got to collect saplings for the sweat lodge. I remembered this area from when we were here the other day." Hank laughed. "No, there's no mystical mumbo jumbo in coming here. I recall that there were some pretty good candidates behind the ridge when we drove back to look for Herb's SUV."

Hank gunned the engine and the Humvee powered through the high weeds. He crested the hill. Hank was right. There were hundreds of saplings of various sizes here. Hank and Lou spent the next two hours selecting, cutting and stripping forty nearly identical saplings and putting them into the back of the big SUV. As they drove back toward the exit, Hank asked, "Would you like me to swing by the…slag pile over there?" Hank nodded across the lake.

"No, thanks." Lou laughed. "Did you think I might want a souvenir?"

Hank stared straight ahead, a small smile tugging the corner of his mouth. As he looked across the lake, a metal glint just outside their vehicle in the grass caught Lou's eye. "Hank, stop the car."

Hank did as Decker asked. Lou opened his door and hopped out. He walked back to where he had seen the glint and there it was. He bent over and picked up a chrome-plated pistol, nestled in the grass. *What are the odds…*

He climbed back in and held the gun up. "Pretty fancy piece, Hawkeye."

"Yeah, we must have driven over it before."

Lou aimed the gun out the window, pulled the trigger and a butane flame shot out from the barrel. Hank looked at Decker and shook his head. "From what I know, police departments aren't issuing mini-flamethrowers as sidearms, so I assume that's not your—weapon."

Reading the inscription on the gun-shaped lighter, "'To Herb with love, Shelley. Viva Cohiba!' You are correct, it's not mine. It was Herb's—a gift from Shelley when he was going through a phase hawking cigars on weekends at regional events, like county fares and demolition derbies. I think I'll take it back to Shelley."

Hank just shook his head.

*****

When Shirley came to, she was tied to a tree in the woods. The woman was sitting on the passenger seat of a car with the door open. She was smoking a cigarette and talking on her cell phone. The man, now wearing sunglasses and a bandana squatted down in front of her. "Now there are two ways to do this. The first way is you answer my questions, I'll untie you, and we all can go about our business. The second way is you answer my questions with a little encouragement." He produced a can of lighter fluid and a zippo lighter and sat them down in front of Shirley. "I will tell you I am not a patient man and I'm not interested in any privacy laws, capisce?"

Shirley was trembling and in a near panic. She couldn't take her eyes from the lighter. "Say yes or no please."

She shook her head and whimpered, "Y-y-yes."

"Okay. Question one—was Detective Lou Decker a patient at your hospital?"

Shirley nodded her head "yes" vigorously.

"Okay. Is he still a patient?"

Shirley shook her head "no."

"Well, that wasn't too difficult, was it now?" Shirley had her head down. She was crying hard.

"Final question. Where did Mr. Decker go when he was discharged and who was he with? I will need a verbal answer this time, uh, Miss—"

"Shirley!" yelled the tattooed woman. "And that was two questions."

"Ah yes, Miss Shirley."

Shirley was hysterical as the man reached out and picked up the lighter and fluid. "Camp Ohiyesa! Camp Ohiyesa!" she screamed. "I don't know who he was with. I wasn't working. I don't know. I don't know." And she broke down into unintelligible sobbing.

The man went around behind Shirley and cut the rope freeing her from the tree. He walked to the car and drove away without another word, leaving Shirley sliding down to sitting position, back against the tree, sobbing.

*****

Decker volunteered to help Hank set up the lodge when they arrived back at camp, but Hank declined. He said that there was a very specialized procedure in setting it up and that there were specific invocations to sing. Hank was insistent that he had been entrusted to perform this chore alone.

Lou went to the office house. Lenore and Shelley were sitting in the living area talking. He turned to go, but Lenore called out to him, "Lou, come on in and join us." As she patted the empty spot on the couch next to her.

"You girls are talking, and I don't want to interrupt."

"C'mon," both women said simultaneously.

Lenny's mood lightened considerably when he came in. This made him smile. Shelley looked up at Lou. "The FBI was here today."

"What did they want?"

"They wanted me to tell them about Las Vegas. They were not very interested in the rest of my story. There was an agent named Taggie and an agent Garvin. They seemed nice, Lou, and told me they might want to talk to you too."

"Okay."

Lenore then asked Lou if he had ever been part of a sweat ceremony before. Lou laughed and then stopped and looked at Lenny. "You're serious, aren't you?"

Lenny nodded her head. "Yes, I am, I would guess the answer is no. However, a lot of Native ceremonies have been co-opted by vacation agencies and shown in a bastardized form to tourists. So I thought it necessary to check. This is a serious topic. It is a sacred time for all the native people involved. It is not entertainment and must be treated with utmost respect."

She continued, "Hank will guide you through the rituals, but, Lou, I want you to understand this is not religious woo-woo or mumbo jumbo. It is a time for purification, healing, and communing with the Wakan-Tanka—God. Lou, you must not think this is anything less or you would do better to skip it." Lou saw that Lenore's face had become hard and Shelley was also looking at him severely. It reminded Lou of Shelley as a little girl standing at her mother's side glaring at him as his mom reprimanded him.

"Lou," said Shelley. "The Shelley you used to know is gone. I'm not that woman anymore. It's not that I suddenly got 'religion,' Lou. Lenore and I have been talking. She's helped me understand who I am, Lou, and the way things really are. I only wish Herb had a chance to know this Shelley." She pointed to herself. "Lou, you *know* that there is more to this world than the way we've been living. You've seen things, Lou. You've seen—" Shelley broke down and sobbed quietly.

Lou was rising up to go over to his sister, but Lenore put her hand on Lou's arm.

"She needs a sister now, Lou." There was love in Lenore's eyes, and Lou turned to go out. At that moment Lou felt a deep emptiness in his heart. He desperately wished to see that love for him in her eyes.

Chapter 33

Sneakers

The next morning Hank was digging the last bit of earth out of a large dish-shaped hole where the Stones would be heated. The sweat lodge was finished and was correct. The stick fence between the fire pit and the lodge was standing firm. Seven ceremonial river stones lie in the shed out of any potential rain awaiting their date with the fire. Hank kneeled down. He prayed silently. *Father God, please. Make our hearts right, for Lord Jesus's glory.* He smiled and leaned back on his heels calling out, "Hi yee Hi Ki ak." He nodded when he saw Uncle standing in the shade watching him. His father said, "Son, I've heard better Indian whoops from the Mexicans they hired in Hollywood." Both laughed heartily.

"Have you noticed that brown car sitting on the road near the entrance. It has been there for about twenty minutes now."

"Yes, I have. They are not very good at surveillance." Hank chuckled. "I keep catching glints from the driver's binoculars. They could scarcely have picked a more obvious vantage point."

"Why don't they just come in? I find it hard to think they are planning to rob us."

"No, Dad, I saw that car earlier today on our trip into town."

"Perhaps they wanted the butter which you purchased." said Uncle with a smile.

"No, at the hospital." Hank related the strange tale involving him "seeing" Shirley in the car.

Uncle said, "Unless Shirley has put on thirty pounds and got tatted up in the last week, I do not think that is her."

As the two men walked toward the office. Uncle offered. "Do you think we ought to go out and say something?"

"Not yet, I want to make a quick phone call first."

He took out his cell to call the hospital. A strange voice answered. Hank said, "Hi, this is Hank Cloud, Is Shirley available?"

The stranger answered, "No, no one knows where she is. She was here earlier this morning, then she was gone. That was sometime late in the morning. She didn't tell anyone."

"Well, if she turns up have her call Hank Cloud at Camp Ohiyesa please. Thanks."

Hank felt his stomach fall to his feet. He questioned the wisdom of using the word "if" rather than "when."

Hank turned on his heel and was off at a sprint toward the car. The driver saw Hank running full speed toward the car with mayhem in his eyes, started the car, and sped away throwing gravel at Hank as he left. Hank managed to get the license number as the car fled. *Minnesota plate-666 LSD—you've got to be kidding.*

Hank walked directly to Lou's cabin. He banged on the door. "Come in. Don't break the door down."

"Lou, remember that car leaving the parking lot at the hospital?"

"Yes, the brown 2010 Subaru."

"They've been sitting on the road scoping this place out for the past half hour."

Lou put down his pen and crossword book. He went and looked out the window. "They're gone now."

"I know. They took off when I went to have a word with them. But, Lou, what did the girl tell you about Shirley in the lobby—exactly?"

"She said Shirley was in the back, but she hesitated, Hank. Now that I think about it, the girl was looking for something, or somebody when she came in." Lou's cop sense was kicking in. "They took her, didn't they, Hank."

"I believe that is so, though I have no proof."

"I assume you've already called the hospital."

"Yes, they say she disappeared earlier today without telling anyone."

Lou was already dialing the MSP. "You didn't get the license plate number did you?"

"I did. 666 LSD."

Lou looked incredulous. "And was 'Hell's Cab Service' painted on the side?"

Hank smiled in spite of himself. "Seriously."

The police dispatcher came on the line. Hank identified himself and gave the officer a brief synopsis of the situation with all the specifics he had. When he gave the tag number, the dispatcher stifled a laugh. "Would you describe the driver as looking more like Freddy Kreuger or Damien?"

"No, honestly, that was the tag." Lou chuckled. He asked the officer to tell Lieutenant Haukom that he would call him later, if the lieutenant came in.

"Roger that."

"Now what?" asked Hank.

"Now we fast and get ready for the sweat tonight. We let the police do their job."

Lou had sat down and already picked up the crossword again. Hank sat down in the desk chair. "Are you ready, Lou?"

"I'll need you to walk me through just what to do, but otherwise, yes. I am taking this to heart, and Hank, don't worry, I won't do anything to embarrass you or Uncle."

"That's not what I mean, Lou. This is serious business." Hank focused his gaze on Decker. "What is it you are so afraid of, that you can't admit that there are bigger forces involved with our lives in this world than what we know or see or touch?"

"I'm not afraid. I've just never seen any proof of that there is a God or that if he were to exist, cares about us in any way."

"Okay. I understand that. But think about something that you *know*. Something that you don't need external, objective proof or an authority to teach you it is so."

"Like what?"

"Your father, Lou, did he love you?"

"Of course."

"Prove it to me."

"Well, he told me so. He provided for me and my sister as we were growing up—"

"People lie. Maybe he was afraid of people's opinion, or he only felt a duty to provide for you or he thought social services would take you away."

"Social services weren't—"

"Don't play dumb, Lou, I think you understand my point. I can come up with all kinds of alternative 'rational' reasons to explain away your statement that he loved you. But your belief is *really* based on your personal experiences, observations and an intangible inner sense—an intuitive understanding of how things are."

"I see this, but what does it have to do with God—or truth for that matter?"

"Man has always looked to a higher power as an explanation for the mysteries of life. Modern scientists say that 'man created God' for that reason. But is that a scientifically justifiable position? No, science does not and cannot prove that God either exists or doesn't exist. So, why does it hold a position either pro or con on the premise. God must by definition exist outside our ever-evolving scientific laws or he wouldn't be God. So if man has persistently demonstrated an innate and universal desire to relate to God, doesn't that put the issue outside of the realm of science?"

"But what about the laws of science that are established and provable?"

"They have nothing to say about God. I can state with some confidence that $E=mc2$. The application of that equation has yielded everything from nuclear weapons to the electricity that powers these lights in our cabins. The scientific process is reliable, but only with respect to certain issues. Lou, you have seen things which do not fit into your current worldview. Modern science might simply ignore such experience or treats those who observe it as crackpots. No, they would say that your observations were tainted, or erroneous. In this way they dismiss the whole topic from consideration. Hence, the sheep plod on in ignorance, thinking themselves wise, to the end of their lives. Lou, scripture says '*the fool has said in his heart there is no God.*' There it is. We both have been to the other side, so to speak, Lou. In your heart, you know *it is real*. Now you need to take the next step. Understand that God is real and there is a war on between good and evil. This world is one of the battle fronts and men's souls are in the balance."

"Lenore, Dad, and I each reached a point in our life's journey when we acknowledged that we needed God, Wakan Tanka, tangibly in our lives and scripture led us to Christ. We then embarked on what some Native Americans call 'the Jesus road'. A sweat is not an attempt to find God or reach out to other spirits. We as Christians don't even use it as a sacrament, but as a sort of 'prayer' for strength guidance and understanding. It is crucial that you understand this before taking part, if not, I would advise you to sit it out. Dad asked me to explain this to you."

Lou hesitated, lost in thought, and simply said, "I'm in."

Hank then went through the basics of what Lou should expect at the sweat. He told Lou that they would only be doing one rather than four sessions. Everyone there would be focusing on prayers to help Lou and Hank deal with what was ahead. This puzzled Lou. "Hank, there you go again. This just sounds, like a, I don't know— like craziness to me."

"Lou, that's exactly what it is. This whole thing is craziness with a capital *C*, but it's real, Lou. You've got to understand this. Real lives are on the line here. Peoples' eternal destiny is on the line. Your life, Lou. You are the fulcrum of this whole episode. Get ready, if you want to live." Lou realized that he was not surprised by this outburst. On some level, he understood that Hank's words were true. Hank stood, walked over, and hugged Lou. He looked him in the eye. "Be strong, brother."

A while later, Lou took Herb's gun lighter over to the kitchen where Shelley was working. "Hi, Shelley, Hank and I found this yesterday when we were gathering saplings. I thought you might want it."

She took the faux gun. She eyed it and asked, "Did Herb think I'd want a victory cigar? Or was he planning to start a forest fire?"

"I don't know. I think maybe Herb thought he could threaten someone with it if he needed to."

Shelley, eyes tearing up, shook her head. "Poor Herb, what was he thinking?" She sighed, placed the gun on the counter and went back to organizing the cutlery. "Thanks, Lou."

Lou walked back to his cabin. He was surprised that Lenny sat on the porch. "Hi, Lenore. You look nice today."

"Thanks, Lou, so do you." Lou reddened. He realized how awkward he had sounded. He mentally kicked himself. Lenore muttered "'Nice,' really." Then she smiled. "Lighten up, Decker, I've brought you some things you will need for the sweat tonight. They are on the bed—and a little present."

He sat on the bench with Lenny. "Thanks, what kind of things?"

"I brought some appropriate items of clothing, a couple towels, and some tobacco. Wear only those things. And I mean only."

"I didn't know we wore any clothing, or I assumed maybe a breech cloth."

"You watch too many movies. This isn't a Tarzan movie or new age séance, Lou. Do not wear any jewelry. Lou, you don't wear hearing aids or have any dental bridges, do you?"

Decker laughed and so did Lenore. "I didn't think so. I guess the pins in your shoulder can't be helped, but nothing else artificial—at all. Don't forget to have—never mind." Lenny looked away across the lake.

"What?"

"Never mind. They sure are chemtrailing in the east today. Wonder what's going on? Hey, don't you want to see your present?" Jumping up and going into the cabin she pointed at something sitting on a towel on his pillow.

Decker walked over to the bed. Astonished, Lou picked up his badge wallet. He opened it up. There was his Police ID. The lamination had protected it. He smiled and spun on Lenore picking her up in a big hug. "Where did you get this?" He kissed her.

She smiled and pulled away. "Down boy. Vernon Blue Legs, Shelley and I took out Uncle's boat this afternoon. We drove it to the area where we fished you out. Vernon was a diver in the Navy. Uncle gives him a lot of business now as a carpenter, so he was eager to do us a favor. He dove in with his tank, wetsuit, and light. He was back up with this in his hand in less than five minutes. Vernon said it was right there on the only sandy section of the bottom he could see. He said you must be one heckuva pilot to land in that spot."

"Thank you, Lenny. This is important to me."

"Well, at least I know you really are who you said you were." Lenny laughed. Decker loved the sound. "Vernon will be at the sweat tonight. You might give him a token gift at some point"

"Tobacco?"

"Yes, that would be fine. Nothing elaborate—just one of the plugs. I've got to go help Uncle get ready, he's already started his preparations."

Lou didn't know what to say to that, so he just said, "Bye." And opened the door for her.

Decker picked up the wallet. He took out and stared at his ID. He was back. Armed and dangerous.

Chapter 34

The Sweat Ceremony

Hank told Lou to wait in his room and prepare himself. He would come get Decker when the ceremony was to begin. Lou sat on the bed wondering what Hank meant, but he didn't want to insult Hank, so he resisted the temptation to do a crossword puzzle. It was just after sundown when Hank opened the screen door. "Ready? Do you have the tobacco and some towels?"

"Yes." Decker held them up.

"I know you have a medicine bundle. Are you wearing it?"

Lou patted the front of his shirt. "I haven't taken it off since Lenny gave it to me."

"Good. Take off the shirt and kill the light. Time to go. I will take you up to Uncle. He will say some words that you won't under-stand and wave a smoking sage smudge in the air around you. When he looks down toward the doorway. Kneel down and crawl in. Crawl around the back of the circle. Sit next to Vernon, I will come in shortly after you, then Uncle will enter, and the ceremony will begin. Do not speak unless you are asked to do so. Don't look anyone in the eye, and, please silence your cell phone."

"What? I wasn't told to bring—"

"I'm kidding."

"I don't know Vernon, but I have a gift for him."

"Leave it here for now. He will be the last one in the circle as you crawl in. He will have a space next to him on his right. Sit there."

Decker's palms were sweating already as he and Hank walked toward the sweat lodge. As he approached, Lou saw the fire pit where the stones were heating. He watched Lenore tending them. She was dressed in a pale, beaded buckskin dress with ribbons and images on it. She looked every bit the beautiful Indian maiden. Along the tree line other men and women stood by quietly. Some wore traditional clothing. Others wore western gear. The women all had blankets. Shelley stood there wearing the sky-blue blanket that Lenore had worn at the powwow. Her face was fixed and unreadable. She even looked a bit Indian to Lou. *Do I look like her?*

Things went exactly as Hank had explained. Soon Lou found himself taking his place in the circle. *Meet someone's eyes? I can barely see my hand in front of my face.*

He felt Hank bump him slightly in the back as he came around to take his place on Lou's right. Uncle then came in and the Lodge flap was shut. It was a bit stuffy in the lodge. It smelled of earth and grass Decker observed, but it was not unpleasant. Uncle began a slow chant in Dakota. At one point said in English, for Decker, "Now we prepare our hearts, Great Spirit. We ask that you be here among your people." He then continued his song. Suddenly he stopped singing and the flap opened. A young man crept in carrying a stone which appeared to Decker to be slightly glowing. As he placed it in the circular area in the midst of the circle, Uncle said, "West." The boy came back and placed three more stones in what Decker assumed were the cardinal points. Uncle said a word in Dakota with the placement of each. A fifth stone was placed in the middle of the four. Finally, two more were brought in. The significance of these was lost on Decker. The lodge flap then was closed again. Uncle reached out and poured a large gourd-like container of water on the stones. Decker was hit immediately by a wall of heat unlike anything he had ever experienced. It hurt to breathe. He felt a momentary panic that he might have to bolt from the lodge, but after several moments, his discomfort began to ease. Decker was hot and sweat was pouring off, *but that's the point of this, right?* Most of the men sat leaning forward. Some were singing together in a quiet baritone. Decker listened. He tried to make out the words, but he realized that it was Dakota and he gave up trying to understand it. He thought the singing was beautiful in a masculine way. Lou felt his mind wander as he sat there. He thought, *I'm afraid this is lost on me, but I am going to stick it out.* After a time, he began to drowse. He floated in a dream. There, in front of him, a man floated in the air. The man pretended to play an imaginary piano wildly. The man's head whipped from side to side. He clacked his large cartoon teeth together repeatedly. Lou was then suddenly out in a farm field. He saw a man bent over at the waist, back to Decker. The man appeared to be picking small plants from the ground and stuffing them into his mouth. Decker tapped the man on the shoulder and the man sinuously straightened and turned around. There was Miguel's face. The man was chewing, not plants, but small people. Decker was terrified as he watched the man begin jerkily jumping up and down in front of him before taking a final great bound up into a dark grey sky where he changed into the dragon. Decker came fully awake. He was afraid he had screamed, but none of the others noticed him. Uncle was looking directly at him. Decker "heard" Uncle say, "Son, I have something to show you." Decker could not hold his eyes open, but somehow watched as once again he was in a field. This one was green with newly cut grass It ran up to the foot of a mountain. On the mountain were giant letters forming the word "Hollywood." Then Lou noticed a man on top of the sign. He was dressed in an Indian costume and Decker somehow knew it was a young version of Uncle. The man was large and powerful. He danced aggressively with a bottle of whiskey waving in one hand and a wad of money in the other. He was dancing for several suited men and beautiful women who were sitting nearby, when several of the women got up to dance with Uncle. He ignored a young woman, dressed in Indian garb who was lying nearby, crying with her head cradled in her arms. Uncle turned Decker's way and Lou saw that Uncle's head had now morphed into that of a wild pig. The Indian woman stood up horrified and tried to get Uncle's attention by grabbing his arm. He shook her off and she fell from the sign. As she fell, Decker saw her face. It was, but wasn't, Lenny's face. The woman got up, brushed herself off and walked out of sight. Decker continued to watch as the dancing became wilder and wilder.

Suddenly, Uncle was alone. He looked about and called out for the Indian woman, but she had gone. Decker then watched as Uncle began walking. He trudged through the slums of a large city with his clothes becoming progressively more worn and ragged and his head still resembling that of a boar. He walked and walked, looking in dumpsters, opening doors only to be thrown violently backward each time. Eventually he walked from the edge of the city into a desert. He finally collapsed and Decker could see sobs wracking the body of this now gaunt pig-headed caricature of Uncle. A man radiating light came along and bent down to Uncle. He whispered some words. Uncle sobbed even harder and nodded his head. The man touched Uncle. Suddenly, Decker watched Uncle here at the lodge hugging the woman and looking out as two children, a boy and a girl, played on the lawn.

Then Decker realized that he was looking at Uncle through the steam and recognized a peace in Uncle's face that Lou was seeing for the first time.

Decker was starkly aware that he did not have that peace. He was very sad and began to weep. He thought of his wife. How he missed her. He remembered all the times he had neglected her or passed up opportunities to tell her he loved her. Now it was too late. He thought of the errors he had made in his life. He thought of his parents. He remembered his father. His father held him on his knee and looked into his eyes much like Uncle and said something to him that escaped his understanding. He tried to ask his father what he was saying but only the babbling of a baby came out. After two attempts he gave it up, but Lou thought he recognized the word "book." Decker then stood over a young man on the ground. Decker forced a handgun into his hand and watched as the young man was cuffed and dragged away screaming at Decker and cursing. Lou felt an avalanche of shame. He began to sob in earnest as he recalled times when he had taken things that did not belong to him or been angry for no reason. He heard thousands of curse words coming from his mouth. He saw a light moving toward him and felt despair. He knew he needed the peace that these Indians, his new family had. The light stopped in front of him *God, or Wakan Tanka or Great*

Spirit, if you are real, show me and help me please. Decker felt a touch lifting under his chin forcing him to look into the face of a glowing, heavenly being. Oddly, Decker was not afraid. He knew the unspoken question and spoke the word "Yes" in reply. He was suddenly wide awake and listening to Uncle chant softly. When Uncle finished, Hank nudged him and motioned for Lou to follow him from the lodge.

As he exited, the sun was coming up. Lenore was still sitting by the firepit. She watched as the men filed out. When she looked at Decker, she smiled. She noted something in his face that was not there before. He looked back at her feeling that he could reach out with his eyes and hug her. When all had exited, Uncle walked to the fire pit and extinguished the flame with the water remaining in his ceremonial bucket.

He clapped his hands and said, "We dine at 3:00 p.m. sharp."

Everyone walked off. Hank turned to Lou. "Go to your cabin and rest now. I'll come get you about 2:30. Don't talk to anyone until then."

Decker turned to walk over to Lenore, but she was gone. He shrugged and headed for his cabin. Lighthearted and focused, Lou knew he was facing a difficult future, but he was now sure he was not alone.

Chapter 35

Reflections

Hank was as good as his word, knocking on Lou's screen at 2:30 on the dot. Decker was lying on the bed, crossword book in hand. "Come on in. What's a four-letter word for 'Nevada town'?"

"Elko."

"Okay. Four letter-word for 'imitate'?"

"Aper."

"Impressive. Not a second's hesitation. I did not realize you were such a man of letters."

"Lou, I've listened to my dad doing those things for fifteen years. The same odd words come up puzzle after puzzle. You can finish that later. You didn't try to give Vernon that tobacco, did you?"

"Nope, and I didn't speak with anyone after the sweat."

"Okay, bring it and I'll formally introduce you. Bring a couple more plugs if you have any extra."

"Got 'em." Lou closed the screen behind him and they headed up to the dining hall. Shelley, Lenore, and three Indian women that Lou did not know were behind the serving table doling out food and replenishing the trays from the kitchen. One of the women nodded at him, then turned and said something to Lenore. The women all giggled and Lenore blushed. Lou decided to put on a big, dopey grin and mug at them.

"Lou, this is Vernon Blue Legs. Vernon, Detective Lou Decker."

"Pleased to meet you, Vernon. Thank you for recovering my badge and wallet." He handed Vernon a plug of tobacco. Vernon held the gift in both hands, looked at it and smiled. He made a gesture moving his right hand palm downward and away from his waist in a sweeping movement. Hank was standing slightly behind Vernon and frowned slightly to get Lou's attention and mimicked the motion. Lou repeated the motion and in his follow through, he knocked a cup of coffee from the hand of an old Indian passing by. The man turned and gave Lou a puzzled look. The women at the food table burst into laughter and the old man joined in flashing a toothless smile, as Lou, Hank, and Vernon also laughed.

"A little extra in that gesture, Detective. Hank must be your teacher." Vernon deadpanned as he got into line. Hank laughed as he and Lou lingered behind a bit. Lou radiated a deep shade of crimson.

The meal was wonderful with most of the famished celebrants lining up for seconds, and some for thirds. Several of the older men came over. They asked Lou how he was doing. Remembering Hank's admonition about not sharing personal experiences he kept his answers brief. Lou did notice that his parade of well-wishers quickly diminished after he handed out his last tobacco plug.

Lou and Hank pitched in to help the women clean up. As Uncle saw the last of the "relatives" off, dusk was on the way. They all walked out to the bluff and sat. The benches were arranged in a circle with a firepit in the middle. Hank went to the log tender nearby. He carried four medium sized cut logs to the firepit. He set three of them down, forming a pyramid. The fourth was a white birch log. He placed this vertically up the middle of the stack. He then got some kindling and paper and set it ablaze with a zippo. Shelley looked at the setting sun, pretended to be startled. "What? Not enough light to use a magnifying glass to light the fire?"

Hank snorted and laughed. "That's right."

Uncle scolded Hank laughingly. "Son, I've told you to keep your flint and steel with you at all times."

Lou put in. "Why was the white log selected to be the upright?"

The fire was blazing as the paper and tinder took and light reflected off Hank's face. "Because it had a square cut end."

Uncle adopted a serious pose. He rubbed the underside of his chin as if stroking a goatee. "Un-huh. 'Sometimes a cigar is just a cigar,' to quote a Western thinker."

Everyone laughed and Uncle started to sing a slow, low pitched song in Dakota. Lou did not understand the words, but the tone and pacing evoked melancholy. He felt a sadness and sense of loss as Uncle sang. His mind wandered. He thought of the loss of innocence that had occurred when his tidy mechanical, scientific, realistic view of the world had been irrevocably destroyed. *Not loss, really, but growth. "There are more things in heaven and earth, Horatio, than are dreamt of in your philosophy." How true.* As Uncle's song then picked up in tempo and as the key changed, strangely, so did Decker's mood. He felt a sense of community and peace. He looked at the others around the fire, examining their faces with the dancing flames reflected in their luminous eyes.

They sat for a long time, no one speaking after Uncle's song ended. Decker was sitting next to his sister. He found that he had put an arm around Shelley and pulled her close to his side. She leaned on him and rested her head on his shoulder. Decker listened to the waves washing the shore below. He could hear crickets and frogs and birds. He thought he sensed a small animal moving behind the bench where Hank sat, staring at the fire. The animal appeared to be hunting something. The animal moved under Hank's bench and now, Decker could clearly see the feline movements of the creature. He could not identify it. Lynx, wildcat, bobcat? Then he looked up at Hank to warn him and the creature's features were superimposed on Hank's face. He blinked his eyes and the image and creature were gone.

He opened his mouth to ask if Hank were aware of the cat but was stopped by Uncle. "The spirit was showing you something, Lou. Like he showed you things last night."

Hank leaned back, stretched and gave an enormous yawn. "This cat is ready for bed."

As he stood up, Shelley did as well. "Me too. Catch you all in the morning." And they moved away together.

Lenore got up and came over to sit by Decker. She leaned against him. He could feel her long, black hair. It was cool against his cheek. He held her close inhaling the scent of apple from her hair.

Uncle looked across and smiled. He stood up and gestured moving his right hand out from the waist turned and walked away. Lenore returned the gesture to Uncle who was already walking away. Belatedly, Lou mimicked the movement and Lenore suddenly leaned away from him with an expression of fear. She met Lou's gaze and they both laughed. "Lucky you don't have a cup of coffee, woman."

"Lou, Shelley says you are going back Wednesday."

"Yeah, There's Herb. Then I need to wrap this—thing up and decide what I'm going to do about work."

"What about work?"

Lou stared at the fire, now burned down to embers. "I don't know if I can continue as a detective on the force and live with myself. Lenny, I'm not the man you pulled out of the water—"

"I know that, Lou."

"The world is in bad shape. Cities are falling apart. Violent crime is everywhere—and now—I know I can't stop it. When I have to break the law to finally put a cold-blooded killer like Garza behind bars, what does that make me? I want to look myself in the eye and not be ashamed."

Lenny put her finger on Lou's lips "Shhh." She leaned in and kissed Lou. "You know I can't go with you." This is what Lou had been fearing. He was going to lose Lenny even before their love had time to bloom.

"I was afraid that you were going to say that. I guess that's why I hadn't brought it up."

"Lou, it's not that I don't want to. I love you, Lou, and I know that you love me. I believe we have a future together, but not yet. Right now, I need to stay here at Ohiyesa."

"I love you, Lenny. You can come if you decide to come, Lenny, there is more than enough help here to keep the camp going."

"That's not it, Lou."

"What is it then?"

Lenny looked deep into Lou's eyes. "It's Uncle… He's dying, Lou."

Lou could not speak. He felt as if he had just been punched in the gut.

"Lou, he has cancer. He's been fighting leukemia for several years. We took him down to Mayo Clinic and they've done wonderfully by him. His prognosis was poor from the beginning, but their treatment—and Wakan Tanka—have kept the disease at bay. Six weeks ago, he sat Hank and I down and told us that his time on this earth was drawing to a close. He was beginning to get sick again and the doctors told him his time was near."

Lou choked out. "How long?"

"He is a very strong man, Lou. The doctors say it that from this point in most people it's two or three months at the most, but Uncle has surprised them so far. He wants you and Hank to see this through. I think this is what is giving him strength. He is praying for you two constantly."

"Doctors don't know everything, Lenny, can't we put all this on the back burner and take him somewhere else. MD Anderson in Houston is a great cancer center—one of the best in the world." *Lou recalled his anguish as his Maggie had died of cancer, going from doctor to doctor, hearing the same non-answers and watching her life fade away before his eyes.*

"No, Lou. He knows of all of this. He doesn't want it. He is at peace. He even jokes about smoking during his days making movies. He says he thought the smoke might get him, but never the radiation he absorbed on location in those old, desolate atomic test ranges. He's taken to calling himself 'the Indian Marlboro Man.'" Lenore managed a sad chuckle. "This…situation…has given him purpose, Lou. He needs to finish his adventure. Hank also needs to see this through. Hank is a warrior. He will bring necessary things to your battle. He has unfinished business with this adversary as well and he needs closure."

"I have no illusions about this, Lenny. We can't expect much help from the police. Heck, we don't really even have a plan yet. What are we going to accomplish, anyway? Vengeance?"

"That's the enemy talking, Lou. You said it yourself. We're called by God to stand in the gap, to stand up against the creeping darkness. You not only have Hank as an ally, you have access to God's power."

Lou was silent. He stood up and walked Lenore to the lodge house. He kissed her and said good night. "I'm not going anywhere, Lou." He smiled and headed to his cabin.

Time to get down to business.

Chapter 36

Preparations

Decker was awakened by a call on his cell phone. It was 5:45 in the morning as he picked it up.

"Decker."

"Morning, detective, Haukom here. Did I wake you?"

"Nope. But you disturbed my deep meditative state, and I had satori in sight. What's up?"

"Well you weren't kidding about the tag number, were you? We put out a BOLO on the vehicle after you called and got a hit last night. A trooper was pulling into a Kwik-Trip outside of Duluth to get a cup of coffee and he caught sight of the vehicle pulling out. He called it in, then waited till they got up the road a bit. He followed them to a side road, doused his lights and followed them back about a mile to a rundown trailer. He called for backup and the SWAT team rolled. They staged nearby and were just getting ready to move when the house literally exploded in flames. My troops noted that there were no lights on when the trailer went up in flames. The fire was burning with a fury that the firemen say would indicate some kind of fuel or accelerant. Meth house? Gas leak? They won't know till they find the ignition point and analyze their samples, but descriptions of the blast did not sound like either of these. Another odd thing was that several of the troops thought they saw fire initially coming down from the sky through the trees as the house incinerated. We found two bodies, but they are unidentifiable. The ME will try to get some DNA and we'll be checking dental records, but there was nothing usable in the premises at all. Ownership records of the property show the land was purchased by a Miguel Lopez in 1983 as trustee for Congregation of Light Fellowship, Incorporated of Delaware. Sounds like your bunch, eh? Everything else burned. The firefighters are looking for a VIN on the trailer, but they are not hopeful.

"We got the car. Matched your description perfectly. No registration, proof of insurance, or other identifying papers on board, but there was a credit card receipt under the seat and the car has already been dusted for prints. Those are being run as we speak. Turns out the plate was homemade." Haukom laughed. "We figure that the man may have spent time in Stillwater honing those skills. It was actually pretty good. The VIN shows that the car was originally sold to a man who we've ID'd as a minister from Fairbault. He died last year, but there is nothing else of interest in the system on him. That's about it, Decker, I guess you can understand that further action on this will take a back seat, right?"

"Of course. Thanks Lieutenant Haukom. Shelley and I will be heading back to Michigan tomorrow. I appreciate all that you've done for us and I guess you will be relieved that we'll be out of your hair."

"Not at all. You've livened up what has been a pretty dull year— or two around here. Hope to see you again, Decker"

"Thanks."

Decker looked at his watch. 5:57. He rolled over and was out in seconds.

*****

Brother Love came into his office to find Miguel sitting in a chair, eyes closed, leaning back and listening to AC/DC's "Back in Black." Love found the music annoying and reached over to turn it off. In mid-reach, Miguel opened one eye and Love found his arm stopped in mid-air. "But thees ees my favorite part, padre."

Love could feel his anger rising. "You are assigned to assist me, not piss me off. I might just talk to your boss."

"Go right ahead, amigo. He'd probably like to hear firsthand about your latest mess."

Love stewed, but he held his peace. He was acutely aware that the higher ups were not the tolerant types, especially when goals were not successfully achieved or their activities were dragged into the light.

"You haven't asked me how my night went, *jefe*. Don't you care for your Miguelito anymore?"

"How did it go?" Love asked unenthusiastically.

"Thank you for asking. I spent the night in Las Vegas and Minnesota, hopefully cleaning up the last loose ends of this fiasco created by your boneheaded henchmen."

"Las Vegas?"

"Our operation there was compromised by developments involving Detective Decker's sister. Your boys not only appear incapable of keeping people from the other side out of our business, but particularly adept at bringing in those likely to turn to that unspeakable light. Word came down that we had to close a very profitable operation in Vegas and move it—to Reno, of all places. We barely had time to load the last truck and fire the place up before the Feds came flying down the road sirens blaring, lights flashing, wearing flack vests with guns drawn. It's been the top story for a couple days now, at least in the uncontrolled media, if you noticed. The Prince of California was, uh, disturbed and I would hate to be the one in his crosshairs if his crew traces the blame. Heh-heh."

"And Minnesota? I thought that was handled." Love was sweating now.

"It is. You might recall the old saying from the 'brethren of the seas'?"

"I don't know who they are."

"Pirates, you nincompoop, pirates! 'Dead men tell no tales.'"

"Oh."

*****

At 9:00 a.m., Decker's phone rang again. This time it was from a number that he did not recognize. "Detective Decker? This is Special Agent Ted Taggie. I came out and spoke with your sister. Did she tell you?"

"Sure. How can I help you?"

"No, dectective, Lieutenant Haukom asked that I pass this update on to you in the interest of interagency relations. Ha-ha. Curtis was my original Training Officer when I was a rookie way back with the MSP. The intel your sister furnished on the facility near Las Vegas and the activities was spot on. In fact, after contacting several confidential informants, we established that the activities of Saturn Communications went considerably beyond providing very expensive cell service to a few gullible subscribers and a 'discerning clientele.' The CIs were not very forthcoming. All seemed afraid to talk about Saturn, but by those interviews and backtracking calls to and from the Saturn group, we obtained warrants to go after them. Unfortunately, as we pulled up, the premises were engulfed in fire. We combed through the remaining debris and it was determined that the whole facility had been emptied. There were no people, little useful equipment, no paper, and no vehicles. We figure they were tipped off. The techs are trying to get latent prints off of the satellite dishes and outside equipment, but whether that will be productive, no one can say at this point. I wanted to thank you and your sister, detective, personally and on behalf of the FBI. This investigation is being kicked upstairs. With recent public revelations about human trafficking, I expect some real interest."

"Thank you, Agent Taggie. And I'll pass this on to Shelley."

At 11:30, Decker's phone rang for the third time that morning. This time it was Martin Hammer. "Hi, Lou. It's Martin."

"Hello, Martin."

"I have some news about Ray Pibble that might interest you."

"I'm listening."

"Clarice, uh, Mrs. Bodkin called this morning. She said that Raymond's mother had called to tell her that Raymond was beaten up outside the pool hall last night on the way to his car. Ray told police that two men from the Congregation of Light came up to him in the lot and threatened him, then beat him up for 'no reason'. There was a witness who confirmed that Ray had been beaten up, but he only saw one man. It appeared to him Raymond was the instigator. The witness said that he could hear Raymond answering questions. They were having a normal conversation, until Raymond began acting crazy. He was looking around wildly and yelling and cursing at imaginary people. Then punches began flying. The man downed Raymond with a roundhouse kick to the head, then calmly got in his car and drove away. The police arrived but didn't arrest Raymond. The officers knew him. They drove Raymond home where he told his mother his version. Ray's mother also said that her son is barely able to walk now. That he is limping and shuffling along and frequently falling down."

"We know these people are brutal, so I guess I'm not too surprised. Sounds like it's only a matter of time till Raymond is back in his chair. I hope he didn't leave it at the Congregation amphitheater. Martin, would I be right in assuming you looked through the book I asked you to send?"

"I scanned a bit of it."

"Did you read my father's account of his last assignment in Laos near the back of the book?"

"I did."

"Had you ever heard anything about this from you father? Did you know that our fathers knew each other?"

"No to both questions."

"Did your father leave any written records of this or any other supernatural encounters in his life?"

"Not that I'm aware of, but I always felt that Dad had a certain quality to his faith that went beyond belief to a certainty. An actual 'knowledge' that I've seen in few other Christians. I can see now where that came from."

"We've met before, Martin. When you were a baby, did you read that part?"

"I did, ha-ha, sorry, but I don't remember you."

"Same here. But it is funny how patterns—" Lou stopped, lost in thought.

"Patterns what, Lou?"

"Oh, I don't know. This'll give us something to talk about over breakfast at Leon's."

"Wow, Leon's. I can hardly wait." Both men laughed.

"We are heading back tomorrow morning. So we should be there by late afternoon. I'll call you then. I'll be bringing a friend back with me, Martin. You might even want to interview him on your show."

"That's cryptic, but okay. If I ever have a show again. Remember, Saturday night is the opening of the Congregation of Light Lakeside Pavilion, so don't make plans. I've got two passes. I'll try to get more."

"Great. I wouldn't dream of missing it."

They hung up. *Lou seems different somehow.*

Lou spent the remainder of the day wandering around the camp trying to stay out of people's way. He and Lenny walked over to the bench on the bluff and sat as the sun started its lazy afternoon decline. "You know, Lou. This spot is where Uncle wants to be buried."

"It's a beautiful spot, Lenny."

"Yes, it is." She looked out at the vista and began to tear up.

"I'll call and keep you updated when we figure out what we're going to do, Lenny."

"Between you, Hank, and Shelley, I'll have a front row seat to the…action?"

"Not exactly reassuring. I wonder if that's how the gladiators' women sent them off to the colosseum?"

"You know what I mean, ha-ha. This 'battle' is not entirely yours anyway. Lou, you aren't anticipating any *real* violence, are you?"

Lou pulled her to his shoulder. "No, but I've been involved in simple arrests that went badly very quickly—and these people are much more dangerous than those." Lou put on a very serious face and pulled Lenny around to face him. "If I don't make it, can I be buried up here too?"

"Are you serious? On Indian burial ground? We'll build a pyre on the bluff above where I found you and scatter your ashes to the deep."

He hugged her tightly and they both laughed. "Of course." She replied, "But you're covered in prayer, Lou. Don't worry."

Chapter 37

Homeward Bound

The sun was still sleeping at 4:30 a.m., when the three travelers tossed their gear into the back of the Humvee. It was cloudless with a full moon about to set—great for traveling. Lou and Shelley each had a small satchel of clothing they had bought in Harbors. Lou had a gun case with the handgun and bullets that Hank had given him. They took a cooler full of sandwiches and snacks that Lenore and Shelley had prepared, along with a large thermos of coffee. Uncle and Lenore were also with them as they stood by the vehicle in a circle. They all put their arms around each other's shoulders as Uncle sent them off with a prayer. They were about five minutes underway when a shadow crossing the moonlight caused Lou to look out his window and up at the sky. Above the trees, an enormous shadowy form was moving in the general direction of the camp. He pulled out his mobile phone and called Lenore.

"Lenny, there may be danger headed your way." He described the sighting and Lenore thanked him with the admonition. "Be careful." Lenore and Uncle knelt down and prayed for protection for themselves, the camp and the travelers. Immediately a half-dozen bright lights were present above Ohiyesa. The creature halted his approach as he saw the lights. A resonant voice sounded. "No further. There is nothing for you here."

The creature flapped its great wings as it hovered. "You are wrong, slave. He knows whom I seek."

The light began to pulse intensely "Do you question the Word of the Father?"

The creature felt a cold pang of fear as he watched the intensity of the lights growing.

The dragon wheeled and headed back southeastward. He called back, "We will meet one day alone, slave." The creature wondered at the warning he had been given.

The trip went smoothly with driving being split between the three. It took less than twelve hours. They had timed their trip to take the morning run of the SS Badger across the lake. Since none had ever been on a real cruise, they explored the old ship with enthusiasm marveling that there were even staterooms and sun decks on the big car ferry. As they disembarked in Ludington, Hank pulled into a souvenir shop with a large sign proclaiming "1,000 pound man-eating clam!" "What? Our family loves these places." They all laughed as Hank tried on a plastic "Authentic President Gerald Ford Football Helmet" painted in the Chinese version of maize and blue. Hank took a cell phone picture of Lou and Shelley cowering below a stuffed twelve-foot tall, stuffed polar bear—an animal not found within 2500 miles of Michigan. Lou sent it to Lenny with the caption "Danger awaits at every turn." After they exhausted the wonders of the schlock emporium, Hank observed, "Michigan is a lot like Minnesota, at least when it comes to souvenir shops."

They drove directly on and turned into Decker's driveway about 4:00 p.m.

Lou was surprised to find Martin Hammer sitting on a porch chair. He had his feet up on the rail, a can of Coca-Cola on a side table, and a paperback copy of *The Grapes of Wrath* in his hand. "Good afternoon."

"This is a bit of a surprise. A good one," Lou responded. He made introductions and everyone went inside. "How long have you been out here?"

"About forty-five minutes. Your home phone rang twice in that time."

Lou walked over and checked his answering machine. There were six calls over four hours from the same local number which Lou did not recognize. A seventh was from Captain McAvoy's office. This call came in twenty minutes ago. A message asked Lou to call back as soon as he was able. Lou dialed the captain's number. "Captain McAvoy's office."

"This is Detective Decker. I got a message to call the cap."

"Yes, please hold, detective."

"McAvoy here. Lou? Glad you're back. How's the shoulder?"

"Fine. Thanks, Captain, it's about back to normal, a little stiff, but I'll be ready for spring training."

"What?"

"A poor joke, Cap. I'm a little stiff but good to go. What's up?"

"Your brother-in-law Herb. His body was stolen from the cooler at Grand City Mortuary last night."

Lou looked over at Shelley who was watching him through the door to the den. A strange look come over Lou's face and she walked toward him. Lou gestured palm up for her to stop. "It hasn't surfaced yet, I take it."

"No. We have a lead but it's weak. Surveillance footage caught two men loading the body into the bed of a pickup. However, they fit the description of two men who showed up earlier at the funeral home earlier in the day asking questions."

Lou immediately thought of Love's two goons.

"They showed credentials from a nonexistent government agency that is supposedly tasked with the oversight of interstate transport of bodily remains. They said they were investigating the company which had delivered your relative's body for sloppy procedures. Mr. Jiggerson, the mortician, said once they ascertained that Mr. Van Doss was there, they asked a few other questions—oddly, all of which they should have known the answer to already. He was about to question them, but they said they were done and left. He said he intended to call around to see if these men were showing up at other funeral homes. However, their arrival had interrupted a meeting with a client, so he put it on the back burner. He forgot all about it till the theft was discovered this morning. I've assigned Turner and Maine to this case, so check with them for updates."

"As for your concerns about the Congregation of Light, we've held up looking into them and nothing has come to our attention, but I'll expect you'll give me the full story Monday morning. Then we can target an investigation, if one is necessary. Don't bother coming in tomorrow. I'm sure your family needs you more than we do right now."

"Roger that. See you Monday, Captain." Decker waved Shelley back into the living room. He came in behind her "If it isn't one thing it's another."

"What's wrong, Lou?" Shelley's face was a mask of apprehension.

"Herb's body has been snatched." Lou outlined the details of the theft to all present as he had received them. They all sat there listening incredulously.

"That explains the other six calls." Martin took a drink of his soda. "The 'Friendly Christian Funeral Home' is probably terrified that you will sue." Martin mused, "or he's deathly afraid of the publicity this will create. No pun intended."

Hank observed. "It's pretty clear where Herb's body is. I think we'll need to do some preliminary recon this evening. If you could show me my room, Lou, I think I'll run an RV session on this." Lou nodded. Martin looked quizzical. Shelley began to weep, and Hank put his arm around her shoulders and led her from the room.

That evening the three men donned dark clothing and headed for Lake Michigan. They drove along the shore until they reached the spot where the elder Hammer had fallen to his death. From this point, they had an unobstructed view of the brightly lit Congregation of Light compound to the north. On the shore was the gleaming new amphitheater. The congregation would face west to view a high rising dais with an altar and pulpit on the shoreside. "There must be seating for a thousand or more people," Martin said as he passed his binoculars to Lou. Behind this was a long, low entry building running north and south along the entire back of the seating area. A large, well-lit parking lot behind the building now paved over spot where the old church had stood. It reminded Lou of major sports league construction. There were stone pillars along the sides of the arena on which what looked like fabric panels were being mounted, but these were mostly down at the moment. There looked to be a framework above for some type of retractable roof.

"That's where Herb is." Hank pointed at far end of the long entry building.

Martin looked at Hank then at Lou, clearly puzzled how Hank could know this.

Lou saw Martin's expression. "Tell you later," he said.

Farther back yet, across the road was a second building, which they decided housed the new offices of the Congregation of Light.

Hank's attention was drawn to movement at the back of the rear tier of seats. "Binocs down. Keep still." Hank continued to look and identified "Four targets. Two are normal sized. One appears to be quite tall and thin and the other bulky. Fat or muscle, I can't tell. I think they're the stooges from the airport. Number three is wearing a suit, but I don't recognize him."

"Sounds about right." Lou squinted but could only detect movement at this distance.

"Miguel is there, Lou."

Lou nodded. "Can he see us?"

"You mean can 'it' see us?" Martin asked.

"I don't know. Keep praying and just lie still." Hank knew that there were natural animals with a sense of sight that would ascertain their presence easily, but he did not know whether the shape-shifting creature had this ability. "No sense in advertising our presence."

In the amphitheater, Brother Love turned to Miguel and smiled. He waved an arm out over the seats "I can picture it now. Every seat filled. A grand spectacle and soul harvest."

"The Prince of California has accepted your invitation. He will expect a sacrifice you know, and it better not be a dead body."

"Which reminds me. Eddie, is Mr. Van Doss being prepared?"

"Yes, boss, he is 'marinating' as we speak."

"In high octane? I want a spectacle. I want a blaze that will be visible to the ISS."

"Uh-huh."

Miguel suddenly jerked his head toward the south. He scanned the horizon and the shore. He looked hard at the dunes. *Nothing but a couple of people standing near an SUV looking out at the lake. If I had time, I'd pay them a special visit.*

"Do you have the weather angle covered, Miguel? Miguel?"

Miguel's attention was jolted back. "Yes, yes. Our friends who run the atmospheric heating apparatus will be bringing a sudden storm across Lake Michigan. The lightning will reach its peak intensity about 9:30."

"Plenty of thunder?"

"Yes, yes. Plenty of lightning. Plenty of thunder. Enough that people will think the earth is going to split."

Dickie asked, "Will it come apart?"

"Not yet, lamebrain."

Hank looked up "Okay, his attention is elsewhere now. I've seen enough. Let's go."

On the way home Hank outlined the preliminaries of a tactical plan to get Herb's body. He also hoped to cause some havoc that would expose the Congregation of Light. "Martin, can you enlist this Mrs. Bodkin and her troops to provide prayer cover. I'll line up Uncle, Lenore, and the Christian community at Ohiyesa to do likewise. Lou, how's your aim?"

Chapter 38

Friday on my Mind

Shelley told Lou the next morning that she had calmed down enough to call the funeral home back. "Hello, Grand City Funeral Home. Jimmy Jiggerson speaking. How may I help *you*?"

"Hello, this is Detective Decker. I'm back in town and returning your call."

"Oh-h-h, detective. I've been trying to reach you."

"I know, and I know why you called. I've spoken with my captain. Mrs. Van Doss is also present. Hold on, please." Lou handed the phone to his sister who stared at the instrument with enough intensity to melt it.

Jimmy Jiggerson gulped. "I want to apologize for this unfortunate accident—"

Shelley launched in. "Accident? Was my husband just lying out where someone driving by happened to find him? Did those ghouls just accidentally choose my husband's body to steal as a crime of opportunity?"

"I'm sorry, ma'am, but these things happen. It's not really my fault."

"Really? Not your fault? Whose fault is it? Mine? Herb's? You say these things happen? When? If this were a common occurrence in the funeral industry, you'd be selling used cars."

Lou was trying to suppress a smile at his sister's explosion. He tried to take the phone from her, but she turned away and jerked it away from his grasp.

"But we're doing everything we can, Mrs. Van Doss—" The mortician was clearly giving up.

"And just what does that mean? Did you put a bounty on the thieves? Are you leading a posse of angry morticians on horseback to find Herb? You've got to do better than this, Mr. Jiggerson. My husband deserves better. I deserve better." Lou finally wrenched the phone away as Shelley leaned in shouting now, "And my attorney will see that I get it!"

Lou hung up as Jiggerson continued to drone platitudes. "We understand that you—"

"Feel better, sis?"

Face red and breathing hard. "No." She laughed a bit. "Maybe…a little."

"Save some of that anger for your speech tomorrow night."

This exchange was interrupted by a knock on the door. "That's Martin. Shelley, we've got to run a few errands. There are a few items Martin says we need for tomorrow."

"Hi Lou, this is Casey Meyers, he was my engineer at WCRS. He agrees that it won't be technically difficult to hijack the internal feed at the 'show,' but the issue will be getting on-site access." Casey turned around showing Lou the lettering on the back of his jacket: WCRS Tech Staff. "This should help me at the compound." Casey then outlined his plans to hijack the internal feed to the audience and substitute Shelley's presentation.

"WCRS is carrying the live feed, so they will have their people there from late morning through the afternoon setting up. Casey plans to show up about noon with his gear and make the connections. He'll drop off a copy of the night's program here, and the IP address to use when cutting into the local feed, then it's up to you." The men headed out to the car. "Where's Hank? Sleeping in?" asked Martin.

"No, he was gone this morning when I got up. Look, no Humvee." Martin then noticed for the first time it was gone from the driveway. They drove to the local Radio Shack where Casey picked up a router, wire, a medium-sized handy box, various electronic components which neither Lou, nor Martin recognized. "I think that should do it. Why don't you drop me off at my place and I'll get started assembling the components. It shouldn't take too long." Martin did as he was asked. He then said to Lou, "Let's run by the theatrical supply and have a look."

Joshua's Theatrical Supply and Costumes was located across town, but well-worth the ride. Lou and Martin looked in awe at the volume of paraphernalia on sale. Lou tried on a cape and top hat. He twirled a cane and Martin observed, "Duke of Earl." Martin put on a stovepipe hat, chin beard and much too long trench coat. Lou asked, "Are you running for office?" Then he made a shooting motion at Martin's head with his finger and Martin stumbled backward. Ultimately, they selected a few specialty items, filling a small bag and headed back to Lou's house.

They found Shelley in the den constructing a set by hanging some old black sheets she had found from Lou's bachelor days. "Wow, back to the '80s." Martin fumbled with his phone for a few seconds. Suddenly the room was filled with the *Miami Vice* theme music. "Book 'em, Rico."

Lou shook his head. "Now, you're mixing in *Hawaii Five-0*." Everybody laughed.

Shelley had also placed a red bulb in a lamp and turned it on. "I'm going for the late-night horror movie TV set look."

Lou set down his bag. "You've nailed it. Just don't freak Casey out."

Hank did not return till late that evening. Lou was cleaning his Beretta as Hank came in with a new camo duffel. It clanked as Hank set it down. "Howdy. Been out to the amphitheater. They have that place locked down pretty tight tonight. People in windbreakers walking all over the place. The good news is they do not appear to be trained up nor armed."

"We should have surprise on our side. Have you been out there all day?" Lou asked.

"Since early afternoon. This morning I went shopping and picked up a few items for tomorrow."

He opened the bag and extracted a long handled matte black tomahawk and a 25-round box of premium .40 caliber Smith and

Wesson ammo. "Don't figure I'll need any of this stuff, but better to be prepared. I also have nylon rope, plastic ties and these beauties." He held up a pair of pale calfskin gloves which he put on and flexed his fingers to show the craftsmanship and suppleness. Hank grinned "They fit like—gloves."

Lou groaned. Martin picked up the tomahawk and hefted it. Decker shook his head. *I hope he's right. I'd sure hate to see him coming at me with this in his hand.* Everyone assembled around the kitchen table and for the next hour they talked over their plan, such as it was, for tomorrow night. Martin had submitted his ticket request for two tickets under the name of Jim Baker. Hank said not to worry, that he would find his own way in. They set up rally points and alternative action plans. Finally, Lou said, "You know all these plans are likely to come undone five minutes into the thing."

Martin looked concerned, but Hank laughed. "Now now, let's not be pessimistic. This is a good plan. Limited objective. Surprise. Nothing too complicated. It should work."

Martin held up his cell phone. "Weather shouldn't be a problem. I've checked three weather apps and they agree. Good lighting, waning gibbous moon, clear skies with a ten per cent chance of precipitation developing around midnight."

"The Hummer is gassed and ready."

"I'm going to work on memorizing as much of this as I can now. Good night." Shelley waved some papers containing her speech, stood up and headed for her bedroom.

"Good night, Shelley. Don't forget to pray." Hank called out, "All of us."

Chapter 39

Showdown

Decker awoke to the sound of huge raindrops pounding his bedroom window as an unexpected squall moved through the area. *Why am I not surprised.* Decker could hear as people moved about the house and he decided to get up. Throwing on a robe, Lou found Hank pouring himself a cup of coffee. "Morning, Lou. Would you like a cup?"

Decker plopped down at the table. "Morning, Hank. Sure, black please."

Hank poured the second cup and carried both to the table. He sat opposite Decker and stared down into his cup. He lifted his head and laughed. "You know this is a harebrained scheme, don't you, Lou."

"Are you having second thoughts?"

"Second? Tenth is more like it." Hank cracked a smile. "Our objectives are…unsettled. We will technically be trespassing, and we will be armed, but at least you will be armed legally."

"You didn't mention that we will be trying to steal a corpse."

"Well, the body doesn't belong to them, so the legal issues involved there are a bit hazy."

"Plus, I don't know if Shelley hijacking their presentation is a crime."

"I see. In fact, we're just three caballeros out to have some fun, take home a souvenir and get some 'religion' in the process. I consider this a fact-finding visit for my meeting with the captain on Monday."

"On the other hand, it's storming outside, when we expected a sunny day. What could possibly go wrong." They were both laughing now.

They looked up. There was Shelley standing in the doorway, leaning against the jamb. "What's with all the racket? How can anyone sleep around here?" She was smiling. "Are you two having second thoughts about tonight?"

"Nope, not me. How about you, Lou?"

"Nahhh."

Shelley asked, "What should I wear tonight?" Both Hank and Lou broke out in laughter.

At 2:00 p.m., a strange car pulled up in Lou's driveway. Decker peeked through the window blinds. It was Casey. He was carrying a case the size of a large tackle box and was whistling as he bounded up the porch steps. *At least Casey is Calm.* Lou looked up to observe that the last remnants of this morning's storm had moved off and the sun was now bright and the sky blue.

"Come on in." Lou swung the entry door open. "How did it go?"

"I decided to go in early. Did not want to run into anyone I might know. It went as smooth as silk. No one even asked who I was, let alone what I was doing? I did get a bit of a long, strange look from this Mexican looking guy, but he was dressed like a gardener or maintenance man, hey, 'the deed is done'. Where is Shelley setting up?"

"In the den."

"Through there?"

Lou pointed. "Yep."

Casey opened the door and laughed when he saw the walls covered by black sheets and Shelley walking back and forth reading from a paper and moving her lips soundlessly. "Queen Jezebel in her lair," he greeted her, noting her crimson dress and golden hoop earrings. "I can only imagine the faces of the faithful when they see you on the jumbotron, instead of that—pervert."

"Here, follow along." Shelley handed him her script. She began reciting from memory. After a few lines, Shelley stopped and looked expectantly at Casey. "Well—"

"Again. From the top. This time try a Dracula's bride accent. And a few tears wouldn't hurt either."

"What?" She laughed. "All I did was introduce myself, why would I cry doing that? Jeez, everyone's a critic."

Casey handed her back the paper and said, "Enough tomfoolery. Begone. Let me set up the equipment. We can do run-throughs when I'm finished. I've decided to stick around and help this evening." Casey had already opened his case and was extracting a small box as Shelley left the room. "Exit stage left."

At four thirty, Martin arrived, and he and Lou began preparing their disguises. Though Hank was unknown to them, Lou assumed that Congregation of Light personnel might be on the alert for him and Martin. Therefore, they would enter separately and proceed to a rendezvous point. They did not want to stand out by appearing outlandish, but a bit of facial revision was reasonable. They took the theatrical hair and gum spirits and started to work. Lou applied a mustache and sideburns. He put on large mirrored sunglasses and a Dodgers baseball cap and was transformed. Shelley did a double take when she came into the room. "Lou?"

Martin had fashioned a bushy graying moustache and goatee for himself. For the finishing touch, he pulled a large afro wig from a bag and settled it on his head.

"Linc! You know, from the 'Mod Squad' on TV!" Lou said.

"Nope, Jimi Hendrix," opined Hank.

"Hendrix didn't have a mustache." Lou protested.

"Sure, he did. Maybe not that thick, but—" Hank was suddenly unsure and changed subjects. "In any case, no one will recognize you two."

Martin suddenly looked thoughtful. "Some of the biggest men in the United States in the field of commerce and manufacturing, are afraid of somebody, are afraid of something. They know that there is a power somewhere so organized, so subtle, so watchful, so interlocked, so complete, so pervasive, that they had better not speak above their breath when they speak in condemnation of it."

"Who said that?" asked Lou

"It's a quote from Woodrow Wilson's book *The New Freedom*. I wrote a paper on the Federal Reserve back in college. I learned that Wilson has been thought to be the political face of the bankers who organized that scheme, but he appeared to me to have been used. It is clear that he was not really involved in the deeper layers. Is this what we're dealing with here—the deeper layers?"

"Lou and Hank looked at each other. Hank nodded and Lou spoke, "I think we need to level with you, Martin. We can't have you going into this unprepared." At this point Lou and Hank described their encounters with the malevolent spiritual force they referred to as Miguel. "I do not know who or what he is, but I am sure that he is not a 'Mexican gardener'."

Martin appeared thoughtful. "He sounds a lot like the entity our fathers encountered in Vietnam, and maybe like Brother Love's attorney at the station." Hank and Lou were both reassured when Martin neither expressed disbelief or an inclination to disengage from their plan. "Anyway, I doubt that he will show himself in front of a thousand people."

"Probably not. And remember, we aren't going there looking for trouble. Our job is to get Herb's body and leave—and do some recon—plus expose Brother Love with Shelley's transmission." Hank laughed and Martin noticed. he was running a hone over the blade of his tomahawk as he said this. Hank added. "For we wrestle not against flesh and blood, but against principalities, against powers, against the rulers of darkness of this world, against spiritual wickedness in high places [Ephesians 6:12]."

"Which reminds me, Mrs. Bodkin and her women's group are holding a prayer vigil this evening to support us." Martin added.

"This would be a good time to pray." Hank began. "Father…"

Departure time approached and the three men headed to the hummer. Lou called out over his shoulder to Shelley. "Remember about two minutes into Brother Love's sermon. Be ready. I'll text you."

"We've got it." Casey turned to go back inside as Shelley stood on the porch waving until the Humvee had turned the corner. Casey had seen how nervous Shelley was about running the electronic gear and decided to stay around for the evening and help with the technical aspects of the process, rather than go home alone to his Xbox.

*****

As Brother Love was getting dressed in his "working man's hero" stage costume, Dickie stuck his head into the room. "Should we take the body up to the altar now?"

"Okay, but don't light it up until I raise my arms and point directly at you from the stage. I will say 'Behold the power.' That's your cue. Are the others under control?"

"Of course, boss. No goof ups this time. Eddie has sedated them already."

"Fine. Make sure you have them up there and ready to go when we ignite Mr. Van Doss…and keep them out of the spectators' sight!"

Brother Love's mind wandered as Dickie left.

He had watched the spirit beings begin filtering in. For the most part, Miguel had chatted with them as an equal, as he watched them take on human appearances and showed them to prime viewing spots in the elevated boxes that ringed the auditorium. However, when the Princes of New York and Florida had arrived, Miguel had suddenly become disturbingly deferential. *I need to watch him when California arrives. I was assured that I was meeting with the Chief Commander himself when I was assigned Miguel. And for the most part Miguel has assisted carrying out the plan in fine fashion, but I'm guessing that maybe he isn't even near the top of the food chain after all.* He looked out through one-way glass over the tiered arena, saw the seats already filling in and smiled. *This should do just fine.*

Hank and Martin dropped Lou off at the main entry gate. Then they parked at the far northern edge of the lot in the third row. This was about 150 feet from the northern entry gate and another twenty-five feet from the long low building which Hank had determined held Herb's body. They had all agreed to meet there right after the program started. By then Hank figured to have gained entry to the building.

Lou entered the amphitheater and was stunned by its opulence. Tonight, the side wall curtain panels were fully raised. The walls widened out at an angle from the front to the back of the arena where guests entered, forming a broad wedge-shaped viewing area. No seat was more than two hundred feet from the dais. The side walls were a heavy gold-veined cerulean blue fabric, lit from the outside they appeared to be carved from lapis lazuli. The stage was raised above the front rows and appeared to be made of hewn granite blocks. In the center of the stage was a massive fifteen-foot square jade base holding a bronze metal bowl twenty-five feet in diameter. There was a pulpit directly behind and over the bowl. The huge base concealed a walkway to a subterranean passage and hid a stairway ascending to the back of the altar. Behind this there was an unobstructed view out over the lake. The fabric roof was retracted, and Lou had a beautiful view of the star filled sky with the nearly full moon just peeking over his shoulder. Lou walked back out and over to the north end of the low entry building as Martin entered through the gate. Lou chuckled as he noticed Martin walking in the middle of a mixed-race church group bearing the writing 'Happiness Church' on their shirts. No one was giving him a second look. Lou waved to get Martin's attention and when Martin had cleared security and turned in his ticket he sauntered over. "Whazza happe*nin*', my brother?"

"Quite a setup they have here. The inside is spectacular. I wonder if Miguel is the groundskeeper?"

"If he is, then he's using bippity-boppity-boo, I just don't see that hombre with a hoe in his hand for any legitimate purpose. We should find our seats. Did you see the door where we meet Hank?"

"Yes."

On entering the seating area Martin gasped at the sight, in spite of himself. "You're right. This is impressive. Brother Love did this in less than four months? That man's team has some skills."

Their seats were center and near the back. A steady bass intensifying beat filled the venue. "'Long Time' by Boston." Martin lowered his face and leaned over to Lou. "That's the tune he's ripping off, a Rock Rollins's specialty. Change some of the lyrics and voila 'Christian Rock Rollins's style." Lou just shook his head.

At this point, a haggard looking middle-aged man stumbled out onto the stage. Even at their distance, Lou and Martin knew that he was clearly intoxicated. Lou thought that he could see some residual white substance under the singer's nose.

Brother Love who had been observing his opening act through the mirrored glass turned to Miguel with a look of disgust. "He's pathetic. What do his followers *see* in this parody of musical talent?"

Miguel made a hand gesture in front of Love. "Look again."

Love gasped as on stage stood a strapping, handsome man gyrating and putting his soul into a well-sung tune. Gone was the aging and drunken clown tripping over his own feet and croaking out off-key rubbish.

"This is what they see. It's part expectation and part 'glammer' spell. Do you think the crowd actually *sees* you, brother?" Miguel was disgusted by Love's egotism and enjoyed using the needle.

"Yes." Brother Love completely missed the irony in Miguel's statement. Miguel rolled his eyes.

Rollins was halfway through his second number—a distortion of Procol Harums's song "A Whiter Shade of Pale" sung as "A Hotter Place in Hell" when Love pushed a button and told the announcer. "That's it. Just kill his mic after this song. I can't stand anymore of this crap." Love headed for the underground tunnel passage to the stage. Miguel spoke to Love's back, "Pity, I had asked Rock to add 'Back in Black' to the playlist. Now I'll just have to wonder what he would have come up with lyrics-wise."

Rollins was upset when his mic went dead. He tried to shoo off the emcee when the man came out to usher Rock offstage as thunderous applause rained. The emcee waved for silence. Then the lights dimmed, and a spotlight lit the base of the giant stone altar. In the middle, the stone split and separated. Smoke drifted from the opening and rolled across the stage. Suddenly Brother Love was standing there onstage. Love stood there for a full minute with arms low and outstretched to his sides. He was dressed in his trademark khakis and white shirt with sleeves rolled up--ready to do the work of his god. He drank in the applause as he raised his head and looked around. There was California. Over there sat New York and Florida. Opposite them sat the Princes of the Mississippi and New Mexico. All had smirks on their faces except California who stared with smoldering menace. "Have we got a show for you." mumbled Love to himself, looking up and around at the dignitaries.

Lou and Hank got up from their seats and moved quickly out to the back. The crowd and ushers were all transfixed by the lights and sound of the spectacle and expectantly anticipated miracles. As they walked, Lou texted Shelley "Now." Things were a bit behind schedule. They could hear Love speaking, introducing his dignities by their human aliases. "From south of the border, Luis Medoza Comacho. All the way from the West Coast." Many in the crowd stood and most were responding with enthusiastic cheers.

The door was ajar, and Lou entered. Martin went off to get the Humvee and pull it up to the exit gate. The scene froze Lou in his tracks. There was a security guard lying unconscious on the floor and three children bound hand and foot along one wall. There was an empty surgical stretcher along the south wall, but Herb was nowhere in sight. Hank was engaged in hand-to-hand combat with the large muscular man. The big man held a torch that he was swinging at Hank with ferocity, but he was much too slow, and Hank managed to avoid it. There was a fourth child on the steps leading down behind the large man. Hank drew his tomahawk and Lou was startled as Hank faked a throw that caused the big man to scream and turn to run away down the steps. Like lightning, Hank was on Eddie and brought the flat side of the weapon against Eddie's head knocking him cold. Lou and Hank untied the children's legs and Lou moved them quickly toward the door. Hank yelled, "You take the kids out. I'm going to check where this tunnel goes, I think Herb is probably at the other end." He turned and bolted down the steps. Having seen the altar, Lou felt nauseous contemplating Herb's fate.

Lou approached the Humvee herding the four children, Martin gave a him a puzzled look. "Where's Herb?"

Opening the back door and helping the children in, Lou could clearly hear Shelley's voice on the PA "We were then taken to a remote Congregation of Light camp where we were held against our will. For several weeks we were forced to perform manual labor and received drugs in our food and drink." Lou leaned in and said, "Change of plans. If I'm not back with Hank and Herb in ten minutes, take get these kids to a hospital and call Captain McAvoy on the way. Tell him where I am and to send in the troops."

Lou turned and raced back into the building. He bounded down the stairway in pursuit of Hank.

Hank had followed the stairs down, along a tunnel and then back up to where he could see out onto the stage. He could hear Shelley speaking but heard Love shout from above, "Light him up, you fool." Hank saw a very tall man on a stairway with a torch raising it to touch off what was obviously Herb's wrapped body in the metal basin. "And get down there and help Eddie bring those kids up, now!" Hank grabbed his tomahawk once again and let it fly at the man's arm. The weapon hit just below the elbow causing Dickie to let out an unearthly howl of pain as his arm flopped back. Dickie dropped the torch into the altar basin, and he fell back against the support wall, dripping blood. Screams erupted from the crowd. Now Hank realized he had a bigger problem. The crowd was now in wild confusion as Miguel rose up over the back of the bowl and began assuming his dragon form. "I know you." The beast roared. Its yellow eyes radiated hatred as Hank prayed silently for help. Hank then realized that all around the arena and between him and the top tier of seats where the demonic dignitaries sat, astounded by this spectacle, were bright lights that pulsed with energy. As the monster drew in a breath to incinerate Hank, a large beautiful luminous human figure stepped between them. The dragon blew fire, and the glowing man appeared to absorb it before it could touch Hank. At that moment, Lou burst from the door behind Hank, and sizing up the danger immediately, Lou yelled, "Duck!" Hank hit the floor as Lou drew Hank's gift pistol and fired. All four rounds went harmlessly through the shining man to strike the dragon in the chest. Lou then heard the report of a rifle coming from behind him. He heard three shots and the skinny man fell and stayed down. The dragon wailed in unholy agony as it felt the impact of Lou's gold-tipped volley. It then collapsed into the bowl where it was engulfed by the raging fire from Herb's burning gasoline-soaked body.

A voice sounded in Lou's and Hank's minds. "The other demons are not a threat to you. We were sent by the Father to protect you and we will keep them at bay. You must go now." As they turned to leave, Lou watched his sister on the Jumbotron still earnestly outlining her story. He also noticed that the skinny man had been crushed under the tail of the demon and reduced to a pile of ashes. Lying on top of the building was a man in camo. He tried to get up, but obviously he could not make his legs work properly and collapsed. "Raymond Pibble." Lou was about to ask Hank to stop and help Raymond, when Hank shouted, "Look!"

Lou turned and saw Brother Love being picked up by a colossal ochre-colored dragon and carried off to the west over the lake. The phony pastor screamed at the top of his lungs. He had two large and growing bloody stains on the belly and chest of his white shirt where he had been hit by Pibble's shots. Lou admired Pibble's marksmanship. Three shots. Three hits.

Decker turned to Pibble again as the veteran put the gun under his chin and pulled the trigger. "No-o-o-o!" Lou shouted, standing frozen with horror. Hank tugged at Lou's arm. "C'mon, *now*. He's beyond our help."

In the distance they could hear sirens and noted that the southern fabric wall had caught fire and was burning fiercely. People were shouting and running about wildly as the flame was quickly spreading. Lou texted Shelley "Stop" as he ran back down the stairs with Hank hard on his heels toward the Hummer. They passed a second pile of dust where the big man had fallen. Lou wondered at this momentarily. Hank threw open the driver's door and pushed Martin to the passenger seat. Lou jumped in the back seat. All the kids were still drowsy. They had clearly been sedated. Hank threw the car into gear and careened off the property to the north on a construction road through the underbrush. He had used this route as cover earlier when doing reconnaissance.

Hank crossed the main shoreline road after about a mile and headed east on a two-lane blacktop, following Lou's instructions, toward Grand Rapids and the nearest hospital. Lou picked up his cell phone and placed a call.

Chapter 40

Aftermath

Lou dialed his boss's cell. Captain McAvoy answered on the second ring. "McAvoy here."

"Captain, it's Decker. I'm on my way to GR General with four kids that I just—liberated from the Congregation of Light compound."

"What are you talking about, Decker. Didn't I tell you not to go bothering them. I don't want to be answering—"

"Excuse me, Captain. You won't have to worry about any complaints from that outfit. Their place is burning like a bonfire and it appears that the leader was shot by some crazy man. I was in attendance strictly as an observer, when I found these four kids wandering near the exit. They appear to be disoriented, drugged, and malnourished, so I'm taking them to the hospital to get checked out."

Hank looked over and raised his eyebrows as he listened to Lou's story.

"A friend in the ministry tipped me off that Herb's body might be there. I didn't have any way to find out and didn't see it, but there were some pretty strange goings on, Cap. I think they might have put some mild hallucinogens in the communion wine. At one point I thought I saw a dragon. It was probably a kite or hologram. Suddenly there were gunshots, and fire, and the place turned into chaos. That's when I found the kids, Captain. My full report will be on your desk Monday morning. If you wouldn't mind, you might ask the investigators to have a look around for Herb's body."

"Decker, why do I feel like there's a whole lot more to this than you are telling me? I'll get someone over to the hospital, and thanks for the tip, Lou. Good night."

Martin leaned back and stared at Lou. "Do you think he really believes that BS story?"

"Probably not. But how's he going to prove anything different. I doubt he'll want to look too deeply. I suggest that you two drop me off when we get to the hospital. Go over to Leon's and have some coffee and pie on me. I'll call when I'm ready to go. I don't think it will take more than an hour."

"I did notice you ignored the role of your Native American brother."

"Just officially. Better that way. But thanks to you both—for everything."

"And who is this friend in the ministry who tipped you off." Martin couldn't help but laugh.

"A detective never names his confidential informants. But I can say that he looks a lot like you." Lou joined in the general laughter, which he realized was at least partially related to coming down from the high-tension events of the evening. Lou then called Lenny. He gave her a more accurate version of the evening than he had given his superior officer. Lou described Hank's role in particularly glowing terms. "He saved at least four lives and probably mine. Lenny you were right about it all. Thanks to you and Uncle for the prayers. I know they were the deciding factor."

Finally, he called Shelley. He repeated the story he had told Lenny. "Shelley, you had the crowd in your hand, and Love was so flustered he couldn't function. I'm sorry we weren't able to locate Herb's body, but the police are on it now and I have to think they will find him."

"I understand about Herb, but poor Ray Pibble," Shelley said sadly. "I didn't know Ray, but I still feel a kind of kinship with him for what that Love gang put him through."

"Yeah, that was a partial victory for the bad guys, but we have to trust God to work things out. I won't be home for a bit. We're just pulling into the hospital and I've got to run. Good job. I'm proud of you."

"Thanks."

Lou got out and guided the kids who were now awake enough to walk and speak, although confusedly, into the ER. The waiting room was crowded, but when the triage nurse listened to Lou's brief summary and concerns, she immediately took them all back to one big trauma room and sent an aide to get stretchers. Lou advised her that the GRPD were sending officers over and she nodded. "I'll try to get the ball rolling and have our social worker on call contact protective services. They'll be in later and we'll keep an eye on them for you, detective. The doctor will be in shortly."

As the triage nurse left, the treating nurse came in rolling a computer. She helped the aide position the stretchers for the children. She was efficient and very caring as she looked over each of the four victims. Lou gave a brief and edited history of the night's events and concluded with the statement that he encountered the kids, on leaving the premises, and seeing their appearance, behavior and being partially tied up had enraged him. She raised an eyebrow. "Human trafficking?"

"I think probably yes."

At this point a doctor came in. "I'm Dr. Coleman, detective. You did a special thing getting these kids to us. Thank you. Two of your colleagues are out in the hall. If you wish, you can step out and speak with them. The nurse will show you to my office so you can have some privacy. Thanks again. We can take it from here."

Decker left the room following the nurse. *I've spent way too much time in hospitals recently.* There was only one officer, he recognized Sgt. Rocco Altomare, a long-time friend and shook his hand. "Glad to have you back in one piece, Lou."

"Hi, Rocky. Who's with you tonight?"

"Sutton. I sent him for coffee. He'll be back in a minute, but we can get started."

They sat in Dr. Coleman's office and Altomare took out a pad and pencil and started a small tape recorder. Decker gave him the same story he had given the Captain, being careful to leave Martin and Hank out of it. He finished in less than ten minutes. "Lou, I think we can handle this. Go home and get some rest. You look tired. I'll call in the morning if we have any other questions."

"Good night, Rock" Lou opened the door and almost knocked the coffee from the incoming officer's hands.

"Good night, Sutton." He walked out of the ER and called Hank to come get him. He sat on a bench looking up at the beautiful sky as he waited. An unbidden thought came to him. *The world is a beautiful and mysterious place when one's eyes are open.*

At 4:00 a.m., his cell phone rang. "Detective Lou Decker, please. This is Sheriff Puente from Ottawa County."

"Hello. I'm Decker. How can I help you?"

"Sorry to bother you, detective, but your captain asked us to inform you immediately—those were his words—if we found the body of a Herb Van Doss. Well, we didn't find his body, but we believe we *have* found his remains. It appears that this cult had burned his body in a large sacrificial brazier or bowl or whatever. I'm not sure what you call it exactly, but anyway it looks like they were burning him in some kind of sacrificial rite when things went wrong and the fire spread."

Decker felt no urge to correct the sheriff's theorizing and let him continue.

"The fire investigator says he has never seen anything like this. The body was reduced to ashes with only a few bone fragments left. He says this is unheard of in an open fire, even when accelerants are used—and he believes they were. The degree of heat necessary to perform this is…impressive. Another odd thing—very odd— there remained an uncharred toe tag, that let us ID him. It's all very strange, but as everyone involved is dead, I guess that wraps things up for you."

"What about Herb's remains?"

"Oh, I'm sorry. Your captain also asked that we call Jiggerson's Grand City Funeral Home, so we called their answering service. Mr. Jiggerson called back in three minutes and he was out here to get the remains in twelve minutes. He must have hit ninety on the way here. He asked that we let you know he will personally deliver the remains tomorrow morning at the time of your choosing. Mr. Van Doss's ashes will be delivered in their finest urn. No charge for the urn or any of his services." The sheriff chuckled. "I know this isn't funny, but he looked as white as a sheet and like someone had put the *fear* into him. He hopes that this will be satisfactory to the bereaved, as do I. Good night, detective. If I can be of any help, don't hesitate to call."

"Thank you, Sheriff, and good night." Lou decided he could wait till morning to tell Shelley.

He awoke at 7:30 to the sound of Hank and Shelley talking with occasional sounds of laughter. He got up and dressed and found them up for the day, sitting on the porch swing and enjoying some fresh coffee. "Morning, Shelley. Morning, Hank."

"Morning, Lou. Hope we didn't wake you. Hank was describing Brother Love's impotent fury at having his program hijacked."

"You looked good up on the big screen, sis. Your set wasn't creepy at all."

"No, not at all."

Lou and Hank laughed.

"Mr. Jiggerson will be swinging by about 9:30 with Herb's remains. It turns out he was cremated."

"Cremated?" Hank and Shelley reacted together.

"Yes, apparently at the Congregation's HQ."

"Oh," Shelley responded.

Hank rolled his eyes at Lou and behind Shelley's back mouthed the word "Bowl?"

Lou nodded slightly "Yes."

He was trying to spare Shelley the details, but she intuited the truth. "Lou, he was going to be the fuel and they were going to sacrifice those children, right?"

"I… I think so."

Shelley teared up. "I'm just glad to have him back. I don't think I want to be here when Mr. Jiggerson comes by."

Hank volunteered to take Shelley out for some shopping, and she agreed. A few minutes later Hank and Shelley emerged from the house. Hank flipped her the Hummer keys. "I know you've been wanting to drive this 'bad boy.' See you later, Lou"

Lou waved. He went in to pour himself a cup of coffee. He came back and plopped down on the porch swing to await Mr. Jiggerson's arrival.

As it happened, Mr. Jiggerson had chickened out. He assigned the delivery chores to a tall, very stern, and impossibly pale, white-blonde woman who addressed Decker with a thick Scandinavian accent. "Hullo, Jah. Meester Chiggerson, he vant me to geeve you dees and tell you hee ees vedy, vedy sorry. Theenk you and gootbye." She handed the urn to Decker, gave a very large fake smile, turned on her heel, and left.

Decker was speechless, but he managed to croak out "Theenk you too" as she got into her car.

She drove off and Martin promptly pulled into the driveway. "Morning, who was that? Queen Ilsa?"

"She was an emissary from the funeral home dropping off Herb's ashes. Beyond that I'm not sure."

"Ashes?"

"Yes." Lou related the call from the sheriff and Martin shook his head. "Amazing. Child sacrifice? These were very sick people."

"Agreed, but remember, some of them weren't people."

"In any case, I came by to tell you that I'm not going back to work at WCRS."

"What are you going to do?"

"Well, I do have a minor in divinity. I think I'm finally going to make my parents proud. I'm going to restart the Lakeside Baptist Church."

"Do you think there are enough people around here to support a new church?"

"I guess I just have to leave that for the Lord… In any case I know I'll have one member in my congregation."

"Let me guess—Clarice Bodkin?"

"The one and only."

"I hope you called her to thank her and her prayer group."

"Yep, last night from the restaurant. That's when I felt the Spirit moving me in the direction of a career change. You know, that voice inside that tells you it's the right thing to do."

"Yes! I do. I'm happy for you. You will make a great pastor."

"What about you, Lou. Don't you start back Monday."

"I'm meeting then with Captain McAvoy, but there are some things that I need to discuss with him regarding my future with the department."

"My advice is not to ask them for a raise right off the bat."

"No, it's not like that. I've got some issues that I need to get off my chest, and, frankly, after what I've seen, I don't know if I can do this job anymore."

"I understand, if you ever want someone to talk to, remember I'm going to be a pastor—and I *have* known you pretty much all my life."

Both men smiled warmly. Martin rose and reached out and shook Lou's hand. "Gotta run, Lou. I'm off to talk to a real estate agent who used to be a member of my dad's congregation. He specializes in Ottawa county land."

"I'll call you, Martin. Maybe lunch Tuesday? I may need a friendly ear."

"White Castle?"

"Or Leon's." Lou grinned.

"White Castle!"

Martin took his leave and Lou went inside. He pulled out his father's book. He reread the story of his life changing event. Lou prayed for the strength to do the right thing.

Decker had fallen asleep in his Lazy-Boy and was awakened by Shelley and Hank on their return. They carried in several bags of clothing and a large duffel. "The urn on the table has Herb's ashes, Shelley."

"Can we go to the lake and empty them this afternoon, Lou."

"If that's what you want to do. Are you sure?"

"Yes, I am. That was Herb's specific wish. Once we were watching a movie. He said it was called *The Big Lebowski* or something like that. He made me pay attention while he replayed a scene that was supposed to be black comedy with friends scattering ashes. Herb turned to me and said in a serious voice 'That's how I want to go.' At first, I thought he was kidding, but he repeated it, and I said 'okay' never thinking it would actually come to this."

"All right… But let's have a little lunch first."

After eating they took Herb's ashes and headed for Lake Michigan. They found the spot where Martin's father had fallen to his death and walked to the edge of the bluff. Hank led them in a prayer, first in Dakota, then in English. Lou felt a need to speak then. "You know how much Herb loved you, Shelley. He was absolutely obsessed with finding you and bringing you home. If it weren't for Herb, none of the things that came of this would have even happened, so we owe him a lot. Me in particular." Lou looked down as his eyes teared up.

Shelley opened the urn and let the offshore breeze take Herb's remains.

As they walked back to the Hummer, Shelley turned to her brother and said, "Thank you. Lou, you know that even though things weren't always smooth, Herb looked up to you… I'm going back with Hank to Camp Ohiyesa, Lou. There's nothing for me here and the family had offered me the cook's job. I called Lenny this morning and accepted. With Uncle dying there is a lot to do to keep things running well and I want to be part of that, Lou."

"I see."

"What are you going to do, Lou? You know Lennie loves you."

"I know she does." Lou looked up and reached out. He took Shelley and Hank into his arms. "I love her too, but I have some unfinished business here, and I need to pray about things." They walked back to Hank's vehicle. Lou looked out over the lake as he climbed into the Hummer. *Lord, help me make the right decision.*

About the Author

John C. Owens MD has had a long career as an emergency medicine physician practicing both in the Detroit area and the hinterlands along Lake Michigan. He served as Van Buren County assistant medical examiner for ten years, encountering many forms of death and homicide. His exposure to mayhem was supplemented by his tenure as team doctor for Detroit's Junior Red Wings. He has long had an interest in writing, beginning with editing, and writing for newspapers in high school and in college. As an adult, he has been a contributor to  the *All-Sports Bulletin* and *Hockey Weekly*. This book is Dr. Owens's first novel.

Dr. Owens currently resides in South Haven, Michigan, with his wife Deborah. They have three adult children. The couple enjoys reading, traveling, movies, and watching their grandchildren grow.

CPSIA information can be obtained
at www.ICGtesting.com
Printed in the USA
JSHW021240070220
4064JS00001B/44

9 781098 025939